The Dragons of Nibiru

Kimani,

Believe in yourself & follow your dreams. Dream Big!!

Lorna

Lorna J. Carleton

Published by
Go Free Directory
29-1945 Grasslands Boulevard
Kamloops, BC V2B 8T3

Copyright © 2017, 2018 by Lorna J. Carleton
All rights reserved.

ISBN 978-1-7750440-7-9

Second Edition 2018

Designed by
Danielle Hebert, Lorna Carleton
and Russell Williams

Fifth Canadian Printing, June, 2018
Printed in Canada by Premier Printing
www.premierprinting.ca

A big thanks to Russ Williams, the best editor on Planet 444. I will always be truly grateful for your incredible ability to take my words and thoughts and make magic with them. Your insights into what makes a story a good story brought this book to life. It would be fodder for aliens if not for you. Thanks for everything.

www.roundlyworded.com

Danielle, with your sublime ability to visualize my words, you created a breathtaking cover, then adorned the text inside with your delightful illustrations. Many thanks for helping bring Celine and the others to life.

www.daniellehebert.com

Devon, Dieter, Pierce and Sarah,
the adventure of this book is for you.

CHAPTER 1

Earth

24,000 B.C.

Huge billows of dust rose from the desolate eastern shores of what would one day be known as the Caspian Sea. Birds of several species took wing, fleeing the roiling maelstrom. A small antelope herd scattered in terror.

High above — but descending rapidly — roared the source of all the commotion: a massive ship, its hull streaked with the friction-flamed scoring of countless planetary landings. Slowing, it came almost delicately to rest in the patch blasted clean by its landing jets.

Moments after touchdown, the aft cargo bay gaped silently, revealing a bewildered mob of humans, all naked or nearly so. Herded none too gently by tall figures uniformed in gleaming white, the mob shuffled dazedly down the ramp.

A young boy of perhaps eight or nine years tripped on the dangling rope which held up his oversized shorts. Landing hard on his knees and hands, he stifled a cry. The woman closest to him was burdened with an infant, but managed to stoop and help the waif to his feet. She held him close, murmuring comfort. A trickle of blood made its way down thin, white shins to bare, dirty feet. Still silent, scraped and bleeding hands clutched to his chest, he allowed the woman to guide him down the ramp.

Blinking at the sudden brightness and puzzled by the strange planet's unfamiliar smells, the humans stumbled off the ramp onto the alien surface and dispersed across the scorched ground. Nearly a thousand of them. Mostly young men and women, with a sprinkling of children and elders. Shuffling, zombie-like; few speaking, a few more weeping.

All were pale-skinned, most with blond hair and blue eyes — features that would one day be deemed "Caucasian," in reference to this very region. The five men herding the hapless immigrants were of the same physical type, tall and athletic, but their uniforms and imperious bearing set them clearly apart from the bedraggled crowd.

"They're all planet-side, captain," the tallest of the wardens spoke into the comm pickup at his left collar. He turned to another uniform standing at the top of the ramp; blast pistol held negligently at his side, he called, "Coca! Tell Clapa to get the dust out of his shorts and offload the container!"

Coca turned, shouts were exchanged, and soon an enormous metallic container floated, humming, up from the bowels of the ship, down the ramp and out to the southern edge of the landing zone. The exiles scrambled to escape being crushed as it grounded in a *whoosh* of hot dust.

"Better let them have a couple more, Clapa — this lot's supposed to survive," yelled Coca. Then, turning, he strode down the ramp toward the huddle of frightened, whispering humans, waving his pistol randomly their way in half-hearted menace.

Soon, two more containers lumbered out of the craft and

settled next to the first. The crowd backed nervously away from the hulking gray boxes, eying ship, crew, blasters and containers with well-founded suspicion. They backed off even further when the tallest warden stepped forward to release the seals on the big boxes.

Catching a glimpse of commotion off to one side, he shouted at one of his crew — "Tatsu! What in all space do you think you're *doing*? Get the hells away from that girl, you bloody idiot!" He stormed over to the offending spacer and shoved him away from the young exile who'd been struggling to escape his groping grasp. Relieved but still fearful, she rushed headlong into the crowd.

"We've got zero time for your crap. Get the hells back aboard and prep for space. You too, Coca. It's time to get out of here." The warden leader turned back to the ship and spoke to another of his crew, halfway down the ramp.

"Quan, give them another blast of memory-wipe. We're under orders to make damn sure this batch doesn't remember a blessed thing about who they are, where they're from or why they're here. Hells, hit 'em with *two* blasts. If we screw this up, we're ash for sure." He stalked up the ramp, Coca and Tatsu close behind.

Quan hurried down toward the confused crowd, then addressed them using a hand-held voice expander. "All right, everyone! Closer together! That's right. No stragglers at the edges. Move in, move in! Thaaaat's right. Closer! Come on, closer than that. Everyone's got to get a good dose of this. Without it, you're dead meat once this planet's diseases catch up with you. And they will — don't doubt it. You grown-ups will die first, leaving the poor kids all alone 'til *their* turns come. Nobody wants that, eh? All right — that's good. Hold still, now. I'm going to let this stuff go. Get as many deep breaths as you possibly can. And make sure those kids do it, too!"

The crowd crushed even closer together, eyes wide and eager for the precious "medicine." Quan donned his helmet, double-checked its seal, then reached around and brought up the long tube-gun slung across his back.

Locking a yellow, melon-sized cartridge into place atop the gun's barrel, he commenced spraying a cloud of yellow vapor out over the heads of the waiting crowd. All stretched upward, desperately gasping in lungsful of the gas, parents enforcing the drill on younger children who hadn't quite gotten the idea.

The whole charge released, Quan counted down a full minute on the timepiece at his wrist, exhorting the throng all the while. "Good. That's it. You've got it. Good, good. Deeeep breaths! That's it."

Now he could see signs of the memory-wipe taking effect. Time for dose number two. He sent a second yellow cloud billowing over the crowd, swinging the tube-gun from side to side so the vapors enveloped every last one of the sorry lot. He smiled; everyone had followed orders. Those that hadn't fallen to the ground, asleep, were utterly blank-faced and glassy-eyed. The whole dosing had taken less than a minute and a half.

Dashing up the ramp, Quan shouted back to his oblivious "patients:" — "Good luck, you poor slobs! You're gonna need it." As soon as he'd entered the cargo bay, the huge ramp-door hissed shut. Seconds later, the massive vessel rumbled briefly, then lifted skyward and was gone. A great gust of air rushed in to fill the space it had vacated, buffeting its erstwhile human cargo and dispersing the last of the yellow vapors.

A moment later, the boy who had fallen on the ramp stepped away from the oblivious crowd, still clasping his battered hands to his chest. Seeing that the ugly yellow fumes had cleared, he gasped his first breaths in nearly two minutes.

CHAPTER 2

Planet Cugini
2016 A.D.

Celine had been near the back of the theatre when the commotion began. She saw Professor Pent slump over his podium, mid-sentence, his several jointless arms gone limp. At the same time, cinnamon-maned Prof. Grout toppled off the edge of the stage. The prestigious instructors, each of a different race, looked ridiculous, mouths agape and sprawled at odd angles.

At once Celine spotted wisps of orange mist drifting across the stage floor and out into the audience. Now students nearer the front of the hall were keeling over, row after row, like a slow tide flowing steadily up the gallery.

Grabbing her sister's arm, Celine hissed out an order, quiet but deadly urgent. "Mia! Mia, listen to me. Clamp your nose and hold your breath as long as you can."

Annoyed at the interruption of an ever-so-vital text-chat, Mia shot back her best scowl of annoyance. Celine shook her; "Do it *now!* And act unconscious, or you've had it." Turning the older girl by the shoulder, she pointed fiercely at the scene below — and the squad of uniformed Repts that had just burst through a side door.

Mia gasped at the sight of the brutish soldiers — and succeeded in knocking herself out with a stiff lungful of gas. Without even time to despair at her sibling's pig-headedness, Celine slumped to the floor in feigned unconsciousness.

Her quick response had spared her a telling dose of the creeping vapor, but she had no idea how long she could hold out. She skirted the edge of oblivion, then felt her head begin to clear. The gas had dissipated quickly.

The Repts, unaffected by the species-targeted fumes, made their way among the sprawled cadets, examining each female. Boys they ignored. Now and then a Rept would point out one of the girls to the humpbacked Rawkls who followed at a respectful distance. As soon as a Rept indicated a body, one of the Rawkl minions would heft it and drape it over a muscular shoulder. With a pair of sleeping students aboard, he'd trundle them out of the hall.

"They said she's in here. Keep looking," ordered the Rept in charge. He was distinguished by dozens of garish badges and buttons spangling his tunic, and a gaudy blue-and-gold lanyard looped over one shoulder. He stooped to turn over a brown-haired girl, then spat, swore and kicked her twice before moving on to the next cadet.

LESS THAN AN HOUR BEFORE, cadets had filled the benches of Lecture Hall 45, chatting as they awaited the start of the advanced cryophysics seminar. It was only one of the hundreds of educational events featured at this year's Draco Advancement Convention. More than just a superb learning opportunity, these conventions afforded cadets from different worlds and academies the chance to network, socialize, and catch up on the latest fashion trends.

Vendors strutted the concourses and plazas, even the corridors between lecture halls and conference rooms, pitching the latest and trendiest this and that. All were vying for the attention — and credits — of the multi-system mélange of cadets. Especially the wealthier and more self-absorbed of the lot, like Mia.

When they'd arrived a few days earlier, Mia and her girl-crew had decided to score matching outfits: sheer bodysuits with a saber-cat theme. Mia had hatched a scheme to top everyone, though: she'd tracked down the same outfit in a shimmering gold fabric — the only one available in the entire sector. She had made the purchase and taken delivery, just hours before the rest of the girls had theirs. Basking in her own craftiness, Mia knew she'd be a total knockout. And *just* the perfect notch above the rest of her crew.

After classes on the day they'd purchased their outfits, the girls had gathered to prep for the evening's social whirl. Hair and makeup fine-tuned, they'd dressed and set out to stun the convention. As the first order of business, Mia led her purring, preening posse to parade before her sibling — all set to savor some sisterly envy.

Celine's reaction was disappointing at best. "You look ridiculous," she snorted. "You'd never be allowed to wear anything that outrageous on duty, or even at official social functions — so I've no idea why you wasted Dad's money on it. That goes for all the other glittery nonsense you've been grabbing up. We're supposed to be cadets, preparing for service. Not a pack of ditzy fashion hounds. Are you serious about *anything* that's going on here?"

Mia just huffed, gave her hopelessly stuffy sister a dismissive wave and led her giggling entourage away, hunting more sophisticated targets.

Celine was right — the convention was serious business and a priceless opportunity for aspiring cadets. Yet, if they were honest, a solid majority of the attendees would admit that much of their attention was focused on the business of landing a mate. For most, the major interest before and after each day's official proceedings, and the total concentration at Convention Week's rich array of social events, was scoping out the field and deploying their flirting skills. This was expected, though, with things as they were in these times. Careers and lives depended upon the mating game.

Each regional academy had its own social events through the year, most with competitions and selection processes to find and rank the most eligible, desirable guys and girls. In terms of looks and pure sex appeal, Mia was one of the hotter prospects from her academy. So was a young man named Hyatt, from another school — the hottie Mia had been plotting for months to make her own. She chattered about him endlessly, much to Celine's exasperation. Celine was convinced that capturing Hyatt was the only thing Mia had any real interest in at this convention. Everything else was superfluous. Worse, the young man had little to recommend him beyond looks, money, swagger, and a conventionally cute ass.

Two years earlier, Mia had left the convention with a fine mate, Tuck MaTuc, a talented kid from a prestigious academy on Pastro. Mia was devastated when the young man was killed just a few months later, during a routine sparring match. Celine suspected that her sister's devastation was at her *personal* loss, though, more than anything else. Now Mia was back, and obsessed with landing her newly chosen mate. Next semester would begin her final year as a cadet, so she had no time to lose.

By any practical measure, Mia was a terrible cadet; but,

thanks to her looks and megawatt femininity, the faculty (nearly all human males) were more than lenient with her. Having a well-known father in the prime of a distinguished military career added still more to professors' willingness to pave Mia's academic path. Finally, everyone knew (though never discussed) that she was a delicate — unaffected by the pandemic infertility that had cursed humankind since the Seeyorg invasion some 275 years earlier. Her status as a delicate added significantly to the special considerations she received. Few delicates lived past the age of two anymore, so Mia was a rarity, held in near-reverence. She managed to slide by each year with a grade-point total which, though largely undeserved, was just adequate to move her up to the next echelon and on toward marriageable status.

Mia considered being born delicate a blessing; Celine thought it a curse. Delicates were born perfect, in the reproductive sense. Perfect genes, perfect blood and bloodline, perfect reproductive system — not sterile. Before the invasion, humanoid births had gone on as usual. Afterward, there were few births to anyone but delicates. By the time many non-delicate girls reached full adulthood, they were sterile. No one was certain why.

Cultivating delicates was a temporary solution for saving many advanced species — human and otherwise — from extinction. For some reason, human bodies made the very best hosts for soul transfers, even if the transferring soul had been inhabiting a non-human body. And among human host bodies, primitives from Planet 444 (called Earth by some of its inhabitants) were the finest that could be had.

Years earlier, it had been decreed that all delicates were to be taken from their parents at an early age and raised in special institutions. This had proved utterly unworkable, as far too many died before even reaching puberty. It was determined that removing them from a loving home environment drastically reduced their chances of survival. Thereafter, all precious delicates remained with their natural parents until they reached marriageable age. They were also well protected, at state expense. Occasionally, some desperate criminal had managed to kidnap a delicate or two, but capture and capital punishment were so close to a certainty that attempts had become rare in the extreme.

Adding to nature's already-powerful reproductive drives, fear of being shamed fueled Mia's mate-hunting obsession. Unmatched cadets entering their final year faced even tougher odds in the mating race, since most pairings occurred during the first few academic years. And to graduate unmatched carried the most mortifying stigma of all — in Mia's view, at least: assignment to the Finishing School for the Unmatched (FSU). Mated academy grads were assigned to a Matched Finishing School, where they went through the final half-year of preparation for service, learning the elaborate etiquette, rules and basic protocols of military service.

The nightmare of receiving an FSU assignment on graduation day haunted Mia. Ordinarily, she'd have had no cause for concern, being a delicate, but she had another reason to worry. After Tuck MaTuc's death, the boys at her home academy — a superstitious lot — had looked on Mia as jinxed. It had also been widely whispered that Celine, Mia's strange, magic-obsessed sister, had cast a spell on her. All the more reason to avoid her, at least as a mating prospect. Mia had heard the whispers about Celine, too, further stoking her resentment of the girl.

Fortunately, few convention attendees were from Mia's academy; the rest were from other planets, other academies. Many knew of Tuck's tragic death, but didn't share the superstitions of Mia's academy mates. Almost no one here knew anything about Celine, or that she was Mia's sister. What they did know was that Mia was hot, fashion-smart, damn sexy and a delicate. Highly desirable mate material. Not just for the trophy factor, either. Matching with a delicate almost guaranteed there would be children — and once in service, those with children were consistently favored for promotions. The capper on Mia's hot-commodity status was the fact that her father held high rank and was racking up an impressive military career.

CHAPTER 3

G.O.D.

Thousands of years in the past, the Galactic Omniplanetary Democratum — popularly known by its self-assigned acronym, G.O.D., had issued a Galactic Edict to the effect that families were permitted only a single child, if their first-born was male; two, if the first was female. The edict sought to limit planetary populations, after overpopulation had triggered a series of devastating pandemic plagues.

First, the caryhnpowh virus had decimated crops on thousands of worlds, with widespread famine following in its wake. After decades of struggle, the crop-plague had been brought under control. But less than a generation had passed before a rapidly-mutating bacterial species spread a dread disease known as eeiingle (or, in some systems, ghavynitis), savaging the battered populations that had survived the caryhnpowh famines.

In the end, Nature had succeeded in returning planetary populations to sustainable levels, but G.O.D. understood only too well that populations have tragically short memories — and long reproductive urges, which good sense and social responsibility alone couldn't hope to keep in check. They knew populations desperately needed replenishment — but feared that unless they exerted careful, strict control, the numbers would again soar past the point of healthy balance, and the horrors of the plagues would return. And so they contrived and launched a vast and intricate program of population-control rules, restrictions, requirements and regulations, complete with stringent monitoring and enforcement mechanisms.

Racial rebuilding began, but in most cases growth was discouragingly slow. Too many children were born with genetically-transmitted defects which ended their lives well before maturity. Rather than compensating with something sensible, like easing restrictions on family size, G.O.D.'s response was to implement an entire set of *additional* rules and restrictions. One such rule was that all mate-matches must undergo exhaustive genetic screening, and then receive G.O.D. approval from the local sector's High Chancellor. Unfortunately, in the Pleiades systems (including the planet Erra, where Mia and Celine had grown up), the High Chancellor was the despised Deebee Scabbage.

Mutual attraction, romance, sex appeal and even good old-fashioned love were still in play, but the future of the race, genetic purity and the fate of worlds could no longer be left to such "haphazard frivolities," declared the almighty G.O.D. Anyone caught fathering or bearing a child outside a lawfully-sanctioned mating was instantly shipped to the desolate prison planet RPF113. No appeal was possible. No parole ever granted. No exceptions made. Ever. Unless, of course, Scabbage found it politically or personally expedient to grant one. In such a case, an exception could *always* be made, and usually was. The same held true for *all* rules, laws, policies, edicts, customs, morals, traditions, common decencies and universal truths, where Scabbage was concerned.

Children of unsanctioned unions were appropriated by the state, their fates forever hidden from parents and kin. The delicates among them were salvaged and given to good families to adopt — but only families on planets far removed from the girls' homeworlds.

One year, a cadet, Marti — an engineering whiz desperate to be matched — had attempted to rig the "kiss evaluator," one of the Mating Commission's mate-pair screening devices. He'd hacked the machine and rigged it so that when he and Elli (his prospective mate) kissed, the device would register their favorability quotient as a highly propitious seven. Unfortunately, his subterfuge had been detected and countered. Instead of signaling a favorable match, the machine gave the lovers a painful shock, sounded an alarm, and the pair vanished in a sizzling flash — teleported instantly (and at vast expense) to RPF113.

Scabbage made very sure the image-capture of the event was shown and re-shown for weeks thereafter, on newsfeeds all throughout his dominion. Later, it was learned that poor Elli had been ignorant of Marti's scheme, but Scabbage could not have cared less. All that mattered was that everyone knew that *he* was in charge, and the penalty for challenging his authority was too gruesome to be faced.

Even a sanctioned mating did not guarantee a couple a child. General fertility continued dangerously low, despite the best efforts of screeners and specialists. In general, males were not as reproductively fragile as females. Those with high sperm counts and favorable genomes — dubbed "producers" — were first in line for promotions in both public and private organizations. A low sperm count or less-favorable genome labeled one as a "degraded being." In most cases that meant a dull, even menial career, regardless of training or native talent. In common speech, the term was usually shortened to "degraded" or "DB."

All this distressed Mia deeply, despite her status as a delicate. She worried endlessly that she might prove barren after all. If a match did not produce children by early middle age, even if the woman was a delicate, the couple almost invariably found themselves assigned to missions in the outer sectors. Mia dreaded the very idea, believing her life would end if she were ever forced to work for a living — or worse, to live without civilization's niceties. Life would be utterly unbearable without fancy clothes, nightclubs, fast shuttlecars and ready access to the most fashionable shops. Outer-sector missions typically lasted a decade or more, as they were never allotted ships equipped for jump-shift travel. To Mia, being assigned such a mission would be akin to eternal damnation.

If a couple somehow managed to conceive while out on a mission, they were sent at once to the nearest major outpost, their former barrenness forgiven. Major outposts were equipped with jump-shift facilities, so the couple could be quickly transported to their homeworld, where the mother and unborn child could be nurtured to term. This was scant comfort to Mia, though.

Celine cared nothing for stupid laws in general, and the mating laws in particular. She considered them illogical, counter-productive wastes, utterly unwarranted. G.O.D. had deemed them the only "fair and sensible" means of guarding against another disease epidemic. Celine deemed them balderdash, and had told Mia so, much to the young delicate's horror.

Celine attended the conventions solely for exposure to new thought, new viewpoints and new technology. She'd spent most of her free time at this year's gathering exploring the many exposition halls, with their displays and presentations.

This morning had featured just such an exploration, in the company of Dardo, a handsome young cadet from Trishbon who thought her quite pretty, and asked if he could come along. He'd been delighted at her easy acceptance, but it wasn't long before he regretted his move. Celine's interest and attention were reserved for the technology on display, with none left over for Dardo's manly charms.

"Wow!" she'd exclaimed, craning her neck to inspect a towering, white-silver cylinder. "This is that new dimensional warp inductor they've just released," she explained to her companion, assuming he'd heard all about it. "The upgrades are *amazing*. Magical! Mmm — just listen to it hum!"

"Yeah. Magical," yawned Dardo.

"No, really — it's just under *five* times faster than even last year's model, and that was already unbelievable," she continued. "Oh, look! They're about to do a live demonstration! We've *got* to see that. I can't wait for them to do a scale-down so I can order one for my little flyer. If I had one in time for my trip to Remini next year, I could be there and back in half the time. Come on, let's get up to Deck 5 for the demo!"

"Aw, sorry. I can't right now, but go on ahead and check it out. Maybe I can catch up with you later," said Dardo, intending nothing of the sort. His radar was now locked on a tall blond who'd winked at him from across the concourse. Celine couldn't have been happier at his departure; now she could take in this place's treasures on her own, without social distractions. Tech treasures, and magical treasures, too.

Maybe this year she'd have enough time to use the simulation deck to try out a new-model incant-baton and cast one of the attack spells she'd learned. Gods! That would be the best thing ever. Maybe even have a sparring match with someone. Hmmm...Mia, perhaps? Celine laughed to herself, envisioning Mia fleeing the simulation deck, screaming wildly as her perfect hair vanished in a trail of sparks and vapor.

Celine had visited a vendor earlier, offering exactly the incant-batons she wanted to try, made of some new unbreakable (and unpronounceable) substance. Even more fascinating were the bookstalls. She was reserving an entire day's free time just to explore them, in search of spell books she'd never seen. She dreamed of finding one that included the obscure Invader Spell — an incantation formulated in the campaign to drive back the Seeyorg hordes, nearly three centuries ago. Properly performed, the spell could freeze an enemy's ships in mid-flight. Or so she had heard. In fact, tracking down this one spell was almost the sole purpose of her planned journey to Remini. But, if she could find it right here...well!

Celine also hoped to locate a copy of the latest book by her muse, Koondahg. Most dismissed his writings as pure fiction, though mildly amusing; semi-plausible yarns of heroic figures from the distant past. Celine knew the truth, though. She'd learned to read between Koondahg's lines, spotting his veiled allusions and cross-relating them among his different published works. If one was clever enough, it was possible to piece together complete spells in this fashion.

Celine loved puzzles, so she'd spent many a night curled up in her dad's study with Koondahg's books. She missed her father. He was so often away on missions these days. Many nights, Celine fell asleep, books everywhere, curled up in his chair, dreaming.

It was some years earlier, in just such late-night sessions, that Celine had first learned to cast spells. From there she'd gone beyond Koondahg to other authors' spell books, grimoires and formularies, expanding her knowledge and sharpening her skills. Spells to shut people up, or to keep them talking. Spells to make people feel sick, and spells to comfort and heal. On and on and on. She'd spent countless nights (and many a free day) reading and practicing.

Sometimes she was guided in her studies by her Mentors. Known in some cultures as angels or guardian angels, these beings communicated to her as voices, perceived inside her head. They were always just a thought away, always ready to help her navigate life's hardships in a crazy universe. They were there to teach her, preparing her to fulfill the purpose for which she'd been born. Celine had never met the Mentors in the face-to-face sense, but she'd spent much of her life in communion with them — her life in this body (even as it formed in her mother's womb) and in many a lifetime before. The four Mentors Celine had encountered were known to her as North, East, South and West.

Celine had grown to love each of them, but West most of all. The others tended to be businesslike and "A-to-B" in their lessons. West's manner was more that of a close friend — joking, teasing, playing, challenging and drawing her out. In truth, Celine had come to love West even as she loved her adoptive parents.

It was on Celine's twelfth birthday that West, during a lesson on perceiving and analyzing sentient beings' vibrations, introduced Celine to another young student, on a planet she called Earth. Jager, he was named. From that day forward, North, East and South took no direct part in Celine's education. West became her only teacher — and Jager was always "present" in her lessons; her sole and constant classmate.

Over time, Celine grew to love Jager. The two became spiritually inseparable — despite their physical separation by so many light-years of trackless void. Celine couldn't imagine life without him, though their only contact was telepathic. This form of interchange was colloquially known as "menting" — mental communication.

West still presided over their daily lessons, but more and

more she acted as catalyst rather than instructor. She would merely suggest a concept or situation for consideration, then let Celine and Jager tackle it together, building on each other's viewpoints and insights. West continually guided and encouraged them to rely upon each other. She also guided them into recalling the lives they'd lived before, and recapturing the lessons they'd learned down the centuries and millennia of their existence. Each had always been the same being, but animating a succession of different bodies and accumulating a broad spectrum of viewpoints in a near-infinite variety of circumstances. They learned of others whose lives had intersected theirs through time, and why. The pair continually amassed and recaptured knowledge, in preparation for their purpose in this life and after — together.

Now, in some strange, strange way, that very purpose had brought Celine to her present plight: hanging head-downward in a dim, dank cargo bay, in the company of a gaggle of unconscious female cadets.

Scanning the hold, Celine wondered if more cadets had been kidnapped than she could see right here. She hoped not. Many royal, noble and chancellery kids, including more delicates than usual, had come for this year's convention.

As her eyes grew accustomed to the dim light, Celine soon spotted her older sister hanging in the next row, and three spots farther from the door. A few of the girls hanging nearby were also their academy mates. Two at the end of the opposite row appeared to be Kohiti, from the Eva Toth Academy. The pair next to those looked like Buga, from the Keeling Cluster. She couldn't make out any more details. But why were there only girls? Had males been taken too, and stowed elsewhere?

"Whatever," she thought, turning her attention to freeing herself. She soon bent her lithe body upward far enough to grab the shank line, then took up enough weight with her arms to loosen and unhook her feet. She swung right-way up, dropped noiselessly to the hold floor and crouched like a wary cat, rapidly regaining her bearings. Her white academy bodypack was still strapped to her back, making her look like a baby beastie huddling in the shadows. She stole silently over to her dangling sister and whispered, "Mia. Mia! Wake up, Mia," gently shaking the unconscious girl. "Please, wake up!"

Celine lifted Mia's shoulders to bring her head more nearly upright, and tried again to rouse her verbally. No go. She gently lowered the girl back to the inverted position. Reaching under Mia's taupe and teal tunic, she worked three fingertips behind the right collarbone, then pressed its front firmly with her thumb. Just as her father had taught her. Covering the girl's mouth with her forearm, she reached around and squeezed an ear lobe — hard.

"Huhhhh...ohhh!" moaned Mia.

"Shhhh. It's okay — I'm here, Mia," Celine whispered, releasing her hold.

At the sound of her sister's voice, Mia quit struggling, then tried to twist her head round for a properly disapproving glare. She couldn't manage it, and had to settle for looking severely annoyed, despite her helpless position. "You get me *down,*" she ordered, "right *now.*"

"Gladly," replied Celine. "But you've got to keep quiet. There may be Repts around." Scanning the hold, she spotted a crate that looked manageable and went to move it. Damn. It seemed to be full of lead. She wrestled it across the deck, cringing at every squeak and rasp.

"Hurry! I'm getting a *headache!*" Mia demanded, as if this were a dire threat to all civilization.

Celine bit back a retort, focusing instead on maneuvering into a good position. "Here. Grab hold of my waist and let me take your weight." Mia was horrified someone might see her in such an undignified position, but did as she was told — maintaining her best scowl of disapproval all the while.

Celine soon had the elder girl down, and Mia bent her attention to dusting herself off, re-adjusting her outfit just so, and restoring her hair to at least a working semblance of perfection. She offered her rescuer no thanks whatsoever.

Suddenly noticing Celine was no longer paying her any attention, Mia wondered what her sister could be up to. The silly thing was just gazing at all the stupid suspended girls. "Typical!" she thought, with a shrug and an eye-roll. Then she began examining the rows of hanging students herself.

"There's my friend, Baylis!" gasped Mia, starting toward a girl in a maroon tunic.

"No. Don't help anyone down," insisted Celine, taking gentle hold of Mia's arm. "Not until I figure out what's going on. Besides, some are sure to make a fuss. Especially those Buga over there," she said, careful to use her best "don't-irritate-Mia" tone.

"Gods!" responded Mia, glaring even more contemptuously. She only barely refrained from saying more, realizing reluctantly that she truly *was* out of her element here.

Celine just couldn't help it; knowing well what she risked, she cooed, "You know, if you aren't nicer, I can always hang you back up," and lit up her most endearing smile.

Mia glared on, but held her tongue — if not her blood pressure. Even *she* could understand that they were in deep trouble. It pained her awfully to admit she needed her "perfect" little Celine right now, but she quickly soothed herself with thought of eventual revenge.

Just then, the cargo door hissed and began sliding open. Mia stood paralyzed, mouth agape. Celine grabbed her arm and yanked her down behind some containers near the closest wall, just as a pair of Repts appeared at the opening.

"See? I *told* you there'd be room in this hold," Prit hissed. "There are two damn empty spots right near the front. Those *bleep*ing idiots were supposed to *fill* this place. Lazy Rehab Project Force bastards! Good thing we've got these two to fill the spots, or Soader would have our heads." The thug slung the girl he'd been carrying upward and secured her with the hook Mia had just escaped.

"Hey, Prit," said Grohs, "this one's way older than we've ever taken before. Why would Soader want it?" Leering at the unconscious human female he carried, the Rept sniffed at her and pawed her breasts. "Do you think she can even breed anymore?"

"How the Xenu should I know, beastie-breath?" barked Prit. "Quit your perverted fiddling and hang her up. We gotta get the hells back to PAC Base. Hey, secure that gods-damned loose crate, too. If that thing flies around in transit and damages any of these pretties, we'll be chow for Soader's pets, sure as we're breathing."

Grohs grunted as he slung the unconscious woman up onto the shank line where Celine had been hanging. Then, opening a wire cage at the back of the hold, he tossed in the loose crate and re-locked the cage. Heading for the door, he turned for one last, longing look at the human he'd been carrying.

"This is a good load," smiled Prit, admiring the bodies and poking at a couple of the hanging girls. He even leaned in for a couple sniffs. "Soader ought to pay us extra this time. There's some good blood and sure breeders here. Especially those Kohiti. I hear he pays top coin for those. C'mon, let's go. We'll be spacing for Shak any minute. As soon as we're away, I need a drink." The brutes lumbered out, and the hold door slid shut behind them.

"Mom!" gasped Mia. "It's MOM!" Mia started toward the mature woman Grohs had just suspended, but Celine grabbed her arm and pulled her back.

"No!" she snapped. She wrestled the struggling but hopelessly overmatched girl over to a heavy, strap-secured container. She managed to loosen a strap, wrap it around Mia's arms and upper body and finally re-secure it. Mia was pinned to the big box. To finish the job, Celine loosened another strap and used it to secure her sister's flailing legs.

"What the hells do you think you're doing?! You *are* crazy! That's MOM!" screamed Mia. "Untie me! NOW!"

Ignoring her sister's rant, Celine quickly secured herself to another container, just in time — the ship gave a jolt that threw both girls hard against the restraining straps. Jerked violently by the initial shock, the suspended girls were now swinging back and forth in slowly-decreasing arcs as the craft more smoothly accelerated.

"Mom! MOMMM!!" Mia screamed, struggling against the straps that bound her.

Celine ignored Mia's protests and frowned deeply, trying to make mental contact with Jager. It was no use; someone or something must be blocking her telepathy. This had never happened before. Never.

How Mia had wished and prayed that her parents had never adopted Celine. Her life would have been so, so much better if it weren't for the strange girl's presence. It made Mia feel unclean, having to live with such a defective, demented monster, spawn of an unsanctioned mating. She desperately hated having to explain to her friends why Celine was...was...the way she was.

"Her real mother had a bad fall when Celine was still in the womb," she often lied. Surprisingly, most kids bought it.

"Aren't you afraid she's diseased?" some would ask.

"Well, the medicals have cleared her twice, but I don't know.... Mom says that after she was born, they kept her in the infant infirmary for a year, just to be sure." More fabrication.

As Mia saw it, her only hope for escaping this intolerable mess and salvaging her ruined life was marriage. Right this moment, though, the source and cause of all her life's troubles was staring across the hold at nothing in particular, a look of calm concentration on her face. "Gods! One of her bizarre, sick-o meditations, no doubt," thought Mia. "This is your fault. I hate you!" she screamed out, hoping to interrupt whatever nonsense Celine was embroiled in. "Our life was fine until you came along. I *hate* you! I wish you were dead!"

Celine turned briefly, with a look of calm understanding — then resumed her concentration. This just further infuriated Mia, and she turned abruptly away with the most hateful, dismissive snort she could muster.

Celine felt sorry for her adoptive sister. She had been the target of Mia's vitriol since their earliest days together, but felt no resentment toward her. The poor girl's emotions were clearly reactive, out of her control and not justified by any actual harm or offense. How terribly painful it must be to live in the grip of such a mental maelstrom.

Celine continued her attempts at reaching Jager, but it was no good. She was well and truly blocked. After several minutes more, she abandoned the effort.

"We should try to get some rest, Mia. It's quite a distance to Shak. This could take hours and hours." Mia grunted a response, refusing to admit aloud that the ever-annoying Celine was right again. She just faced as far away as she could, and tried to get at least somewhat comfortable. Both girls were soon asleep.

"MIA. MIA!" WHISPERED CELINE, as loudly as she dared. "Wake up, Mia."

"Hmmm. Wha...?"

"Shhhh. Quiet. We're landing. We've got to pretend we're unconscious so they think someone strapped us in like this. Okay?"

"All right. Whatever," grumbled Mia, wanting to argue but thinking better of it. For now. A moment later, she was terrified to hear the hold door humming open.

"Move it! Get these pukes out of here and into their cells. It's time to eat and I don't want my break cut short 'cause you morons are too damned slow," barked a greasy-smelling Rept, brandishing a long, shimmering rod. "Move it, turds — or I'll give you some o' this."

Three big workers — two Repts and one shaggy-furred humanoid — lumbered into the hold. The Rept in charge released the locking mechanism on the shank line so the girls could be unhooked and taken down. The work party got busy carrying girls out of the hold, two at a time — one slung over each shoulder. Down the ramp they hauled the still-unconscious kids. The Repts dumped their burdens none-too-gently into a large cage which rested at the center of a transbeam platform; the third worker was carefully gentle with those he carried.

"What the blazes is this? What kind of flaming idiot lashes cargo like *this?*" roared the Rept in charge. "Get the hells over here, Otto, and unlash these last two. Throw 'em in the cage with the rest. I'm reporting this crap for damn sure. That Prit is going to lose his job. Ha! Then *I'll* get it, and finally get the bleeding Xenu out of here. That'll teach that damned loser."

The shaggy Otto hurried over and unstrapped the two girls, lifted them gingerly onto his shoulders and bore them down to the now-crowded cage.

"Lock it up tight, Otto — if any of them get away, we're ash," ordered the Rept. "Make damned sure it's sealed, then send it planet-side." He stalked off in search of chow.

"Yes, sir. Yes, sir," answered Otto, bowing again and again. He locked the cage, checked it twice, then stepped to the console beside the transbeam platform. "Right away, sir. Right away," he muttered, though the Rept was long gone. He worked the controls through the activation sequence, gave the side of the console a thud with his massive fist, and watched as the cage was enveloped in swirling iridescence — then disappeared.

CHAPTER 4

Shak

"Mom! Mom!" cried Mia, shaking her mother's unconscious form.

Celine was standing at the door of their dank little cell. She peered to the left, down the long, dimly-lit corridor, littered with trash. Here and there, faint drifts of vapor wafted up from cracks in the concrete floor. Three of their surly captors sat at a rickety, three-legged table beneath a bare light globe at the corridor's end, wreathed in a cloud of noxious cigar smoke.

"W-where am I?" moaned the girls' mother.

"Mom! Oh, Mom!" cried Mia. Remi, still dazed, sat up and pulled the sobbing girl close. Mia shivered against her mother like a tiny child, with no hint of embarrassment despite her seventeen years. Celine turned to watch the pair for a moment, then returned to her study of their circumstances, looking for some way out.

"What do they want with us, Mom? What are we going to do?" cried Mia.

"We're going to be their slaves," answered Celine,

dispassionately. "Judging from their chatter, there are women from Carriere, Curt, and Keskinen in the cells down that way," she explained, gesturing to the left. "Hutters and Fillions, too, up to the right. They all look like slaves; shackled and shabbily dressed. I assume that's what's in store for us. Sex slaves would be my guess. Mom and I for sure, but maybe they'll try you out as a breeder at first, Mia."

Celine turned around to see if they'd heard. The pair glared back at her, but she was unaffected, expecting no less. Remi realized Celine was probably right, so she just held Mia tighter. Mia opened her mouth to launch a protest, but Remi gestured for quiet, shook her head gently and stroked the girl's hair.

Celine sat down on the floor and began taking stock of what she had with her. She pulled item after item out of her bodypack and arranged them before her, nodding thoughtfully. She had also zip-sealed various useful items into the linings and straps of her clothing and boots, and these she reviewed as well.

Most of her clothes, much to her mother's dismay, were military uniform whites. Just like her father's. For years, Mia had moaned about Celine's woeful lack of fashion sense, but her complaints had fallen on deaf ears. She'd eventually given up, coming at least somewhat to grips with what amounted to a law of nature: Celine would do whatever Celine *wanted* to do.

Mia's biggest worry was that other kids would tease her about her weird sister. They had, at one time, but rarely did so anymore. A few years back, a boy had teased Celine about her fascination with magic. Laughing and pointing, he'd said she was so old-fashioned that she'd never land a mate; she was just too weird. The next day, he ended up at the medic's with an array of fractured limbs and ribs, complemented by assorted contusions and a most admirable black eye. All the result of accidentally falling down an embankment, he swore. No one bought the story, but no one pressed the point, either. The kid had been stuck in a healing vat for four days; thereafter he avoided Celine studiously — as did almost everyone else. No one had seen Celine so much as touch him, but speculation spread quickly, and in short order, kids at all the surrounding academies knew to keep a respectful distance (emphasis on the "respectful"). Secretly she became known as "Celine the Wrecking Machine." Despite their discretions, Celine learned of her new title, and quite liked it. It made her seem more powerful than she felt. One kid even wrote a bit of a song about her, and it spread in secret among her peers. She discovered it, too, and was even more pleased. She was becoming a mini-legend! She hummed it to herself as she rummaged through her pack.

<blockquote>
Celine, Celine,
The Wrecking Machine
Beats up the boys and is awfully mean
Breaks both their arms
And fractures their legs,
So stay, stay —
Or she'll turn you to eggs!
She practices magic
By day and by night,
So stay far away,
Or you'll feel her spell's bite
She'll use her dark magic
And cast you a spell
Knock you out cold and then
Send you to Hell

Celine, Celine,
The Wrecking Machine
Killed all her mates
</blockquote>

And now reigns as queen.
Practices magic by day and by night,
So stay away, stay —
Or be banished from sight
Stay away, stay —
Or she'll cast you a spell,
Knock you out cold
And then send you to HELL!

Next to the fragile, fashionable Mia, Celine looked out of place. Always had. She took top female athletic honors year after year, often outshining most male competitors her age. She was like one of the Atlantean gladiators whose statues now lined the corridors of G.O.D.'s headquarters in every sector. Her physique and bearing weren't her only unusual attributes, though. Unlike almost everyone around her, she had deep green eyes and dark chestnut hair.

Most Pleiadeans were blond-haired and blue-eyed, so Celine stood in sharp contrast. Different though she was, her beauty was literally striking, at an almost subconscious level. No one would openly *admit* to being stricken, however. There was too strong a social agreement that being different was unacceptable, tantamount to some sort of dread disease.

Celine was well aware of her own difference, the senseless stigma it carried, and the fact that so many were inwardly conflicted at their own reactions to it. She could scarcely have cared less. If anything, it was a plus: people left her alone to do as she pleased. And what pleased her most was learning and practicing magic.

There was no one on Erra who could or would help Celine with her magic. For years, she had had to rely completely on the telepathic tutelage of her friends, the Mentors. Since they had introduced her to Jager, she now had his enthusiastic help as well. Learning and practicing together, their progress had more than doubled its pace. Much to the Mentors' satisfaction.

Though once held in high regard, magic had become thought of as old-fashioned (if not absurd) on the worlds under High Chancellor Scabbage's control. Very few practiced it any longer, openly or otherwise. Books and recordings on the subject could still be found, but they were regarded as little more than amusing fantasy. Scabbage himself had been the source of this turn of opinion, when he decreed that the serious study and practice of magic were strictly forbidden. Simple illusionist's tricks were permissible as entertainment, but even these were generally frowned upon.

Some years before his ban on the subject, Scabbage had badly, badly botched a particular sequence of spells he'd attempted to cast on a girl he was sweet on, named Lisam. So serious was his misapplication of basic principles that the girl had been badly destabilized, and finally died.

Some speculated (ever-so-privately) that Scabbage's attempts, overt and covert, to end the practice of magic were a veiled attempt to bury his own crimes. Others thought he was afraid someone might attempt to use magic on *him* — something he could never abide. No matter (to him) that so many had benefited and *could* benefit from competent magicians' honest work. No matter that so many had long valued magic so highly. He insisted it had to be phased out and ultimately quashed, at all costs. He even went so far as to issue an Official Policy to the effect that anyone found using magic outside certain strictly delineated circumstances was to be imprisoned, immediately and at once, on RPF113.

Of course, everyone knew very well that since the passing of the Founders — the scholars, statesmen and administrators who had long ago established the government's working structure — it had been utterly against Policy for anyone to set *new* basic Policy. Orders or programs could be issued to apply established Policy in new circumstances, but these were strictly temporary and could never contradict, alter, evade or subvert original Policy in any way. No one was even vaguely willing to point this out to the High Chancellor, though. That would be suicidal.

Just to add to the insane paradox, there was no being in all the broad universe more continually, rabidly insistent that Policy be followed — to the last letter, always and forever, period, shut the ____ up, you degraded ____! — than Deebee Scabbage, High Chancellor.

So people just sucked up or ignored the mind-bending contradictions and let Scabbage do what Scabbage did. The alternative was to speak up, and anyone who'd ever dared do *that* had disappeared forever. Often along with their families and close friends.

Policy did not state anywhere — nowhere in all its ancient, etched-titanium tomes — that there was anything whatever illegal about magic. All such prohibition was strictly Scabbage's. And Celine knew it; she had done her homework. So she had no qualms about practicing her magic, secure in the certainty that she was abiding by *true* Policy. It actually helped that magic was now considered silly and old-fashioned in her sector, and even shunned. That made it safer for her to practice, so long as she was discrete about it. Fortunately for Celine, the sectors outside Scabbage's domain were not magic-averse. She took advantage of this every time she travelled, particularly during her yearly trips to the Draco Advancement Conventions.

"Perfect!" said Celine, completing her inventory. All her hidden assets were still there, including a tiny light-orb, water purification button, fire starter, assorted power crystals and other handy items. Her left boot's side panel concealed a six-inch blade with a slim, elegantly formed handle. In the right boot was an incant-baton, carved from a desert Joshua tree, ready for spell casting. All safe. She smiled.

Mia had been watching her insufferable sister fawning over the ridiculous gadgets and toys she seemed so in love with. "Really, Mom," Mia whined, "does she have to do that now? She should be finding us a way out of here!" Remi just hugged Mia closer and stroked her arm, as a mother would sooth a small child. Even she was sometimes perturbed at Celine's insistence on doing as she pleased. Unlike Mia, though, Remi understood *why* her adopted daughter was so strong-willed — and how important it was to accept it.

CHAPTER 5

Princess Linglu

Having completed her inventory, Celine set about returning each item to its proper place.

Her father had taught her that most security scanners missed items that were strictly organic, so she had carved her knife from the horn of a creature native to Rinder. A massive, snow-white beast, it was similar in form to Earth's rhinoceros, but three times its size. Males of the species shed their single white horn at the close of their mating season, then promptly began growing a new one for the mating cycle to follow. Her incant-baton was also entirely organic. Though thinner and more delicate than most, it was as potent as any. It would be invaluable should the time come when magic must be brought into play.

Unfortunately, the one item that didn't appear in Celine's inventory was her most prized: her communication stone. The flat, smooth disc had been concealed in the lining of her helmet, the one element of her kit lost in the kidnapping.

With everything stowed neatly, Celine resumed her

attempts to reach Jager, West, or any of the other Mentors. Sitting on the floor with her back against a wall, eyes closed, she frowned with the telepathic effort. Remi noticed, and looked on, puzzled at what had her daughter so absorbed.

"No luck," thought Celine. Not the faintest connection. Her probing was still blocked, utterly.

Abandoning her efforts, she looked about and noticed her mother's puzzlement and concern. "Mom, don't worry. Things will be okay." She relaxed, took a deep breath and began reviewing everything that had transpired since she'd settled in to hear that cryophysics lecture, back at the convention. She felt strangely queasy. Not in a particularly bad way, just an odd twist on excited anticipation. It looked as though, after all her years of preparation, the moment the Mentors had been grooming her for had arrived.

It seemed to Celine that she'd always known her life would be far from normal. Even as a toddler, she had had a faint inkling that she was *different* from the big, kind people around her — and not just different in size. When, on her eighth birthday, she had had a remarkable, life-changing dream — one which she much later learned was known as The Dream of Atlantis — she instinctively kept it a secret from her parents, and from everyone else. Not that she was in the habit of discussing her dreams with others; it was just that she knew *this* one must be kept to herself.

She had recognized that the experience was deeply significant, but not *why*. She had understood that it confirmed her difference from her family, from her schoolmates, from everyone. And somehow she had known that her future path was now irrevocably set.

The Dream centered on the history and fate of Atlantis, a planet concealed for eons in the double-star system some Earth astronomers had designated Theta Tauri. Once she had dreamed it, her interests and priorities had shifted. Ever since, the only things that had truly mattered to her were training, magic, Jager, the Mentors, and the purpose they shared. All these things were integral. Inseparable. And, necessarily, secret. Secret even from her beloved father.

Only one other person had ever had the Dream. For centuries on centuries, some of the finest minds in hundreds of systems had sought its significances and secrets. They wrote volumes of theories, and wished and prayed they could experience it themselves. They studied and speculated on what it meant; on why the young man Schimpel had had it, and not someone older, or a royal, or a priest, or a member of another race. Or why and how the Dream was connected to the primitive planet Earth, and the Ancients who had lived there before their cities were destroyed by the Brothers.

Schimpel had been an undistinguished young man, the son of a fish merchant. Yet he had saved a great dragon — the only heir to the Nibiru throne — from death in the jaws of a vicious rogue dragon.

The planet Nibiru was home to a race of highly intelligent dragons, known for their wisdom, their prowess in the ways of magic, and their devotion to collecting objects of great beauty and value.

Nibiru orbited Sol — Earth's Sun — in a highly eccentric path that took it far, far beyond the most remote of Sol's more conventional children.

Ordinarily, any planet with such an orbit would be a dark and frigid waste-world; it would almost always be too far out in deep space to benefit from the Sun's warming rays. However, the All of All — an ancient race of highly advanced beings — had chosen Nibiru for a special role in their plans to guide this universe's development. When they found the planet, it had just a single, cold moon. They created a second moon, not much larger than the first, but with many of the characteristics of a tiny star. This "false sun" provided the light and warmth that had allowed Nibiru to develop a rich, thriving ecosystem. It was the perfect home for the creatures the All of All brought there — ancestors of what would become a noble race of sentient dragons.

Nibiru passed relatively close to Earth's orbit during one stretch of its own long trek around the Sun. It was during such close approaches that Nibiru dragons would travel through a tube-chute vortex — a naturally-occurring "wormhole" in the fabric of space and time — to visit the lovely blue planet, legendary among them as a retreat for rest and recreation.

Visiting dragons returned to Nibiru near the end of their planet's close pass. They avoided staying on Earth for extended periods; while there, they aged much more quickly than on their homeworld, due to differences in the planets' atmospheres, electromagnetic fields, and common minerals. They had to pay close attention to the time window for a safe return to Nibiru; if they were careless or encountered unexpected delays, they could be stranded on Earth for hundreds of its years.

Princess Linglu's father, a member of Nibiru's ruling family, had promised his daughter in marriage to a cousin whom young Linglu detested. She made a terrible scene when she learned of the plan, hoping her father would relent. Her ploy didn't work — the wedding remained scheduled for the last day of spring, a year and a half hence. Linglu decided to travel to Earth until the appointed time, to wallow in her sorrows. She took with her an entourage of fourteen servants, including her father's favorite chef, much to his anger.

One autumn afternoon, Linglu and her servants were picnicking on the shore of a beautiful lake. The servants, figuring they were on vacation too, over-ate and fell asleep, sprawled about the picnic site. The princess was delighted at her

unexpected freedom. She wandered to the water's edge and settled on a broad, flat rock to bask in the sun and enjoy the peaceful scene. She neither saw nor heard the rogue dragon until it was much, much too late. He captured and imprisoned her, then demanded an outrageous ransom — and her throne — in exchange for her return. The demands were unthinkable; Linglu knew it, and accepted a lifetime of captivity as her royal duty.

Forty-eight warriors — dragons, humans and others — perished trying to rescue Linglu from her evil captor. The dragons among them made the attempt out of a sense of honor and selfless duty, with no thought of personal gain. The non-dragons came for various noble reasons, but most also harbored an unspoken hope. Each wished that he or she might be so instrumental in the princess's rescue that she would make them her Companion, take them with her to Nibiru, and reward them with some of the unimaginably vast treasure to which she was heir.

Legend tells that one midwinter night, the young Schimpel had a mystic dream, rich with revelations. Among them was a method by which a malicious dragon might be defeated. Knowing well the story of Linglu's captivity, he vowed to use his new knowledge to free her at last. Motivated only by a sense of justice and duty, he had no thought of reward beyond the satisfaction of having done what was right, against all odds.

When those close to him heard of his intentions, they either advised against the attempt, or begged him to reconsider. Schimpel would hear none of it. After assembling the weapons, gear and magical tools he would need, and practicing until their expert use was second nature, he secured passage on a small ship bound for Earth. Once there, he tracked down and challenged the evil beast, defeated it in heated battle, and humbly informed Linglu that she was free to return home.

In the months before the tube-chute would be available for her return, the two became the closest of friends. So very close, that shortly before the day set for her departure, she invited the young man to become her Companion: to form a spiritual bond with her. He humbly accepted, and the two were linked — the first such linking to take place anywhere but on Nibiru.

Schimpel was never seen on his native world again, though he paid one brief visit to Earth, many years later. Though his story soon spread throughout the sectors, Schimpel never revealed the details of the Dream to anyone. It disappeared with him when he passed away on Nibiru. In his subsequent lives, he never revealed who he had been, nor the secret he carried. He knew the legend well: one day the Dream would come to another, and that other would become a dragon's Companion, just as he had.

Over the centuries that followed Linglu's rescue, many warriors, adventurers and fortune hunters travelled to Earth, seeking to befriend a visiting dragon. They reasoned (or just blindly hoped) that by doing so, they would influence the Powers behind the Dream to reveal it to them. None ever succeeded — so none ever travelled to Nibiru, either. Direct travel to the planet by space ship was useless — it was shielded by a powerful hex that prevented landing. Transbeam transmissions were similarly blocked. The *only* known way for anyone but a dragon to make the trip was as a dragon's chosen Companion. And only one whom the Dream had visited could ever be so chosen.

Scabbage was among the many who dreamed of gaining access to the immeasurable wealth of Nibiru. Of course, the wretch knew nothing about true friendship or bonding of any kind — much less the profound bond of Companionhood. His plan was to learn the secret of the Dream, and then subvert a dragon into linking with him. Next, he would accompany the trusting creature to its home planet, annihilate as many dragons as necessary, and claim the planet's treasures for himself. Each year, Scabbage paid out huge sums to researchers, directing them to discover how the Dream could be triggered. This had been going on for centuries, with no result other than thousands of dead or devastated research subjects — and researchers.

Scabbage promised fabulous wealth to anyone who had the Dream and reported to him. Few believed he would ever actually part with the promised riches, but still there were thousands who worked, prayed, conjured and connived through the centuries, all in the hope of inducing the Dream in themselves. Occasionally someone would come up with a scheme to make it appear he'd had the Dream, and present himself to Scabbage for the reward. In every case, the schemer was quickly exposed as a fake and exiled to RPF113.

No one had experienced the true Dream in all the centuries since Schimpel's time. Not until now. When Celine realized the truth of what she'd experienced, she also recognized that revealing the fact would put her family and everyone who knew her in grave danger. And so she had kept it as her most closely guarded secret.

That is, until the Mentors introduced her to Jager. Jager, who had experienced the Dream as well. The Mentors explained to both young people that the Dream was a tool they had created, as part of a grand plan for achieving their benevolent aims. Celine and Jager realized that they must be the "Moon" and the "Hunter" the legends described; they had been chosen and charged with a sacred responsibility. When the Mentors indicated that the time was right, they would fly across the stars in a white chariot. It was their destiny.

While still in the womb, Celine had been aware of people nearby, and had attempted to communicate with them. She soon discovered they weren't aware of her, and had little or no telepathic ability. She did have one bit of success in her efforts. She repeatedly told her mother-to-be that she wished to be called Celine. Evidently, she got her subliminal message through: within minutes of her birth, her mother announced to the proud father that the little girl would be named Celine.

It wasn't until she was older — and well versed in legends and lore — that Celine realized *why* she had been so insistent about her name. West praised her for making the connection, but advised her to keep her realization secret from everyone but Jager, whose name was similarly significant. Both were pivotal pieces of an ancient puzzle and prophesy which spanned space from the Pleiades to Atlantis. Locked within their genetic code and the matrices of their minds were skills, perceptions and abilities that would make them potent agents in the Mentors' crusade against the Brothers.

Two beings of the same race as the Mentors, the Brothers had been banished from the All of All for their aberrant and evil ways. The vicious pair had engineered a universal catastrophe that would bring all sentient beings under their suppressive control. They had been patiently working to execute the scheme for centuries.

As Celine and Jager grew through childhood and adolescence, they did their best to appear normal, careful never to use their rapidly-growing abilities in ways that others might notice. When in strictest privacy, both strove hard and long to increase their knowledge, and to expand and sharpen their skills.

CHAPTER 6

Otto

Celine sat near the front of the cell, deep in contemplation, apprehensive about the daunting task before her. She looked at her mother and sister, huddled at the back of the cell like a couple of beggars, then surveyed the corridor they would soon have to traverse. First, she must get them all out of this stinking cell, and then away to safety. She had managed to keep her abilities secret for ages, but today that might have to change, if she was going to pull this off.

Remi and Mia were more worried about their capture than Celine. Celine understood their situation was just the universe working in its mysterious ways. She knew that, as always, she was exactly where she *should* be; where she *needed* to be.

Remi and Mia were not parts of the puzzle, though, and not equipped to deal with the sort of dangers confronting them. She had to get them to safety so she could operate freely.

Come to think of it, no — the need to get them to safety must be part of what *should* be, too. No sense pondering such intricacies, though. It was time to plan and to act. She wished she could consult Jager and West, but her connection with them was still blocked. She must come up with a plan on her own, and execute it. A *good* plan.

A week passed with no change in their situation. They were still locked in their cell and the daily routine was just as dreary. They'd thought that if they behaved, they might be granted some freedoms. Maybe even permission to join the other slaves, working in the prison gardens. Celine had hoped so, as it would give her many more options for an escape plan. But it didn't happen. Nothing happened. On one hand, that was fortunate — at least they weren't harmed or abused. On the other hand, it left her almost nothing around which to build a plan.

There was one small variable in their circumstances: one of the guards, called Otto, spoke to them more often than the others. He had an almost friendly bearing, quite in contrast to the harsh surliness of the rest.

Otto didn't dare admit it to anyone, but he had taken a shine to the new prisoners. They didn't seem to fear him. They even thanked him when he brought their food. And they smelled good, too. He began lingering after delivering their scanty meals, just to be near them, hear their voices and enjoy their scent. It felt almost like having a second family.

Celine sensed Otto's affection. She could see he felt sorry for them, and that he wished there were some way he could ease their lot. Here was the opening she needed. She formulated a plan, and explained it carefully to her mother and sister.

All guards wore translator units, so Remi and the girls could understand Otto easily, and he could understand them in turn. Over time, they had learned a bit about him. "How is your son doing, Otto?" asked Remi one afternoon, munching a brattle from the meal he'd brought them.

To her surprise, Otto went sad at her question, and began to sniffle. A few tears seeped out. "Augusti is mostly weller now.

That's a good. But I only gets to talk to him on the 'visor. I don't gets to go home for five more months. I sure misses him."

"Ohhh, poor Otto! That's terrible. How can they *do* that to you? What a brute your boss is, keeping you away from your family! I don't know what I would do if I were you. I couldn't stand being away from my girls for so long. How do you manage to be so strong? You must hate it."

"Yes, ma'am, I misses them. I do," sniffed the massive guard. He flopped to the stone floor, took his woolly head in his hands and went into a mournful pout. The sight of such a powerful creature, armed and uniformed, pouting piteously was just too much; Remi had to hold back a smile.

Reaching through the bars, she, put her arm across a hairy shoulder to comfort him. "Now, now, Otto, it's okay," she soothed. "Would you like to see your family? I think I could help with that."

This only made Otto cry! Remi and the girls were horrified; what if other guards should hear, and come to investigate? What if some other prisoner complained? It could mean the end of Otto's assignment, and their one small hope would be gone. Luckily, the rest of the guards were either asleep or caught up in a rowdy card game. All the cellblock's other prisoners were out working in the fields, or as sex toys in the nearby garrison. So no one heard Otto's blubbering.

"Waddaya...mean...you...you h-helps me?" asked Otto, between sighs and sobs.

"Otto, I can guarantee you a reward for helping us. A new job, too. I swear it," said Remi. Otto just stared at the woman, his sobbing stilled and his forehead creased in a muddle of hope and puzzlement. "Well, Otto, what do you think?"

"You means it? You means you can get me home to see my Augusti? And get me a other job?"

Mia and Celine struggled to keep straight faces at the

melodrama. Thinking it a good opportunity to ease the tension between them, Celine gave Mia a conspiratorial smile — but her sister just turned away. "Oh, well," sighed Celine, turning back to listen to her mother and the guard.

"Yes I can, Otto. You just have to do some small things to help us get away. Once we're safe, I can reach my husband and ask him to help you. I know he will reward you handsomely and get you a decent job near your family. This I promise you on the lives of my girls."

"You promises on your *girls?* Oh, I know you tells me the truth now. You loves 'em. I see it," answered the guard. "But how do I helps you get outta here?"

Remi couldn't remember a sweeter question. "So good, Otto, so good. Now, this is what you do," answered Remi, and she carefully explained the simple plan the three had devised.

Their plan under way, they slept well that night. But morning brought disaster. Soader had ordered that the three prisoners be transported at once to the Dulce underground compound on Earth. Otto cried when he reported for duty, to find Remi and her daughters being marched down the long corridor by a pair of surly Repts. His hopes crushed, tears crept down toward his hairy jowls.

Otto had always thought escape from his wretched posting was impossible, and had resigned himself to his lot. Hearing Remi's simple plan had changed all that. He saw he didn't *have* to stay here forever. They couldn't keep him. Not if he didn't let them. And so he made a plan of his own — and quietly stole away the following morning.

Soader and his minions were busy preparing for the Titan Portcullis's opening, now just weeks away. So when Otto's disappearance was reported, Soader shrugged it off. The scum wasn't worth the effort to track down and terminate. If they didn't open that portcullis in time, Soader's plans would be trashed. No way was *that* going to happen. So Otto was free to live out his days, happily at home with his growing family.

Fate wasn't nearly so kind to Remi and her daughters just now. Two Repts, one tall, one short and stout, dragged them roughly from their cell. Through the long, dark cellblock corridor, down several flights of stairs and on through a dim, damp tunnel they were herded, prodded viciously at every slightest stumble or hesitation.

"Eieeee!" screamed Mia, tripping over the decaying corpse of what appeared to have been a young girl. A long hank of faded blond hair trailed across the stone floor from atop the rotting head. Landing hard on hands and knees, Mia saw what had caused her fall and struggled to regain her feet. Instead she slipped on a patch of slime and fell backward onto her hands and butt. Terrified, she scuttled backwards like a fleeing crab, desperate to distance herself from the decomposing form. She only succeeded in ramming into the tunnel wall, flanked by two more inert bodies — young girls again, blond just like the first.

"Mom!" Mia shrieked. *"MOM!!"*

The Rept guards looked on in contemptuous amusement.

"Shhhh! Quiet, dear. It's okay," Remi soothed. "We're all right. Shhhh. Now, let's go." She helped Mia to her feet, putting arms around the trembling girl to steady her, and barely smothering a violent shudder of her own. Celine stood by, expressionless — but thankful that Remi was there to manage the burden of her sister.

One of the Repts grunted "Break's over. Move it," and the painful shuffle through the tunnel continued. Finally, they were yanked to a stop at the entrance to a large, domed room.

"Git inside, filth," slurred the taller Rept, shoving Mia. "Move!" Mia stumbled again, but Remi caught her. Celine followed the two into the room, still showing no sign of her thoughts. The second Rept gestured toward a crude platform at the room's center; Celine stepped up onto it. Remi followed, leading Mia. The Repts stepped up to flank the Pleiadeans, and the shorter spoke into the comm pickup clipped to his collar. Soon cobalt swirls of shimmering energy enveloped the group, building in intensity until they vanished with a pop and a flash — transbeamed to a matching platform in a spacecraft high overhead.

The moment the transfer was complete, the Repts lashed the women together with binding wire, spat from a gun-like projector. The wire stung and held them tightly, but stopped short of breaking tender human skin.

"OWW! You're hurting me!" cried Mia, but the Repts ignored her. Instead they led the three to a cargo bay, shoved them into a small, filthy cubicle and slammed its door shut.

Celine remained calm. She knew they were in no real danger. It was clear their captors knew of her telepathic abilities — why else go to the trouble of blocking her? They must also be aware of her importance and value, or they'd have been treated as expendable slaves.

Though she'd confirmed her menting was still being blocked, Celine resolved to try reaching Jager and West from time to time, on the off chance that the shielding might go down at some point. She knew wielding any magic was out of the question for the moment. It was too likely to draw unwanted attention. And if it wasn't already known about or suspected, revealing her skill could just make their situation even worse, and greatly reduce its potential value.

"No noise, or you pay," hissed the smaller Rept, spittle flying at Celine's face but splatting harmlessly on the cubicle's transparent side. The other guard punched a button on a panel beside their new prison, enveloping them in a pale orange mist — a mist all too familiar to Celine. In seconds the three slumped to the deck, unconscious.

"Ha," rasped the Rept. "Gave 'em too much. They'll be out for a couple of days."

"Well, good, I say. I hate their whining," grunted his partner. "I don't know what makes these blasted bitches so precious that we had to go to all this trouble. Their kind don't make for good transfers, nor for breeders neither. Too thin. I've no idea what in Xenu's name that scum Soader is up to, or what he wants with 'em."

"Yeah, I hear ya. I hate humans, too. We'll have useable transfer stock soon, though. Earthlings! Then we won't have to deal with primitives or Soader anymore. I'm counting the days." The pair trudged out of the hold.

Minutes later, the craft accelerated sharply, slamming the drugged-out Pleiadeans against the cubicle's back wall.

CHAPTER 7

Dulce Compound

New Mexico
Earth

Two days later, Remi and the girls woke to find themselves locked in yet another cell. There was an important difference from their earlier accommodations, though. This cell held a fourth person. She was human, rather tall for a female, and with graying auburn hair.

Celine had been the first to awaken. She'd opened her eyes to find a strange woman bent over her, humming softly and gently tending to a cut on her arm.

Noticing the girl was awake, the woman paused in her ministrations. "Hello," she said. A battered translator unit was strapped around her thin neck, its old-style earpieces protruding slightly from her ears. "My name is Shellee. Here — drink this. It should help."

Celine sat up and took the dented tin cup. It was obvious at once that Shellee was a long-time prisoner. She had the pallid skin of an underground dweller, nearly translucent. Her faint odor suggested a death home — the sort where bodies are stored before disposal. Her face and attitude were those of someone utterly weary of life, perhaps even yearning for a quiet death to end an existence stripped of hope. "Where are we?" asked Celine after a couple sips, regarding Shellee kindly.

"Beneath Dulce. Level seven. That's two miles down."

"Earth?"

"Yes. Dulce, New Mexico. North American continent. Do you know where that is? Do you know anything of Earth? You might know it as Planet 444."

"Yes, I know a bit about it. Thanks."

Celine turned to see her mother and sister beginning to stir. She let Shellee tend to them. Mia, true to character, screamed when she first saw the stranger, and pulled harshly away. Remi came to the rescue, calming the young girl. Soon both were sharing from the old cup, while Shellee swabbed their cuts and sores with a pungent, greenish salve.

Celine left them, moving to the back of the cell to retry her telepathy; still no luck. She realized she might have to use magic if things did not start to improve soon. At any time, their captors might find her mother and Mia useful in ways she didn't want to contemplate. Particularly the beautiful young delicate, Mia.

Celine reflected a while longer, then turned to their cellmate. "Shellee, who's in charge of this place? Please tell me whatever you can about their set-up."

A disheartening pall came over Shellee as she spoke. "First, I must tell you that Soader, the one who runs this place, put me here with you as a spy. He'll use anything you say against you and your people. Even if I don't want to tell him, he has ways of extracting information." She lowered her eyes, avoiding Remi and Mia's venomous looks at this revelation.

"It's okay, Shellee, I know," responded Celine, gently placing a hand on the woman's thin arm. "I don't want you harmed, so please do *not* try to hide anything from them — tell them whatever they want to know. Promise?"

Shellee looked deeply into the girl's eyes for a few moments before nodding gently and responding. "Okay, I will. Thank you. I've been in these cells for a bit longer than twelve years now. There are thousands of others here, too — mostly Earthlings. The Repts and Greys do all the work, but Soader's the big boss."

"Who imprisoned you here, and why?" asked Remi.

"My husband."

"What?" gasped Remi. "Your husband?!"

Now Shellee looked directly at Remi for several seconds, as if taking the woman's measure. Then she averted her eyes. "My husband is Deebee Scabbage. A High Chancellor. He was once a good and sincere man — or I never would have married him. But as he rose to power, he became harsh, even cruel. For years now, when anyone has done anything he's interpreted as a challenge or embarrassment — whether it was actually meant to be or not — they have disappeared. Like me. I embarrassed him badly once, by accomplishing something he'd failed at."

Now Remi and Celine recognized the woman, but only barely; she had once been quite robust and lovely, a far cry from her present state. Yes, it was Shellee, the High Chancellor's wife of many years past, when Celine was just a toddler. She'd appeared often in the newsfeeds. They recalled the reports about how the woman had been killed in a tragic accident.

"A lot of those under his rule think he's wonderful," Shellee continued. "Not surprising, since he's extremely clever at PR and can really turn on the charm. Most people who have to work anywhere near him cower when he's around, though. They fear they'll be beaten, screamed at, strangled, demoted, disgraced or sent away. They don't dare just leave, either; they know his people will track them down and haul them back, and then they'll *really* be in trouble. If you desert and he doesn't order you brought back, it can be even worse — he's likely to ruin your life, even harass or harm your family.

"Officials and government workers who he doesn't despise too much, and who seem like they might someday be useful, he sends here. Those who seriously piss him off end up in a place they call 'The Hole.' You mostly never see them again.

"So yes, my husband sent me here. Up to now, I think being his wife has kept me safe, but I don't think that will be true much longer."

Remi was shaking her head slowly in disbelief as Shellee continued. "Being here so long, I understand a lot of what goes on, and why. The main thing is, Soader has Greys conducting breeding experiments. They usually use abducted Earthlings, but some subjects are offered freely by cults, or the Illuminati, or other such groups. Sometimes when they're low on subjects, the Greys just ask my husband for more. He's always happy to send them disgraced followers — people he's accused of incompetence, or of questioning his actions or authority. Or new subjects are just abducted, as you were."

Mia asked, "What are these breeding experiments for? What are they trying to do?"

"They're trying to produce Earthlings with heightened telepathic and other spiritual abilities. They need them as host bodies for soul transfers. Without transfer bodies, the Repts and Greys would become extinct, because they can scarcely breed anymore. They can't transfer to just any body, though. The DNA has to be exactly right, and the inhabiting spirit has to have progressed far enough, spiritually, to trigger a specific level of pineal gland activity. That's pretty complicated, I know. But that's how they've got it worked out. If a Rept or Grey takes over a body that doesn't meet all the right specifications, they're trapped. They lose their memory and end up as primitives, like most Earthlings are. Oh — and if the pineal gland hasn't been triggered correctly, it's even worse for the new inhabitant. They stick in that body forever, even after it's dead and rotted. Like a ghost, pinned to a useless corpse. Talk about hell! Apparently, several advanced races have already gone extinct, so the Greys and Repts are desperate. Other approaches they've tried haven't worked, or don't work anymore. The Earthling protocol is all they've got left, and their time is running out."

"But, why Earthlings?" asked Remi.

"Humans were brought to Earth thousands of years ago, by *your* people, in fact — Pleiadeans. So Earthlings are really displaced Pleiadeans. Earthlings, Pleiadeans, same people. The ones transported to Earth were all memory-wiped so that they and their descendants would remain low-profile until G.O.D. needed them. If they'd just been dumped on Earth with their memories intact, they would have developed advanced technologies far too quickly, caught the attention of other societies, and been exploited before G.O.D. was ready for them.

"Pleiadean DNA works best at developing disease antibodies, which is why they were chosen by G.O.D. to be preserved on a hidden, primitive planet. Years later, Repts came to Earth and inseminated many Earthlings to make human-Rept hybrids, so you find some Earthlings with Earthling-Rept DNA. Not long ago, I heard that cataclysmic circumstances in the Pleiades had forced a change to the timetable for many advanced aliens. That caused a huge change here in the tunnels. It's why you were abducted," Shellee said, speaking directly to Celine. The two exchanged looks and knowing nods. Remi and Mia didn't quite understand, but they were still too distraught to care.

"I know," Celine responded. "But why did they capture my mother and sister as well?"

"I don't know," Shellee replied. Remi was about to speak, but was cut short by a loud commotion up the tunnel. She turned to see a burly figure walking toward them: Soader. He looked like exactly what he was: a cross between a Rept and a human. His reptilian side had dominated, in terms of physical features. The result was far from an attractive sight. Two Greys armed with blasters followed the hybrid, a few yards behind.

"Hi, ladies," Soader laughed. "Getting to know each other, I hope?" All four women were silent, glaring. Mia clung more tightly to her mother. "Wow, you're gorgeous," Soader leered, eying Celine and Mia and licking his lips.

"Get your pervert eyes *off* them, you worm! Stay *away* from them or you'll regret it," Remi railed.

"Har har!" laughed Soader. "Feisty! I see why that puke hubby of yours nabbed you. And quite the looker you are, too — just like your tasty kiddos. I like women like you. We'll have to have some fun later. There's a positively huge bed in my shuttlecraft up at Salt Lake. Well-stocked bar, too. Even have some special elixir you could share, if you're a good girl," he said, imagining Remi with the bloody brew dripping down her chin and onto her breasts. Remi spat through the bars, glaring red hatred. The repulsive hybrid only laughed harder. Spinning around, she pulled Mia with her to the farthest corner of the cell.

"Haaaarrrr! Your two little girls are mine, pretty lady. Both worth a bundle, too — especially that ripe little breeder bitch you're coddling so very sweetly. I'm surprised she hasn't been scooped up before now. Yeah, I might have to use her personally. I always like to keep my, uh, *hand* in; take direct part in the important research we're doing here, don't you know.

"Saaaaay! I should maybe get started right away, don't you think? Use the pair of 'em tonight to help charge the emotion-condenser tubes that much faster. We could use some new meat on the sex-dream experiments, too. Blondie there looks like she would prove herself useful there. Haaaarrr! Yes, yes — I'd love to hear her groans and moans. Har haaaarrrr!

"First things first, though. They can pitch in and help charge those condensers. They're nearly full, but every little bit helps. In a week or so I'll have enough charge stocked up to open the Titan Portcullis, and then everything will change. Everything! I gotta tell ya, when I come up with a plan, it's fabulous."

Remi's hateful glare had only intensified. "Oh, but I see the lovely lady is mad. Feeling left out — that's it! Not to worry, you tasty little thing. I promise to use you, too. No need to feel left out. Harrrrr!"

Remi turned away and held Mia tighter.

"Now, take a guess, Mommy Dear," Soader continued. "Do you know what happens to everyone stuck on Earth after I get through that portcullis? Harrrrrrr! That's right, doll face. *Kaboom!* Blown to the stars. Every stinking Earthling, Grey and Rept — *gone!* That means you, too. But don't worry, it won't happen right away. Not until your pathetic excuse for a husband shows up to rescue you. Arrogant slime that he is, I still wouldn't want him to miss out on all the fun. Har haaaarrrr!"

Remi just kept her back to Soader, not knowing what else to do. Mia began to cry. Remi was relieved; it gave her something else to concentrate on. Anything but that hideous beast outside their cell. All four women breathed easier when Soader finally left.

The next morning, a Grey raked his blaster back and forth across their cell door, jolting the women awake. "Git up!" he barked. Shellee rose first and walked straight to the door, then stood with her arms stiffly at her sides, chin lowered and feet spread. Celine understood Shellee's purpose and did the same.

"Mom, please come here," Celine said.

Remi slowly stood, got Mia up with an effort, and led her to line up with Celine and Shellee.

"Mom, what's happening?" Mia asked.

"No talking," barked the Grey, banging his blaster against the bars. Another Grey approached, shackles and chains clanking in his hands. The first Grey unlocked the door for his partner, who stalked in. Shellee offered an ankle and was soon shackled. Celine followed suit, but when the guard came to Mia, problems began.

"Mom, please don't let him touch me," wailed the girl. The guard responded with a swift blow to her shoulder with his blaster butt, knocking her to the ground.

"Stop. *Stop,*" interrupted Shellee. "She doesn't understand. Let me talk to her."

The Grey grunted assent; Shellee helped Remi get Mia to her feet, then gently whispered, "It's okay, Mia. It's all right. Just do as they ask, and everything will be okay." Mia nodded, puzzled but somewhat calmed by Shellee's manner and reassurance. The Greys finished shackling the group, then led them out of the cell and down the corridor.

They had walked only a hundred meters or so when they passed the opening to a wash-chamber; inside they could see toilets, basins and shower heads ranged along the stone walls, and two drains set in the floor. Shellee spoke deferentially to the Grey leading them, asking for just a few moments' pause so the prisoners could attend to their business. The guard muttered in disgust, but agreed to a short break.

The four women shuffled into the chamber, used the toilets (a vast improvement over the crude fixture in their cell) and washed hurriedly. The water was cavern-cold, but it was such a blessed relief to wash, they scarcely noticed. When the Greys ordered them out, they obeyed promptly and resumed their shuffle down the long tunnel, one guard leading and the other behind.

After several minutes, the distant sounds of human voices

and clanking chains could be heard from farther down the tunnel. What excited the prisoners, though, was the array of aromas. Food! Soon the tunnel emptied into a broad, low-ceilinged cavern, occupied with perhaps thirty long tables, each flanked with benches. Most of the benches were occupied by Earthling females, intent on the bowls of food before them.

About a dozen Repts and Greys were scattered around the chamber, leaning against the walls as they watched their feeding charges and battled the urge to doze off. At the big room's center was a glass-walled circular booth. A narrow counter ran around its inner wall, interrupted by four doorways, ninety degrees apart. Eight Repts sat at the counters on low stools, facing outward so they could keep watch over the prisoners. Most were clearly bored nigh unto death, picking at their claws or doodling idly. A couple of them — rookies — feigned dutiful alertness.

Remi and the girls were famished. It had been three days since they had eaten anything but a few stale brattles, so they had no complaints at being shoved toward one of the tables, occupied but for four empty spots. At each place was a battered metal bowl loaded with food. *Warm* food. A cup full of some sort of brownish fluid was set in front of each bowl. They joined their fellow prisoners and dug in, glancing around apprehensively as they processed each mouthful.

Today's menu was gruel. Remi, Mia and Celine suspected that was the menu *every* day. Shellee knew it was. The stuff was awful by any civilized standard, but it was nourishing and usually at least tepid, if not quite warm. The four ate eagerly, easing the hollow, desperate ache of empty stomachs and restoring some strength. The nameless beverage they sipped worked wonders, too. It seemed to contain some sort of stimulant herb.

Some of the other women at the table were talking quietly

among themselves. Once immediate hunger was satisfied, Shellee joined in. Her companions didn't understand the language being used, and Shellee was the only one of the group with a translator unit, so she gave Remi and the girls a running account of the conversation and relayed their questions and comments.

Most of the women looked as though they had lived underground for years. Many were also pregnant. They were of several Earthling races, a rich mix of colors and sizes. There were no babies or children to be seen, though. None. And no males.

A horn blared, startling the newcomers and quelling all conversation. The veterans got up at once and began forming lines along the side of the chamber. Shellee and her companions followed their example. "Tell your mother and sister not to say a word, no matter what they see or what happens. And make them understand that those who rebel are never seen again," whispered Shellee over her shoulder.

Celine relayed the message to Remi, and asked her to pass it on to Mia. Now there was silence in the ranks, the women stolidly waiting for the next step in the routine. More Repts arrived, carrying long, shimmering goads. One made a wicked jab at the woman closest to him; her piercing scream filled the space, echoing.

Celine chanced a quick glance around and noticed the very pregnant prisoners all stood together in just one of the lines. The next consisted of women who looked to be about six months along. She guessed the rest of the lines followed a similar pattern. Those in the row she and her companions occupied were mainly middle-aged and older women. Celine could see that many of them had scabbed knees and bandaged hands. That could only mean one thing: hard manual labor.

One of the Repts walked over, grabbed Celine and Mia and shoved them toward a line of young girls. Remi cried out and tried to pull them back, but the Rept swung around and struck her with the tip of his goad. She fell to the floor, shrieking in agony; at once Mia added her own terrified cries to the din.

"No, Mia! Quiet!" warned Celine. Too late. The Rept goaded Mia in the leg, and now she screamed for real, thrashing on the stony floor beside her mother.

A huge Rept lurched through the entrance to investigate the commotion. When he saw who was screaming, he yelled, "What the hells are you doing, you cretin? Not *these*, fool! It's Soader's orders — don't damage them. Don't *hurt* them! You want to get us all sent to the Box? Or put on his damn pets' dinner menu? Get them back to their cell. NOW! Before I send you to the Box myself!"

The chastened Rept barked instructions to the Greys who had brought the cellmates to the eatery. The lead Grey growled an order at Shellee, who spoke in turn to Celine. The two helped the moaning, shuddering Remi and Mia to their feet, and soon all four were being herded back up the tunnel that had brought them.

CHAPTER 8

Mission to Earth

"Unbelievable! Now we're ordered to go shut down TS 428 *again*," the commander ranted. "It's supposed to be a soul transfer station, not a circus. What kind of bloody morons have they got posted there, anyway?"

He continued reading the dispatch on his comm pad. "The insufferable idiots are sending *Rept* souls to Earth, instead of humans! Incredible."

Tossing the comm pad aside, he continued his rant. "We're *supposed* to be making sure Earth survives. With those incompetent dolts sending Rept souls into the population, they'll have advanced nuclear weapons in a matter of decades. That will make sixty-seven nuclear planets in this sector. *Our* sector. G.O.D. will be outraged — and they'll have every right to be. They'll have our asses in ice cubes for a hundred millennia!

"We're bloody well not going to let *that* happen! Get your butts moving and put this ship on a course for Earth. Now — before I change my bloody mind and freeze you all myself, for the next *billion*." He grabbed up the comm pad, shoved it into an ensign's hands, and yelled, "Jessup! Get us moving. At once!"

"Aye, commander. Right away, sir."

Jessup turned to a red-headed young man at the helm console. "Peggers, standard course for Earth. Take us out." In moments, the docking grapples tethering the massive ship released their hold, a deep vibration reverberated through the vessel, and it began moving out of the station's vast docking bay. In less than a minute, the white and gray bulk of the Erra Portcullis Station was receding behind them. The interstellar cruiser *Queen Asherah III* was bound for Earth. The small, blue planet had been under close observation for 13,800 years. Soon it would be under attack.

The commander stood on the elevated command platform at the rear of the bridge, watching his crew. His pride in them was not often visible, but he knew every one of them was eminently competent; they'd proven it time and again, and they all had his trust. He wondered if he'd been a bit harsher than necessary just now, but pushed the thought away. They had been searching for months, without turning up even the faintest clue. He had nearly lost hope, but now it had been rekindled and he was impatient.

Commander Rafael Zulak watched his family walking across the corner of his console screen in an image-capture, then looked back over his bridge crew. Damn, he missed Hadgkiss. Their last ship had fought off two Era-Aola fighters and won, but not without casualties. His First Officer, Major Dino Hadgkiss, had been badly injured and was still in rehab, learning how to use his new bionics.

Times like this were the hardest on Zulak; his wife Remi had always been a great comfort to him, seeming to understand any situation that involved people. She always managed to say and do just the right things to help him regain control of his temper. He missed her terribly.

His eldest daughter, Mia, looked like her mother. Silken blond hair, deep blue eyes. Surely, she'd be a wonderful breeder when the time came. It was his youngest that he missed most, though. Zulak had never admitted it to anyone, but Celine was his favorite. She had always been difficult, making up her own mind about everything — which only made him even prouder of her. He saddened at the sudden memory of their last conversation. "Dad, you're not being fair," Celine had asserted. "All the other girls in my class will be at that party. If Mia asked, you'd let *her* go. It's not fair and it's not right. And you know it." She'd stormed to her room and slammed the door.

That was the last time he'd seen her. What an idiot. The argument had started over a boy. He'd been jealous of a Godsdamned boy he'd never even met. He knew he was acting like a child, but couldn't control himself. "You're being stubborn, Celine, and you're not listening to what I'm saying!" he'd called after her, to no effect.

Celine had grown up with no friends, so he should have been happy for her — at last there was someone she liked. Instead, he'd acted like a Lunndein ass, foolishly jealous of some pimply kid, light years away. He deserved to lose her. But she did not deserve to be kidnapped. He clutched the turquoise crystal necklace he kept always around his neck — a surprise gift Celine had given him a couple of years earlier.

Jessup's voice jolted Zulak back to the present. "Sir, in position at Portcullis 4."

"Peggers, are we prepared for entry?" asked Zulak.

"Yes, sir. All systems ready, sir."

"Excellent. Enter!" ordered Zulak, glancing again at the image-capture of his family. He was on his way to save them, and Soader was none the wiser — he hoped. Zulak knew the Bali

Transfer Station had not been operational for years, so in an act of pure and foolish politics, G.O.D. had permitted — "temporarily," of course — redirection of Rept souls-in-transit to Platform 5 of Transfer Station 428, on Earth's moon. Recent reports, however, showed numerous instances of soul misdirection from that platform. That *had* to be deliberate. It was just the sort of devious treachery that was Soader's stock in trade. And it was Soader who had Celine.

It would also be totally in character for the wicked, twisted creature to lure Zulak back to where their feud had begun. He was near certain he was flying into a trap, but didn't care. He just wanted his family back. He wanted his little girl safe.

The ship had entered the portcullis station, and was now in position for jump-shift to Earth orbit. "Sir, ready for jump-shift, sir," Jessup announced.

"Thank you," responded Zulak.

"Sir, all stations report jump readiness, sir," said Peggers.

"Good," acknowledged Zulak calmly, considering the circumstances and his temper. He knew that the moment they arrived above the planet — even before they began executing their official mission orders — his crew would scan the globe in search of his family. It was a routine they had followed since the kidnapping. That Earth was today's destination made Zulak more hopeful than ever. Soader had been spotted there, and that vastly increased the likelihood his family would be there, too. Zulak smiled grimly, and in his resounding voice issued the order: "Launch!"

"Launch, sir! Aye-aye!" Peggers replied. He flipped up the safety cover over the jump-drive switch and gave it a push. A deep, reverberant hum filled the ship, rising in intensity for several seconds. Then it was as though all the air in the vessel vanished for a fleeting moment — then returned with a sharp, palpable *whop*. An azure globe, half-swathed in brilliant white whorls of cloud, appeared on every forward monitor. They had arrived at Planet 444. Earth.

Zulak was out of his command chair at once, making his way across the bridge.

"Jessup, Madda, follow me. Peggers, have Sreach and Deggers meet us at Transbeam Station 3. Tell Doc Deggers to bring his kit. If the planetary scan comes up with anything even remotely interesting, I'm to be notified at once." He stepped into the lift, Jessup and Madda close behind. *"Queen,* transbeam level," he ordered; the lift doors slid shut and the team was on its way.

As the lift gathered speed, the ship spoke. "Commander, your tension index is rising. I recommend you take a stroll on the imaging-deck before transbeaming to the surface. Or perhaps a swim, preferably with your favorite mermaids." Soothing harp and woodwind music had begun playing softly in the lift chamber. Zulak ignored her, staring straight ahead and waiting impatiently to reach their destination. "Very well," the ship continued. "Please note that I shall be obliged to include your response in my transcripts."

"Madda, make sure we have extra transport buttons and blasters," Zulak ordered. "Jessup, full alert at all times. Shoot first, no questions. Got it?"

"Yes, sir."

"We don't know what we'll be facing, but I sure as Xenu don't want to walk into any trap," said Zulak, remembering his first encounter with Soader; he rubbed the nerveless stub of his lost left pinky. The lift door hissed open. The team stepped out, turned right down the corridor and soon approached Transbeam Station 3. Sreach and Doc Deggers arrived moments later from the opposite direction. No one spoke; expressions said it all.

Entering the room, Zulak addressed the young officer

manning the transbeam console. "Doyle, have you set coordinates for the Death Valley site?"

"Aye, sir."

"Have you got a location for Remi and the girls?"

Doyle shook his head. "No, sir. We haven't been able to isolate them. I'm afraid the tunnels are too deep for fine resolution."

"Dammit, Doyle! Up the power, then. I want their location!" demanded Zulak, knowing as he spoke that he was being unfair. Doyle and his team knew their business, and would have tried every possible trick to find them.

"Yes, sir," answered Doyle. "I'm prepared to bring you down under some covering trees near a little-used tunnel entrance."

"Good," Zulak said, efforting to rein in his impatience.

"I'll let you know the moment we locate your family," Doyle added. At that, the five stepped onto the transbeam platform. Doyle swept his hands across the console in a precise sequence. A loud hum filled the room. Swirls of flashing iridescence grew around the landing party, their intensity increasing as the hum rose to a high electronic whine, then ceased. The platform was empty.

The landing party hit the surface at high alert. Doyle had picked the spot well — through the surrounding foliage, they could see the hills where they'd find the tunnel entrances, but were themselves hidden from view. They could hear faint sounds coming from the nearby village — a honking car, barking dogs, some kids at play.

Each touched an icon on a sleeve panel, adjusting the appearance of their uniforms and gear so they would be as inconspicuous as possible. Despite their mix of races and sizes, they managed to look like a pack of leather-jacketed Earthling bikers — at least from a distance, to a casual observer. Their helmets prevented telepathic penetration, and had one-way visors that concealed the wearer's skin color. For the tall, fair Pleiadeans, skin color wasn't an issue. It was a different story for bronze-green Madda, and for Sreach, the Arcturian. Sreach's pale, fern-colored skin and large, almond-shaped black eyes would have startled the natives, to say the least. Gloves concealed her hands, with their three long, jointless fingers.

"Sir," said Jessup, pointing at a screen on his right sleeve, then toward a line of low hills to their north, "my map shows the Grey compound is a mile north from here, mid-way up that ridge."

"Good. Take Deggers and Sreach. Climb up to the entrance. Madda, you come with me," ordered Zulak.

"Sir? We're to split up?" asked Jessup.

"It'll be all right. We'll be back soon. There's something I must do," responded Zulak.

"Understood, sir. How long do you need?"

"If we're not back in thirty, beam to the ship."

"Yes, sir. But...sir?"

"Just do it. I'll explain later." Rafael didn't like to be cryptic, but he had to keep their minds empty of his plans. If Soader caught any one of them, he would extract *everything* they knew.

Zulak had plenty to keep secret. Before their arrival to Earth that morning, Admiral Elias Stock had relayed the news that Earth's troublesome primitives were now a protected species. Zulak hadn't yet passed this information on, despite the personal risk involved in keeping it quiet. But right now, he couldn't afford to have his team hobbled with worries over possibly damaging an Earthling, and so facing prosecution.

Jessup and the others slipped into the shadows of the rocks and pines. Zulak turned to Madda: "Okay, Madda. It's time." Madda smiled grimly, seated herself on the ground, bent forward at the waist and folded her arms over her head. Soon her body began to quiver, then to squirm, and finally to thrash about on the needle-carpeted forest floor. Zulak politely turned away. Soon Madda's form had shifted utterly. She now appeared to be the brutish Soader's identical twin. Madda was a Chameleon Rept.

"You okay?" asked Zulak. Madda uttered a few small sounds, but did not answer right away. Zulak waited patiently, knowing she needed a moment to adjust.

Soon Madda spoke in Soader's deep, guttural voice. "Yes, Raff, I'm okay." She knew that using his childhood nickname would reassure him. They had been fast friends since Primary.

"Ah. Good, Madda," Zulak sighed. "You don't have to do this, you know."

"I know, Raff. No worries. I hate Soader as much as you do. Remi and the girls are like family; you know I'd do anything to get them back." She raised herself to her feet, awkwardly at first, but gaining better control of her new form with each movement she attempted. "Well, I guess we should go meet the others."

The balance of the party had reached the Death Valley underground entrance, and were waiting in the shadows. Zulak and Madda signaled Jessup they were on their way. Madda kept her head down as best she could. Normally Zulak was taller than she, but as they approached the team, there was no way to conceal the fact that she now stood a head taller.

"Sir!" Jessup gave a half-stifled shout, mindful of the need for concealment, but deeply shaken by what he beheld: his commander, accompanied by the very psychopath they were here to track down!

Zulak raised his hand in the command gesture to stand down. Jessup and the others hesitantly lowered their weapons, rattled by the turn of events. "It's okay. This is Madda, shifted. I decided we had to go with Plan B. I'm sorry for keeping you in the dark about just what that is — especially since I can't pull it off without you." Madda caught his brief, apologetic smile as he said this, and broke into a smile of her own. It had been months since she'd seen so much as a feeble grin from her friend and superior. "Okay, here's what we're going to do," Zulak began.

The team listened intently, yet remained alert for the slightest sound or movement around them. Once everyone understood the plan in general and their individual roles in particular, they stole through the shadows toward the entrance to the enemy compound. Across the small valley, the rooftops of the popular Furnace Creek resort gleamed in the light of the rising moon, just now clearing the mountains to the east.

"Okay, this is it," said Zulak, clearing his suddenly dry throat. His thoughts were full of Remi and the girls, imagining them safe in his arms. He forced down the momentary reverie and returned his full attention to the task before them. "Madda, as 'Soader,' will trick the guards into leading her to Remi and the girls. Do what you must, but I ask you to avoid killing if you can." He laid out the plan in detail, then asked for questions. There were none. "Good. Let's get on it."

First, they must deal with the guards at the front gate — and their dogs. This would be a neat trick, as the Grey's beasts (technically not dogs, but the concept held) were not the typical, ferociously effective guard dogs common to most civilized worlds. Nope. Each was at least 325 pounds of ravening, psycho-savage animal. They were known far and wide as "beasties."

Nature had engineered the beastie to rend and consume its fellow creatures with terrifying efficiency. Then she had gone one step further, encasing the animal in some of the most effective living armor in the animal universe. Once locked in a beastie's bear-trap jaws, it was more merciful to shoot the victim than attempt rescue. The death would be just as certain, but far, far less agonizing. Beasties do not simply kill their victims outright. Once they have their prey clamped in their powerful jaws, they gnaw slowly, drawing both physical nourishment, and the raw life energy effused by the victim's terror, pain and struggles to escape. This is why beasties always prefer live food. Only in dire need will they consume non-living flesh.

The landing party was ready. Zulak sauntered up to the Grey guard who was lounging against the guard station door. "Hey, man! What a day," spoke Zulak in the Grey's tongue, strolling toward the entrance as if he did it every day. "Have you seen Dante?" he asked, hoping to throw the guard off with a non-sequitur.

"Who the Xenu is Dante?" the guard challenged. "And who the Xenu are *you?*" He moved toward the alarm button on the nearby console; the beasties raised their hackles. But before the guard could reach the button, Sreach emerged from behind a boulder and hit him with her stunner. The two beasties lunged for the Arcturian, but she stunned them mid-flight with two more quick shots. She rarely missed.

"This is too easy. Something may be wrong," thought Zulak. "Sreach, remain here," he said, watching Jessup and the others drag the inert beasts behind the guard station. He leaned the guard up against the wall. "Deggers — truth serum."

The medic produced a hypo from his kit and thrust it against the Grey's neck, injecting a measured dose. The stun was wearing off; the Grey was soon awake, but vacant-eyed from the drug. "Where are the prisoners kept?" demanded Zulak. "Where are the Gods-damned prisoners?"

"Where am I? Who are you? W...what's happening?" slurred the guard.

Zulak's control was usually exemplary, but he was short on

rest and long on anxiety over his family. He backhanded the guard so hard he fell over. Madda gasped. Zulak's move was totally unnecessary — the drug would compel answers, and they would be true, to the best of the guard's knowledge. "I'll ask you just once more. Where are the Gods-damned prisoners kept?"

"Tunnels!" croaked the guard, spitting blood. "They're in the tunnels! Bottom three levels. South end."

"The Pleiadean females — where are they?"

"What? There aren't any. No Pleiadeans. No Pleiadeans!"

"You *lie*. Pleiadean females. A mother and her two daughters. *Where are they?*" Zulak shouted, shaking the Grey like a rag doll.

"Sir," offered Deggers, with an effort to sound inoffensive. "The drug always works. He's telling the truth; at least it's the truth as he knows it." Zulak was stunned. He'd been certain his family was here. He dropped the guard. Deggers moved past his commander and injected the guard with memory-wipe; the Grey promptly fell asleep.

Zulak thought for a bit, then spoke into his comm pickup. "Doyle, bring us up." Seconds later the team stood on the transbeam platform.

"Sir, there's no activity at the station. Your incursion appears to have gone undetected," said Doyle, scanning his console. Zulak grunted an acknowledgement and headed for the lift, the others following close behind.

"Commander, your blood pressure remains elevated," said *Queen Asherah*. "You must report to sick bay at once. Dr. Deggers, please escort the commander." Both men ignored her.

The lift deposited them at the bridge, and Zulak strode forward. "Helm, take us to Dulce. Now," he barked. Peggers, taken aback at the commander's intensity, couldn't respond aloud

— his throat felt as though the officer was throttling him. So he activated the jump-shift instead.

A short while later, Peggers's strained voice interrupted Zulak's musings. "Sir, we're now above Dulce compound."

"Good. Madda, Jessup, follow me. And call the others." Zulak rushed to the lift.

Soon the party was back on the surface, just out of sight of the Dulce compound's main gate. Knowing there was no time to waste, Zulak had planned a direct, in-and-out action; he expected their presence would be detected at any moment. If found, they could lose their only chance of rescuing his family. They would go in, put transbeam locator buttons on Remi and the girls, and beam everyone out. He could only hope his family was not being held in the compound's lowest levels. He had been in those vast natural caverns years ago, when trying to capture Soader for G.O.D. edict violations; he knew their tunnels were studded with deadly gas mines.

The team advanced to the main gate, captured its pair of guards before they could sound the alarm, and sedated their beasties.

"Drug them both," ordered Zulak. "If one doesn't have answers, the other will." Deggers injected the guards, the truth drug taking effect almost at once. "Where are the Pleiadean prisoners?" demanded Zulak, shaking one of the guards violently. "Out with it. Now!"

"Soader always keeps Pleiadeans way down on the seventh level," muttered the drugged guard. "In cells near the tunnels."

Not what Zulak wanted to hear, but it was what it was. "Deggers, wipe them and put them out. Then you're coming with us. Sreach, you too. We're going to do this all together, and we're going to do it fast. In and out."

The Dulce bunker complex had seven levels, reaching two miles down into the planet's crust. At either end of the complex, two huge black elevators served all seven levels — but Zulak had no intention of using them. Too much chance for trouble. Touching his comm pickup, he spoke to Doyle: "Zulak here. 'Port us to the seventh level. We'll find Remi and the girls and get transbeam buttons on them. As soon as that's done, I'll signal again. 'Port everyone up at once. Understood?"

"Aye, sir," replied Doyle. The team disappeared from the gateway, re-materializing in the cellblock, seven levels below. They were in a corridor, about fifty feet from a cell that held several women, and close to a shuttle-train docking platform. The team's sudden appearance surprised two guards, but before the Greys could react, Sreach had stunned them both; they sprawled on the tunnel floor. Two more guards heard the commotion, but they too were neutralized the moment they ran into view. The landing party moved down the tunnel toward a large cell.

The prisoners, alerted by the noise of the struggle, had retreated to the back of their cell and cowered against the stone wall. One of them saw the second pair of guards go down, and signaled her cellmates. They now cautiously approached the front of the cell.

Zulak arrived and peered into the dimly lit enclosure. He couldn't believe his eyes — there were Remi and Mia! Yanking off his helmet, he called to them.

"Rafael! Rafael!" cried Remi, incredulous; the two rushed to the cell bars.

"Remi! Mia!" he shouted again, overjoyed. But where was Celine? "Celine! Where's Celine?!"

Sreach quickly disarmed the cell's locking mechanism, along with a couple of booby-traps set to terminate any would-be escapees. The door opened, and Zulak rushed in to embrace his wife and eldest daughter. The rest of the team stood watch over the emotional reunion.

"Where is Celine?" Zulak managed to ask again, pulling back slightly from the still-crying Remi.

"Some Rept-hybrid took her a few hours ago," she sobbed. "Soader, they call him. I'm sorry, Rafael. I tried to get him to take me instead, but he just laughed. He said you'd understand why he took her. What did he mean?"

"In a minute, darling," said Zulak. "Tell me what else he said."

"He said he'd changed his plans; then something about condenser tubes, and needing Celine. Who *is* he, Rafael? What does he want with our girl?"

"An old enemy," answered her husband. "Can you tell me any more? Anything at all?"

"He told a Grey to prep an underground train to go to some place called Salt Lake. He has a shuttlecraft stored there. He told me so a few weeks ago — said he wanted to take me there for some 'fun.'" She began to cry again. "And he said he was going to trick you into killing us all. What does he mean, Rafael?"

Zulak remembered the network of sub-surface shuttle tubes crisscrossing this region. He also knew why Soader had mentioned Salt Lake. The hybrid was baiting him. He'd expected Rafael to try to rescue his family. That's why he'd left Remi and Mia here, and taken Celine with him. He wanted Zulak to follow him. Well, Soader was going to get his wish — and then regret ever having wished it.

Zulak had pursued Soader to his Salt Lake haven once before. It was then that he'd been forced to decide between keeping his entire crew alive, or killing Soader's only child, Hiko. He'd chosen the latter, and Soader had sworn revenge.

Jessup and Sreach quickly attached transbeam locator buttons to Remi and Mia's collars. "You have to give Shellee one, too, Raff. We owe her our lives," explained Remi. Zulak nodded, and Sreach gave Shellee a button.

"Sir, we need to get out of here *now!*" Madda urged. She had spotted a faintly yellow vapor seeping from vents a dozen yards down the tunnel. Gas mines. No time to wait for her commander's reply. "Doyle, beam us up at once. Now, now, now!" she barked into her comm pickup. She turned to see Zulak rushing toward her, arms raised and face contorted in protest. But there was no other way. There were only seconds before they would all be dead, nervous systems fried by the deadly gas.

"No, Doyle! No!" screamed Zulak. Too late — the team vanished, along with the women they'd rescued. A moment later, they materialized on *Asherah*'s transbeam platform, Zulak's arms still held high in desperate protest.

"Peggers, take us to Mars orbit. Now!" demanded Madda through her comm pickup. Peggers jumped to comply, and in seconds the great ship no longer circled Earth; it had slid silently into orbit above Earth's rusty-red neighbor, Mars.

Zulak was stunned. He'd rescued his wife and eldest child, but his precious Celine was still captive on the world they'd left behind. Recovering his wits, he demanded Doyle transbeam him back at once, but Madda put a hand on his arm. "Sir, no. I understand, but we *must* regroup and re-plan. We'll find her. We'll bring her back. I know it. You know it." Zulak nodded, his composure gradually returning.

Madda spoke again to the helmsman. "Peggers, take us home. Erra. Standard orbit."

Zulak held his wife and child. The rest of the landing party stood by, recovering from the ordeal. The only one not badly shaken was their new guest, Shellee. Instead, she was elated, an incredulous grin spreading from ear to ear. It was the look of one suddenly liberated from long, cruel, and undeserved captivity.

CHAPTER 9

A Change of Plans

The evening before Zulak's raid at Dulce, Soader was having a bad time of it. He sat slumped in his desk chair, amid the rat's-nest clutter of his office. He re-read the report on his console for the twentieth time. His condenser tubes were empty! Drained! The fruits of his years of hard work had vanished in one bloody night. "Who in all hells would let that happen?" he cursed. "Don't they know who I *AM?*" He took another long drink of bloody elixir and gave a thunderous belch.

The big Rept-hybrid proceeded to drink himself into a dazed dream of his younger years, reliving the more lurid details of his most daring misdeeds. Chief among them was the heist he'd pulled with his cousin, Hobbs. The one that had landed him on the "most wanted" list for the first time. Quite an accomplishment for a mere adolescent. Had anyone looked into his office, they would have seen a drunken Rept stumbling about, dancing with himself and holding heated discussions with people who weren't there. Eventually, he passed out on the floor, face-down in a puddle of spilled elixir.

THE HEIST SOADER HAD SO fondly (if fuzzily) recalled was an epic adventure, to be sure.

"Hard right, Hobbs. *Hard!* The bastards are gaining," yelled the young Rept-hybrid, studying the shifting display on the screen before him. "Hard!"

Hobbs had already hit his controls, snapping the craft ninety degrees to the right. Only the inertial buffers kept every life form aboard from being squashed into jelly by the shift. "Okay, now what?" Hobbs asked.

"There! Into the crevice in that asteroid," Soader barked. The little ship swung toward a big asteroid looming to its right. "No idiot, not that one. The one right there!"

The shuttlecraft heeled a few degrees left and bore down on another craggy mass of space rock. "Right. That one. Get us in there deep. Good! Good! Now hang us along that wall. Right. Right. Perfect. They won't see us here. Cut her off. Shut it all down," ordered Soader, rubbing his clawed hands together.

The boys held their breaths. "I think we did it," panted Hobbs, coming down from the high of the chase.

"Get the cloak up," ordered Soader. "Get the gods-damned cloak up, you effin fool!"

"Sorry. Forgot," replied Hobbs, scanning the panel above and hitting the proper switch.

"Good," Soader commented, more to himself than to his companion. He stood, gripped the back of his chair and studied a monitor.

"I think we did it. They haven't spotted us," thought Hobbs. "Good thinking, Soader! Great place to hide," he said aloud. He smiled, but only briefly. "Too bad you killed those guards, though. I don't think we can go back home now."

"Shut your feed hole, moron," growled Soader. "They got

what they deserved. Anyone stupid enough to work a diamond reservoir on Gat II is practically *begging* to be fried." The young Soader made his way to the large container secured at the back of the shuttlecraft's small cabin. Unlocking and lifting its hinged lid, he broke into a broad smile at the gleaming, glittering cargo within. Laughing like an Asho sheeple at a trough of its favorite rice and beans, he grabbed handful after handful of the glistening gems, letting them fall back through his fingers onto the glowing pile. He even thought about climbing in and wallowing in the treasure.

"Besides, we'll be famous now," he puffed, still playing with the multi-colored stones, their perfect facets catching and refracting every ray of light that struck them. "We've just pulled off the biggest heist this side of the Letz Cluster," he laughed. "And we're just kids!" Shoving a handful of gems into a pocket, he went forward again, returning to his seat just aft of the main control console. "Now let's go find some girls!" laughed the young master thief.

Watching his cousin's antics, Hobbs felt a sick twinge of apprehension.

SOADER WOKE UP STARING at the ceiling, annoyed, stiff and sore. He had slept on the floor all night. He hauled himself to his feet and looked around to see if there was any elixir left. No, dammit, he'd downed it all. He staggered to his desk and barked into the comm link for a Grey to bring him something hot and strong to drink, and something for his pounding head. He plopped down in his chair, head hanging heavy. He didn't move, didn't dare think — just waited for the Grey to arrive. He *did* remember the awful news on his console last night, but he wasn't anywhere near ready to confront that yet.

The Grey appeared and scuttled across the floor, shaking in

fear. He'd seen what the boss could do on mornings-after like this. He gingerly set a tray on the edge of the desk and backed away a pace, hands clasped in front of him, hoping to be dismissed before Soader decided to use him for a punching bag. Again.

Soader growled something unintelligible, but that was all he could muster. The Grey had no idea what the Rept-hybrid had said, so he tossed off an all-purpose acknowledgement, spun around and made for the door as quickly as he dared, back and shoulders tensed against possible flying objects. None came, and he managed to get through the door and close it, heart pounding.

Soader took a sip of the hot drink the Grey had brought, then downed the whole collection of pills sitting in a dish at one side of the tray. "The idiot's learning," he thought, sipping some more of the hot, stimulant beverage. There was a big jug of it on the tray this time, not just a pitiful little flask, like last time. He finished the first mugful, poured himself some more, and sat back to daydream. Anything to put off looking at that console again.

Early on, Soader had accepted his role in life. He was a natural-born criminal, and he liked it. He'd begun committing petty offences before he could even walk. His first significant bust came at the age of five, when he was caught stealing his grandma's most precious keepsakes. At ten, he raped the six-year-old girl next door, and succeeded in shifting the blame to a hapless schoolmate. At fifteen, he killed four guards in a jewel robbery — his first murders. Before his thirtieth birthday, he was already wanted dead on twenty-two planets (alive on none). On the run for centuries now, he added to his infamy with every passing decade. Goldenrod "wanted" notices flashed his sardonic smile on the bulletin-panels of every planet in several sectors. Yet somehow Hobbs, his accomplice and cousin, was never mentioned. Never.

A distant crash jolted Soader's attention back to the present. The console flashed in front of him, demanding attention. With a sigh, he sat up and tapped it, calling up the first urgent message — a new report about the empty condensers. After just a glance, he wished he hadn't. It was no use. He couldn't control his rage. He lurched up, hoisted his huge chair above his head and heaved it over the desk toward the opposite wall, shattering a set of shelves and sending their contents flying. He still burned at the thought of his drained condenser tubes. All of them!

"What the Xenu am I going to do now?" he roared. "Who the hells would do this? I bet that damned, damned, damned Zulak has something to do with it. He's going to pay, that bastard!" he shouted, stalking out from behind his desk, snatching up another chair and heaving it after the first. He stormed out of the office and down the corridor, ranting as he went, and struggling to understand what was going on.

"Zulak will pay! He'll more than just pay, I'll slice his family to bits and feed them to the prisoners. Yes! YES! Or, no! I'll feed them to my pets! Yes, that's even better. That's what that shit deserves. Then they can rip *him* to pieces. Haaarrrrrrr!"

Nearby guards, hearing the demented tirade, slipped quietly out of sight. One was too slow about it; Soader rounded a corner, came face to face with the terrified Grey, and promptly jammed a claw-tipped finger through each of his eyes, killing him instantly. The chance to vent his fury gave Soader a flicker of relief, but he was still far from rational. Wiping his bloodied hands on his uniform, he headed for the eatery. A good feed of Earthling would do the trick, he thought.

Twenty minutes later, appetite sated and back under control again, Soader licked his fingers pensively, and came to a fresh resolve. "Time to change things. Right now!" he declared, to the universe in general, a sneer spreading across his half-rep-tilian face. "Time for effin Zulak to pay. For *everything*."

The Rept-hybrid returned to his office. Someone had hurriedly cleaned up the mess and replaced the broken chairs. "Now, how the Xenu can I open the gods-damned Titan Portcullis with empty tubes?" he muttered. "If I don't get it open on time, the Brothers will kick my ass all the way to RPF113, no question. And how can I get back at that bastard, Zulak? Dammit, I need more time." He mumbled and growled on for several minutes, then began to laugh uncontrollably. "I know! I know! Why didn't I think of it before? Haaaarrrrrrrr! I'm brilliant! Phobos! PHOBOS!!"

He leapt up and barked a string of orders into the desk comm link. Three Greys stepped into the office, knowing it was now safer to venture close — Soader had fed. "Vic, bring my things and meet us at the train. Max, send orders to prep my shuttlecraft. Mullins, get our people to see that Phobos is fully stocked for at least a two-month stay. The three of you meet me in the tunnels in five minutes."

Soader was pleased with himself. With its natural shielding, Phobos was the perfect place to hide out. A few minutes later he boarded an elevator, announced his destination, and admired his reflection in the mirrored side-wall. "Such a clever, handsome guy," he proclaimed. The elevator stopped and he stepped out, heading down the corridor toward the cells and adjusting his translator unit as he strutted. Soon the three Greys fell in behind him at a cautious distance.

"Now, aren't you all pretty?" he cooed, smacking his lips and blowing a lewd kiss at the caged women. "You're such prizes." It had been so clever to put his new prisoners into Shellee's cell, he thought. Shellee always did as he asked. She knew that if she didn't, her husband would hear about it, and come to set her mind right. Soader smiled at the thought of the credits the wretched wench's husband was paying him to keep her on ice.

"Shellee, have you been a good girl for me?" he purred, giving her a conspiratorial wink when she nodded her response. Soader was still irritated at losing his precious energy store, and baffled at how such a disaster could have occurred. Seeing Shellee reminded him of her husband, Scabbage, which made him angry all over again. He stood, lost in his thoughts for nearly a minute, staring vacantly into space and muttering at random. The women huddled as far from their captor as possible, waiting and watching in fear.

Soader began pacing up and down in front of the cell, mumbling non-stop, "Scabbage, that bastard! He and those *bleep*ing Brothers promised me their stinking plan couldn't fail. They said it would be easy to open the damn portcullis. Liars! Effing liars. They promised everyone would die. Zulak included! I hate them all! Bloody, effing liars!" Soader screamed his final thoughts aloud, startling the caged women with his outburst. They remained huddled in a corner as the Rept continued his psychotic harangue. "They will pay. Everyone is going to pay. Zulak is going to pay. I'm going to kill that bastard, but first... what?? How do I get back at that shit and make him *suffer*?"

The women stared at him in fear, unable to make much sense of his garbled yammering and too afraid to move. "Girls," Remi whispered, "if he says anything to you, humor him; don't do anything to aggravate him any further. He's completely lost it."

Soader took no notice of the women, or anything else in the objective world outside his twisted disaster of a mind. He just continued pacing, halting suddenly now and then to stare in silence, or fire off a new rant. "Gods damn Zulak! It's his fault. He's the reason my Hiko is dead! Hiko, I'm so sorry," he sobbed. "It wasn't my fault your mother died! It was his! He infected her with eeiingle. *He* did it. He killed you, too. I'm sorry,

Hiko — soooo sorry!"

The women exchanged puzzled looks and shrugged. "Yes, Hiko, he'll pay!" Soader ranted on. "I'll *make* him pay. Yes, he's going to die. Soon, dear daughter, soon. He'll suffer too, Hiko, I'll make so sure of it. He'll pay. He'll *pay!*"

Abruptly ceasing his frenzied pacing, he stood at the cage door for several minutes, head lowered, glazed eyes fixed on nothing. Then his head snapped up and twisted violently from side to side, back and forth, eyes wide and wild, scaring the women afresh. One of the Greys loudly cleared his throat. The sound triggered something, and Soader's head went still, eyes agape in a manic stare.

"Celine! Yes, Celine! That's it!" he thought. She would come with him to hide on Phobos. Brilliant! Scabbage and the Brothers would keep him safe if he had the girl along with him. No one would dare risk harming her. No one! Har haaarrrr! She would keep him safe until he could get through the port-cullis. She could go through the portcullis *with him.* Perfect!

Soader's demented reverie wore on. "Damn it to all hells, I wanted to see his face when I killed his family right in front of him." He burst out with a great guffaw; the women just watched in silence, their initial fear morphing into a sort of horrified pity at the demented spectacle. The Rept continued his musing and mumbling. "She'll help buy the time I need, and I'll *still* kill Zulak. What a perfectly ingenious plan!"

Suddenly, the spell was broken. Soader ceased his muttering, and his eyes focused on the real world before him. He leered at the women, drooling, then barked at one of the Greys, "Open this gods-damned cell!" The guard complied; Soader shoved his way past and into the cell. Remi stepped in front of her daughters, blocking his approach. "Out of my way, old bitch!" he ordered, threatening to cuff her aside.

"Keep your paws off us and get out of here," Remi

commanded. "Wait 'til my husband comes. You're going to regret what you've done."

"Har haaaarrrrr!" laughed Soader, spitting out a gob of blood-tinged phlegm. It barely missed Remi as she shied out of its path. "Your *bleep*ing husband will *die* before he ever rescues you."

Remi raised her hand, claw-like, to strike at Soader, but one of the Greys grunted a warning and aimed his blaster squarely at Mia's head. Remi lowered her hand as Soader pushed past her and grabbed Celine by the arm. "Keep your filthy, filthy hands off her!" Remi shrieked.

"It's okay, Mom," Celine said, calmly. "He won't harm me. I'll be all right." She allowed Soader to lead her out of the cell.

"No! Celine!" cried Remi — but somehow she knew her daughter was right. The monster would not harm her youngest. Her shoulders slumped in despair as the cell door clanged shut, a sound that would reverberate in memory for months to come.

Mia gasped in the background. "No, Celine! Listen to Mom!" she called, surprising herself with her sudden concern for her sister. Shellee remained silent, knowing she could do nothing. Celine just kept on walking, following Soader down the tunnel, while the Greys kept their blasters trained on Mia. The three women could only stare in impotent horror as Celine was led away. When she was gone, Remi and Mia fell together, crying.

Later, her composure somewhat restored, Remi reassured her elder daughter. "Celine's right, he won't hurt her." The Zulaks had done their best to keep Celine safe all these years. They'd done it out of a sense of duty at first, having no choice but to honor their solemn agreement. It wasn't long, though, before they had grown to love the strange little girl as if she were their own child.

Late on a rainy evening, fourteen years before, Admiral Elias Stock had appeared at the Zulak's door with a tiny child in his arms, trying in vain to shield her from the downpour. The child looked like some sort of abandoned pet; she was clad in filthy rags, and her skin and hair were so dirty it was hard to tell where they ended and the rags began.

The admiral had implored the Zulaks not to ask questions — just to keep the child safe, for the Gods' sakes. He left as abruptly as he'd arrived.

The Zulaks imagined they'd only have to care for the girl for a short while. Surely Stock would return for her, or send a trusted aide to retrieve her — just as he'd done a few times before. The longest any of the poor waifs had been with them was four days. When the admiral called a week later to say he was on his way to see them, they assumed it was to take back the little girl. They had cleaned her up, fitted her with some clothes Mia had outgrown, and fed her well. She looked quite presentable, and had even begun to cheer up, coming out of her initial haunted silence.

The admiral arrived, but instead of coming empty-handed as he always had before, he had a suitcase in one hand and a tablet computer in the other. "Here," he said, handing the suit-case to Remi. "These are some things I picked up for Celine," he smiled. "I don't expect you to pay for everything, of course, but once the adoption has gone through, you'll be on your own." The couple could only stare, bewildered.

"I know you're unable to have more children, so this is a good solution for everyone. Besides, Rafael, with your new promo-tion to commander you can easily afford to support another child. Come, let's sign these documents." He motioned them to follow as he strode to a table and set up the little computer.

Rafael and Remi looked first at each other, then at the strange little girl sitting quietly in their lounge. The child had her back to them, but when they looked at her, she turned at once, looked straight at them and smiled as broadly as her tiny cheeks would allow. The Zulaks turned to each other once more, and shrugged. Somehow this was all meant to be, and there seemed nothing they could do about it. Not that they wanted to. "I guess we have that second daughter we've prayed for!" Rafael said. Remi responded with an incredulous smile, pulling her husband to her in a brief, fierce hug before they hurried after the admiral.

The couple had no doubt that Admiral Stock had very good reasons for placing the child in their care. He had asked them to keep her safe, and they had dedicated their lives to that purpose — both for the child herself, and out of the certainty that her safety was also crucial for far broader reasons than they knew. Stock had only vaguely hinted at who the girl's parents might be, and from time to time Rafael and Remi shared their guesses on the subject. If their best guesses were true, Celine had been correct: Soader would never dare to harm her.

"TOO BAD I WON'T SEE ZULAK die, but at least I've got what everyone is after," Soader laughed, eyeing Celine. "Damn! You're even more gorgeous and sexy than I remember. Will I have fun with *you*," he leered. He bent down to Mullins and whispered something; the Grey turned and waddled back up the tunnel toward the cell.

"Max, zip her hands and throw her in the train cage when we get there. Vic, wait for Mullins, then take us to my shuttlecraft," he ordered, continuing down the tunnel toward the small train waiting at the platform. He sat in one of the front passenger seats while Max poked his goad at Celine, herding her into a cage at the back of the musty car. He locked her in and sat facing her, grinning and waving his goad. Vic took the controls and soon had them hurtling up the track toward Salt Lake. Soader was so pleased with himself, be began singing a near-senseless ditty learned in his twisted childhood.

Eggs and ducks
Ducks and eggs
Which comes first
Before them stays.
He who kills
Outlives the five
Fuddle dee dee
Fuddle dee die

Shoot the monster
Kill the queen
Slay the dragon
Free the fiend.
Cut them up
Eat them 'live
Cast a spell
See them fly
Fuddle dee dee
Fuddle dee die

Shoot the girl
Kill the beast
Slay the leader
Make her peace.
Chop them up
Burn them 'live
Fuddle dee dee
Fuddle dee die

You shall be free
You shall be FREE!
Fuddle dee dee
Fuddle Dee DIE!

Celine sat quietly, ignoring the Grey who sat watching her, eager for any movement that would justify another goading. She watched the tunnel lights flash by as they zoomed along. Under any other circumstances, she would have enjoyed such a ride. She could hear Soader singing (if that was what his mangling of the tune could be called), and snarling the occasional comment or order at the Grey driver. She tried menting Jager and West several times, to no effect. Though not in fear, she had never felt so alone.

A few hours later — at the same time as Zulak was landing on Earth — Celine and her captors were aboard Soader's shuttlecraft, bound for Phobos, one of Mars's two tiny moons. It was actually a hollowed-out asteroid, placed in Mars orbit as a monitoring station, staging platform and hideout, complete with shielding against radiation and telepathic contact.

"What's your problem now?" demanded Soader of the annoyingly calm Celine. He sat next to the small cell that held her, while the Greys piloted the shuttle.

"I'm hungry. The crap you fed us yesterday wasn't fit for maggots. I want something decent, and I want it right now," demanded Celine. "I also want out of this cage. It stinks, like everything else you touch."

"Har haaarrr!" laughed Soader, jerking his chin toward the bench in her cell. "There's a human food kit under there. Ration it; that's all you get. Once it's gone, you'll have to eat what I eat." He laughed at the thought of the girl confronting the choice between starvation or dining on Earthling.

Celine just stared at him coldly. She'd decided on annoyance as the best tactic.

Back when they'd arrived at Salt Lake after the train ride, she couldn't believe her luck. One of the Greys had forgotten to activate the blanket shielding when they'd exited the train. As they walked the hundred yards or so to the waiting shuttlecraft, she'd leapt at the chance to contact Jager. "Jager! Jager! Soader has me on Earth, at a place called Salt Lake! He's taking me to Phobos. Tell West where I am, and that I'm okay. Tell her to contact my dad. Mom and Mia are being held in a cavern under Dulce."

"I hear you! I hear you, Celine. We're coming!" Then she was back under active shielding, and the connection was lost. But she couldn't help grinning at having reached her friend.

"What are you smirking about?" probed Soader. Celine just smiled serenely, annoying him even more.

She thought of her father. How she missed him! She hoped Jager and West could rescue her before Soader took her too far. She had overheard the Rept-hybrid ordering one of his Greys to take them to Phobos, and then mutter something about preparing for the Serpens Universe. She knew that if they passed through a portcullis, there was no coming back. The Titan Portcullis was always sealed unless there was someone waiting on the other side, ready with a code to hold it open when sufficient energy was applied to bridge the gap between universes.

All cadets had to study about the Serpens Universe, and the Babau who inhabited it. The vicious creatures — reminiscent of Earth's piranha, even though they were not aquatic — had come through the portcullis fifteen thousand years before, raiding, pillaging and spreading disease. They had finally been vanquished, and the portcullis sealed against them. So Celine knew the importance of keeping the Titan Portcullis closed. She mustn't let Soader know of her apprehension, though, so she grinned again.

"I asked what you're smirking about. Out with it, little bitch," growled Soader.

"Nothing you'd understand," she replied, and began munching a brattle stick from the food kit.

"Don't get smart with me, or I'll make your miserable little life...uh...miserable! Besides, you realize, don't you, that when your father tries to rescue your pathetic mother and sister, they're all going to die?" He hoped that would get to her, but there was no visible response whatsoever. She just looked blandly back at him and continued to munch. "That's right! Before we boarded, I sent orders for their cell to be rigged. The instant that door opens, the whole place gets flooded with gas. Har haaarr! They're all dead meat! One whiff of that stuff and it's over," he laughed. His gloat was a short one, though — Celine still showed no hint of a reaction.

Celine did react, inwardly. Somehow Soader knew her father was heading to Earth. But how? Then it struck her: he must have ordered the Grey to leave the telepathic shielding down when she was being transferred from train to ship. What a fool she'd been! He'd played her. He had either known or suspected that she was able to ment — and that if she could, she would call for help at the first opportunity. And, of course, her father would be the one to come for her. Her father's reputation for being overprotective was a joke among their close family and friends, but it was known to many he worked with, too — and Soader would surely have a spy among them. So now she'd set her parents and sister up to die!

Guessing her thoughts, Soader taunted her. "You didn't think I was stupid enough to leave the telepathic shielding down by accident, did you? Harrrrr! You Pleiadeans are all the same. Always think you're smarter than everyone else."

Suddenly Celine saw it. Of course Soader had known she

was telepathic! Why else would there have been shielding around her constantly, ever since she'd been captured at the Draco Convention? What an idiot she'd been! Her stupid, stupid carelessness would cost many people their lives! There was only one tiny consolation: at least Soader wasn't telepathic; if he'd been able to "hear" her, the consequences would have been far, far worse. And it would have added a huge new element to the challenges she faced.

Celine quickly regained her composure, hoping that if she played stupid, Soader would wonder whether she'd actually contacted anyone. She tried again to reach Jager and West, but no luck. All she could do was continue to munch her brattle and stare coolly at Soader, hoping to annoy him. She said a prayer for her family's safety while maintaining her bland stare.

"If I were in your sorry situation, I'd be a bit more worried about being orphaned, and having to deal with *me*," Soader growled, his annoyance growing under her unblinking gaze. "You stupid kids and Earthlings are all the same," he huffed, then stormed out of the room. Exactly as Celine had intended.

CHAPTER 10

Gone

"West! West! Do you hear me?" Jager yelled.

"I am here, Jager; how may I help you?" the Mentor asked.

"It's Celine! She's called me. She's alive, but she's in trouble! She was here on Earth — Soader had her at a place called Salt Lake, but now he's taking her to Phobos. Her mother and sister are being held underground in New Mexico — someplace called Dulce. We need to find her father," Jager's thoughts came all in a rush.

"Oh, what wonderful news. I am so relieved to know she is alive. I have friends who can get word to Commander Zulak. You must get your family to the bunker right away, though, as I fear you all are in danger. To accomplish that, you must do as I tell you. All right?"

"Yes, West."

"Your parents and brothers have had hypnotic commands instilled in them. You must speak their trigger phrase in just the right manner to initiate their response. Do you understand?"

"Yes."

"Good. You must maintain the emotion of cheerfulness while speaking this trigger: 'A forgotten friend has arrived to take our family on a trip.'"

"Okay, I've got it. 'A forgotten friend has arrived to take our family on a trip.'"

"Perfect. This trigger was instilled for your protection. Once you say it correctly, they will pack their belongings and accompany you to the hiding place. They will pack two bags each; you should do the same. Pack only necessities and valuables. Unfortunately, it is unlikely that you will ever return to your home."

"Okay, I understand," said Jager, not overly surprised at what West was saying.

"Someone from Commander Zulak's ship will come for you tomorrow, so give your family the command at breakfast. They will act normally and be quite cooperative, but keep an eye on them until you arrive at the bunker. Once there, double-lock it to keep them inside, and don't let them out for any reason. Is that understood?"

"Yes. Double-lock, keep them inside."

"If anyone questions any of the family before you get them to the bunker, they will reply that you all are going to visit a sick relative."

"Okay."

There was a deafening silence, and then West spoke again. "Jager, there is one unpleasant fact I must tell you."

"I think I know what it is," said the young man, sadly.

"I imagined you would expect it," replied West. "We have no choice, you know."

"I know," said Jager. "When will it be done?"

"When Major Hadgkiss transbeams them aboard *Asherah*, it will be done as part of the transbeam process. When they appear on the platform, they will no longer remember anything about their lives on Earth. They will not know who they are," replied West. "At the same time, the process will give them new memories, new lives. Everything will seem natural and normal to them. There will be no physical, mental or spiritual discomfort. They will not suspect anything unusual has occurred. We will beam you separately, so that you are not memory-wiped."

"Will...will they still remember me?" the boy asked.

"We are sorry, Jager, but no. They will not. I know that is very hard, but it cannot be safely avoided. You will have a new identity as well, and will live with Major Dino Hadgkiss, Celine's godfather. We have papers ready for you, stating that you are a nephew, from a planet several light years from Erra, and that your family were all recently killed in an accident. You look very much like a Pleiadean, so there should be no difficulty. Commander Zulak will not know that you are Celine's friend."

Jager lowered his eyes and went silent. West waited patiently for a while, but finally had to interrupt his thoughts.

"I am sorry, Jager, but there are other matters I must attend to now. If you need me at any time, though, please call."

"Okay. Thank you, West. Goodbye."

Jager stood for a while, digesting the reality of what was about to happen to his family and his life. Looking around his room, his eyes came to rest on a wall chart of the Pleiades and neighboring star groups. He grinned. He'd never been one for regrets, or getting stuck in the past. He decided to say a fond but firm goodbye to much of his life, and to move cheerfully forward from this moment. He would miss his family terribly, but the opportunity to be aboard a spaceship and to visit another planet was a fantastic trade-off. He would also be on the same planet as Celine, once she returned to her home. He rushed from the room. His parents were in the den, reading; his younger brothers were already in bed.

"Everything all right, Jager?" asked his mother, as he regarded them from the doorway.

"Huh? Oh, yeah — sure, Mom. Just been studying too long. I'm going to get something to drink and then head to bed. See you in the morning."

"Good night. Have a good sleep," answered his mother and father together.

CELINE HAD SO ANNOYED SOADER that he stomped away, barked a couple of unnecessary orders at the Greys and disappeared into his cabin. The flight to Phobos lasted until the next afternoon. Max skillfully docked the craft, and Soader dragged Celine out of her cell and down to the aft exit hatch. Letting go of the girl momentarily, he activated the hatch mechanism. As the doors were opening, he grabbed Celine again and turned to step out onto the landing platform. He'd gotten one foot out the hatchway when BAM — a flying fist caught him in the jaw and knocked him straight back through the open hatch onto his ass.

"Daddy!" screamed Celine, trying to push past the prostrate Rept and join her father on the landing platform. "Dad!" But Soader grabbed her ankle and hauled her back. Vic had just entered the hatch area behind them; he got off a blaster shot that kept Zulak from charging into the craft. The Grey slapped a switch and the hatch slammed shut. "Daddy!" she screamed again, trying to wrench her leg from Soader's grasp. "Dad!"

"Shut your face," Soader bellowed, rising from the deck and wrapping his arms around the struggling girl. Pinning her in a smothering bear hug, he hauled her up the short corridor and into the ship's tiny transbeam bay. "Secure her!" he yelled at

Vic, who had followed the pair. The Grey yanked a restraint gun off a rack on the bulkhead, aimed it at the girl and fired the instant Soader released her. She was enmeshed at once in a fibrous restraining web. Immobilized, she fell to the deck.

Soader hefted the now-helpless girl onto the small transbeam platform, stepped back, folded his arms and admired his handiwork. "Let's see your Daddy Dear find you now," he laughed. "He'll never know where I've sent you. Neither will I, for that matter. Neither will anyone else. *Ever!*"

"Dad!" screamed Celine. "Dad! Help! Daddy!"

"You're going to suffer, Zulak," muttered the Rept, working feverishly at the transbeam console. "I'll make you suffer just like you did me. You're going to watch your beautiful girl die, just as you forced me to watch my Hiko!" he shrieked.

A transparent cylinder descended from above the platform where Celine lay. It slid into a groove in the deck around the platform, sealing the girl inside. The transbeam was ready.

Soader heard a muffled blast from the rear of the craft; Zulak had breached the hatch and rushed aboard, working his way forward. The Rept waited, his clawed hand poised above a raised dial at the right of the transbeam console. When he judged that Zulak was only yards away, he spun the dial hard, then released it to spin freely. It continued to rotate as he hit the beam's activator switch. Zulak burst into the small space and froze, horrified. There was Celine, bound and struggling frantically against her restraints inside the transbeam chamber. Her eyes turned toward him, wide with terror, imploring.

"Too late!" crowed Soader. The girl was rapidly being engulfed in the swirling iridescence of the active transbeam. In little more than a second, she vanished.

Zulak lunged for Soader's throat, but not quickly enough; the Rept had already hit a key that would obliterate all record of the transbeam's projection. Now there was no way in the universe to discover where Celine had just been sent. Even Soader had no idea of her destination — he had deliberately looked away when spinning the dial, so even a hypnotic probe could not recover the information. Celine could be anywhere in the universe. Anywhere. She was well and truly lost. And, short of a miracle, she would be lost forever.

"Where did you send her?" roared Zulak, grabbing the Rept-hybrid by the throat. *"Where have you sent my daughter?!"*

Soader managed a half-laughing croak past the enraged commander's grip. "I have no idea! She's gone! No record! No coordinates! Ha-haarrrrrrr! GONE!!"

Zulak threw the creature to the deck and grabbed the sides of the console, scanning it in desperation and working its controls. It looked like the Rept was right — he could find no record of the projection that had just taken place. Not a trace.

Rafael turned to see Madda standing in the doorway, weapon trained on the still-laughing Soader, who lay sprawled on the deck. Two G.O.D. Police officers edged past her and grabbed the Rept. Binding him hand and foot, they gave each restraint a yank vicious enough to draw blood.

Soader wasn't fazed. "Harrrrrr, Zulak! I've been waiting to see that look on your pathetic face for years! It's so, so precious! Worth everything and anything! Harrrrrr! Now you know what you put me through, you bastard! Now you feel what I've felt all these years and years and years. You deserve to lose her, you worthless shit! And it's all your fault! She'll die because of you. All because of you. Everyone will die because of you. Everyone — everywhere! All dead, all dead, all dead! And all because of you! Har har haaaaarrrrrrrrrrrrrrrr!"

"Shut him up," grated Zulak. "Shut. Him. Up." An officer jumped to comply, jamming a gag across the creature's mouth and tying it much too tightly.

"Sir, we'll find her. I swear it," promised Madda, her hand

on her commander's arm.

"We'll have him memory-probed sir," said the police captain. "Once we have the information, he'll be transferred straight to RPF113. Permanently."

Zulak nodded a response. He still stood over the console, now staring helplessly at its displays and controls. He'd gone numb. Utterly numb. His shoulders were drooped, his breathing short and shallow. The police hauled Soader away, still laughing spasmodically through his gag.

"Commander, we must leave at once," spoke Madda. "Sir..." Gently but firmly, she guided Zulak out of the ship and back to the landing platform. There she signaled *Asherah*, and almost at once they were transbeamed aboard.

Remi was waiting for them in Zulak's quarters, pacing, a drink in hand. The moment she saw her husband's face, she knew Celine must be gone. Her drink fell to the deck. Rafael held her in exhausted arms as the tears flowed.

"We'll find her. We'll find our Celine," soothed Zulak. No sooner had he spoken than the turquoise crystal necklace around his neck began to glow. He heard a faint voice, female, its source seemingly inside his own head. The voice was Celine's! Definitely, definitely Celine's. "Celine! Celine!" he cried, springing away from his wife and clutching at the crystal. "Celine!" He carefully unclasped the necklace and held it in both hands. It still glowed faintly, but the strange luminescence was dimming. In a moment, it was gone — and so was the voice. "Celine!"

CHAPTER 11

Major Dino Hadgkiss

"Great, Dino! Really great. You keep this up you'll have full use of your hands in a few days," encouraged the biophysicist at the officer's side.

"Thanks," responded Dino, watching his left fist as he turned, opened and closed it.

"It's hard to believe how quickly you've gotten control of your new legs, too. Usually quadruple amputees take months to learn their bionics. I've never seen anyone catch on so quickly," she said. "I'm sure you'll be back to work in a couple of weeks."

"Thanks. I really couldn't have done it without you," smiled Dino, continuing to flex his bionic left arm and hand. "This actually feels better than the real thing," he laughed. "So do these legs." The door to the training room opened and Zulak stepped in. He walked straight to Dino, warmly embracing his closest friend.

"Rafael!" exclaimed Dino, holding the man at arm's length. "It's good to see you. How are Remi and Mia doing?"

"Under the circumstances, they're both doing well. I'm worried about Remi, though; she blames herself for what happened to Celine. She's not sleeping or eating well, and I think she's doing it so I won't blame myself. Which of course she knows I'm doing anyway" Rafael said, staring out the window at a pair of lovebirds on a nearby branch. Abruptly Rafael turned to his friend. "Dino, I don't..." His voice choked to a halt, tears welling in his eyes.

"Rafael, I'm told you're actually worried about whether I'll be willing to come help kill that bastard. Nonsense!" exclaimed the major. "I read all about his escape from that prison shuttle, before he could even be probed or wiped. That simply isn't possible without help from high up in G.O.D.," he continued. "I love my goddaughter as if she were my own, and of course I'll do whatever it takes to get her back. *Whatever* it takes. When we dissect that filthy reptile, we'll find out who his inside connections are, and terminate them, too." All the while he flexed his new hands and pounded fist into palm, the loud smacks punctuating his heated declaration.

"I know, I know, Dino. Silly of me even to have thought it," Rafael replied. "Oh, and Remi insisted I remind you you're always welcome at our place."

Dino smiled, nodded and crossed the room to the rehab tech, Somi. Bending down from his seven-foot height, he planted a gentle kiss on her blushing forehead. "I'll be leaving now. Thanks so, so much for all your help," he said.

"Sir, you *can't* leave. You haven't finished your rehab! You have to have authorization to leave."

"No worries, dear. I've got my authority right here." He clapped Rafael on the shoulder — too hard; it made the senior officer wince and stumble.

"You *sure* you have those things under control?" asked Zulak, rubbing his shoulder with an amused but half-worried smile.

"No worries, mate. I'll have it all down perfectly, real soon," laughed Hadgkiss. "I've got to — I have a very important Rept neck to wring!" The men chuckled, nodded once more to Somi, then strode from the room and down the corridor, Dino in the lead. Reaching the Cybernetics Center courtyard, they prepared to part ways.

"Meet me at the *Queen* tomorrow, 07:00. We're going hunting," said Rafael.

"Gladly. But would you care to join me at Callaghan's?" asked Dino. "Illidge and The Tunnel Dwellers are playing tonight, and I want to say hi to their bass player, Pooka. You remember Pooka? From Finishing School?"

"Yeah, sure, I remember her. See you there. I want to go check on Remi first."

"Okay. Later!"

At 07:00 sharp, Rafael and Dino stepped through the lift door and onto the bridge of *Queen Asherah III*. The entire crew was ready and eager.

"Major Hadgkiss, welcome back," said Madda, bowing gracefully. "I take it you'll be reassuming your old post of First Officer. I've kept it warm for you!"

"That's right. And thanks, Madda. I knew you'd make me proud while I was away." He crossed to the station Madda had vacated for him, and settled into the old, familiar seat. "Xenu! The tactile in these new hands gives me the feel of the station better than my 'real' ones ever did. Wild!"

Madda resumed her own former station and awaited orders from Zulak. She had also resumed her native Rept appearance. She was well aware that most of the crew disliked and distrusted members of her race, but she wore her "own skin" proudly, knowing that she, as an individual, had earned their respect. Besides, she knew that not all Repts were bad, and she wanted them to keep that fact in mind. Her face darkened at the thought of how they'd failed to save Celine, and that they might not be able to recover her. If there was any crew that could, though, it was *Queen Asherah*'s.

Rafael took time to greet each of his bridge crew, then called for the senior officers to join him in the chart room in five minutes. He left his station, entered the small chamber adjoining the bridge, and closed its doors. The chart room was not actually used to store charts; it was more a planning and meeting space, but it had retained its name out of ancient maritime custom. The sailors of space cherished the traditions of their predecessors, who sailed on oceans and seas.

Zulak had formed a plan to find Celine, and he needed his closest team to help execute it. He'd just settled into his seat at the head of the small conference table when the comm link on a monitor buzzed, and Admiral Stock's image appeared. "Good morning, sir," said Zulak, "I was just about to confer with my officers. Let me send them away and then we can talk."

The officers didn't need to be asked; they all stood and quickly filed out. Again, Zulak addressed the admiral; "I'm surprised to hear from you, sir. What's your pleasure?"

"I'm surprised to be talking to you, too, commander. I've just received urgent orders from very high up in G.O.D. Command to dispatch you to a planetary satellite, PS 428 — old Luna, you know — and P 444, Earth, to provide overwatch on preparations for a harvest. Why a planetary satellite and a backwater like Earth, I have no idea. I'm sorry, Rafael, but you'll have to put off your search for Celine for the moment. G.O.D.'s orders."

"What the hells?" gasped the commander. He wanted to say more, but couldn't trust himself to be diplomatic — and he'd already said far too much. "My apologies, sir. Begging your pardon. Of course, sir. But..." He couldn't help himself. "What in the worlds is going on?"

"I know it makes no sense, and I wish I didn't have to do this, but Command has stressed that you are to follow these orders without deviation, or face immediate relief of command." The old officer was clearly pained to have to deliver such a dire threat. "Do I make myself clear?"

Zulak slumped, unable to believe what he was hearing. This could *not* be happening. What was he to do? He had to find Celine. He had to bring her home. He had to set right everything he'd destroyed. And he had to do it all *now*. He couldn't possibly waste even a day babysitting a mundane bloody harvest prep. His girl was missing — and he knew that wasn't just a personal disaster. It had become all too clear that her importance went far beyond any private concerns. Further even than he might ever understand. And he knew the admiral was fully aware of this as well.

"Commander?" Stock prompted.

Zulak stared at the image on the monitor for several seconds more, then reluctantly replied. "Aye-aye, admiral. You have made yourself quite clear, sir. But if I may speak frankly, sir, ..." He let fly his real feelings on the matter, in language so colorful it would have made a pirate spacer blush.

Hearing the commotion within, Dino jumped to the chart room door and called to Zulak, "Permission to enter, sir!"

"Enter!" barked the commander.

"What the hells is happening?" Dino asked in a strained whisper, as the door was still open behind him.

Rafael paused while the door hissed shut. He gestured toward the monitor, which still showed the admiral's stern visage. "I just told the admiral here to shove his orders where the stars don't shine, then take a flying leap to the purgatory zone on a humpbacked Rawkl." Zulak's voice was tightly controlled, yet concealed none of his fury.

With that, he slapped off the monitor, pounded the door switch, strode from the chart room and straight off his ship.

CHAPTER 12

Scabbage

Scabbage stood before a deep bay window overlooking his lavish gardens, high in the hills above Devocht. Hearing the comm link's chime, he stalked imperiously to his expansive desk (he constantly practiced his "I'm in command here" bearing, whether anyone was around to see it or not), seated himself ever so authoritatively and stabbed at a button. "Scabbage." He managed to make even the statement of his name sound imposing. He listened for perhaps twenty seconds, then screamed, "I don't care if you were given different orders. You do as I tell you, or you're beastie chow. Got it?? Get your asses moving. Catch that shuttlecraft. Kill the officers and take the prisoner. He had better be at the Mars outpost by 14:00, or you're all toast."

He listened again, briefly, then interrupted, "I told you, I DO NOT CARE if it's a G.O.D. shuttlecraft. I don't care if they're G.O.D. Police. I don't pay you to think. I pay you to do what I order. You do as I say, or you'll never see your family again. Never. And I'll smear your name across this whole sector so badly, no one would ever vote for you again. No more Chancellery. Get it? Hells, you'll never get a job *anywhere* when I'm done. Not even as Acting Deputy Assistant Weed-Control Technician In Training."

Wiping flecks of spittle from his chin, the little man glared at the now-silent comm link, then batted the device from his desk. "Gods-damned useless morons," he growled. He began to stand, but was seized by a fit of coughing and gasping that forced him back into the chair. The seizure passed, and he sat muttering to himself. "Time's running out. I've got to hang on until My Birthday; they have to see me receiving that award in *this* body. It won't be the same if I get it in a new body — everyone knows *this* one. It's in all the current image-captures and statues. After the ceremony, I'll transfer to the Jager kid's body — providing they hurry their worthless asses up and bring it to me!"

"Pe-ann! Pe-ann! Bring my elixir! Now! Move!! What's your effin problem, you degraded bag of dung?" A bloated, hump-backed Rawkl shuffled into the lounge, carrying a large serving tray. It bore a jug of elixir, in the shape of an exaggeratedly curvaceous human female. Next to the bottle was a matching tankard, already filled with the thick, crimson liquid. The Rawkl set the tray on a small table, beside a dark leather reclining chair.

"You put my medicine in there, right?" Scabbage demanded. She nodded. "Then get out of here. I don't want to see your sorry pie face the rest of the day." He grinned, sniffled, hoisted the tankard and took a couple of swallows. "Crap. The idiots probably haven't thought to order another shipment of this stuff. There's got to be plenty of it for My Birthday celebration next month. If some degraded slob doesn't screw it up, it's going to be the best yet. Highest-ever attendance, too — straight up and vertical — or heads are gonna roll."

He leaned back in the big recliner, adjusted it for better comfort and resumed his slurping. Between swallows he took a moment to admire the trophies ranged about the big room. Jars containing some of the more important heads he'd taken over the centuries. Embalmed eyeballs strung like beads, festooning framed image-captures of his hunting exploits. Like one of his favorites, which depicted him hacking the limbs from a yearling grassbuck he'd taken on a trip to Ronae. Or the slash-and-burn raids he'd led on a series of tribal villages. So many treasures, so many treasured moments.

His most prized possession was still at his bedside, though: an intricate, exquisitely detailed white crystal sculpture of a Nibiru dragon and Companion. He fondled and kissed it every night before sleeping — except on those evenings when he was too high to manage anything more than a wobbly collapse onto the bed, usually with the considerable assistance of a minion.

"I wonder what they'll be giving me for this year's Birthday," he mused, as he drifted into a gorged slumber.

Hours later, he woke to a voice blaring at him from the comm link, still on the floor where he'd batted it.

"Scabbage?" came Soader's guttural voice. "Scabbage, where the Xenu are you? Are you *there*? Asshole! What the hells am I looking at? Is your comm link on the *floor*?"

"Huh? Hunnhh," mumbled Scabbage, painfully propping himself up and wiping dried, reddish drool from his chin. "Soader? Soader! So glad to hear your voice. I assume everything on Mars is to your liking?" Scabbage steadied somewhat. "Don't be raising your voice at me. Don't forget who I am, reptile. Or that I'm only lenient with you because we're cousins. You wouldn't want me pissed at you next time your ass needs rescuing."

"Yeah, yeah, don't threaten *me*, you overgrown chameleon,"

Soader barked. "You need me as much as I need you, shithead. Pick up your gods-damned comm link. And explain why the hells you cut it so close. Those cops on 428 almost had me in the memory-wipe. I could've been blanked and dumped on RPF113."

"Yeah, well, you weren't, were you?" laughed Scabbage, picking up the comm link and putting it back on his desk. "No worries, Cuz — I'll look after you. As always. By the way, you make damn sure you get that girl back. We must have her. The plan won't work without her. Nothing will."

"Yeah, yeah. Shut your hole. I know what I'm doing," Soader growled. "I'll find her. Don't forget, I got to where I am with no help from you. You just keep me supplied now, and everything will be fine. Got it? I could decide to keep the entire treasure to myself, so you better play nice."

"Ha!" laughed Scabbage. "*Now* who's making threats? Haaa! And don't ever forget, I'm the only one who knows why your parents got rid of you."

"Shut the hells up, moron. I could do this without your help. Remember that. *And* make you even shorter than you already are!" threatened Soader, knowing mention of his cousin's stature would irritate him even more. "Have you heard anything yet?"

"No," growled back Scabbage, straining to hold his tongue. He knew he really did need Soader. Without him, the plans might not succeed. "But if and when I do, I'll call. Now get back to the plan. Don't take that kind of risk again, or I'll send you to '113 personally." Scabbage realized that although Soader was dangerously unbalanced and unstable, in this case he was correct. The demented half-Rept really *could* carry all this off on his own. That was something Scabbage did *not* want; not with the stakes what they were.

CHAPTER 13

Magic

"Dad! Daddy!" screamed Celine, struggling against her restraints. She began casting a spell to dissolve the restraining mesh, but it was too late — the transbeam sequence had begun. Soon she was fully engulfed in a whirlwind of scintillating plasma. It spun faster and faster, until, before his eyes, Zulak's pleading daughter disappeared.

Focused on the coordinates Soader had randomly dialed, the transbeam deposited Celine on a planet's surface. It was night. She could see stars above, but no constellations she recognized. It was a bit cold, but bearable. The air smelled odd, but that was to be expected when arriving on an unfamiliar planet. She seemed to be breathing without difficulty, and felt none of the illness or disorientation that would suggest a poisonous atmosphere. Fair enough — she seemed to be okay, for the moment.

She reached around and pulled out a small, pink crystal she'd hidden in her bodypack's lining. With the crystal in her open palm, she rubbed it gently with a finger and began chanting, softly and steadily. After perhaps a minute, she called aloud for her father. She heard a brief, startled reply, then silence. She repeated the chant several more times and called again, but there was no further response. She had lost the connection — but she *had* made contact, however brief. And her father's reply had indicated he knew it was she who was calling to him. He knew she was alive. Hopefully, he could also figure out where she was, and what was happening to her.

She had just begun exploring her new surroundings when she heard a warm, soothing voice — in her head. "Enter, young one," it said.

"Enter what?" she thought. As if in answer, a small shimmering, swirling circle of multi-colored points of light materialized a few feet away. Over the next few seconds the ring expanded until it was slightly taller than her body. "A tube-chute vortex!" she thought. She had never seen one before, but she'd read about them often enough. She hadn't really believed they existed — and had plenty of well-educated company in that disbelief. Yet here one was, or seemed to be. Was she just hallucinating?

"Enter, young one," the voice urged, once again.

"What the hells?" Celine thought, and approached the glittering ring. She reached out a hand toward the opening — if it really *was* an opening in any normal sense — and found herself drawn straight into it. At once she was enveloped in the swirling mass of colors, and had the odd sensation of forward motion, as though she were being carried along in a swift, roiling current of liquid, shot through with clouds of bubbles and frothy wisps of color. The experience was strange at first, but she had no serious feeling of alarm or discomfort. She could still breath normally, and the temperature felt neutral. After a little while, there came an occasional jolt — a sudden, brief feeling of being shoved or tumbled about by shifts of the "current." She'd flow along smoothly, then be buffeted to one side or the other, upward or downward. Once several of these had passed, she discovered she could sense when a "bump" was about to occur, and could shift her body to compensate for it. It wasn't long before she had herself under control and was "riding the flow" in relative comfort — no more jolts or tumbles, no more disorientation.

Now she tried for mental contact with West and Jager, but her menting was being blocked. The tube-chute must be shielded somehow. Still, she made several more attempts before giving up. Gradually, the current's fluctuations grew stronger, to a point where considerable concentration and energy were needed to keep oriented and in some degree of comfort.

The turbulent passage went on for what seemed like hours. What had at first been strangely pleasant had become a nightmare, and the weakening girl wondered when it would end — and where she would find herself when it did. She did not know how much more she could endure.

Suddenly, the tube and its rushing contents simply vanished. She was back in the open air at last — but it was open *mid*-air: she was free-falling toward...what? She barely had time to swing around for a look downward before she splashed deep into a pool of shockingly cold water. At least she hoped it was water! It certainly felt like water, and she hadn't started dissolving or anything, so it was probably okay. She pulled for the surface and came up with a gasp. Wherever she was, it seemed to be nighttime. She could see stars and a smallish moon at quarter-phase above.

She sensed a very slight flow to the water, so she must not be in a pool after all. She was right — she'd landed in an eddy along the bank of a broad river, and was about to be carried into the main current. Tired as she was, she knew she had to get to shore, so she began to swim across the current toward a reedy bank she could just barely make out, some forty or fifty feet away. She could hear the roar of rapids in the distance, and thanked her Gods and Goddesses for dropping her in a calm spot. She reached the shore, but was too exhausted to stand. She hauled herself through the reeds and onto a sandy bank, then lay still, resting. Clouds swept in and blotted out the moon and stars, and it began to rain. Gently at first, but rapidly rising to a downpour. She could hear nothing above the rain's rush — not even the rapids downstream.

Celine had regained her breath, but little strength. She wished she could just lie still for a while, but it was cold, and a stiff wind made it feel even colder. She had to find shelter and get dry soon, or she would be in much more serious trouble. She dragged herself up the bank, shivering all the while. She tried to stand; no way. Looking around her, she could see almost nothing; the clouds had blotted out the stars and moon. She managed to get up on all fours and began crawling toward a darkish mass, barely discernible inland and slightly downstream. She hoped it would turn out to be an embankment or hill, or perhaps a stand of trees. Anything that might offer some sort of shelter. She made her way slowly toward it over the rough terrain, navigating around or over logs, boulders and other obstacles.

Finally, she was close enough to make out that the dark shape was a long, low hill, with a steep embankment at its base. As she drew nearer, she spotted a darker spot at the bottom of the embankment, to the right of her current position. She made her way toward it, hoping it would be a cave. An empty one.

On reaching the entrance, she stopped and listened intently. She heard nothing but the rainfall, still strong and steady. She couldn't see more than a few feet into the dark space, but didn't want to risk using her light-orb; too much chance of attracting unwelcome attention. There were no alarming smells, mainly just the odor of cold, damp rock. She could tell there had once been fire here, though — and cooking.

There seemed no immediate threat, and in truth she had no choice: she had to get inside and get dry and warm. Now. She would have to confront whatever might be hiding in the shadows within. The rain lashed down in a new burst of intensity, urging her forward.

Every nerve and sense at highest alert, Celine stepped farther into the opening. She paused for a bit to let her eyes adjust. Still nothing visible within. Three tentative steps more, with a hand held out before her, just above head height. She stopped, listened, and peered into the darkness. More nothing. Now she judged she was far enough inside to risk a light. She brought out her light-orb, cupped it in her hand and activated it at its lowest level. She spread her fingers enough to let a few rays play in a faint beam, and swept the space. Nothing remarkable — and no eyes reflecting the orb's faint glow.

Satisfied for the moment, she opened her hand, raised the orb's intensity and made a rapid inspection. Dry. Reasonably level, even floor, with a random scattering of twigs, leaves, rocks and gravel. The cave appeared to extend back maybe seventy-five or eighty feet, narrowing gradually as it went deeper into the hillside. The air within was fairly fresh, and there seemed to be a faint breeze at her back — so there must be some sort of opening in the cave's roof or walls, allowing ventilation. Relieved but still wary, she shrugged out of her bodypack, propped it against the nearest wall, removed her boots and began stripping off clothing.

Once she'd shed the soaked outer layer, she stopped, pulled the comm crystal from its pocket and tried to reach her father again. This time there was nothing but silence. She mented strongly for West and Jager, but got no response. Well, at least she knew she'd gotten through to her father earlier. A hopeful start.

She had given Rafael his own comm crystal a few years before, as a seemingly ordinary holiday gift. In fact, the jewel was anything but ordinary: it carried a powerful spell of communication and connection. A spell Celine had placed upon it under West's tutelage, in preparation for precisely such a moment as this. Her father thought of it only as a pretty keepsake, knowing nothing of its function. She had made him promise to keep it with him always. Always. As for the stone's apparent failure to function just now, perhaps it was due to some sort of electromagnetic effect of the storm. Explanations would have to wait, though.

Celine hoped the cave's ventilation would be sufficient to allow a fire, without danger of accumulating smoke or fumes. She realized smoke would escape, potentially drawing unfriendly attention, but she'd have to risk it. She rounded up some grapefruit-sized rocks and arranged them in a circle about two feet across. Then she gathered leaves, twigs, sticks and branches, piling them next to the stone circle, arranged by size. In the center of the circle she made a small mound of the most delicate bits, then built an open-sided cone, outward and upward with gradually thicker and longer twigs and sticks. When it reached a little more than a foot high, she took the fire-starter from her pack and lit the fine tinder at the center of her fire-set. Soon she had a small but cheerful blaze going.

Stripping off the rest of her clothing, she pulled a tightly-rolled tunic from the bottom of her waterproof pack. She unrolled it and used it to whisk the worst of the dampness from her body, careful not to let the tunic itself become wet. That done, she pulled it over her head and smoothed it out. Now to attack the task of drying the soggy clothes she'd just removed. She set up some larger rocks and sticks close to the fire circle and draped the damp garments as best she could, facing the fire. Soon a faint steam was rising from the fabric. "Better. Much better," she sighed. She'd begun to feel human again.

Next up: something to eat, and then some much-needed sleep. Fortunately, Celine had thought to stuff a human food kit from the shuttlecraft into her bodypack. She brought it out, opened it up and spread its contents in a flat space near the fire. "Not much," she said aloud, inspecting the little array. She chose a brattle, sat on the floor and began to munch. Picking up her light-orb, she took a longer look around the cave. Others had definitely been here. She could see charred spots on the floor, only faintly visible beneath settled dust. There were also a few drawings here and there on the cave walls, most in black or gray and shades of red. Most were fairly crude, little more than stick figures representing humans and various animals, along with a sprinkling of symbols and geometric designs. It was hard to tell from a distance, but a few looked like they were quite intricate, finely executed and more colorful. Celine got up to inspect a group of such drawings, almost at the back of the cave. Coming closer, she stopped short. Now she knew where she was. She had been transported to Nibiru!

The paintings before her depicted dragons. Dragons of different types and colors, across a section of wall and up onto the ceiling. Dragons flying and fighting, some carrying human Companions, against a background of planets and stars. To one side there were depictions of humans and dragons celebrating a birth. Celine found one of the paintings disturbing. It showed several red dragons, one with two heads and rendered at nearly twice the size of any of the other types. It called to mind one of Koondahg's books, in which he explained in detail the several types of dragons, and their similarities and differences.

In the mural before her, one of the beasts was biting off a

human's head, while another red dragon seemed to be dancing with delight beside a bonfire. At the center of the fire was another human, tied to a stake and screaming in agony.

While studying this painting, simultaneously amazed and repelled, Celine glanced to one side and caught sight of yet another depiction, a bit deeper into the cave. She moved toward it, holding her light-orb high. What she saw left her stunned, mouth agape. It was an elaborate symbol, far more skillfully executed than anything else she'd seen here. A symbol she had seen back home on her native world. A symbol of purity, truth and abundant survival: A young man and woman stood facing one another, kissing, their arms interlocked. There was a purple halo above each figure's head. A horizontal figure "8" — the ancient symbol for infinity — embraced them, each encircled at the waist by one of the figure's loops. What surprised Celine most, though, were the additions to the symbol as she'd always seen it: At the feet of the kissing pair were two small children, embraced by another, smaller infinity symbol. One was a blond-haired, blue-eyed boy, dressed in rags and with bloodied knees and hands. The other was a little girl with long, brown hair and green eyes, similarly dressed. Standing close beside the humans were two dragons, one white and one blue, with a pair of dragon eggs at their feet. The figures were arranged in such a way as to give the distinct impression that one was looking at a family portrait. Or rather, an extended-family portrait.

Celine stared at the elaborate painting for a long while, transfixed. At length, she became aware that the fire had begun to die behind her. She came to herself with a start, suddenly struck by how very tired she was. She took one last look at the symbol, then returned to the fire, stoking it with more of the sticks she'd gathered.

After eating a bit more from her meager stock of rations,

she arranged her pack, spare clothes and some dry leaves to form a sleeping place, at least a bit more comfortable than the raw cavern floor. She sat and watched the waning fire for several minutes, reflecting on the day, and what might lie ahead. She felt a calm certainty that things were about to improve — though others who'd just seen paintings of humans being exterminated by huge, red, twin-headed dragons might have felt very differently indeed. She lay down and was asleep almost at once.

CHAPTER 14

Fianna

The following morning, as the new day's light crept into the cave entrance, Celine was startled awake by what sounded like the huffings and snortings of a great beast, just outside. She sprang from her sleeping-place, scooping up her knife and incant-baton as she rose, ready to defend herself against whatever came through the opening.

"Ahhh, but you are quick!" came a deep but distinctly feminine voice from just beyond the opening, which was now in shadow. "By the smell of you, you are clearly intelligent, and not the least fearful. But, can I trust you?"

"Who are you? What do you want?" demanded Celine, straining to see who or what was blocking the cave entrance. Sniffing the air, she judged it was an eater of fish.

"What do I want? That depends upon what *you* want. So, young human, what *do* you want?"

Celine had more patience and skill than most with puzzles. That had been instrumental in deciphering the many cryptic writings she'd studied, detailing the ways of magic. But that was different from playing potentially deadly word games with unknown creatures. "Show yourself, and tell me who you are and what you want," she demanded. She brandished her blade, more to stoke her own courage than to threaten the unseen intruder (who couldn't *see* the blade, after all).

"Oh, you are a prize. You are a prize!" laughed the shadows once more. The sound was deep and resonant, without a hint of menace. "All right, you win. I mean you no harm, so please put aside any weapons and have a seat. I shall only show myself if you will promise not to attack. I have no desire to harm you, though I surely might, if you were to attempt an attack. You see, I have not learned fine control and delicate restraint with my means of defense. Now, do you agree?"

This mysterious voice from beyond the door had tweaked something in the recesses of Celine's mind; something familiar yet foreign, as if it were an echo from another lifetime, long ago. "Oh...ah...all right. I agree," she said, sitting down on the rocky floor and setting her knife and incant-baton close by.

The shadow at the door darkened almost completely, and into the cave flowed a beautiful white dragon. Once fully inside, wings folded close to its body, it paused and looked at Celine directly. The large, glittering eyes were classically reptilian, yet somehow conveyed warmth and a calm curiosity.

Celine had always been deeply fascinated by images of dragons, but never could she have imagined the sheer, soul-wrenching beauty of the creature before her. The scales were brilliant white, glistening even in the cave's dim light. Every plane, every curve, every angle of the creature's great form was beautiful in itself, and each blended into the perfect harmony of the whole. The creature's movements were silken-smooth, exquisitely balanced and precise. The overall impression was of immense power, held in perfect, delicate control. Celine suddenly gasped, realizing she had stopped breathing quite some time ago — and had no idea when.

"I greet you, child." The rich, mellow voice filled the space. Celine wondered at the experience: not only was she perceiving the speech as sound, but also as a sort of spiritual vibration, deep within body, mind and soul. It was wonderful, and it was quite beyond anything she'd experienced, in this life or any other.

"I am called Albho Fianna, and that is my name. It means 'white warrior.' By my friends, I am called Fianna. The same you may do, if our talk here goes well. Who might you be, and what might be your business in my home?"

Celine had read all Koondahg's dragon books three times each, and knew that white dragons were rare, white females even more so. If she remembered correctly, only one white dragon hatched in every ten thousand years, and just one in four of those was a female. Celine was in awe, to her very core. More amazing still, this creature seemed identical to the dragon in her dream. The girl was so stricken that she hadn't even noticed that the splendid beast was speaking in her own native language, without benefit of a translator.

Firmly but gently, the dragon interrupted Celine's fascinated reverie. "I have asked you questions, child. Please tell me, who might you be, and what might be your business in this, my cavern home?"

"I b-beg your pardon, Albho Fianna," said Celine. She bowed low, knowing that dragons expected members of other races to treat them as though they were royalty. She'd read that if one didn't treat them so, one could be judged an enemy very quickly. An enemy, or simply supper. "I was brought to your planet against my will. I have used your cave only to rest and to get dry and warm. I was lost, and am most thankful for your cave's gracious shelter on a harsh and rainy night."

Then Celine recalled that it was important to give a dragon

a gift at your first meeting. If the gift was accepted, you were friends — and only extreme circumstances could ever threaten that friendship. "I regret that as a lost traveler I bear little of value, but I wish to offer you the gift of a song, if that would please you." The dragon was silent for a time, gazing intently at the girl. The sounds of its deep, measured breathing filled the cave.

Finally, the creature's eyes brightened, she smiled an almost playful smile, and she spoke. "I accept the gift you offer."

Relieved, Celine cleared her throat and began to sing a favorite song from her childhood. It was fortunate that she had a fine, strong singing voice. Dragons do not appreciate poor singing.

The princess and the boy
The princess and the boy
Where have they gone
The princess and the boy?
Some say together, some say not
Some say lovers, some say lost

The princess and the dragon
The princess and the dragon
Where have they gone
The princess and the dragon?
Some say white, some say black
Some say for good, some say for bad

The princess and the prince
The princess and the prince
Where have they gone
The princess and the prince?
Some say up, some say down

Some say back, some say now

Her and he
Him and she
They and them
Where are they now?
Where could they be?

When the song ended, the girl and dragon were still for a time, watching each other — Celine seated on the floor, Albho Fianna resting on her haunches just inside the cave's entrance.

Albho Fianna broke the silence. "A fine cave, is it not?" she asked, rising, stretching, and stepping closer to Celine — much as a panther does before pouncing. Celine remained utterly still. "Do you like my paintings?"

"Yes, I quite like them," Celine replied. "Did you do them?" she asked, though she knew the images were ancient, and the dragon before her was fairly young — there was still fuzz on her chin.

"Ha! You flatter me," laughed Fianna, knowing precisely what Celine was up to. She took two more steps toward the girl. Celine remained composed, showing no outward sign of fear. "They were painted by my grandmother's Companion, a Pleiadean warrior. Schimpel, he was called. Perhaps you know of him?"

Celine knew this was the dragon's polite way of indicating it knew where she came from. It also meant that she must now allude to her enigmatic dream. "I once dreamed of a lovely dragon princess. She was terribly lonely because she had been separated from her dearest friend. The dragon princess had searched for her lost friend for ages, without success. She had given up hope, and lost the will to live. She flew off to find a suitable place to die.

"After a time, her flight took her over an unfamiliar valley, with a lovely lake glittering in the sun. She decided to spend one more afternoon in the world, and landed on a knoll to bask in the summer warmth. After a time, she heard a distant cry and turned toward it. The cry came again, and the dragon princess rose and walked toward the source of the sound — a nearby wood. She heard the cry once more; it sounded like her friend!

"She leapt forward and into the wood, only to be swallowed by a huge pit-trap and snared in a net at its bottom. Though she realized she had been tricked, she did not struggle. She gave up utterly, thinking this just one more proof that it was time for her to pass on."

"What happened next?"

"The dragon princess curled up at the bottom of the pit as if to go to sleep, waiting for her evil captors to end her life," answered Celine.

"Did they kill her?"

"Yes, they killed the lovely dragon princess. Her spirit freed from the captive body, she flew away to resume the search for her friend," Celine replied.

"And did she find her friend?"

"Yes, she did."

Fianna had been moving slowly, gradually closer to Celine throughout the story. Celine had noticed, but made no attempt to back away. When Fianna had come to within inches of the girl, the dragon bowed.

Celine was thrilled to her core. The traditional signal! The formalities were complete!

Now the two could drop their ultra-polite reserve, and speak as friends. They talked for hours; it was as though they had been friends for many lifetimes, and were happily catching up after a long separation. Oddly, Celine thought, it was the same sort of relationship she enjoyed with Jager.

As the day moved along, the pair left the cave and settled in a grassy spot in the sun, beside the river that passed nearby. Celine's stomach began to growl, so while the conversation continued, she finished off what little food she had.

Suddenly, Celine realized that in her excitement, she'd forgotten all about her worries over her father, Jager and everything else. "Oh, Fianna," she exclaimed. "I'm so sorry, but I must find a way to reach my family and friends. My telepathy and communicator charms don't seem to work here, so I don't know how to contact them."

"Unfortunately for you, our planet is shielded so that others cannot find us. I am sorry, but you will not be able to reach anyone while you are on Nibiru."

Celine was crestfallen at the news, but the feeling vanished quickly. She had a strange, calm confidence that everything would be okay, and that circumstances and events that were worrisome at first would turn out for the best. She was surprised at her own optimism, but accepted it cheerfully.

"Do you know that you are the first human to visit Nibiru since Schimpel?" Fianna asked. "It is quite exciting. Our legends tell of a young girl, a descendant of Schimpel, who would follow him to our world and rescue us from doom as a race. This is why I was so delighted, but not surprised, at your arrival."

Celine listened politely. She knew dragons considered it rude in the extreme to interrupt when another was speaking. One of Koondagh's books had included a lengthy discourse on dragon etiquette, with explicit details on successful communication with the noble dragon-folk.

"You may not be aware of it, but we dragons are in grave danger. Our eggs no longer hatch — they have been hexed. If there are no hatchlings soon, our race will vanish. My brother and I were the last to hatch, but he disappeared many years ago; I am left as the youngest of our kind, and the last female of breeding age.

"The older dragons are losing hope. I must find a way to help them and to prevent our extinction. There remain a few unhatched eggs, under close guard, but there is little hope of their hatching; they are already thousands of years old."

Fianna continued, "Legend says the spell to remove the hex is hidden on Earth. We're waiting for Nibiru's orbit to take it closer to the planet, so that I may safely travel there. When our planets are separated by too great a distance, one so young and small as I cannot hope to survive the journey. Further, no dragon's magic will function to its full potential until he or she has been joined with a Companion — and as you see, I am Companionless, just as are all our people now living.

"And yet, I am the only hope for all my people. I must journey to Earth and find the Book of Atlantis, which holds the key to reversing the hex. I must also find a mate. It is much to do, and I am near despair."

Celine sat quietly, nodding now and then to let Fianna know that she heard what the dragon was revealing, and that she understood her new friend's plight, pain and sorrow.

"I am Princess Albho Fianna Uwatti, born of the line of Nibiru dragon royalty. I am the last alive in the line to the throne. Yet if there can be no more dragons in my realm, I have failed before I have even begun my reign." Fianna bowed her head, sighing. Several minutes passed before either of them spoke again.

"What has happened to your leg?" asked Celine, changing the subject. Much earlier, she had noticed the creature's twisted and undersized left front limb, though she'd politely refrained from mentioning it. She would not ordinarily have been so forward as to mention it at all, but now she was certain her arrival on Nibiru had been no accident. The knowledge gave her a new boldness, a willingness to follow her feelings and instincts. She and Fianna were *meant* to meet. They had mutual purposes. Deep purposes. Each, in her way, must save her own kind. And they must work together to do it.

"Ah, my leg. My older brother deliberately mangled it once, in what was supposed to have been a play fight. I knew at the time that he was jealous of me, but had no idea how deeply. Not until he bit me that day, then flew off and left me bleeding badly. I never told our parents what really happened. I lied instead, saying I had been ambushed by a bearcat and only barely escaped. They sympathized and inquired no further, but I think they had their suspicions."

"I'm sorry to hear that, Fianna. I've a sibling like yours; a sister, Mia. She didn't try to bite my leg off, but she might as well have," laughed Celine, and Fianna joined in. "But listen: I know some healing magic," Celine offered. "Perhaps I could help heal your leg."

Fianna leapt to her feet. "You would do that? You could truly do that?"

"Yes, I think so. I can certainly try. I don't have all the things I'll need right now, but when I've gathered them, I'll do all I can to mend your leg."

The pair spent the rest of the day and nearly all the next talking on and on, ranging far and wide in the subjects they explored. Fianna told Celine about the great community of dragons farther down the valley, in and around a place called Dragon Hall. She explained that she herself preferred living alone. She enjoyed her freedom, and found it wearying to be around many of the older dragons who had become depressed and dejected in recent centuries.

As they talked, Fianna helped Celine to clean the home-cave; Fianna admitted she had let it lapse. Once the cleaning was done, the two dragged in some tree branches and reeds, and Fianna watched in fascination as Celine fashioned a bed for herself. Next, they brought in large armfuls of long grass, and bundles of lush bush-boughs to create a new bed for the dragon. The bond between the two grew stronger by the hour.

Late in the afternoon, their day's projects completed, Fianna asked Celine if she would like to accompany her on a flight the next morning.

"I'd love to, dear Fianna, but how can I fly with you? I have no idea how; and please forgive me, but your scales look so sharp!"

"Ah, you are quite right, my friend. I have a solution, though. I will show you in the morning," Fianna said with a smile.

The dragon left the cave that night as Celine slept, and flew off across the starry sky. She returned at dawn, with a smooth, graceful saddle clutched in her one good front paw. She explained that it was the very saddle Schimpel had used when flying with her grandmother — as her Companion. Surprisingly, the saddle was in excellent shape despite its great age, bearing few signs of its long and distinguished service.

Fianna explained how to secure and use the saddle, and laid out the basics of flying with a dragon. Celine quickly recognized that one did not *ride* a dragon, in the sense that one might ride a horse. Horses and similar animals were intelligent and sensitive; there was no question of that. Dragons were not animals, though. They were *people*. Just as aware, intelligent and developed — individually, socially and spiritually — as any of the other known sentient races. So, one did not "ride" a dragon. When invited to do so, one shared flight with a dragon.

Once Celine felt confident enough to give it a try, she and Fianna made their first flight together. The experience was beyond anything Celine had ever imagined. The pair practiced

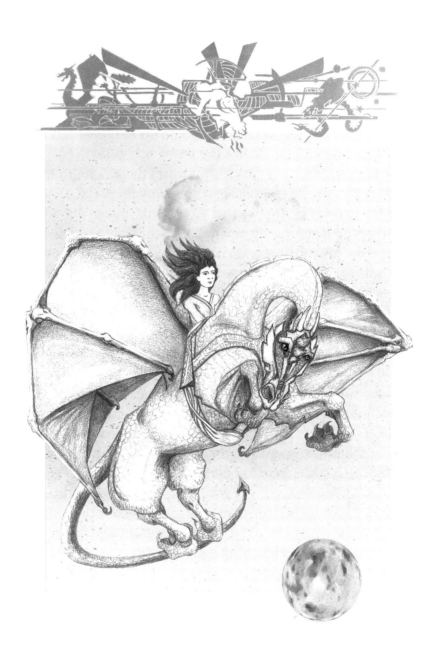

flying together for hours every day. It was a glorious time for them both.

In hopes that the shielding Fianna had described might not be completely impervious, Celine sometimes tried to use her telepathy to reach Jager or the Mentors. Every attempt ended in failure. She had no better luck with her communicator crystal, trying to contact her father. There was no denying that she missed her friends and family. Her growing bond with Fianna, however, and especially the exhilaration of their flights together, pushed such thoughts to the very back of her mind.

She had never had such a friend. Precious though they were to her, even her relationships with Jager and West couldn't compare. Those connections had always been purely mental and spiritual. Her bond with Fianna added the elements of physical presence, physical contact, and shared physical effort. As the days literally flew by, Celine thought of her family, West and even Jager less and less. Fianna was right here, right now — and the two were becoming inseparable.

One day, while resting after a particularly intense session of maneuvers, a large, green-hued dragon appeared in the eastern sky, flying toward them. Celine watched in wonder as he approached, then landed just yards away. As he folded his magnificent wings, Celine had a flash of recognition: this must be Orgon the Wise. She knew of him from stories Fianna had told, about the last of her kind still living on Nibiru. Celine realized she must now observe the same polite rituals she'd followed when first meeting Fianna. Introductions were made and protocols meticulously followed, but soon the three were immersed in conversation.

Orgon departed near the end of that first day, but thereafter rejoined the two friends daily, helping them with their lessons. With his keen observations, wise suggestions, firm insistence, and praise for demonstrated competence, Celine and Fianna improved more quickly and gained far more skill than they would have on their own. Orgon well remembered the stories Fianna's grandmother had once told around the courtyard fire — tales of her exploits with her Companion, Schimpel.

Up until Orgon's arrival, Fianna and Celine had only been practicing general flying skills and maneuvers. Orgon began coaching them in more and more of what he referred to as tactical maneuvers, geared to such things as escape and evasion, and gaining and maintaining positional advantages in combat. Neither Fianna nor Celine found this new orientation odd. It seemed natural, considering the history of dragon-human flight. They also thoroughly enjoyed the new challenges it brought to their work.

Once the young dragon and her friend had become proficient at offensive moves, he began teaching them more defensive maneuvers. They loved the new viewpoint and techniques. The two steadily gained expertise in attack avoidance, sudden reversals, rolls, stalls, energy conservation moves, and — a big favorite — the evasive spiral. That one was particularly tough to master, but they practiced it over and over (and over) until they finally had it down.

Late one summer afternoon, Orgon gave them a new and different sort of task. "I want you to fly to the top of the ridge you can see on those mountains to the west," he said, pointing to indicate the spot. Sit there and watch the sun go down behind the range you'll see farther on beyond it. The moment the sun dips fully below the far crest, fly straight up into the clouds, as fast and as high as you possibly can. When you are far above the clouds and there is scarcely any air to breathe, stop climbing and glide."

"Then what?" asked Fianna, but the ancient dragon's only response was to spread his time-worn but grand wings and climb steeply upward and out of sight. Fianna and Celine thought this odd, but just shrugged it off and flew to the ridge Orgon had pointed out. There they sat, idling away the last of the day and watching a flock of young inglit practicing with their newly-fledged little wings.

Seeing the sun touch the far ridge, Celine spoke to Fianna: "Time to get ready." She rose, dusted off, secured her bodypack and climbed into the saddle. She hung on extra tight as Fianna gathered herself to launch. When the sun's last ray vanished behind the mountain, Fianna leapt skyward, straight up. They passed through the few thin clouds above them and continued to climb; soon they were higher than Celine had yet flown.

Fianna's ascent slowed until finally the air was so thin she couldn't climb any farther. She leveled off, hung motionless for a moment, then went into a long glide. The view was unspeakably gorgeous. Celine thought to herself, "It's breathtaking!" Then she laughed — it truly *was* breathtaking! There wasn't sufficient air pressure up here for either of them to breathe properly, and she could sense Fianna beginning to struggle. She realized she must act, or they would very shortly pass out.

She pulled out her incant-baton, then fumbled with a small satchel until she found a pea-sized, dark-green crystal. Now she began a chant — though it could barely be heard in the thin air. Audible or not, the incantation worked. Soon they were suspended in the center of a crystalline bubble, full of air at breathable pressure. Because Fianna's wings no longer had contact with the surrounding air, she couldn't glide. They began a gentle descent, prevented from plummeting straight downward by the buoyancy of the crystal bubble itself. Fianna partially folded her wings and the two relaxed a bit, catching their breaths. Celine explained what she had done, and what they should do next.

Once they were refreshed, Celine spoke a few syllables and the bubble vanished. Fianna re-spread her wings, and they began a long, lazy spiral downward, drinking in the spectacular views as they went.

After a while they found themselves looking over the night-shrouded landscape of a valley close to home. Fianna turned toward their cave, and soon they were safe inside, settling for the night.

Their lessons and practice continued for months. Orgon would give them a task, never explaining the reason for it, nor its expected outcome. They would always do as he asked, and each time they came away with new knowledge, insight and skill.

One day, Orgon sent them several mountain ranges away and told them to land on a particular ledge, near one of the peaks. They found the ledge, landed, and settled down to wait. Within moments an enormous flying creature swooped up from below and passed above them. Its wingspan was at least seventy-five feet, and it was armed with a thick, powerful beak and wicked talons. Once above and behind the pair, the beast wheeled and dove straight at them, screaming. Fianna barely had time to react, shifting at the last second; the impact that would otherwise have crippled her only succeeded in jolting them badly and knocking them from their perch.

They tumbled through the air toward a craggy ridge below, until Fianna managed to twist 'round and get her wings out to catch the air, arresting their crazy descent. They had only barely regained a bit of orientation when the monster was upon them once again, shrieking hideously. Fianna pulled to one side and out of reach of the creature's talons, but slammed into a rocky abutment in the process, nearly crushing Celine and giving herself massive bruises that would take weeks to heal. They were still alive, though, and she regained anxious flight after rebounding from the mountainside.

The beast made another screaming dive, but now they had

their bearings and balance, and managed to maneuver out of its reach again without damaging themselves in the process. While the beast recovered from its latest assault, Fianna flew straight upward, putting some blessed distance between them and their attacker.

"What *is* it?" shouted Celine.

"I do not know, but it means to put an end to us. Hang on!" responded Fianna, diving first in one direction, then another.

At one unexpected, jolting turn, Celine lost her hold and hung out of the saddle, clutching it desperately. "Fianna!" she screamed. The dragon made a compensating move that landed Celine squarely back in her seat, where she quickly strapped herself down.

Fianna and the monster maneuvered across the sky in a living dogfight, the dragon continually fighting for an altitude advantage. Celine hung on for dear life and kept her friend apprised of the beast's whereabouts and actions. Finally, they managed to get well above it, with their position concealed from the beast by a wispy straggle of cloud. They watched it through the cloudy mist, Fianna adjusting their position continually to stay out of its sight for as long as possible.

"I know what it is!" Fianna shouted. "A stigr! A mythical monster created by magic. Orgon must have put it here as a challenge and test. They're nearly unbeatable! Hang on, Celine." Fianna dove through the concealing cloud, darting and rolling randomly from one heading to another, and shifting the angle of her descent — leaving the stigr no way to predict her path and launch a strong assault.

Celine recognized it was now her turn. Pulling the incant-baton from her boot, she began chanting. Meanwhile, the stigr had gauged their general course and was flying at them, gaining on them gradually despite Fianna's continued evasions. Celine continued her chant as the beast approached.

When the stigr was almost upon them, Celine yelled, "Fianna, hard right — NOW!" At the same instant, she flicked her wrist and a stream of flame and sparks shot from the end of her incant-baton, straight toward the rapidly-closing beast. The fiery blast caught it square in the chest.

The great creature screamed in agony and wheeled away. Its massive chest had been split nearly its full length, and the beast was beginning to disintegrate. It gave a choked, tortured roar, but managed to spin round and dive toward the two companions once more. They evaded easily, and the monster sailed harmlessly past, now thrashing and flailing as Celine's spell slowly but steadily tore its body apart. Fianna brought them to rest on an outcrop and the two watched as the stigr crashed into the rocky slope, broken utterly and silent at last.

Fianna and Celine looked at one another in a strange mix of horror and triumph, neither speaking a word. Launching herself from the mountainside, Fianna glided down to the valley far below, landing beside a quiet river. There the two spent the night, resting, recovering and reflecting on their recent brush with death.

Next morning, they flew home, where they found Orgon awaiting them. After acknowledging their respectful bows, the ancient dragon rumbled, "I can teach you no more."

He was quite correct. His methods had brought the two young friends to almost perfect integration, and superb mutual ability. No matter what problem arose, they confronted it together, blending their skills and abilities for an elegant solution. They could now teach themselves anything new they might need to know, drawing on the deep knowledge they had gained under the old sage's guidance.

Orgon spoke to them a while longer, then concluded: "You are now your own teachers, as always it should be with Great Dragons and their Companions."

The three joined in a wonderful feast Orgon had arranged at Dragon Hall, with all their favorite foods and many more besides. Dragons from far and wide arrived and joined in the celebration, invited some time before by Orgon, in certain anticipation of the event. It had been years almost beyond count since Nibiru had seen a Dragon-Companion pair, and the significance of the occasion was lost on no one — not even Celine, though she was new to the fabled planet.

After a while, Celine and Fianna flew up to a ridge above the party, watching the happy celebration. Both were deep in their own thoughts; feeling older, knowing they now were somehow responsible for every dragon they saw below, and the rest of Fianna's race besides.

CHAPTER 15

Ready or Not

Suddenly, Celine's contemplative mood broke. "What is your brother's name?" she asked her friend. "Where is he now?"

"Ah, Companion," said Fianna. "His name is Ahimoth, and he is a black dragon. In an ancient Earth tongue known as Hebrew, the name meant 'brother of death' — but today it carries no such dark significance among our people. It is simply the traditional name given to a male black dragon. Black dragons are rare in the extreme, and considered surpassingly handsome — so it has become a name of distinction. Nevertheless, when my brother learned of the name's ancient meaning, he was stunned. He felt that it carried a curse upon his life, so he took steps to change his name to one with no sinister significance, past or present: Leothe.

"Some years later, he left Nibiru to travel to Earth. That is where he is today, as far as I know. That is where he meant to go, but in truth I have never been certain he arrived safely."

"How could he travel to Earth when he was so young?" Celine asked.

"Well, our people are long-lived. Our planet's eccentric orbital path takes it close to Earth only once in a very great while. The last time that happened, he attempted the trip. He was too young to risk the journey alone, but another dragon, older and stronger, offered to travel with him."

The two sat for a while longer, watching as the last of their guests departed. Then they headed down the valley to their cave and slept the night through.

Exactly a year after the day of their first meeting, Fianna gave Celine a special gift. Dragons only give such gifts to those who have proven they will be loyal friends for life. Fianna's gift was a firestone — a strikingly beautiful sapphire. She lifted a scale below her left wing, revealing the sparkling stone. Plucking it from its hiding place, she set it in her Companion's hand.

Celine stared in wonder at the glowing stone, marveling at the soothing warmth it emanated. From her long studies of dragon lore, she knew what she must do next. She built a small fire, then drew her knife and made a three-inch-long cut along the inner side of her left forearm, midway between wrist and elbow. She grimaced at the pain, but managed to keep silent. Picking up the gem, she closed her eyes, kissed it, then inserted it firmly in the center of the wound.

Next, she heated her knife blade, holding it just above the dancing flames until a faint red glow appeared along its length. Bracing herself against the shock, she pressed the blade against the wound, sealing it with a hiss and a plume of pale smoke. The smell of her own burning flesh startled her, almost as much as the searing pain. Excruciating though it was, it lasted only a few moments; Celine was proud to hold herself to no more than a gasp and brief groan.

The ritual completed, she turned to Fianna and threw her arms around the gracefully bowed neck, tears now streaming down her face. Tears of happiness, though, not pain. "I love you too, Little One," the dragon responded — without uttering a sound.

"Oh! Oh, my! I can *hear* you!" cried Celine, jumping back in amazement. "I can hear you! In my head! My telepathy *does* work!" she laughed. She leapt forward again to hug Fianna even harder, then broke away and danced around the clearing.

"Yes, Companion. Because you had the Dream, and because a year has safely passed since we first met, we are able to link in this way. There will always be this connection between us now, even if we should be worlds apart, physically. This is the way of dragons and their Companions."

Celine and Fianna celebrated through the whole evening. After a huge and luscious meal, they laughed, told stories and joked for hours. Celine went into the cave and returned wearing a reed-grass skirt she'd woven, and put on a show as though she were a dancer from Ryuku. Fianna laughed so hard, she feared she'd pop out a scale or two. It was the most splendid evening they'd ever shared. After many hours, the two fell asleep, Celine curled up between Fianna's forelegs. They were far more than just friends for life, and both felt they had *always* been together. They knew in their souls they always would be — always and forever.

Still, each had a strange feeling, nearly imperceptible yet undeniable, at the back of her mind. They both had it, and each knew the other had it, too. It was the idea that *something* was still missing — something that would make their linking even more complete. But neither would know what that something was, just yet.

The next afternoon, the two took off to visit their venerable mentor, Orgon. They had perfected a particularly difficult diving spiral maneuver earlier in the day, and were eager to demonstrate the new skill. They'd found their new, closer connection made all their familiar moves easier and more certain, and opened up all sorts of possibilities they'd never even imagined. Suddenly, Celine asked her friend, "What's that sound?"

"It is the Horn of Disaster," mented Fianna. "I have heard it only three other times in my whole life. Something terrible must have happened." Fianna tightened her profile and leaned into the effort of flight, nearly doubling her speed. They had already been fairly near to their destination, Dragon Hall, so within minutes they spotted it and dropped from the sky. They found a crowd of dragons gathered in the enormous courtyard, with Orgon standing on the Cynth Pedestal above the group. The pair were amazed to see a large clutch of dragon eggs resting on a royal-blue cushion at the foot of the pedestal. Lye, the Nanny, watched over them, her body and tail encircling the precious, living treasures. The rest of the Dragon Council stood behind the pedestal, on a wide ledge used only for important ceremonies and emergency meetings.

"Welcome, Fianna and Celine," said Orgon, as the two landed lightly beside the pedestal. Celine slid quickly from the saddle and stood close to her friend, a hand resting on Fianna's flank.

"What has happened, Uncle?" asked Fianna, looking along the ledge at the clearly worried council, their heads shaking and great wings twitching. Looking down to the courtyard just below, she could see the dragons assembled there were just as agitated. Fianna had only rarely seen such behavior. A few were also huffing smoke. The eldest of the group, Old Haggis, had even allowed a few bursts of flame to escape his jaws. Those closest to him moved gingerly aside, but none presumed to tell him to mind his manners.

"Your attention please, my people!" bellowed Orgon. "Hush!" Everyone went still at once, watching him in worried anticipation. As Orgon slowly scanned the whole gathering, a deep wave of sadness came over him; there were so very few of his people left. He could not hold back a tear, much to the crowd's fresh dismay. Dragons rarely cry. And when one does, it is a certain omen of doom.

"Uncle, what is wrong? What has *happened?*" gasped Fianna.

Orgon looked away from his lovely niece. Her face was too poignant a reminder of the tragedy now facing their kind. His face still averted, he replied, "Another egg has died. We have no more time to lose. We must recover the Atlantis Spell and remove the hex that was laid upon our precious eggs. We must have hatches, and we must have them soon. If we do not, I fear the last of them may die before another year has passed — and with it, all hope for our future as a race."

Now Orgon lifted his face to Fianna and Celine. Bowing, he said, "The Council has met, and has made its decision." He spread his great wings to their full extent. The sun glinted from their edges, and his deep green scales glistened.

"Oh, no!" mented Fianna to Celine. "This cannot be happening. Not *now!* We are not yet ready!"

"Ready for what?" asked Celine, aloud.

"They want us to travel to Earth, to recover and return with the Atlantis Spell. It is too soon — the planets are still at a dangerous distance — but I fear we have no choice. We must go now, or we may never need go at all."

"Ohhhhhh!" Celine thought back. "You're right. We can't be ready for that — not yet! What can we do?"

"Ready or not, we *must* go," answered the dragon. "'Ready' is a luxury we can no longer afford. You and I are the final hope for all the dragons of Nibiru. Legend foretold this, and now we must comply with that which is written."

Celine stood silent for some time. Finally, she thought, "All right, Fianna. I'm with you, but I will not hide it: I'm scared. I'm very, very scared. Can we possibly make the trip? From all you have taught me and all that I have read, there seems little chance that we'd survive it."

"I too am fearful," replied Fianna. She turned toward Orgon again and spoke, "Oh, wise Uncle. Respected Council. We accept your charge. My Companion and I will leave for Earth tomorrow night, when the moon is at its highest. We will find the Atlantis Spell and return. Our people's precious eggs shall live to hatch, and our race shall survive and flourish."

"Thank you, Fianna, and Companion Celine," intoned Orgon, bowing deeply — first to the dragon and then to the girl. "We shall aid you in your quest as best we can, with our prayers and our magic."

"As you know, our legends state that millennia ago, fleeing from a Rept army, the Atlanteans hid their ancient spell books, along with a great treasure. It remains hidden — as far as anyone knows — in a great city, in the Earth country now known to many there as Turkey."

All were silent as Orgon continued. "It has long been the custom that each time a dragon visits Earth, he or she spends time in search of the hidden spell books. Since we have never needed them so desperately as we do now, the searches have often been less than serious. Now there is no choice. We must find them. They must be brought home to Nibiru. You, Fianna, and you, Celine, must visit our long-time friend Nessie, in her deep lake home. If anyone can help you to find the books, it is she." Orgon bowed again, and then concluded, "May our gracious and beloved Gods and Goddesses watch over and guide you, Princess, and you, Companion."

The assembled dragons broke from their solemn quiet and began to cheer. They all knew the legend well: a dragon princess and her Companion would one day find the spell books, the hex would at last be broken, and the future of their race assured.

Tables were whisked out and loaded with food and drink,

and a celebration of new hope began. All were happy, excepting only the two apprehensive young travelers, and their aging mentor, Orgon.

Later that evening, after most of the other dragons had retired, Celine asked Fianna to come sit down beside the dying fire. When the dragon was comfortable, Celine rolled out a woven reed mat by the fireside, then placed on it a wide, empty dish, and a wooden bowl, half-filled with moist, pliable clay. Taking a collection of small satchels from her bodypack, she opened one after another and placed some of the contents of each in the dish — dried herbs, berries and roots, as well as other small items. She had earlier set a small cauldron of water to heat over the fire; now she added the dish's contents to the boiling liquid, a careful bit at a time. Soon a fragrant vapor began to rise from the little vessel.

Celine turned to Fianna, saying, "Time to mend your leg, dear friend. Seeing as we're going on an important adventure tomorrow, the moment has arrived."

Celine ladled most of the boiling mixture from the cauldron into the wooden bowl and mixed it thoroughly into the moist clay. Next, she scooped up a handful of the warm mixture and spread it gently on the dragon's withered foreleg. She continued until most of the leg was covered with a thin layer.

Now, with the dragon looking on in fascination, Celine added wood to the fire, then placed a carved, wooden star medallion on a flat rock beside the reed mat. It was a token she had made to represent the Mentors and Jager; it symbolized their constant presence and support.

With an improvised broom she'd cut from a nearby shrub, Celine swept clean the area around both the fire and the dragon, creating a large circle that was clear of stones and debris. She threw some dried sage and sweet grasses into the flames, bringing forth a soothing, scented smoke. Now, holding a long, pointed stick and walking backwards, Celine drew a circle just within the border of the area she had swept clean.

Next, she sprinkled a thin trail of salt just inside the circle, all the way around. Taking a small, silver bell from her bodypack, she rang it three times, waited for the space of several breaths, then rang it once again. This she repeated two more times. Drawing out her incant-baton, Celine turned once more to Fianna. "Close your eyes," she said. When she saw that the dragon had done so, she closed her own as well. Now she began a chant, rocking from side to side with its cadence, the incant-baton held high.

Gods and Goddesses
Watching over me
Watching over thee
Give to me give to me
A leg a leg
for my friend
for the friend with me
Give a leg give a leg
One two three
Give a leg give a leg
To me to she
She'll use it well
She'll use it free
Give her a leg
Give her a leg
My friend, my friend
The friend with me
It's attached to her left
It's attached at the knee
Give her a leg
Give her a leg
One two three

Gods and Goddesses
How mighty are ye
Give her a leg
Give her a leg
One two three
Give her a leg
ONE! TWO! THREE!

Fianna suddenly flinched, then began to squirm and moan. Celine gently stroked her flank, then spoke. "We must sit here quietly, eyes closed tight, and meditate until the fire has gone, Fianna. I know there is pain right now, but it will be all right — it is just a natural part of the healing. Your part is to hold in your mind the new leg you've wanted for so long. Picture it there, whole and perfect. Know that it is there, and soon it will be."

She resumed her chanting:

Leg growing out
Leg growing strong
Give to her give to her
Painless growth
Pure and long
Blood flowing through
Bone growing strong
She wishes nothing more
Than to be whole again
Pure and long
Her long-lost dream
Whole again whole again
One two three
Please grow true
Please grow strong

As white as pure
And pure and long

Celine stroked her friend's side as she chanted softly on and on for hours, while the fire reduced to coals and embers — then finally nothing but warm ash. Now she opened her eyes, and asked Fianna to do the same.

There, in the pale light of the gathering dawn, where a sad, withered limb had been, was a beautiful white leg, whole and perfect. The companions looked to each other in wonder, tears running down both their joyful faces.

CHAPTER 16

Jager

Repts and Greys have been experimenting on human-oids, particularly Earthlings, for thousands of years. One fourth-generation product of those experiments was a real stand-out: a young man by the name of Jager. Jager Chet Cornwallis, to be exact.

Born in the aliens' experimental station located under the tiny town of Dulce, New Mexico, Jager was conceived in vitro — a "test-tube baby" — and brought to birth in the womb of a surrogate mother. Each day she was connected to machines that supplied nutrients for the growing child, easing the burden on her own body. Once the fetus had reached a fairly advanced stage of development, new machine connections were introduced, this time leading directly to the fetus itself. These carried full mental images, complete with all sensory perceptions, emotions and information. Their purpose was to educate the developing baby in advance of its birth.

Jager's genetic parents knew nothing of the station at Dulce. All their business in connection with the boy's conception, birth, and early years was conducted at a respectable, seemingly ordinary fertility and family clinic in nearby Santa Fe. Actually, although it did deliver ordinary services to locals, the clinic was primarily a front for the Repts' and Greys' Dulce underground operation, all under Soader's control. And, as a matter of "insurance," Jager's parents had been drugged and hypnotized during one of their first clinic visits — just to ensure they would cooperate fully, and never suspect anything unusual was going on, or try to pry or interfere.

At birth, Jager had been turned over to his genetic parents, but scheduled to return regularly for testing and evaluation. From the very first of these visits, it was clear that Jager was a special child; his response to pre-natal training had exceeded expectations — considerably. And so he was tagged as a potential prime candidate for future Rept or Grey soul transfer, and subjected to even more rigorous treatment and testing.

Physically, Jager's appearance was quite normal for a child of his genetic background. Blond-haired, blue-eyed, well-proportioned, with a flurry of freckles across his pink nose and cheeks. He grew as any child would, and lead a fairly normal existence — or so it seemed on the surface. A much closer look would have revealed quite a different picture.

Jager's young life was not truly his own. All important events and details had been carefully planned and pre-arranged. What he ate, where he went to school, who he befriended, his interests and activities, his career aspirations. Even his eventual choice of a mate was to be pre-determined and deftly engineered.

As a child, he was regularly visited by late-night intruders who stole into his bedroom, sedated him, took readings and measurements, and implanted fresh hypnotic commands and suggestions.

Fortunately for young Jager, he wasn't entirely at the mercy of Soader and his crew. Unknown to the Repts and Greys, there was another group that had taken a keen interest in the boy, and watched over him continually: the Mentors. The same beings who had secretly nurtured Celine from the day she was born.

Beginning just weeks after his birth, Jager interacted daily with his Mentor friends, telepathically. They coached him through his outward development — learning to crawl, walk, speak and so on. They brought him along at a rate only a bit quicker than a normal child's, so as not to arouse suspicion in the aliens who thought the boy was under their complete control.

Meanwhile, on a strictly mental and spiritual plane, the Mentors taught Jager a great deal about life, his own abilities and potentials, and how to protect and defend himself against attempts to tamper with his mind and memory. He learned to wall off a part of his mind to create an impenetrable mental space, undetectable to anyone else and impervious to discovery by any drug or hypnotic probing. Here he stored all his interactions with the Mentors, along with his true private thoughts, intentions and aspirations. One day, this would be the mental vault in which he'd safeguard his entire relationship with his soulmate, Celine.

Warned by the Mentors of what to expect, Jager learned at once to pretend cooperation with Soader's experimenters. As far as the aliens could ever tell, he was responding to their tests and treatments exactly as expected; he seemed to be the ideal subject. In truth, Jager remained unaffected by their meddlings. He was occasionally annoyed, but more often amused at their deluded antics, and their utterly unwarranted pride in their "success." The boy was always at least one step ahead of the aliens' sinister scheming.

Like Celine, Jager never met the Mentors face to face — yet

they played a huge part in his life. These benevolent, powerful beings were among the last of their race (known as the All of All) to remain in this universe. They were sworn to protect all Ancients: races they had guided and nurtured for countless millennia.

The Mentor known as West introduced Jager to Celine on the boy's fourteenth birthday – which just happened to be the girl's twelfth. From that day forward, the two youngsters were inseparable, though their homes were light years apart.

For the time being, the Mentors kept one bit of information secret from their young charges: thousands of years and many lifetimes in the past, the two had been soulmates. The Mentors had separated them long ago, veiling the lovers' awareness of their relationship and separation. The purpose of this benevolent subterfuge was to keep the precious pair hidden from the Brothers, who sought to capture and exploit them for their own evil purposes.

When one of the pair — the one now named Jager — had suddenly surfaced in the Grey's experiments on Earth, the Brothers were delighted. Not long after, they stumbled on Celine. They thought this "coincidence" to be nothing more than confirmation of their own supreme cleverness, and perhaps just a tiny bit of good luck. The possibility that another power might have influenced events never made it past their overarching arrogance.

When they heard that Celine had been located, the Brothers called on their creature, Deebee Scabbage, to kidnap the girl and bring her to them. Scabbage knew his masters wouldn't demand he nab some brat without damned good reasons, so he dug around and discovered a bit about who and what this girl was. Knowing of Soader's earlier run-ins with the girl's adoptive father, Zulak, Scabbage hatched the perfect plot: leverage the hybrid's hatred for the man and have Soader haul her in.

Soader was speechless when he heard that Celine was Zulak's adopted daughter. Right on cue, he leapt at the chance to grab the girl, and began planning a way to pull it off with maximum painful impact on her unsuspecting father. His only disappointment was that Scabbage forbade him to kill the little bitch, or harm her in any way. Still, he'd have a measure of revenge on Rafael, and that would be reward enough. For now.

The Brothers enjoyed watching their plans fall into place. They were using all those involved — Jager and Celine included — as pawns in an even broader scheme, to which everyone was utterly oblivious. Or so the Brothers thought.

As Jager grew and learned, the Mentors gave special attention to his interest in magic. They taught him deeply, encouraged him to study further on his own, and led him in exercises and drills to develop his skills. The boy secretly practiced magic, black and otherwise, in a hidden room in the family's mansion.

Jager discovered that his greatest skill and most cherished ability lay in healing. He even began thinking of his healing skill set as an entity in itself — and he gave it a name: Lazarus.

Jager first discovered this healing gift one summer evening, walking home after a rugby match. He came upon a small dog, lying on the roadside with a broken hind leg. "Hey, little fella," he said to the whimpering pup. "Let's see what's wrong here." He placed a hand gently on the injured limb. "It's okay. I'm not going to hurt you." He focused his attention on the leg, and concentrated deeply for several moments.

"Hey, hey, little guy! Don't struggle. It'll be okay." He was about to reach out to gently restrain the little dog, but stopped short. "What do you know!" he exclaimed. The dog stood, its limb now sound and whole. It licked Jager's astonished face, and trotted off down the road, tail wagging cheerily. Jager had never been more proud of himself.

From that day forward, he practiced and explored his new skill, though he did his best to keep it a secret from others, along with the rest of his special abilities. He soon noticed his own injuries healed far more quickly than others', and without any special attention or treatment.

He realized he must pretend he was wounded and in pain for a while after everyday mishaps, to avoid attracting unwanted attention. One day, on the rugby field, he sprained his ankle during a particularly violent play. His teammates gathered round and helped him get up, then one of them supported the boy as he limped painfully off the field. By the time the two reached the sideline, though, Jager's ankle was back to normal. He was about to shout out about it and show his mates, but caught himself just in time. Instead, he continued to limp, and put on a convincing show of suffering. He allowed himself to be taken to the school nurse, moaned and grimaced as she probed the "damaged" ankle, and even let her tensor-bandage it and provide him with a crutch. He hobbled around for a whole week before gradually "getting better," setting aside the crutch and asking for the bandages to be removed.

Jager eventually found he could even bring an animal back to life if it had just died, and wasn't too severely injured. He could perform such revivals even at a distance. And then one day he discovered this remarkable power extended to departed humans, too.

One winter evening, his parents received a call that Robert, a sickly boy who lived a few houses away, had died of pneumonia earlier in the evening. Hearing this, Jager went to his own room, sat on the floor, and searched mentally for Robert's spirit. He found the boy lingering over his now-lifeless body, which was lying on a gurney in a hallway of his family's home.

"Whatcha doin', Robert?" asked Jager, addressing the hovering soul.

"I'm trying to get back in my body, but I can't," Robert whimpered. "Hey, I thought I couldn't talk to anyone. I tried to talk to my parents, but nothing happened. I called and called, but they couldn't hear me. Why can you hear me?"

"Because we're both kids," answered Jager. "Adults can't hear kids outside their bodies." He figured a little white lie was okay, under the circumstances.

"I don't want to be dead. I miss my mom and dad," said Robert.

"All right," Jager replied. "Here — just slip back in," and he gently guided the boy back into the body. Then Jager focused on the body itself, coaxing it back to full function. In moments, the boy began to cry — to the utter amazement of his parents, and the medical team who'd come to take the body away. For the rest of the week, the big news around the town was how the doctors had accidentally pronounced a boy dead.

Jager was proud of his accomplishment and skill. All he had to do was get into communication with a departed soul, help it to examine the body's energy chakras and coax them back to harmony, restore the spirit's willingness to animate the body, and *voila* — life returned. The body's normal healing processes were no longer impeded by the spirit's upsets, so they soon took care of any physical damage.

Jager practiced and practiced until he could work this supreme magic consistently, even at great distances. "There!" he congratulated himself at last. "Lazarus is ready."

For his last few years before college, Jager's parents (still under the aliens' influence) sent him to Eton, the famous English boarding school for boys. After the initial adjustment to being in a new country, at a different sort of school than he was used to — not to mention completely new sports! — Jager came to enjoy the challenges of boarding school life. He followed the curriculum Soader's minions insisted he pursue, and did well in all his classes.

His photographic memory came in very handy, and the Mentors' training in analytical thought and clear expression made his schoolwork easy. Once again, he had to make a show of being normal, though. He routinely commiserated with classmates about the tough subjects and difficult assignments. Now and then, he'd even deliberately underperform in classes and on exams, confident in his true knowledge and not wanting to seem too bright an academic star.

Despite the school's rigors, Jager made plenty of time for his deepest interest: magic. He spent many a spare hour in the special hiding spot he'd found, poring over dusty old tomes and practicing spells. And every night, through all his time in England, he enjoyed long mental conversations with Celine.

OVER THE YEAR SINCE *Queen Asherah* had brought Jager and his family to Erra, he had resumed his custom of nightly study — and his nightly ritual of calling out to Celine. He never lost hope that one night she would answer.

Tonight was the anniversary of his first meeting with his soulmate, and her birthday. Today, she turned seventeen. The concept, "she *would have* turned seventeen" never even occurred to him. He was calmly, completely certain Celine was still alive. He felt it. He knew it. She was out there somewhere, and she needed him.

Jager and West talked every day, each hoping the other would break the joyful news that they'd heard from Celine — but so far, that news hadn't come.

Throughout his year on Erra, Jager had also worked with members of *Queen Asherah*'s crew in a secret search for the lost girl. Despite the strain of not knowing where his young love might be, the work with Major Hadgkiss and his compatriots had been fascinating. He avidly soaked up everything they could teach him about the universe and space travel.

Happily, Jager's parents and siblings had also settled in well, living in a richly multi-racial district that even included other Earthling families. Before long, life on Erra had come to seem comfortably normal for the Cornwallis family. Jager had no contact with them, and thanks to the mind-wiping they'd received, they wouldn't have recognized the boy even if they had encountered him. Sad though the situation was for Jager, he understood why it was necessary. He was content to know they were safe and happy.

It wasn't long before Jager and Dino became quite close. No one ever questioned the cover story about Dino being the young man's uncle. More than a few felt sympathetic toward Jager, believing that he'd been orphaned. Jager fit in famously with the *Queen*'s crew, and with the people he met on the Fleet base and in the surrounding community.

Then, one evening, his soulmate's long silence ended.

CHAPTER 17

Dragon and Companion

Celine stood in the center of their cave, looking over their half-packed belongings. "Fianna, I just wish we had more time to prepare. We need to practice fighting maneuvers, and...and...I'm just worried about the tube-chute."

"I worry as well, but the passage will be different this time. I will be there with you, so do not worry. Dragon magic is powerful, we have had at least a bit of time to prepare, and we have the entire clan behind us. We will make the journey to Earth safely. I am certain of it."

"All right. If you're sure," said Celine, though still hesitant. "How long will it take to get through?"

"In the time of our outer world here, it will take one day and one night. This is the reason we will leave tonight, when our moon is high. Legend tells us that if a dragon does not make the journey safely, the moon will not appear the following night. Such a missing moon is a signal for those left behind on Nibiru, telling them it is time to send up prayers that the lost souls may find their way back home. It has happened only once that a soul was lost, but we watch nonetheless. Do not worry, though," smiled Fianna, "I shall see you there safely, and back home again, too. Besides, I happen to know that your concern is not only for yourself." She winked.

"Okay. You're right," said Celine. "But I still think I've every reason to be concerned."

"Have faith!" smiled Fianna. To any human, a cheerily smiling dragon is an irresistibly amusing sight, and Celine couldn't help but laugh and lighten up. She appreciated her friend's efforts to reassure her.

Celine returned Fianna's smile, then went back to her packing. Since her arrival on Nibiru, she had added considerably to her collection of dried herbs, roots, flowers and other medicinals and magicals. She had been surprised to find that Nibiru had more to offer than even her native Erra, which was renowned for its bounty.

When out swimming one evening, she'd even found several rare and potent crystals, glistening beneath the water close to shore; they included a precious silvery one she had only ever read about, never seen.

Fianna suggested that Schimpel himself may have left the crystals to be found later, since he had shared the cave they now occupied with her dragon-grandmother, and frequented the same swimming spot.

The suggestion prompted Celine to launch an extensive search of the cave and its surroundings. She was delighted to find a hidden cache, in a small recess at the back of the cave. It contained two incant-batons, several white candles, incense, polished stones, bottled salts and potions, a few empty bottles and some essential oils. There were also a few handy items, such as an incense burner and a small, intricately-carved hand bell, wrought in silver. The entire store was secured in a small-ish iron cauldron, sealed against time and the elements.

Schimpel had even left a grimoire. Though it showed signs of much use by its former owner, it didn't seem to have badly deteriorated over the centuries. The little book had a soft but sturdy leather jacket, tied closed and with several black and white feathers entwined in the cords that bound it.

Celine was speechless at the find. She had felt lost on more than one occasion, without a grimoire to help her in casting spells and creating charms and talismans from high-magic-potential items she found now and then. That evening she said a prayer of thanks to the spirit of Schimpel. To commemorate the occasion, she also added a colorful image to the others she'd painted on the ancient cave's walls.

Of the several paintings she had placed there, the first was her favorite. It showed her tumbling down the tube-chute; to its right was a depiction of her first meeting with Fianna. Celine had always loved to paint, so when she'd found a variety of colored berries growing near the cave, she had gathered them, then mixed them with water, powdered clay and bird's eggs to create a colorful palette. Then she had fashioned a set of brushes from sticks, hair and feathers, and set to painting up a storm.

At first, Fianna had objected to Celine's adding their story to the cave's records, thinking it might be bad luck. Celine convinced her it would not bring danger, though, and would help lighten the mood of their rocky quarters. Fianna relented, admitting that the new images really did brighten up the cave. She even tried creating a few images of her own, and did a fine job of it, for a dragon. On the ceiling, she painted a scene of one of their training flights, which Celine supplemented with more such views on the wall directly below.

Celine now stood staring blankly at the paintings, turning her white knife over and over in her hand. She had recently engraved the knife's grip with an image of a dragon; now she ran her fingers over the image's planes and ridges, contemplating all that had happened since that awful day at the convention. She had thought less and less about those times and people in recent months. Looking back at them now, she realized she hadn't seen her family in more than a year. Her eyes welled with tears.

Fianna noticed her Companion's grief. "Do not cry, Little One. You shall see your family again. I know it," she soothed. "You and I were meant to meet. We are meant to travel to Earth. These things are foretold in our legends. They are and have been predestined. This is the way of our universe. I have known these things since the day you arrived in my home. You shall see. We shall find the Atlantis Spell and rescue the precious eggs and the dragons' race. I shall find a mate, and you shall be reunited with your family and the young man you love. The legends tell it, and the legends do not lie."

"Thank you, my dearest friend," said Celine. They stood awhile, admiring the paintings; though they were far from masterworks, they captured their wonderful times here together, and that was what mattered.

"We shall soon have new stories to paint!" declared Fianna, and the two stepped out of the cave to enjoy the fresh breeze that had come up. She made no mention of it, but deep down, Fianna felt Celine might never return to Nibiru.

"That we will," sniffed Celine to her smiling friend. "I'm sorry. I just miss them all, and knowing that I'll be able to use my telepathy once we reach Earth is making me nervous. It's been a long time since I've had any contact with them at all, and I have no idea how they are. I feel badly that they had to grieve my disappearance, and wonder whether I'm even alive. Worse, some of them may have died since our parting; that would be unbearable to learn."

"I understand. I miss my parents, too," said Fianna. "I know that my pain is different from yours, since it is almost certain that my parents are dead, and I have come to accept that. And yet I do understand."

"Thank you; I know you do. What happened to your parents? I've never asked, as I thought the polite thing was to wait until you told me. I really want to know, though, before we enter the vortex tonight."

"Of course," Fianna replied. "I was still quite young when they disappeared. My brother Ahimoth was still on Nibiru at that time. I believe that what happened to my parents contributed to his decision to leave. It all happened during the season of flowers, on the far side of the world. My parents flew there to gather some rare herbs that grow in only one small region, and only during the season of flowers. Each year, a different dragon volunteers to make this trip. My parents chose to go together. They had been trying without success to have another egg hatch, and thought the trip would do them some good — especially my mother.

"They never returned from the journey. When they had been gone weeks longer than expected, Orgon himself led a search party to discover what had happened. All the party found was the place my parents had bedded down, and a large collection of herbs they had set to dry in the sun. My parents were nowhere to be found, but there were signs of a great struggle: dried pools of blood, charred foliage, broken and toppled trees, and so on. One of the party also found several of my father's golden scales in one of the bloody patches. That was long, long ago," Fianna ended, lowering her head in sorrow.

"I'm sorry, Fianna. I didn't know," said Celine, sharing her friend's pain.

Fianna sighed, then came to herself. "Enough! It is time to lighten the mood!" She loped over to their nearby swimming hole, scooped up a mouthful of the frigid water and returned to spray it all over her friend.

"HEY!" yelled Celine, jumping up and glaring at the grinning white dragon. Fianna mented the girl an image of herself, defiant, indignant, dripping and bedraggled, wearing a look more searing than dragonfire. Between the mental image and the dragon's grin, Celine couldn't help herself. She burst into laughter, and Fianna joined her. The pair laughed and laughed until they were rolling in the grass, holding their bellies.

When they'd calmed down and caught their breaths, Celine said, "I don't believe it. I even miss my troublesome sister. There's no way I will ever tell *her* that, though. And don't *you* dare to, either! Ha! But now let's go for one last fly-over of Dragon Hall, shall we?"

Fianna grinned back and nodded. The girl reached up and stretched her arms around the dragon's neck, hugging her tight. Then she climbed into the saddle, using the new-restored leg Fianna held out to her as a helpful step. The dragon had taken to wearing the saddle almost constantly. She was proud of it. It made her feel majestic, reminding her that she was a princess. A dragon princess, with a Companion!

The pair were soon flying low over the rolling hills, casually winding this way and that, following the river's course. Celine sat tall and lifted her hands above her head, laughing, loving the rush of the wind in her face.

Fianna did a sudden but graceful roll, causing the girl to grab for a handhold, laughing all the harder. She felt supremely lucky to have such a wonderful friend, and reminded herself she must present Fianna with an extra-special gift when all of this was over. She would never again have a friend like Fianna. Never again.

Dragon and Companion soon spotted the small but steep mountain that shielded Dragon Hall. They descended and began a slow circle, high above the courtyard.

A few dragons had resumed the festivities that had begun the night before, and the scene was alive with colorful flashes in many hues, reflections from the revelers' shiny scales. The entire community had been hoping for decades that a solution would be found for their perilously aging eggs. Now the prospect of a happy resolution, perhaps just days away, brought many to joyful tears. It was as though the long years of worry and gloom were boiling away in the cheers, singing and dancing, all echoed by the merry gurgling of a fountain of their traditional holiday beverage, set up for the occasion in the courtyard's center.

On watch duty, Tamar spotted Fianna and Celine circling above, and began fanning the air with her wings, in greeting. Soon everyone had joined in, creating quite a spectacle for the circling pair, and raising a tremendous updraft in the process. Even Old Haggis was there, fanning with the best of them (but panting harder than any). His efforts worked loose a mighty belch that managed to set some of the nearby brush alight; everyone laughed, even Fianna and Celine, as they glided to a graceful landing on a projecting ledge above the crowd.

"You're so fortunate, Fianna, to have such a caring community. I will do anything in my power to help you all," vowed Celine.

"I know, dear one. And I would do the same for you and your people."

They sat on the ledge for a while, watching the revels below. Then Fianna called to the crowd, "Thank you all! We shall see you tomorrow!" and sprang into flight, heading for home.

"I suppose we should get back to our packing," Celine said, as they landed lightly in front of their stony dwelling. And so they set to work. Celine tended to most of the work — dragons have never been known for their skill at such mundane chores as stuffing saddlebags.

Months earlier, Celine had found a staff at the back of the cave, buried in a trench which had been carefully concealed. Now Fianna dragged it out and Celine strapped it beneath some of the bags. The long, stout staff was obviously meant for a man, but Celine wanted to bring it anyway; she had a strong feeling it might come in very handy. Just touching it also brought her a sense of strength and comfort. Quite mysterious, she thought.

"Once on Earth," said Fianna, "we must make the short trip from the tube-chute's terminus to a place Earthlings call Loch Ness. It is the residence of one of my water dragon cousins, Nessie. She will give us all the information we will need before heading to Turkey. She keeps abreast of news and events on the planet — in particular, anything even remotely bearing on the treasure."

"Please tell me more about this Atlantean treasure," asked Celine, as she settled on the porch rock at the cave entrance.

"Well, it holds the answers to many of the mysteries of this part of the universe," Fianna began. "One of its artifacts is a large and elegantly-crafted chest, wrought from pure gold and set with jewels and gems. Legend says that the chest is so beautiful and bright that even a dragon must shade its eyes to look upon it.

"The chest is said to contain many treasures. Among them are two books: an ancient grimoire known as The Book of Atlantis, and The Book of Mu — a compilation of mystic riddles and puzzles. To properly use The Book of Atlantis, one must first solve the correct Mu riddles and puzzles, in the exact order of their presentation. As you have heard, one of the spells in the Atlantean book has the power to reverse the hex that has been set upon our race's precious eggs.

"Many years ago, two beings known simply as the Brothers made their way through space to Nibiru. By the most heinous treachery imaginable, they managed to gain access to and hex every living dragon egg. They did this to seize total control of the planet and all its dragon-people.

"Next, they tracked down and killed every dragon Companion they could find, and demanded that the council make them Companions themselves — the *only* Companions. They knew that as Companions, they would have access to all our hidden treasures, and any more we might amass in times to come. They swore that until and unless we made them Companions, the hex would remain in force, and our people would be doomed to slow extinction. What they did not know — and the council did not reveal — was that one Companion remained alive: Schimpel.

"Among themselves, the dragons agreed that they must never give in to the Brothers' heinous demand, but they pretended indecision, and pleaded with the Brothers for time to consult and consider carefully. The Brothers grudgingly agreed.

"During the period of consideration, two of our people, posing as traitors, tricked the Brothers into entering the tube-chute vortex by making them think one of our richest treasures was hidden within it. Feigning deep disaffection with the Dragon Council, and pretending to divulge a dark secret, the two said that contrary to legend and 'common knowledge,' it was not necessary for a human to be bonded as a Nibiru Dragon's Companion in order to pass through the tube-chute. This 'rule' was nothing more than a clever fabrication by the dragons, they said, a way to prevent anyone else from ever sharing in their vast treasure horde."

This latest revelation instantly raised a serious question in Celine's quick mind, but for the moment she restrained the impulse to ask it, preferring to let Fianna continue.

"The greedy Brothers believed every word," Fianna went on, "and they eagerly stepped into the vortex. They were instantly whisked off-planet and on their way to Earth; at the same moment, all the members of the Dragon Council put forth their powers, erecting an impenetrable shield around the entire planet. Nibiru was thereafter secure against the Brothers, and anyone else who might ever attempt to raid it.

"My grandmother and the others thought their dragon magic would also be potent enough to reverse the hex upon our eggs, but they were wrong. Unfortunately, the Brothers had the Atlantean books with them when they entered the vortex, and so the secret to the hex was lost.

"Not long after, my grandmother and her Companion, Schimpel, traveled to Earth to recover the books. The Brothers had re-hidden the precious volumes in the Atlantean tunnels from which they had stolen them. They thought that none of the Atlantean priests who had originally hidden the books remained alive, so the tunnels would be the safest possible place to hide them. They were wrong, though — there were still a few priests left, living in hiding. When the Brothers had gone, the priests retrieved the books and hid them in a new, more secret place. They also formulated an elaborate plan to move the books to new hiding places at random intervals, to further secure the precious volumes against theft. The Brothers have been trying to recover the books ever since.

"All this brings me to the most important reason that I am certain you are the girl of which the legends speak."

"What is that?"

"It is written that only the White Moon Princess may penetrate our shields, and travel the tube-chute alone. If you were not that princess, you would not be here today. Further, you are, I assume, aware of what your name means in the language of Earth. Yes?"

"Of course," Celine replied. "It is the name of a goddess of the moon — Earth's moon."

"Correct! The White Moon, to be precise," Fianna replied. "You, my dear, are the White Moon Princess."

Celine sat for a long while, considering all she had just been told. Fianna made no move to disturb her. They sat together, looking out across the river and the moonlit landscape beyond — one running her thumb up and down her knife handle, the other patiently awaiting a response.

"This explains a lot for me," Celine finally announced. "It answers questions I've had for a long, long time. Who I am, where I came from, why I seem to be so different from others, why I had the Dream of Nibiru, and why I so cherished my name. You're right, we were meant — destined — to find each other, to bond and to travel to Earth together."

Without another word, Celine went back to her packing. Soon everything was in readiness, set neatly by the mouth of the cave. "We're all set. I don't know about you, but I'm exhausted. It's been quite a couple of days."

"Yes, it surely, surely has been. I am tired, too — and seeing as there are a few hours until it will be time to depart, I propose we have a rest. Orgon will send someone to make sure we arrive promptly, so we can rest without worry of missing the appointed time." At that, the two friends curled up together under their favorite tree, and soon fell fast asleep.

They woke a few hours later to the *whoosh* of a dragon's landing. "Greetings, Orgon!" said Fianna. "You have come yourself?"

"Tamar asked to come, but there is something I wish to tell you without other eager ears about," responded the great green dragon. "Is everything prepared?"

"Yes, we have only to strap the items you see here to the saddle." She noticed the aging dragon's worried expression and asked, "What troubles you, Uncle?"

Orgon did not answer at once; instead, he looked up at the

scattered stars, and at the moon, now almost at its zenith. Both Fianna and Celine waited patiently for his answer. Finally, with a hesitant swallow and grunt, he spoke. "Another egg has perished." He bowed his great head.

Without a word, Celine and Fianna rushed to the cave entrance and quickly finished strapping the last of their equipment to the saddle. Celine leapt to Fianna's back, and they turned to address the green dragon. He was nowhere to be seen. He had already begun his flight back to Dragon Hall. Fianna leapt into the air to follow him. It was the fastest passage to the courtyard she had ever achieved.

As they set down on the ledge behind the Cynth Pedestal, they could see dragons already gathered along the long ledge facing the rear wall. All were staring at a trickle of water which flowed down the wall's shiny surface. Suddenly, the wall itself seemed to vanish. It had been, in fact, an illusion, magically generated. Now all could clearly see what had actually been there all along. What had seemed a mere trickle was in fact a small waterfall, plunging from high above into the most amazing pool Celine had ever seen. Its shimmering liquid ("Is it really *water?*" she wondered) swirled continually, flickering in cool shades of blue, green and lilac, and infused with galaxies of tiny, sparkling bubbles. At the whirlpool's very center was a tiny swirl of intense pink.

"It's...so beautiful!" sighed Celine. "If we make it back, we'll have to paint this on the wall of our cave."

"What is this 'if we make it back', Companion? Bite your silly, forkless tongue! No such thoughts. Understood?" said Fianna, half-jokingly. Celine smiled and gave her friend a nod.

Fianna continued, "Yes, the vortex is breathtaking to behold. We call it Dini, after a beloved matron-dragon of long ago. My mother shares the same name; it means 'swirling beauty.' But quickly — the vortex remains open but briefly. We must enter it soon. Are you prepared?"

"This is all happening so fast," replied Celine, "but I am ready whenever you are."

Though Celine hadn't noticed it until now, the assembled dragons had been humming rhythmically for some time. Meanwhile, one of the elders had placed a bundle of dried leaves and twigs in a small pit close to the vortex, and set it alight; now she fanned their fragrant smoke toward Fianna and Celine.

"What are they humming?" Celine asked.

"An incantation to guard us in our passage," the white dragon replied.

"Fianna, our dear princess," spoke Orgon, his voice firm and strong. "We all are grateful to you and your Companion for what you now set out to do. The legend will be fulfilled. You will return with the means to break the hex and quicken our eggs. Fly swift, fly strong, return whole. We love you both. Our prayers and thoughts will be with you through every moment until your return."

The crowd's chant grew louder, and they began to reinforce its rhythm with sweeping wings and stomping feet — all in unison. Even Old Haggis joined in.

Gods and Goddesses of the light
Guide our princesses through this night
Guide them safe, hear our song
Guide them now, and all night long
Land them gentle at the end
Guide them safely
Home again

"I'm ready," Celine said, hugging tightly to Fianna's great back. The dragon leapt straight upward, whirled about, and dove straight into the swirling mass of colors, vanishing into it without a sound. Seconds later, the vortex entrance itself vanished — but the gathered dragons continued their chanting, on and on throughout the night, intent that the young white dragon and her Companion make the journey in safety.

At dawn the chanting ceased and the dragons went their ways, all praying silently to see the moon rise the following evening.

CHAPTER 18

Teamwork

"Help! Fianna!" screamed Celine, mentally, as the two tumbled up the chute. Somehow, the girl had been jolted from the saddle as they entered the vortex; now her only connection was one leg, caught in a saddle strap.

"I am here!" the dragon called. She rolled gently to bring the saddle back under her Companion, then arched her back slightly, landing Celine firmly in place once more. "There you are! Strap yourself tightly, now. We're through the worst, but the spinning will not stop, and there will be bumps and bubbles. Our passage will take a few hours. Just hang on; I will take us safely through."

"You will take us through? No chance! We fly as a team, remember?" Celine replied, with a laugh.

And so the pair worked together to smooth the passage as best they could, through the maelstrom of liquid color.

At one point, there was a sudden, twisting jolt that spun the dragon wildly. "Celine! I can't stop it!" mented the dragon.

"Hold on!" the girl called back. Struggling against the

gut-wrenching forces, she drew out her incant-baton, waved it in a hasty pattern, and croaked out a chant:

> Gusts blowing up
> Gusts blowing down
> Many fluids up, many fluids down
> Control the power, control the power
> Give me control

> Gods and Goddesses of the sky
> We'll not give up
> Let us fly
> With wings of white
> We'll continue our flight
> Gods and Goddesses of the sky

Fianna began to recover as the girl continued:

> Gusts blowing up
> Gusts blowing down
> Dragon fly up, dragon fly down
> Wings in, wings out
> Give me control
> Spin, spin, spin
> Slow the spin
> Spin, spin, spin
> Slow down the spinning
> Stop dragon's fall
> Give me control

> I cause the wind to stop
> Its airy powers to drop
> I control the power

I control the power
You gave me the power
I now control the fall

By the chant's end, Fianna was back in control. The airy fluid spun as wildly as before, but dragon and Companion rode it like the most expert surfers who ever lived.

"Brilliant!" Fianna called. "I thank you for reminding me we are a team. You are no idle passenger, no passive lump in the saddle. If not for you, we could have been thrown from the vortex, out into the void!"

"That's just what Companions are for," laughed Celine, as they churned onward.

After what seemed like days and days, the swirling forces eased somewhat. Then, with no warning, the journey was over: The vortex simply vanished, and the pair found themselves high in the air, tumbling down toward a slate-blue body of water.

Fianna managed to right herself just in time to avoid plunging into the chilly waters. They flew low, just above the lake's surface, their reflection flashing over the calm, early-morning water.

"Are you all right, Celine?"

"Yes. Very tired, but okay. You?"

"Exhausted, but that shall pass. This is Loch Maree. It is only twenty minutes' flight to Loch Ness, but I don't have the strength to make the journey right now. Let us find a spot to rest until tonight."

"Good idea. Maybe one of those islands has a place we can hide."

"You are right. Let us check the largest, first."

Fianna turned gently, and soon set down near some large rocks and a stand of old oaks. A bit of exploring turned up a serviceable hiding spot — a sheltered area beneath an over-hanging ledge, obscured across its front by dense brush.

"Perfect," said Celine. "If it's all right with you, I'm just go-ing to sleep. I'm so tired, I don't even care about eating."

"Me, too. I shall catch us some fish, later on. For now, I will race you to sleep!"

"Ha! All right: ready, set, go!" joked Celine, and the friends curled up together. They slept soundly through the whole day, waking just as the sun began dipping behind a far-off peak.

"It will be dark shortly, so I had better get busy about those fish," announced Fianna. "But, do you want some?"

"No, but thanks for asking," replied Celine. "I don't want to start a fire, and I'm not in the mood for raw fish. You go have a good feed and I'll be fine with some nuts and berries I packed. You said it would take about twenty minutes to fly to where your cousin lives, right?"

"That is correct. Loch Ness is to the southeast, about fifty miles. Earth's air is thicker than Nibiru's, so it will take us a bit longer to cover distances here. After we find Nessie, we will fly to Turkey, a journey of two nights. I do not want to travel during the day; the risks are too great."

"Okay. Even at night, I think we should fly above the clouds, to stay out of sight — whenever there *are* any clouds. The air will be thinner that high, so while you're fishing, I'll try out the bubble spell we've used. I'm not sure it will work in exactly the same way here. We don't want to get way up there and *then* find out it doesn't work right!"

"That is a splendid idea. I believe we should fly as far as Germany tonight, to reach the safety of the tunnels."

"Tunnels?"

"Yes, an ancient underground network."

"Oh, I know the tunnels you mean. The ones on what was once called the 'European Highway,' between Scotland and

Turkey. I studied them in Primary; amazing. I remember reading about one in Turkey, under a place called Derinkuyu, that was big enough to house more than twenty thousand people. Maybe someday I'll be able to come back to Earth to explore them."

"You may get the opportunity sooner than you expect, my friend. The treasure we seek is hidden in one of those very tunnels. Atlanteans built them as a safety measure when first they came to this planet. They came here, you know, fleeing the Rept hordes that were ravaging their home planet, Mu."

"Yes, I know of the planet, and the story. The exiles from Mu built an empire here, with its seat on a continent they named Atlantis. Their network of intercontinental tunnels was enormous, and they even built whole cities underground. When the Repts eventually caught up with the Atlanteans here, some escaped in starships, but many more hid under ground. Unfortunately for those who stayed, the Brothers, who were in league with the Repts, caused a great flood by diverting an asteroid called Biminis and slamming it into the planet. Atlantis was destroyed, and all but a few of those hiding in the underground cities and tunnels perished."

"Ah! I see you know a great deal about Earth. Your knowledge may soon prove quite useful," said Fianna.

"Thank you! I found the studies fascinating. I also learned that after the Flood, the Brothers flew over all the planet, poisoning the atmosphere to kill off any survivors. Only native Earthlings and Rept-hybrids could process the poisons. A few Atlanteans and other colonists escaped, like those who'd built a civilization in Peru, in one of the southern continents. Some peoples living in the Pleiades today are descended from the escapees. Others settled elsewhere, such as on Mars."

"Maybe you are related to some of them," laughed Fianna. She said it jokingly, but both were aware it could very well be the truth.

"And now I must find myself some tasty fish," the dragon said. Celine watched her fly off, then opened her pack to dig out a meal of her own.

Suddenly, she gasped — her telepathy! Earth had no shielding, so it should work here! She was embarrassed that she hadn't thought of this the moment they'd arrived. Still, she would wait until Fianna returned to attempt a contact. She preferred having the dragon present, to help explain the situation to Jager and West.

A short while later, as Celine was scooping some water out of the loch to wash down her breakfast, Fianna swooped in and landed beside her. "Ah, I feel so much better," the dragon said. A hearty belch escaped her, and both laughed at the sound. "The fish here are quite tasty. I have made a glutton of myself, but I do not know when I shall have another opportunity for a good feed. Have you eaten all you need?"

"Yes, I feel much better, too," Celine replied, standing. "Hey, I think it's time we reach Jager and West, and ask for their help."

"That is a splendid idea," Fianna said. "We should do it right now, before we travel to Loch Ness."

Celine nodded agreement, and then shouted — mentally — "Jager! Jager! Can you hear me?"

"Celine? *Celine!!*" he responded, in the mental equivalent of a joyous yell. "Is it really *you?!*"

"Of course it's me, Captain Silly!" laughed the girl.

"Oh, my Gods!" gasped Jager. "I'm so happy to hear you! Where are you? Are you all right? Where have you been? We've been worried sick. I knew you had to be alive, but we couldn't find or reach you — we've been searching every day!" The young man's thoughts came all in a rush; tears of joy spilled down his face. "Why didn't you call? Why? Are you okay? Does

West know?"

"I'm so sorry, Jager," replied Celine. "I know it's been an awfully long time, and it's been *horrible* not to be able to reach you! Please let me explain, though. After Soader transbeamed me, I ended up on a planet that's totally shielded against telepathy. It's called Nibiru — I'm sure you've heard of it. Anyway, I haven't been able to get off the planet until now, so I've been cut off from you, and West, and everyone. It's been horrible!"

"Are you sure you're all right? And if you're off Nibiru now, where *are* you?"

"Yes, I'm fine. Don't worry, I'm really okay. I'll explain more in a minute, but first, please tell me: Did West let you know about my family? Are my parents okay? And Mia? Did Dad rescue them? Oh, please, please tell me — are they all right?"

"Yes! Oh, yes, yes — they're all fine. Your mom and your dad and Mia, too." In his happy relief, he couldn't resist a playful jab: "I'm fine too, just in case you're interested."

"Oh, that's so good to know. I've been so worried about them. And you, too — of course! I'm sorry, I just had to know if they were okay. The last time I saw my mother and sister, they were being held hostage."

"Hey, no worries, no worries! I understand. I was just teasing," replied Jager. "I'd feel the same way. I'm just out of my head, hearing from you again. And so, so relieved to hear you're alive and okay. You're really all right, right? You're being straight with me?"

"Yes, Jager, I'm fine. I'm so, so happy to hear you, too. But look, I know we have an incredible amount of catching up to do, but it will have to wait. The fact is, I really need your help — right away, if it's possible."

"Okay, but first tell me where you are so we can come get you now, now, *now.*"

"Oh, Jager, I'd love it if you all would come, but there's

something I absolutely have to do first. I can't explain it all right now, but I know you'll understand when you hear the whole story. First, you asked where I am. I'm on Earth."

"Earth! Well, that's a surprise! How did you get to Earth from Nibiru?"

"I'll explain it all soon. Right now, I have to introduce you to a new friend. Jager, meet Fianna. She's a dragon. The last Princess of Nibiru. She tells me she can ment with both of us, because you and I have such a close connection. She says it's because we're...mates." Celine suppressed an embarrassed giggle. "She has been my companion, protector and closest friend through all of this past year. If it were not for her kindness, care, courage and skill, I wouldn't be alive to speak with you."

Jager was stunned at the revelation, but recovered quickly. Fortunately, his wide-ranging studies had included dragon lore, so he had some idea of the protocol for addressing them —though he'd never imagined he'd have to put the knowledge into practice. "It is a pleasure and an honor to meet you, Princess Fianna," he said. "I thank you for your kindness in caring for my dear and special friend, Celine." Despite the formalities, he couldn't resist a bit of a joke. "I sincerely hope that she was not too troublesome; she can tend to be a bit trying at times."

"Ha-ha!" laughed Fianna. "No more trouble than I would be, if she found me stranded on Erra." The three laughed. The ice was broken, and the formalities relaxed.

"Speaking of homeworlds, Celine, I should tell you that I'm now on Erra," said Jager.

"What?!" gasped Celine. "On Erra? Why? How did you get there? Do my parents know about us? What's going on?"

"There were some major complications after you disappeared from Soader's shuttlecraft, and the Mentors decided it was time for me to disappear. They arranged it so my family and I were brought here to Erra. Things aren't bad, though.

Overall, they're great, actually. The one unfortunate thing is that my family had to be memory-wiped. They no longer know me. They don't even know I exist. I guess I'm a sort of orphan."

"Oh, Jager, I'm so sorry to hear that."

"It's okay. It was a bit hard at first, but I was never really close with my parents or brothers. And I've been so busy that I hardly ever think about them anymore. The important thing is, they're safe and happy.

"Hey, here's another great thing," he continued. "I live with your godfather, Major Hadgkiss. Everyone thinks I'm his orphaned nephew. I get to work on the *Queen Asherah*, and I see your dad all the time. Dino knows all about you and me and the Mentors, but your dad has no idea."

"Wow! That's amazing. Almost unbelievable, but I guess I'm getting used to believing unbelievable stuff! Now, before I get to what I need from you, we should call West, so she knows I'm okay, and what's going on."

They called to the Mentor, who was overjoyed to learn that Celine was safe. Celine briefed Jager and West on the circumstances on Nibiru and Earth, and with Fianna's help, the three worked out what to do next.

They also discussed G.O.D.'s plans to harvest Earthlings, and the hundreds of Rept harvest ships now bound for Earth. Many aging Repts desperately needed new bodies to inhabit — including the Rept High Chancellor, Pratt. He had been especially anxious because the young Earthling whose body he had claimed as his to take over — a male named Jager — had gone missing from his home on Earth. Pratt had dispatched a search party to find the boy; after more than a year's hunting, they had finally located him on Erra. What Pratt did not know was that Scabbage had also designated Jager (or his body, at least) for his next transfer.

"Wait. West, are you saying that both G.O.D. and the Repts

are out to harvest Earth?" asked Celine, incredulous.

"Unfortunately, this is the truth, Celine. G.O.D. is not quite as bad as the Repts; G.O.D. only means to harvest a select group of Earthlings — the more spiritually advanced. The Repts will take anyone. But it's all a grave situation. Also, as you know, galactic law classifies Earthlings as primitive, so harvesting them is acceptable. No offence meant, Jager."

"None taken," he replied.

West continued, "Since you have been missing, things have changed drastically in our part of the universe. I am afraid that there is another war brewing."

"So I heard. That isn't good," Jager spoke up. "So, now there are a few of us here on Erra who are determined to stop both the Repts and G.O.D. The Repts don't have jump-shift capability, so it will be weeks before they reach Earth. G.O.D. is another story. Someone within G.O.D. has blinded or subverted the ethical members of the council. Celine, last year your father was ordered to set up harvest stations on Earth and its moon, PS 428. This happened shortly after you disappeared. Rumor has it that he refused because he didn't know who to trust anymore, and didn't want any part of the destruction of a civilization. Those same mission orders are back on the table."

"That's awful! Things are worse than I thought," said Celine.

"I'm afraid they are," Jager continued. "G.O.D. research found that most primitive bodies are harmful to advanced spirits. As you know, G.O.D. still designates Earthlings as primitive, despite the fact that some Earthling bodies have been the very best transfer hosts on record. Specifically, bodies whose birth inhabitants were spiritually and intellectually advanced. So those are the ones G.O.D. is most interested in. They want them for transfers, and for breeding programs, too — to make more of them available."

Celine shook her head, stunned at what she was hearing.

She and Fianna looked at each other. Their mission was becoming more important and more treacherous before it had even begun. The four continued their discussion. Fianna and Celine were torn. They knew this talk was important — input and help from Jager and West enormously increased their chances for success — but they were increasingly anxious to be on their way to Turkey. Somehow, they kept their impatience in check.

The discussion made Celine realize she could not tell her parents the truth about what she was about to do. They would not understand; her father, in particular. She had no doubt that if he knew, he would travel to Earth to stop her. She was momentarily lost in thoughts of her father when West addressed her.

"Celine?"

"Yes, I'm here."

"As I mentioned, I will be on Mars with the other Mentors if you need anything."

"Thanks," answered Celine. "Soader and the Brothers — where are they?"

"Please don't worry about them; let the Good Energy deal with them. We've been waiting years for this opportunity, and we won't fail this time."

"All right, I'll try not to worry," Celine responded. "Jager, do you have a story to tell my parents? They mustn't know about this until it's over."

"Don't worry. I'm was born an actor, and I've been fooling people my entire life. Your parents will have no idea what's going on. Besides, I already have them eating out of my hands — even more than Mia does!"

"Well, okay," Celine replied. "But you'll have to fill me in on your story, so I can play along. I don't want to mess things up by saying something I shouldn't."

"Right you are, clever girl. Here's what I'll tell them..."

IN ANOTHER NEARBY NEIGHBORHOOD, Rafael Zulak's evening routine was similar to Jager's, whenever the commander was at home. He studied hard, searching for any scrap or thread of information that might lead to his lost little girl.

Whenever Zulak came upon a new report of Soader's whereabouts, he would look for any plausible reason to travel there — either commanding a patrol with the *Queen*, or aboard another vessel. If he could catch up with Soader, he reasoned, his chances of finding Celine soared at once. The Rept-hybrid was the key; of that he was quite sure. So far, every attempt had failed, though. He always arrived to find Soader had already departed, destination unknown.

It was another evening at home, and Zulak had been locked away in his study for hours, glued to his console. At last he gave up — he just wasn't going to find anything tonight. He shut off the console, tidied his desk and opened the study door. There was Remi, arms folded across her chest, waiting silently.

"Rafael, I don't like to see you like this. You have to stop it, dear. I insist. I cannot take *any* more of it!" she cried.

"I'm sorry, Love. But this is not just about you or me. You *know* it isn't. I'm doing this for Celine. Damn it, Remi, we owe it to her as much or more than we owe it to ourselves. We can't give up. We've got to bring her home."

"I know, Rafael, I know. But there must be some other way. What about Mia? We owe her, too. She's our true daughter, and she deserves parents who treat her that way. She's alive. She's right here under the same roof. And yet you sometimes act as though she doesn't exist. That's not right!"

Rafael's face reddened and he began to pace, struggling to maintain control. "Damn it, I don't need this right now. You know that! What the hells?" Remi buried her face in her hands and cried.

Instead of comforting his wife as he knew he should, or apologizing to Mia, who had been watching their spat from the top of the stairs, Rafael stormed out of the house, slamming the door behind him. He was fully aware that he was acting like a child, but damn it, he was scared and didn't know what to do. "Honestly, though," he thought to himself, "it's not just that I'm scared. It's that I hate myself for the way I've been behaving, and for being an utter failure at finding my daughter. That slamming door was like a slap in my own face. A slap I deeply deserve. Remi's just too good a woman to have delivered it herself."

If only he had killed Soader years ago, when he'd had the chance, and every justification he could want! Then none of this would have happened. For just a moment, he regretted ever having agreed to take Celine in. If he hadn't, today she would be safe under some other family's roof, with a father who took proper care of his own.

And there it was again to torment him: the awful image of Celine, struggling on the transbeam platform, pleading for his help. He relived the terrible scene again, as he had hundreds of times before. If he'd just terminated the blasted Rept before he'd spun that dial! He'd *had* a clear shot. Everything would have been fine now, if he'd taken it. But no — regulations were regulations, and nothing else mattered.

He cursed himself once more, with a fresh, raw self-hatred. His pathetic — no, *pathological* devotion to "policy" had cost him his daughter, the respect of his family, and his respect for himself. What made it even worse was that the policy he'd supposedly been following so faithfully actually allowed him discretion in circumstances like that. So he couldn't even blame policy. *He* had hesitated. *He* was to blame. No one else.

Nothing else.

And now it was a year — almost to the very day — since Celine had disappeared. An entire year, and he'd failed to find her, or even a clue as to where she might be. And now he was taking his frustration out on his loving, devoted wife! The only person close to him who seemed to be doing well was Mia. She had a new mate, Hyatt. She looked more beautiful and seemed happier than Zulak had ever seen her.

So now Rafael found himself back at Callaghan's. He'd sought refuge there more and more frequently as the year had worn on. He slumped into his usual booth, and before long, his usual drink appeared before him. He downed it at one go. It was soon replaced, and the sequence repeated. Again and again and again. He'd become so accustomed to the stuff that three or four no longer clouded his thinking much. They just numbed his inner pain down to a dull ache. Content with that, he sat for a long while, lost in thought.

A voice startled Zulak out of his pensive fog. "Sir, please come with me." Zulak turned toward the voice's owner: a tall, blond young man, standing beside the booth. Jager. He wore a crisp, white uniform, in stark contrast to the commander's crumpled civvies. The boy was grinning broadly. "We've heard from Celine!"

CHAPTER 19

Ahimoth

"**M**ake sure it's sealed," barked Soader to the Grey at his back, helping him suit up. The Grey hesitated, toying with the idea of booby-trapping the suit so Soader would die. He knew that if he succeeded, though, some other vile Rept would just take Soader's place. Maybe an even worse one. He couldn't *imagine* a worse one, but it would be just his rotten luck. Besides, if his treachery were discovered, he could end up on RPF113. Or dead. He closed the suit, double-checked the seals and stepped back.

"Sealed," he grunted.

"Get me my blaster," Soader ordered, then strode to the entrance of the dark tunnel. The suit was heavy, but it was equipped with automatic power-assists so that it didn't hamper the wearer's mobility. The Grey brought his blaster, and he entered the dark tunnel.

As the massive tunnel door swung shut behind the Rept, a new murderous thought occurred to the Grey: he could bar the door, locking the wretched Soader away forever! But damn

— there were cameras everywhere, watching. He'd never get away with it.

"Gods-damned, effin scum," muttered Soader, slowly making his way down the tunnel, using his helmet light to pick his way through the rocks and debris littering the floor. There were also plenty of bodies to avoid, in varying stages of decay. Animals, the occasional Grey, but mostly Earthlings — young boys.

He moved down the shaft for about twenty minutes before coming to a fork. Taking the passage to the left, he continued on for another five minutes, then turned right at a "T." Finally, he reached the tunnel's end: a steep bluff overlooking a cavern that stretched for miles, lit by an artificial sun-ball placed hundreds of yards above, in the domed ceiling. A river meandered across the scene below, with trees and lush meadows on either side. Small herds of antelope and other beasts grazed here and there. Birds flew overhead and hopped about in the trees and shrubs. Their pleasant calls gave the place a dreamlike quality.

Soader turned to his left and carefully made his way along a steep, narrow trail cut into the side of the bluff, down to the cavern floor. Reaching the bottom, he walked out into the meadow, scanning the whole scene. "I know you're here," he shouted, "show yourself!" Silence, except for the sounds of the scattering animals. "It's time to earn your keep. So get the Xenu out here, or your sister is as good as dead."

There was a *whoosh* of wings behind him, then a deep bellow: "Keep your face on, half-breed. Here I am."

Soader turned to see a big, imposing black dragon perched atop a small mound, two hundred feet behind him — blocking his exit and clearly in an unfriendly mood.

As with any people, there are good dragons and bad dragons. This particular black dragon felt, deep down, that he might once have been good. Yet his parents had named him

Ahimoth — which meant "brother of death," in an ancient language. His parents meant no harm in this. They were merely upholding one of the longstanding traditions of their proud people. It was born of legend, and the reasons for it had been lost in antiquity. Few still knew the name's historic meaning, and fewer still granted it any serious credence.

Nevertheless, when the young dragon learned of his name's old significance, he was overwhelmed with a foreboding that it would dictate the course of his life. He felt irrevocably doomed to be a bringer of death and sorrow, whether he wished to or not. Tragic events would one day reinforce his belief.

Growing up, Ahimoth had tried his best to ignore his name, but eventually a few other youngsters learned of its old meaning, and the whispered word was passed around: "Beware the black dragon!" Of course, it wasn't long before Ahimoth became aware of the rumors. He put on a show of laughing them off as silly superstition. Inside, though, he considered it all far from silly; it cut him deeply.

Early in his adolescent years, his cursed name cost Ahimoth dearly. He had developed quite a crush on a lovely young dragon named Joli, and courted her avidly. He had a rival for Joli's attentions: a slightly older dragon named Vin. When Vin learned what the black dragon's name had once meant, he used the knowledge to his advantage. He convinced Joli that, admirable and worthy though Ahimoth might be, he was fated to live up to his name, sooner or later. The scheme worked: though she had long favored Ahimoth, Joli now chose Vin to be her sole suitor. She met with Ahimoth and tearfully informed him of her decision, and the circumstances that had prompted it.

Ahimoth was furious, and challenged Vin to a duel of honor. The two met at the appointed place, observed the traditional dueling protocols, and vaulted into the sky to begin the fight, surrounded — at a safe distance — by friends and the required formal observers.

The battle began, and the fighting was fast and fierce. So fierce that neither the combatants nor the observers noticed that a storm that had been looming nearby had veered in their direction. Suddenly it was upon them, lightning flashing and thunder roaring so loudly it drowned out the bellows of the battling dragons. At first, the storm just added to the excitement, but then tragedy struck. A monstrous bolt of lightning speared Joli squarely through her graceful back, killing her instantly and filling the air with the stench of incinerated dragon flesh. The fighting ceased at once, the combatants staring in horror as their beloved's charred and lifeless body tumbled toward the plain below.

Compounding the tragedy, there were no eggs on Nibiru ready to hatch at the time of Joli's death, so her spirit was given up as lost forever.

Ahimoth would never be the same. He abandoned his home for a sparsely populated area on another continent. Hating his cursed name more than ever, he changed it to Leothe, a made-up name with no significance, in the desperate hope that this might alter his fate. He vowed that when Nibiru's orbit brought it close enough to Earth for a crossing, he would make the perilous trip. He would go there to search for Joli's spirit, on the remotest of remote chances that she had gone there in search of a viable egg. Ahimoth/Leothe knew he was neither old nor strong enough to attempt the trip safely; his chances of surviving the passage were horribly slim.

Survive it he would, though. Just barely.

While he was waiting for the planet to move into range, his former rival, Vin, had managed to locate him. Vin was as crushed by Joli's death as Ahimoth was, and had sought him out to share his grief and try to make amends. Ahimoth/Leothe had refused Vin's entreaties at first, but finally relented. He told Vin of his plan to travel to Earth, and the older dragon vowed to make the trip with him, promising that if they found Joli, he would step aside, satisfied to know she lived.

Two years later, the planets were close enough for the dragons to dare the tube-chute. Vin was battered almost to death before they had been in the vortex two hours. Leothe fared little better; when the tube-chute spat out the pair at its Earthside terminus, he was unconscious, broken and near death himself. The fall to the planet's surface nearly finished them off. Such was their condition when Soader found them.

The Rept-hybrid had a device which detected the presence and pinpointed the location of any dragon that might appear on the planet. He responded at once when the locator alerted him to the two youngsters' arrival. Racing to the scene, he was beside himself with delight to see that one of the dragons was a black. The creatures' unconsciousness was a big bonus, too — there was no need to subdue them.

Soader immediately had a team of Greys transport the broken pair to deep caverns he'd set up to hold any dragons he might be lucky enough to capture. It took another group of skilled Greys several weeks to nurse Leothe back to consciousness and relative stability. Vin — held in a separate cavern — remained in a coma far longer, and his eventual recovery was much slower.

During Leothe's convalescence, Soader exercised all his wiles to befriend the dragon. He learned much about conditions on Nibiru, and the workings of the tube-chute vortex.

Leothe thought Soader was just being kind, and, like most adolescents, he was glad for a sympathetic ear. He never suspected his "benefactor" would soon use everything he'd told the half-Rept against him, and to Nibiru's gravest detriment. The naïve dragon went into considerable detail about the dragons of his homeworld, including his beautiful sister, Fianna. Soader drooled at the thought of how much the white dragon could be worth to him.

When Leothe asked about the fate of his traveling companion, Vin, Soader lied shamelessly: "I'm so very sorry, but your friend was dead when we found him. We tried to revive him, but it was no use. We cremated his remains, with all proper ceremony. I'm so sorry for your loss." The dragon wept at the news.

When Leothe was almost fully recovered, he felt the urge to explore the planet he'd managed to reach. Within minutes, he discovered he'd been trapped. He was on Earth all right, but shut up in a subterranean cavern. He screamed his rage at Soader's treachery — and at his own hideous foolishness for confiding in the despicable wretch.

Each day he flew from one end of the cavern to the other, exploring every inch of the place in hopes of finding a way out. His efforts were futile; he was Soader's prisoner. He swore that no matter how long it took, he would have revenge upon the vile Rept. He was so angry that he changed his name back to Ahimoth and vowed to prove the legend true: once he had escaped this trap, he would be death's closest brother — and Soader would be his first victim.

Soader had anticipated the dragon's rage, however, and devised a way to turn the violent emotion to his own advantage.

"Nothing you could say or do could *ever* convince me to help you," Ahimoth snarled, when Soader came to present his proposal — garbed once again in his impervious suit.

"Haaaaar! I wouldn't be so sure, big boy. I've something here that might interest you, in spite of yourself. It belonged to your dear, snowy-white sister, Fianna. She followed you to Earth, you know, in the pathetically charming hope of bringing you home to Nibiru."

"What are you blathering about, scum?" the dragon roared, spitting fireballs at the Rept. "My sister is too small and too young to travel to Earth. You're lying, as usual," he growled, leaping forward and landing closer to Soader, furiously fanning his wings. Both the fireballs and violent gusts bounced harmlessly off the heavy, shielded suit.

"Quite true," Soader agreed, "but you'll be *so* sorry to hear that she attempted the passage anyway, poor thing."

Ahimoth gasped in horror, fearing the worst. Soader was just toying with him, though. "You'll probably be glad to know she survived the trip. Though not in the best of condition, I'm afraid. See? Here's a scrap of one of her precious little wings. It's a pity; I'm sure she was once perfectly lovely." He held up a few inches of a dragon's wingtip; it glistened white in his hand.

"What have you done to her?" roared Ahimoth. "WHAT HAVE YOU DONE?!" He blasted the Rept-hybrid with a searing plume of dragonfire, though he knew it would do no damage.

"Haaaaarrr!" laughed Soader. "I knew that would get your attention! Now there's something you are going to do for me, or I'll be forced to take more than just a bit of her wingtip. And let me say, she is beautiful, even if she's damaged. Why, even the smallest scale of her would fetch me a tidy pile on the markets. So, do as I say, or I'll start cashing her in. Oh! And don't get any nasty ideas. It's all set up so that if anything, shall we say, *tragic* happens to me, she'll be killed, just as dead as she is pretty. And so will you! Haaaarrrrr!"

Still laughing, Soader walked straight past Ahimoth and began climbing back up the steep, winding trail. The dragon just stood where he was, his great, black neck bowed in defeat.

Then, slowly, a grim smile appeared on Ahimoth's finely scaled face, and he straightened to his full height. At last, the true significance of his name was clear. It had been there all along, but he, and everyone else, had grossly misinterpreted it. Yes, he was the Brother of Death. But not random, wanton, senseless death. No. The truth was plain, and it filled him with a powerful new purpose. For as long as he remained alive, he would bring death — painful, horrible, everlasting death — to anyone who ever dared harm his precious sister.

AHIMOTH HAD NEVER PERMITTED Soader to fly with him, of course. But the Rept had the dragon by the tail now. He could force the big black to link with him and allow him to ride. Soader laughed in triumph at the thought, and continued his climb toward the cavern's exit. How clever he'd been to bleach the wingtip of that blue dragon he'd found alongside Ahimoth. He'd already sold off hundreds of the bleached blue scales, raking in a small fortune. They appeared to be totally authentic. Only a curious expert's closest scrutiny with a powerful microscope and spectrometer would ever reveal their few remaining nano-traces of blue pigment. Soader figured he would be long gone in the Serpens Universe before anyone discovered they were fakes. If anyone ever did.

"Haaarrrr. The blasted beast will have to link with me now. I'm going to be a dragon rider! Nibiru's treasure will be *mine!* I'll take it all away to Serpens. They'll *never* find it — not when it's a whole universe away! I've outsmarted everyone, as usual. Haaaaaaaaarrrrrr! I'm going to be stupid, galactic, filthy *rich*, and rule the whole Serpens Universe forever!"

CHAPTER 20

To Earth

Only a minute earlier, Commander Rafael Zulak had been sitting at Callaghan's bar, slumped over a beer and mentally replaying the argument he'd just had with his wife. Now he was jumping around the bar like a cadet, laughing, crying, and hugging Jager. He slapped the younger man on the back, over and over — hard enough to make Jager stumble, despite his scuttleball-player build.

"She's alive! She's alive!" yelled Rafael. He dashed out of the pub and down the road toward his home, Jager close behind. Neighbors peeked out windows and stepped out onto porches to see what all the commotion was about, so late in the evening. Some who knew him joined in, yelling and dancing with Rafael down the street — "She's alive! Celine's alive!"

Reaching his home, Rafael banged through the front door, just as Remi rushed into the room, wakened by the din outside. Soon husband and wife were dancing around the house, hugging, kissing, and laughing. Even Mia was caught up in the excitement.

Dino, Madda and others soon arrived, and before they knew it, there was one crowd inside their home, and another out in the garden.

"I don't know what to say," laughed Rafael, cheeks still moist with tears. "It's *such* a relief to know she's alive! Our Celine is alive! My Gods, if I was a more religious man, I'd be on my knees thanking the Founders," he laughed, giving Remi another big hug.

"I still don't understand why she's not coming straight home," said Remi, as Madda embraced them both, planting big Rept kisses on their cheeks.

"I know, dear, I know," Rafael said, pulling away from Remi and Madda, and gently patting his wife's hand. "I don't understand it either, but Celine said the friend who saved her life needs help. She's her father's daughter, you know," he winked, "if someone needs help, she's right in there."

Nothing could have dampened his joy. Now he could fix everything. Now he could make up for all his mistakes. Things were going to be fine. He would have his Celine back. Pleiadeans would have their talisman back!

"I know, but I'm her mother. I have a right to want my daughter home safe, and fast! Why didn't she call us? That still doesn't make sense," Remi pouted.

Dino overheard, and came to Rafael's rescue. "Hi, Remi. I can answer your question," he said. "You know how it is, she being a teenager — not always thinking logically. She did try to call both you and Rafael, but I guess she couldn't get through — so she called her godfather. Makes sense, don't you think? Anyway, when she called, I was busy. Luckily, Jager happened to be there; he answered for me. He knows how desperately we've been looking for her. I guess she was going to try calling you again after talking to Jager, but she had to go help her friend, back in an area where there aren't any comm stations.

That Planet 444 is a pretty primitive place, so it's practically a miracle she found a station at all. She asked Jager to apologize for her, but I guess in all the excitement, he forgot. You know how kids can be."

"Well, I'm still hurt, but since she's okay, I'll quit complaining for now. You're going to go get her as soon as *Asherah* is ready, right?" Remi asked, hesitantly, looking back and forth between Rafael and Dino.

"Yes, dear, we'll get back to *Asherah* and go get her. As soon as we can — I promise!" her husband responded, still grinning. He knew it would be difficult to convince Fleet to allow it, but he would make it happen somehow. It was a good thing Admiral Stock owed him a couple of favors.

More friends and neighbors had heard the news and come to join the impromptu gathering. Before long it was a full-scale party that lasted well into the wee hours.

Near dawn, after almost no sleep at all, Rafael made his way to Fleet Headquarters. It seemed like a lifetime since he'd been there. He looked around, his feelings mixed at seeing the familiar facilities and faces. Soon he'd reached the office he was looking for. The secretary announced him to its distinguished occupant, and ushered him through the big double doors.

"Come in Rafael, come in," said a tall, graying man, turning away from a large window. "Come, sit down and tell me how Celine was found." The admiral gestured toward a big padded guest chair in front of his imposing desk. "I heard that she is well. I'm so happy for you and Remi."

"Thank you, sir," said Rafael, sitting down. The older man gestured toward a flask of water on the desk before him; Rafael accepted and opened it, gathering his thoughts before speaking. "Apparently, Celine has been on Planet 444 this entire time. Earth. As you know, it's a primitive place, and the transbeam landed her in remote mountains where few natives live, thousands of miles from any civilized settlement. Her comm pickup had been taken away, so she couldn't contact us. One of the mountain dwellers found her and took her to her village, high up in an Alpine valley. The long winter kept them snowbound there for months. The friend who saved her asked Celine to help find a brother who'd been missing for quite some time. Well, you know how honorable Celine is; she agreed. They've been unable to find the missing brother, and now she's asking for our help to locate him, to repay the mountain people for rescuing her."

Of course, the whole story was a fabrication — though Rafael didn't know it. Jager had made it all up. There was no way he could have told them that their young daughter had traveled to Earth with a dragon, through a tube-chute vortex. He'd have been hospitalized for observation at once. All anyone needed to know at this point was that she was alive and safe. Jager had promised Celine to keep the truth to himself for now, due to the importance of what she and Fianna were doing. He'd agreed with her reasoning and her plan.

"She's a daughter to be proud of, Rafael. She'll make a great commander someday."

"Thank you, sir. She does make me proud. I suppose I should get to the reason I've come, though I imagine you've guessed it."

"Yes, I have. I'd be doing the same if I was in your boots; I have two daughters and three young granddaughters, now. Celine is precious to us all; I, more than anyone, am aware of that. I'm happy to do it, but I'm pulling a big string for you here, Rafael."

"Yes, admiral. I know I don't deserve such a favor, but I thank you, sir," the commander replied, just now noticing the old man's new crop of wrinkles and thinning hair; he really was aging fast.

"I'm also doing this because I know that if I didn't, you'd take the *Queen* without permission — and that loyal crew of yours would back you all the way. You would probably deserve the court martial that would follow," laughed the admiral, "but your crew wouldn't! So that's that. But come look at the view from my balcony — there's some new construction I want to show you."

For a moment, Rafael hesitated, puzzled by such an odd request at a time like this. The admiral noticed his confusion, and gave the commander the slightest of conspiratorial winks. Rafael got the message at once, and instantly played along. "Oh, yes! I've been wondering how that project has been coming along."

The two men stepped out onto the large balcony and over to a railing, where they could take in the vista below. Between the whistle of the brisk breeze and the sounds of traffic above and below, it was difficult to make oneself heard here — and for any possible bugs to pick up a conversation. Pretending to point out something down below, the admiral leaned in close to Rafael and said, "Go get your daughter and bring her home. Leave at once, before someone from Fleet or G.O.D. tries to stop you."

"Sir?"

"Strange things are happening. Things I can't control," responded the admiral. Now he pointed in a new direction, toward another construction site; Rafael continued playing along, looking enthused and asking questions. After a bit of this, the admiral leaned close again. "I don't know if I'll still have my position when you return, or if I'll even be alive, for that matter. I've lost most of my power, and many of my connections have disappeared. You mustn't speak of this to anyone, or answer to anyone else in Fleet. I don't know who can be trusted anymore. Now that others know Celine is alive, they will expect you to try to recover her. There are those who want her almost as badly as you do, so trust no one. She would not be safe on Erra; you and Dino will have to figure out where to take her instead. We're being infiltrated at an alarming rate, so you must be very careful who you trust, even among your own crew. Dino's nephew — the one called Jager — is no longer safe either. Protect him as if he were your own son, Rafael."

"Sir?"

"No time to explain. Be careful. I know things have been rough for you and Remi lately, and I fear they will be getting rougher. I trust you and Dino to make the right decisions, no matter what arises. I know you realize Celine's importance to everyone. Unfortunately, 'everyone' includes some very bad characters. Some of them would stop at nothing to get hold of her or the boy. Make very sure Jager stays with *Asherah*, Rafael. And tell Dino all about this conversation. He'll know what must be done. Understood?"

Rafael was a bit taken aback by the admiral's unexpected revelations and advice, as well as the sudden interest in Jager, but he nodded agreement. He followed the old officer back toward the office, wishing he could ask more questions.

"Spectacular view, isn't it?" the admiral asked, as they stepped through the doorway to the patio. "I can hardly wait to see those towers completed. As I mentioned, I'm happy for you and Remi; give her a hug for me. Now, go get your daughter."

"Thank you, sir," Rafael responded, as cheerfully as he could manage. Salutes were exchanged, but so were hugs — Admiral Stock was a close family friend of long standing. As they hugged, the admiral covertly slipped something into Rafael's jacket pocket. Rafael noticed, but gave no outward sign that he had. The admiral watched the younger officer leave, and whispered a prayer as the door shut behind him.

As Rafael walked toward the lift, he took notice of everyone, on full alert for anyone acting suspiciously. The admiral's assistant smiled; she seemed to be the only one paying any attention to him. She went quickly back to her work.

Rafael had never seen the admiral act so strangely, but he trusted the man, regardless. The commander decided to take precautions, starting now. Reaching the lift, he stepped into the empty car, but told it to take him to the eatery instead of the foyer, as would normally be expected. It was a simple trick to see if he was being followed. He stepped out of the lift when the doors opened and walked over to a teala vendor's booth.

He bought a teala and sat down to chat with some friends having breakfast. When they got up to go back to their offices, Rafael made his way to the restroom facilities, taking note of everyone he saw. He remained in the restroom for several minutes, then made his way to the main entrance, lingering to talk with the doorman before leaving the building. The entire time, the object in his breast pocket was consuming more and more of his attention. He almost looked at it, but restrained himself; he feared that discovering what it was might cause him to react badly, drawing the attention of anyone watching him.

The farther he got from Fleet's offices, the more he fixated on the mysterious object. He decided he had to get to the safety of his ship, and find out just what it was. Catching a shuttlecar, he asked the driver to take him in the direction of the hangars, and drop him off at a spot a few miles before they would reach them — a little routine he'd often followed in the past. The driver stopped at the designated spot, and Rafael got out. "Thanks. I'll walk from here," he said.

"As you wish, sir," replied the driver. "I heard the news about your daughter, sir. That's great. I hope she'll be home soon."

"Thank you. Enjoy your day," said the commander, and he watched the craft disappear. He thought it a bit odd that the driver had seemed to know who he was, and his connection to Celine. The man wasn't familiar to him. Probably just served on one of his ground crews or some such. No matter — but he was glad he hadn't checked out the object in his pocket while in the man's presence.

Zulak tried to look casual as he walked along. He checked his watch, mopped his brow, took out a tin of mints from a pants pocket and popped a couple into his mouth — and slipped the tin into his breast pocket, instead of back into his pants. A while later he began to sweat, so he stopped and removed his jacket, draping it over his arm. While he was stopped, he took out the mint tin once again, also picking up the mysterious object along with it. He opened the tin, took another mint, and slipped the object inside before closing it and returning it to the original pants pocket. He wanted to make sure that whatever the admiral had slipped him wouldn't show up easily at gate security. The tin of hard candies should obscure it well enough. He'd almost snuck a look at it, but held back — there was every chance he was under observation, with equipment powerful enough to identify whatever the object might be, if he were to reveal it. He slung the jacket over his shoulder and walked on, thoughtfully sucking his mint.

Now the base security gate was in sight. He knew his crew would already be aboard the *Queen*, preparing her for tomorrow's early departure. Dino would have seen to that. Zulak arrived at the gate, acting businesslike but unconcerned. He presented his identification, and, at the guard's direction, passed through the scanners, holding his breath. He was careful not to look too relieved when the "all clear" indicator flashed and the gate opened. He hurried to *Asherah*'s berth and went aboard.

Making his way to the bridge, he exchanged greetings with the crew. All were clearly delighted at the news that Celine was alive, and that their commander had returned. Turning the bridge back over to Dino, Rafael retired to his ready room, close by the bridge. The door slid closed behind him, and he settled into his chair to call Remi. She was at home, preparing for Celine's return, sprucing up the girl's room and baking some of her favorite treats.

"Good, dear. I'm sure Celine will like that. Bake some of *my* favorites too, will ya?" kidded Zulak. "Yes, the cookies with the rueberries. Exactly. Love you too. We'll bring her home soon. Bye."

Leaning forward and clasping his hands before him, Rafael considered all that had gone on in the last few days. He'd dared to believe he was on the verge of righting so many of his past mistakes: He was close to putting Soader away for good, bringing his little girl home, and hopefully mending the rifts in his family's happiness. Still, a heavy sigh escaped him. He had an awful, unexplainable feeling. He should be overjoyed; instead, he felt a creeping apprehension and a thin, brittle nausea. Admiral Stock's words and actions hadn't helped matters.

Pushing his misgivings aside, he pulled the mint tin from his pocket, opened it and plucked out the mysterious whatever-it-was. A package — some sort of fabric tape or ribbon, wound around and around into an elongated egg shape. He found the end of the wrapping strip and carefully began to unwind it.

Soon the contents were revealed, and he laid them out on the desk before him. A small, pinkish crystal. A flat, oddly-shaped metal object, which he recognized as the key to an old-style mechanical lock, of a kind he'd once seen on Earth. And, finally, a rolled-up scrap of paper inscribed with a few seemingly random letters and numbers. Gods! What the Xenu did this junk have to do with anything? With a shrug, he retrieved an empty envelope from the desk drawer, placed the strange objects inside and slid it into a pocket.

"Jessup, kindly bring me some teala," he said into the desktop comm link. "Oh, hells. And a plate of those spice biscuits, too." The snack arrived a few minutes later. Rafael tilted back in his chair, took a sip of the hot liquid and bite of biscuit, and tried to relax — hoping to settle both his stomach and his anxieties.

He mulled over the plans he and his crew were about to carry out, looking for any flaw or fatal omission. He knew that when he found the right thing, his gut would settle at once. He'd been through this scenario many times before, and had come to trust his gut — literally. One time he'd dismissed this same sort of visceral upset, in not dissimilar circumstances. It had nearly cost many lives, his own included. Only a flash of insight and instant response had averted. But they had also resulted in his killing Soader's only child.

It was the hardest thing Zulak had ever done. He — and numerous others with no emotional connection to the incident — had reviewed the event in minutest detail. The conclusion was always the same: There was nothing whatever that Zulak could have done that would have had a better outcome. Still, he had killed...a child. The memory had haunted him ever since.

But back to the present. He could find no flaw in the plans, and the gnawing upset in his gut was growing worse. He tapped the comm link. "Mr. Hadgkiss, please join me in the ready room."

"Sir," responded the major, stepping through the still-opening portal. "What can I do for you, sir?"

"It's okay, Dino. I just need your viewpoint and advice." Zulak was pacing, hands clasped tightly behind, a glisten of perspiration visible on his tensed forehead, face and neck.

"The admiral and I had a most unusual conversation earlier today." Pulling out the envelope, Zulak continued. "He insisted I tell you about it, and slipped these into my pocket just before we parted." Carefully arraying the odd objects on the desk, he asked, "Does anything there mean anything to you? Anything at all?"

Dino stepped closer and examined each object carefully, even though he'd recognized them at once. "Yes, unfortunately, they all mean something," he replied.

"Oh!" said a surprised Zulak, unaware that his fingers were fidgeting with the turquoise crystal hanging at his neck. "Well, maybe this will make sense to you, too: he also warned that we had to recover Celine fast, before someone from Fleet or G.O.D. tried to stop us."

"Yes, that makes sense — and you can thank the Gods he was able to warn you," replied Dino. "Celine and Jager are in grave danger, Rafael. So is anyone who's anywhere near them. We're going to have to be very, very alert, and prepared to act."

"The admiral said as much," said Zulak. "So what the hells is going on, Dino? What was he talking about? And how is your nephew involved?"

"I'll explain — but if you'll excuse me for a few minutes, there's something I must attend to on the bridge, immediately."

"Of course — but what is it?" asked Rafael.

"As the admiral advised, even our own crew can't be trusted. I'll have a discrete sweep conducted."

"Very good," acknowledged Zulak. "Have Sreach run blood tests on the entire crew, too. I'm sure she can come up with some plausible reason, so any spy isn't alarmed."

"Good idea," replied Dino. He turned to leave, then saw that the commander had more to say.

"I've got that sickish feeling in my gut again, Dino. You know the one. I'm worried I've missed something, and things are going to go all to hells. I need you to promise me something."

"Of course. Anything, Raff. What is it?"

"Take care of Remi and the girls, if anything happens to me.

Promise?"

"Hey, hey, what's this? Nothing's going to happen to you, pal. You've just got the jitters. Don't worry — nothing will happen," Dino responded, with a slightly forced chuckle.

"I know, but I want your promise all the same."

"Sure, sure; okay. I promise. I'll take good care of Remi and your lovely daughters. Even that hustler Hyatt, that Mia plans to marry," he laughed.

"Thanks. You're always welcome at our place — you know that. I know it's been hard since Mosi and your son died."

"Yeah, thanks, but enough of this sad crap, eh? Give me one of those awful-looking biscuits, would ya?" He took the biscuit Rafael held out, popped the whole thing into his mouth and strode from the ready room, chewing with enthusiasm.

Zulak turned back to his console, which now displayed the plans for their upcoming mission. But, despite his efforts to concentrate, his thoughts kept turning to Celine. She was in danger! He should be on Earth *now*, looking for her. If it didn't take so damnably long to prepare the ship, he *would* be there. She could be hurt before they ever arrived. Hurt, or... He couldn't bear to consider it further; he forced his attention back to the tables, maps and images before him.

In a while, his stomach had eased a bit. With a sigh, he went to work re-calculating the jump-shift numbers. He knew before he started that they would be correct — his navigators were utterly reliable — but he did it anyway.

Satisfied with the calculations, he decided to brush up on portcullis travel. Earlier, he'd overheard Dino's nephew asking someone a question about it, and he'd been startled to realize he couldn't have answered it. He prided himself on being deeply knowledgeable about his ship and its operations, and would have been sorely embarrassed if the question had been directed at him. Being knowledgeable was a matter of personal pride, but he also knew it was a crucial element of leadership. He called up the subject on the console, and settled in to study.

CELINE HAD BRIEFED JAGER AND West on what she and Fianna had been through since their arrival on Earth. Jager had briefed Dino, and Dino had briefed Admiral Stock.

Hadgkiss knew exactly where the ship should go to find Celine, once they arrived at Earth: the Vogelsberg Mountains, in the region Earthlings now called Germany. Hadgkiss didn't like to act without his commander's knowledge or contrary to his orders, but in this case, the admiral had directed him to do so, if circumstances clearly demanded it. Not out of disrespect for Zulak, but because both understood that the commander was unavoidably compromised by his close personal and emotional involvement with some of the parties involved. Further, Rafael was ignorant of Celine's origins, and her importance in galactic affairs.

"WEST, ARE YOU THERE?" asked Jager.

"Yes, I'm here. Everything is in readiness," she answered. "North, East and South are with me. Please inform me when you have arrived at Earth."

"Of course," replied Jager. "I will. But I'm nervous and worried for Celine and Fianna."

"So am I, in my way," mented West. "But I believe the element of surprise will act in our favor. We should be on the scene in time to protect them — before Soader can arrive."

"That's a relief. Thank you," replied Jager. "It's almost time to leave. I'll contact you soon."

CHAPTER 21

Vogelsberg Mountains

Celine was overjoyed to be talking with Jager and West, but a vague uneasiness still gnawed at her. "Now that we have a plan, I guess Fianna and I should say goodbye and be on our way," she said, feeling apprehensive.

"I agree," said West. "Please, Celine, stay in touch. Call immediately if you find yourself in any trouble."

"I will, West," the girl replied.

"You are right, Celine," thought the dragon. There is a long flight ahead of us. We will not reach the German tunnels tonight if we do not depart soon."

"All right," said Jager. "I'll say goodbye on one condition: I call you every two hours, at least. Agreed, Celine?"

"Yes," she said, rolling her eyes. "You sound like my dad." She managed a laugh.

"Who cares? We want you to come home — and in one healthy piece," Jager replied. "I've really missed you. I'm not kidding, Celine. There were times when I lost all hope that you were still alive, and I had no idea what to do. So please indulge

me in a silly little thing or two. Like letting me know you're alive, once in a while. Especially while you're on the most dangerous trip of your life!"

"I agree with Jager," said West. "Do take care, and stay in touch."

"We will. I promise," replied Celine. "You're right, Jager. I wouldn't have wanted to be in your boots. I'm sorry."

"Apology accepted," said Jager. "Your dad and I should be there early in the morning, on the day after tomorrow. Be safe until then. Once we arrive, we'll be able to shield you with our cloaking system. I'm sorry it can't be sooner, but there are things we must deal with before we can come. Keep your senses about you. I want to finally hold you for real, and kiss those lips I've been dreaming about."

"Ye...yes! Don't worry. We'll be careful. I'm looking forward to seeing you, too," responded Celine, flustered and blushing. "Good-bye, West."

"Good-bye, Celine, and Fianna. Fly strong, fly safe," said the Mentor.

Celine turned her still-reddening face away from Fianna, and tried to focus on gathering their gear and packing the saddlebags. "I'll be ready to go in a couple of minutes. How about you?" she asked the dragon, her face still warm.

"I am ready when you are," answered Fianna, struggling to hide a huge grin.

Celine soon had everything in its place. She tied the last saddlebag closed and quickly climbed up, securing herself into the comfortable saddle. Then dragon and Companion launched out over the waters of Loch Maree.

"As soon as the moon moves behind the clouds, I shall climb higher. It is a short flight, so I do not want to go too high; just enough so that we will not be seen," mented Fianna.

"Sounds good," answered Celine, her face still red, and now

smiling broadly. Soon the two were cruising above the clouds; before long, it was time to descend again. The cloud cover was thick enough to make the night below quite dark, so Fianna made a quick dive, levelling out into a flat glide just above the calm waters of Loch Ness. Fianna spotted the landmark they were looking for — a high crag near a sheltered bay — and set down near the shore below the crag, in a stand of Scots pines. Celine climbed down, walked the short distance to the lake, and sat down on a rock beneath the shadowy crag. Fianna followed close behind, but walked to the water's edge.

"Nessie, can you hear me?" mented Fianna, concentrating on the dark waters as they glimmered in the moonlight. "I have come from Nibiru, bearing the blessings of our clan."

A few minutes later, the surface of the calm waters, about forty feet from shore, roiled and then broke. Up, up came a long, graceful arch of a water dragon's back, glistening as it rose to greet the night sky. Ahead of the gliding arch, the creature's head now breached the surface, rising to about fifteen feet above the water as the dragon slowed to a stop a few yards from shore. A striking pair of chartreuse eyes regarded Fianna and her Companion. The dragon's neck, and the portion of her back that could be seen, were a beautiful, brindled mix of dark blues, browns and grays.

"Nessie, it is an honor and a pleasure to meet you," said Fianna. "I am Princess Albho Fianna Uwatti, daughter of the Great King Neal Tawni Uwatti; last of the royal dragon line of Nibiru."

"Princess, it is likewise an honor and a pleasure to meet you. Who is this in your company? She is not from this planet, I see."

"This is my Companion, Celine, of the Pleiadean planet of Erra. We have come in search of the lost Book of Atlantis, and the Book of Mu."

"Ah, this is a goodness. The legends are being answered. Welcome, Companion Celine. Long have we awaited your coming."

Celine bowed, and she and Fianna stole quick glances at each other. "It is a rare pleasure to make your acquaintance, Nessie," Celine replied, bowing again, as one does upon first meeting a dragon. "I hope that I will live up to the legends of which you speak."

"It is my hope that you shall do so as well, young Companion. It is said that you and Fianna must succeed — for if you fail, not only will the dragons of Nibiru pass into oblivion, but so will the Earthlings. They are a very disturbed people, who have lost their way."

"Thank you, Nessie. These things we understand. And we must begin our travels on this planet as soon as we may," interjected Fianna. "May we ask your guidance?"

"Of course, Fianna."

"We seek directions to our first destination, the tunnels of Germany. From there we will travel to Turkey, to search for the Atlantis Chest. Can you also advise us how to enter the tunnels in which it is rumored to lie, and how to find our way within them?"

"Yes, certainly. Look to the European Highway and its tunnels," Nessie counselled. "You will know the one to choose, when first you see it. But before you depart on your quest, please allow me to remind you of some of the salient points of the legend. Being mindful of these may save you when all hope seems lost.

"Before leaving Earth," the water dragon continued, "the Atlantean prince, Deet, hid the Atlantis grimoire and the Book of Mu, along with his people's treasure. He did this so that they would be available to his descendants, should Atlanteans ever return to this planet. The prince left behind several of his most loyal servants and their families to guard the treasure — a task they faithfully performed for centuries upon centuries. Then the Brothers returned to Earth, in search of the treasure and grimoires. Fortunately, neither they nor their minions were able to find what they sought."

"Have you ever seen the Brothers?" interrupted Celine — instantly dismayed at her own rudeness. "I'm so sorry to interrupt, Nessie; that just slipped out. I apologize for my rudeness, but I must confess that I have been deeply worried ever since arriving here on Earth. You see, somehow I know that something terrible will happen soon, and the Brothers will be at the root of it."

"Celine?" broke in Fianna, in surprise. "Why have you not mentioned this before?"

"I'm sorry. I know I should've said something, but I've felt so confused. You see, some of my ancient past-life memories have been surfacing; I think my exposure to Earth's air must have triggered them. And now I'm worried. I haven't told anyone because I've *caused* so much worry in this past year, I wanted to have more information and more certainty before I said anything."

Celine turned to Nessie, and, careful to follow the proper etiquette, addressed her once more. "I apologize once again for interrupting you, Nessie. I hope you will forgive me, and continue your generous counsel."

"Thank you, Celine. I understand your concerns, and all is forgiven," the water dragon replied. "In answer to your question, yes – I have learned that the Brothers are hiding on one of Saturn's moons, Titan. I have also heard that they are in collusion with a vicious Rept-hybrid with whom I believe you are familiar: Soader."

"Soader!" the girl exclaimed.

"Yes," answered Nessie. "He, too, seeks the ancient

grimoires and treasure. There is also this: he has beguiled a great red dragon, with which he flies as if he were its Companion. A huge, red dragon, a mutant with two heads." Both Celine and Fianna gasped, but neither spoke; they digested Nessie's words in respectful silence.

"As you see, you and your Companion have come at a crucial time, my cousin," continued the water dragon. "Many planets, many systems — even whole sectors would be in grave peril, if either Soader or the Brothers were to obtain the spell books. I hear much of what goes on, on this planet and elsewhere. So do my many sisters and friends on this world, as we traverse its network of water tunnels. Quite recently, I learned that the Brothers have found the Book of Serpens, and plan to subjugate the Serpens Universe before attempting the conquest of our own. And so, we must work quickly. The fates of universes are at stake."

"Indeed we must," agreed Fianna. Turning now to her Companion, she said, "I, too, have an answer to your question, Celine." The dragon looked to her blue-hued host, who nodded permission to continue.

"Celine," Fianna continued, "perhaps I should have told you this earlier, but I did not wish to cause you more worry. I am sure you will understand, once you hear it. I, too, was aware that the Brothers were seeking the treasure of Atlantis. As you may not know, among the secrets within the Book of Atlantis is the key to reaching Nibiru. If either Soader or the Brothers find that treasure before we do, the problems we face will be gravely worsened. We must not fail."

"Fianna is correct," said Nessie, before Celine could respond. "My understanding is that G.O.D. has known of the Atlantean treasures for centuries, and has considered them safe here on Earth. It appears that G.O.D. was correct — the treasures have remained hidden — but I fear their belief is no longer valid. The Atlantean priests who guard the tunnels and treasures have moved the treasures numerous times over the long years, to keep their location a mystery. However, Soader has recently had most of the priesthood killed. He could not pry their secrets from them, so he filled the tunnels with poisonous gas and blocked all their exits. It was a senseless act, but typical. Soader is now said to have Greys and Repts searching day and night for the treasure, so take great care in exploring the tunnels."

Celine touched the medallion dangling from the leather thong around her neck. The smooth cherry wood comforted her. Next to it hung a carving of a small white dragon and Companion. The medallion was meant to keep Jager and the Mentors safe; the carving, to protect herself and her dragon friend. She continued running her fingers lovingly over the precious talismans, humming a spell for everyone's safety.

"Thank you for your gracious audience, Nessie," said Fianna. "As a member of the royal family of Nibiru, I give you our blessing, and wish you a long, bountiful and happy life." Nessie bowed her graceful head.

"There is one more thing I must relate before you leave, Princess," said Nessie, with a grin. "There are other dragons on this planet. Nibiru dragons."

"My brother?! Have you heard news of my brother?" asked Fianna, standing and stretching to her full height, wings spread wide. "Is he alive?"

"Yes, I have heard news of your brother; and yes, he lives," the water dragon replied.

"Celine! My brother! He is alive!" exclaimed the white dragon. "We must find and help him!"

"Oh, Fianna! This is wonderful! Yes, yes, we will find him," replied Celine. "Once we have found the spell books, it will be our new quest."

Nessie spoke up, "Alas, Fianna, Soader holds your brother captive. He is imprisoned in a deep cavern, far across the ocean."

"No!" said Fianna. "What are we to do?"

"You will know, when the time comes; I am certain of it," Nessie replied. "In that place, Soader also holds the twin-headed red dragon of which I have spoken — the one he rides." Celine and Fianna stood silent. They had not expected to find Soader on Earth, much less in the company of a red dragon.

Nessie continued, "Finally, I must tell you that Soader possesses an instrument that alerts him to the presence and location of every dragon on the planet. He has used it in the past to find and capture some of my water dragon friends, as well as more than one flying dragon. Now his only interest is in the flighted members of our clans."

"This is not good news, but we thank you for relaying it, Nessie," said Celine. She exchanged looks with Fianna; it was time to leave.

The two thanked Nessie for all the information and said their good-byes, then flew swiftly southeast, over more of the Scottish Highlands' beautiful hills and mountains. "Fianna, I am so happy to hear about your brother," mented Celine. "We'll go looking for him as soon as we can. Maybe West and Jager can help us. Let's call them right now, to let them know what Nessie said. We need to tell them about Soader, too." Fianna agreed, and Celine contacted West and Jager.

"You've got to be extra careful, Celine," insisted Jager, "and you *must* call instantly if Soader shows up. Promise?"

"Yes," replied Celine, "you don't have to worry about that! I'll call the second we see him. He will *never* take me prisoner again."

Celine and Fianna were both in much better spirits after their talk with Jager and West, and continued south and east toward Germany with fresh resolve.

"It's quite dark with the moon behind those thick clouds," said Celine. "Do you think it would be safe to fly lower, and maybe make up a bit of the time we've lost, talking with West and Jager?"

"I think you are correct," thought Fianna. "It would be good to get at least as far as western Germany before the moon sets. If we don't make it to a tunnel entrance, we might have trouble finding a safe place to rest for the day. There are some old, abandoned castles scattered about that we could perhaps use."

"That sounds good," replied Celine. "Whenever you need a rest, let me know, and I'll use a spell to help you go on a little farther.

"My father and the *Queen* won't arrive until sometime tomorrow night, after we've landed. We'll have to be extra vigilant until then. We're on our own now, except for whatever support West and the other Mentors can give us, from Mars." She leaned forward and gave Fianna a hug, holding the position fondly as the friends flew onward, just beneath the cloud deck.

Celine's thoughts leapt back and forth, between her worries about Soader and the Brothers, and her uneasiness about meeting Jager in the flesh for the first time. Would their meeting be as she'd been imagining? Their relationship had been easy while they were separated by four hundred light-years. They hadn't even known if they would ever meet, and that had taken a bit of pressure off the relationship, too.

Now she felt as if she had no control over what would happen. They *were* going to meet. She *was* going to be with her soulmate. Would he still want her, once he'd seen her in person? After all, she wasn't tall, slender and beautiful, like Mia. Sure, there'd been boys who seemed to think she was pretty enough, but she thought of her face as fairly plain, and her figure as more athletic than alluring. And would she still want Jager? Maybe he looked like a Rawkl! She began to laugh. She was sounding just as catty and shallow as Mia at her worst! "Time to just be myself," she thought.

Jager contacted Celine several times during their flight to Germany. As she and Fianna neared their destination, he greeted them once more. "Hello to you both, ladies. I hope all is well. We're very nearly ready for launch. We'll be there soon, to assist you bold adventure seekers, and bring you home.

"Celine, you should have seen your father's reaction when I told him we'd heard from you! He just about jumped out of his skin! Then he dashed straight home to tell your mother, and word spread fast; I think half of Devocht knows you're alive. I *may* even have seen a bit of a smile from Mia, but it could've just been gas," he laughed. "Is there anything you'd like me to bring you?"

Celine began to blush all over again, but caught herself and shifted from "giddy young lover" mode, back to "serious cadet on a mission." "Our journey is going as expected, thank you," she replied, with a bit of forced formality. "Thank you for the offer. I could really use a fresh uniform, and a decent hair brush. Oh, and a tooth brush, too! Ha! I hadn't realized how much I've missed such things. I'm afraid you're going to find me looking like an asteroid bum."

"As you wish!" Jager replied, half joking. "I'll see to it that everything is ready, well before you come aboard. That is, if your father hasn't taken care of it all already! I have to tell you, I'm amazed at how much I've missed you, girl. Very strange, considering we've never even met, face to face."

"Thanks. I missed you, too," answered Celine, now more at ease. "How are my parents doing? Are they suspicious? Did you manage to convince them with our story?"

"They're doing well. Not suspicious in the least. Your

mother's annoyed that you're not coming home right away, but she's been busy helping Mia with her wedding plans and preparations. If it weren't for that distraction, I think she'd be impossible to live with."

"Ha! I'm glad to hear my sister hasn't let me down. Life continues for her. I'm happy for her, though. Really. I know she'll be so much more at ease, living away from me."

"Hey, don't say that. You're a peach. Mia is, well...just Mia."

"No worries. I know it was hard for her, having to put up with me as a sister. Heck, I'd find it hard to have *myself* as a sister. I just want her to be happy."

"Well, you're sweeter about her than I could be! Listen, don't worry about our first meeting. I promise not to bite. Not immediately, anyway." The two enjoyed a good laugh. They were back to their accustomed closeness — soulmates reveling in each other's company. Mental and spiritual company, at least.

"I've some duties to attend to," Jager explained. "I'll be back in touch in a couple of hours, though. Stay safe, and watch out for crazy Repts and their beasts. Bye!"

"Bye," said Celine, smiling. She turned her attention back to her dragon companion, who'd been flying onward throughout the young lovers' conversation. In fact, the time that had elapsed amounted to no more than a few seconds, thought being instantaneous. "How are you doing, Fianna?"

"I am doing quite well, thank you. I have become used to travel in this Earth air. I move faster than I would have expected. It requires energy and attention, but it can be surprisingly exhilarating. You will be happy to know we are ahead of our schedule," the dragon explained. "I cannot stop thinking about my brother, though. I do so hope that he is well and in good spirits."

"I understand, and I hope so, too," the girl answered. "We'll find him, Fianna. Don't worry."

"I thank you," mented back Fianna. "I believe you are correct — though finding him will not end our efforts, I am quite certain."

"You're right. We're going to have to be totally alert for any sign of Soader's presence or activities, from now on. And for his minions, too."

"In that you are correct. It is well that Nessie warned us of his dragon-locating device. The knowledge that he has it — and the fact that he probably doesn't suspect we know about it — gives us at least a small advantage. We can safely surmise that he has detected our presence on the planet. Oh! It also occurs to me that he is likely on his way to intercept us at this very moment," said the dragon, picking up her speed to match her newly-heightened sense of urgency.

Celine acknowledged her friend and retreated to silent contemplation. She was concerned about their conversation with Nessie regarding the Brothers and Soader. Celine knew she was no match for either, on her own. Even with her dragon companion, she was in grave peril. The only thing that eased her apprehension was the knowledge that the Mentors would be close, monitoring events and ready to intervene if it proved necessary.

Several hours later, Fianna spotted the broad, conical mountain that Nessie had mentioned. She'd said it acted as a protective fortress. The moon was barely visible as the dawn began spilling over the Vogelsberg Mountains; they were laced with tunnels, cut through the volcanic rock — some wide enough for a shuttlecraft to pass.

The tunnel entrance Celine and Fianna sought was on the southern end of one of the many terraces across the mountain's flanks.

"There is the place we are meant to land," said Fianna, "hold tight!" She spiraled down to the rocky ledge, then came to a landing noticeably more abrupt than her usual graceful touch-downs.

Celine slipped from the dragon's back and rubbed her saddle-weary thighs. "Thank you, my friend," she said, patting her friend's side affectionately. She could sense how tired the dragon was.

"Wow! What a view!" The two friends stood looking out over the vast park below. All was quiet, but for their breathing, and faint forest sounds from below. The lights of a ski hill still sparkled, but began winking out as the pair watched; the night was at an end. A few villages and chateaus were visible, here and there across the landscape. The mammoth blades of a modern "wind farm" turned slowly in the morning breeze, feeding power to the Germans' electrical grid.

From below them and to the right, Fianna heard a series of high, whistling sounds — short bursts in rapid succession, above the range of human hearing. Nessie had told her to be alert for this; it was a warning that the tunnel entrance would be open in two minutes. Once open, the passage would re-close after only twenty seconds. They had to get to that entrance, and fast.

Fianna told Celine that the signal had sounded, and urged her to mount up at once. Celine complied; the dragon sprang into the air and maneuvered down the mountainside to the tunnel entrance. It was so well disguised as part of the native rock that Fianna almost missed it. She landed gently, and the friends waited for the tunnel to open. In less than a minute, the big doors slid away to either side, revealing the tunnel's mouth. Dragon and Companion passed through, and the doors slid quietly shut behind them.

There was a soft light inside, provided by orbs set in the cavern's ceiling. There was a faint, fresh breeze, adding to the impression that they were inside a pleasant building, not a cavern carved from a rocky mountainside. Celine sensed the magic of the ancient place.

Numerous trails crisscrossed the hard-packed floor of the entrance area. They decided to take the most worn, which appeared to lead straight into the mountain and downward. The tunnel walls narrowed and lowered as they went along, to the point where Fianna was nearly forced to crawl. Celine was about to suggest they go back to the entrance chamber and choose another route, when they came to an opening in one side of the tunnel that led into a spacious, high-ceilinged room. It was clean and dry, and even had some simple human furniture, and what looked like a dragon's bed filled with clean straw.

As they passed into the space, Celine sensed that the opening was protected by an invisibility hex. It must somehow be selective, she realized, since she and Fianna had seen the entrance as soon as they came upon it. The hex didn't feel to Celine to have an evil origin, but she remained cautious.

Examining the room's contents more closely, Celine gasped. "Someone has been here recently. These blankets and clothes haven't been here long. And there's food that's still fresh," she said. Then she noticed a folded piece of paper, partially hidden by a plate on the small table. She picked it up, and froze. Her name was hand-written in the folded paper's center. She dropped it instantly. Her knife and incant-baton were out and ready before the paper reached the floor.

CHAPTER 22

Dragon Rider

Leaving Ahimoth to wallow in his misery, Soader made his way back up toward the tunnel entrance, chuckling as he went. He reached the massive door, pushed it open, and was instantly furious to find no one there to greet him. "Where the hells is that gods-damned Grey?" he yowled. He stabbed at the comm link next to the entrance and bellowed, "Someone get the hells down here and help me out of this gods-damned suit. Now!"

A Grey showed up within a minute, out of breath and spouting apologies. He helped the seething Rept out of his heavy suit, bowed deeply and scurried away without asking if anything else was needed. In any other circumstances, Soader would have punished the Grey for his laxness, but after his fresh triumph over Ahimoth, he was in what passed, for him, as a cheerful and forgiving mood.

That night, Soader barely slept; he was too excited at having convinced a Nibiru dragon to carry him, an achievement and honor few beings of any race had ever experienced. In truth, he

could scarcely have cared less about the honor factor. A dragon was just an animal, as far as he was concerned. All that really mattered was that he would now be able to travel to Nibiru and pillage its treasures. There were only two ways to reach the eccentrically-orbited planet, if one was not a dragon: as a Nibiru dragon's chosen Companion, or alone, after experiencing the legendary Dream. Dragons from other worlds could survive passage through the tube-chute, but only Nibirian dragons could link with a non-dragon and bear it safely through.

There was one small detail that wasn't mentioned in any of the legends or lore Soader had studied, though. No being with Rept-specific DNA could pass through the planet's shielding, even if linked with a Nibiru dragon.

After Soader's previous attempts to link with a dragon had failed, he had hit upon his scheme to force Ahimoth to create the bond. Gloating over his accomplishment, Soader was still troubled by the thought that he should have linked with Ahimoth at once, back there in the cavern — as soon as the dragon had capitulated. The thought of the dragon agonizing through the night over what it had agreed to — betrayal of its race and homeworld — was just too delicious to pass up. And so Soader had chosen to wait, and let the beast stew in its misery.

He could not wait for long, though. Tomorrow — or the following day, at the latest — he must return to the cavern, link with the dragon and depart for Nibiru. Otherwise, all his plans would collapse. First, however, he had to track down that damned Zulak's spawn, Celine. Time was running out. If he hadn't found the girl before tomorrow morning, he would be forced to contact Scabbage and wheedle out any information the bastard had. Not a pleasant prospect, but this had been such a great day that even the thought of speaking directly with the despicable creature couldn't dampen his mood. He finally fell asleep, for one of the most restful nights he'd enjoyed in ages.

After breakfast, Soader headed to his office to call Scabbage. Reaching the office door, he heard Scabbage's voice calling *him* over the comm link. "Soader? Soader! Answer me!" bellowed the High Chancellor.

"Well, well. If it isn't the royal troublemaker himself," snided Soader.

"Watch your damned tongue, maggot. I could end your existence in an instant," barked Scabbage, "never forget that." Then he fell into a violent coughing fit. Soader grumbled and wisecracked under his breath through the painful two minutes of the hacking bout. At last Scabbage regained control. "She's alive, Soader. The Zulak girl has surfaced. On Earth, of all places. You are to locate and secure her at once."

"What?" said Soader. "Earth? How in hells did she get to *Earth?*" He was suddenly quite willing to continue the conversation — not that he hated Scabbage any less.

"Yes, the girl's apparently on that damnable Planet 444 right this minute. All I know is that she's in a cold, mountainous place. But I'm not solving this for you — it's *your* job. Find her!" Scabbage broke out in an even harsher coughing fit. Soader took the opportunity to consider how he'd go about locating and taking Celine — and what her capture would mean for his future. His life was really turning around! Unbelievable! He hoped it would continue. Then he might be able to....

"Soader! Soader!! Did you *hear* me?" yelled Scabbage.

"Oh...no. What?" asked the Rept, more annoyed at being interrupted than embarrassed for ignoring Scabbage's near-death coughing experience.

"That Earthling, the one I want for my transfer, was also just located. He's on Erra. You're going to love this: he's with Zulak. On Zulak's ship!"

"What?? With Zulak?" replied Soader, now at full alert.

"Heh! Yes. With *the* Commander Rafael Zulak. And they're on their way to Earth to fetch the girl. So get your ass moving and find her before they do. And if Zulak happened to meet a tragic end while they're visiting Earth, well! Wouldn't that just be too, too bad?"

Soader would ordinarily tell Scabbage where to shove his "orders," or shoot back some sarcastic retort, but not today. Things couldn't have been better if he'd planned them. Zulak was coming! All he needed now was a simple ambush, and all would be right with the universe. With *all* the universes!

"Remember, you have to grab that boy, too — and bring both of them to me," nagged Scabbage, interrupting Soader's reverie.

"Yeah, yeah. Right. Got it," replied Soader, cutting the connection. "Haaarrrrr! What a day! Inconceivable!" He leaned back in his chair, called for some elixir, put his feet up and had a good laugh. "I can hardly believe it. A chance to get even with that shit, Zulak. And *he's* coming to *me.*"

The comm link sounded again. "Soader! Soader! Are you there?" asked a squeaky voice.

"Yes. What is it? Good news, I hope — for your sake."

"Yes, yes. I found out something about that girl you said you were looking for. She just left Scotland. She's on her way to Turkey to look for the spell books. Supposed to be stopping in Germany on the way. And you're not going to believe this part: she has a dragon! She's riding on a *white* dragon!"

Without so much as a grunt of acknowledgement, Soader cut the connection and sat staring into space, stunned.

"How can this be happening?" he muttered, incredulous. "How can *everything* be going my way?" He laughed and laughed. "A *dragon!* Haaaarrrrr, the gods are watching over me." He jumped from his chair and rushed to the cabinet where his dragon locator was kept. Pulling it out, he powered it up and tuned it. Sure enough, it registered a new dragon on the planet. "Yes, the gods are watching for sure," he laughed. Switching off the device, he barked at the comm link, "Mullins, get my dragon gear ready. Now!"

AFTER SOADER LEFT HIM, Ahimoth was motionless for hours, brooding over how he could possibly escape from his horrible promise. "I *cannot* link with that vermin. I'd rather kill myself," he thought. "It would be unforgiveable to take scum like that back to Nibiru." Thirsty, he flew down to the river. In the middle of a long draft of the cool water, he stopped suddenly and raised his head high above the current. *Current.* Flowing water. He began walking along the riverbank, smiling.

"The river comes in through the mountain, flows through the cavern and out again. It comes from somewhere, and then goes somewhere. Hmmm...." Excited, he leaped into the air and flew along the river's course toward the far end of the cavern. There the river disappeared into a tunnel, wide and high at its mouth, but quickly narrowing. The dragon settled on the bank and listened, ears cocked toward the river tunnel. "Ha! I can hear it! I can hear it! I can *do* this!"

This might be his escape route. Yes, he might very well be killed in the attempt, but that would be better than having to link with that foul Rept, and betraying his homeworld. Still, he was in no hurry to die — and a small, inner voice was telling him he would not. It repeated that he must escape, to save his sister.

His thoughts turning to Fianna, a sadness settled over the black dragon. "Where are you?" he asked, aloud. "Is he torturing you? He cut off your wing tip!" He hung his great head, silent. Minutes passed, but then he snapped upright, his eyes sparkling clear. He was resolved: he *would* find Fianna. He *would* save her from harm. He was *born* to protect her — to bring death to any who would harm her.

Free of his worried funk, Ahimoth realized Soader would return soon. He must make his escape at once. Without another thought, he waded into the large pool at the tunnel's mouth. Knowing he was watched, he pretended to be taking an afternoon swim. He made a few dives, swimming underwater one way and then another. After establishing this little pattern, he took a deeper breath and dove once again. This time, he made for the opening in the cavern wall, following the river's current. In moments, he was enveloped in darkness. He was inside the mountain channel!

The darkness was complete, and he was in the grip of the powerful, coursing current. Panic welled up — terrifying memories of being battered and tumbled in the tube-chute vortex. The small voice within him spoke soothingly, though, urging him to be calm, save his strength, allow the river to carry him to the light and freedom. He willed himself to relax, and discovered the current, though strong, was smooth and even. After several minutes, concern rose up again. Like most dragons, he could easily hold his breath for ten minutes or more — but would the river pass into the open again before that time was up? There was nothing he could do about it, so he relaxed again and flowed with the rushing waters.

Just as he was beginning to feel the need to breathe, the river shot out into the open again. He popped his head up, exhaled, then drew a fresh, deep breath. Looking forward along the river's course he was startled to see...nothing! In a flash, he was propelled out into open air — the river had dropped over a sheer cliff in a roaring waterfall. Tumbling downward, Ahimoth quickly righted himself, and began to open his wings to take flight. Before he could spread more than a third of the way, he plunged into a deep pool.

He folded his wings again and swam from the churning confusion at the base of the falls. Reaching calmer water at the pool's edge, he cautiously raised his head above the surface. He found himself, not in open country, but inside another cavern. It was similar to the one he'd just left, but seemed slightly larger. It, too, was artificially lit, but by a network of glow orbs set in the ceiling high above.

The sounds and smells were also similar to those in his former prison, with one important difference: he sensed there was another dragon here. Not Fianna, nor any other dragon he knew. He swam out into the current again, and along the stream's course, remaining submerged except for his nostrils, eyes and ears.

He'd gone only a short distance when he had a fresh surprise. He could hear Soader's voice nearby! He stroked against the current at once and moved shoreward, stopping behind a group of half-submerged boulders. He cautiously peered around the rocks and saw Soader, perhaps fifty yards away. Lying at his feet was a dragon.

An enormous, red dragon.

A dragon with two necks arching from its great shoulders, each neck ending in a ferocious-looking head. Both heads faced the Rept-hybrid, their eyes wide and staring.

RED DRAGONS ARE NATIVE to the planet Kerr (Planet 676, in the Pan-Sector Planetary Catalog).

Like several of the dragon species inhabiting this side of the galaxy, Kerr dragons are able to exert some control over space-time vortices. Millennia in the past, they had discovered and learned to control a vortex that had a terminus on their own planet. They'd used it ever since, to visit their fellow dragons (they thought of them as cousins) on Nibiru, and even to travel to Earth.

Unlike Nibiru, Kerr is not shielded or hidden, and any race capable of interstellar travel may visit there. Almost no one ever does, though. Kerr's dragon people generally dislike off-planet visitors, and have been known to kill them on sight, now and then. Because there is nothing on Kerr that anyone particularly wants, aliens tend to avoid it.

Soader had an excellent reason to visit Kerr, though — at least in his twisted estimation. He figured that if he could gain the confidence and cooperation of a Kerr dragon, he might be able to leverage the relationship to get close to one of its Nibiru cousins. He also guessed that his reptilian form would be similar enough to the dragons' that they would tolerate him. Tolerate him better than members of the more mammalian races, anyway.

He took a ship to Kerr, sent down a flock of reconnaissance drones, and began a covert survey of the planet's inhabitants, looking for a likely target for his little subterfuge. It took months of patient snooping, but he finally found what looked like the perfect candidate: a mutant dragon that had been exiled to a deserted island, owing to its chronic antisocial behavior.

The creature was huge — nearly half again as large as others of its race. That wasn't its chief mutation, though. Instead of a single neck and head, it had two. Each head had its own personality, one going by the name of Narco, the other called Choy. Narco was the dominant member of the pair — Choy always deferred to his decisions and choices. And, in matters of control of the big body they shared, impulses from Narco's brain always took precedence. Strangely, though they were two distinct personalities, the pair generally preferred to be addressed and referred to as a single entity.

Soader cautiously approached the massive creature, eventually gaining its willingness to engage in conversation. Pretending to sympathize with the outcast mutant's plight, Soader weaseled his way into his confidence. Though suspicious at first, the dragon's longing for friendly contact got the better of its judgement.

One evening, when the dragon was upset over a failed fishing expedition, Soader saw his chance. Sympathizing and soothing the big creature, he gradually, gradually managed to hypnotize him. With the dragon now under his control, Soader induced him to call up the vortex and travel to Earth. Specifically, to an enormous underground cavern he'd prepared for the purpose, near the off-worlders' facilities at Dulce.

Just as instructed, Narco rode the vortex to the Earth cavern, and settled down to await Soader's appearance with new instructions. The dragon was happy enough in his new situation; there was plenty of room, a pleasant, constant climate, a fish-laden stream running the length of the cavern, and plenty of tasty game. All in all, it was a much nicer place than his desolate island back on Kerr.

A month or so later, Soader took a spaceship to Earth, and was delighted to find "his" dragon had followed his orders to the letter. He rewarded Narco with good food and high praise, further cementing his control over the creature. However, when he attempted to convince the dragon to carry him in flight, he hit a wall; Narco flatly refused. This didn't stop Soader for long, though. He simply watched and waited for a new opportunity to hypnotize the dragon, seized the chance when it presented itself, and soon had the thrill of riding the great creature up and down the considerable length of the cavern.

That was not the last time Soader would use his hypnotist's skills to manipulate his huge, twin-headed prisoner.

"LOOK DEEP, DEEEEEP INTO MY eyes," Soader purred, gazing intently at Narco's face, less than two feet away. "Thaaat's right. Verrry good. You're feeling lighter now. You feel as though you're drifting, drifting pleasantly."

Ahimoth was close enough to see that the dragon's eyes were glassy — empty and flat, as if the great creature were in a trance — which was exactly the case. He marveled that Soader could ever have managed to lull the dragon into allowing itself to be hypnotized. Whatever his devious means might have been, the half-Rept had done it.

"Now, here is what we will do," Soader continued, his tone resonant and oily-smooth. "We will fly together again, as we have flown so well before. We will travel to Germany to find her — to the same place you have so recently been. If she is not there, we will fly on to Turkey. You will enjoy the challenging flight. You will enjoy carrying me, just as before. You will relish the chase, and the capture. We will leave immediately. We will fly hard and fast. Now I am going to count from five to one, and then you will awaken, refreshed and ready for the journey. Five, four, three, two, one." Soader snapped his fingers. Both faces came alert, eyes bright and focused. The dragon shifted a wing, allowing Soader to strap on a saddle that had been lying nearby. The Rept swung up into the saddle and the dragon reared up, ready to take flight.

Ahimoth was astounded at what he'd just witnessed. He was overjoyed to know that Soader was leaving. That would make his search for Fianna all the easier. Strangely, though, the quiet voice in his head urged him to follow Soader and the red dragon. Ahimoth was horrified at the idea — following these two would mean putting off his search for his sister! The voice repeated its advice, though — calm, reassuring and insistent.

So, when the red dragon leapt into the air and flew straight upward, Ahimoth waited a few moments, then emerged from the stream and followed, careful to remain directly behind his huge kinsman, in his blind spot.

Looking past the red dragon, Ahimoth could see it was heading for a large, round, black opening in the cavern's roof. We must be inside an ancient volcano, he thought — and that must be a vent to the surface. They entered the black vertical opening, more like a chimney flue than a tunnel. They continued upward, Ahimoth at what he hoped was a safe distance behind. Soon a spot of light appeared in the blackness above and began growing steadily: the opening to the surface!

The red dragon burst from the opening, flew upward for another several thousand feet, and then veered sharply to the east — toward the Atlantic Ocean, and Europe beyond. When he emerged, not far behind, Ahimoth stopped in the shadow of a spur of rock, allowing the red dragon and rider to get far enough ahead that they would not notice him trailing behind.

Soader and his enslaved dragon flew for hours, landing once so that the dragon could rest and drink from a lake. Ahimoth did the same, keeping out of sight. Soon they reached the continent's eastern shore and shot out over the ocean. The flight over water was grueling; by the time they made landfall on a remote stretch of the French coastline, the black dragon was near exhaustion. He landed in a woodland meadow not far from where Soader was making camp, and collapsed in the shadow of a stand of ancient beech trees. He was well enough concealed and far enough from Soader and the red dragon that they should not detect him, but close enough that his keen ears would pick up the rush of wings that would mark their departure.

As he rested, Ahimoth reviewed what he had heard Soader saying to the red dragon. He had no idea who might be the "she" Soader was after. It must be someone important, to risk such a journey. He worried again that it may have been a grave mistake to follow the pair. He was consoled by the thought that if Fianna was being held back at Dulce, Soader could not torture her while he was away on this mad search. The dragon prayed that, wherever she was, his sister was not in pain or peril.

Now Ahimoth recalled the German tunnels his parents had visited many decades before. Perhaps that was where Soader was going. Maybe that was where Fianna was being held — not beneath New Mexico! The thought bolstered his spirits, but unfortunately it also lulled him into a doze, which soon gave way to deep sleep.

Hours later, the dragon woke with a horrified start. Had he slept through Soader's departure?! A furtive inspection confirmed Ahimoth's fears. The dragon and the Rept were gone, and their sleeping place was cold. They must have left hours before. The black dragon cursed himself mercilessly. How could he have been so hideously, criminally negligent? Soader could be in Germany by now. Or well on his way to Turkey. Or anywhere!

Getting a grip on himself, Ahimoth recognized that self-recriminations weren't going to solve anything. He had to do *something*, and fast. But what? He hastily reviewed the situation, then smiled. He had a new plan.

CHAPTER 23

Thaddeus Greer

Celine stood in a crouch, ready to spring, her knife and incant-baton at the ready. She listened intently for any slightest sound that might betray the intruder's location. All she could hear was the pounding of her own heart. She bent cautiously and picked up the paper from the floor, wondering again at her name, written across its folded face. She placed it carefully on the table to her right, handling it as if it were dangerous, then turned a slow circle, straining to catch any noise and scanning every inch of the room.

"What is it, Celine?" asked Fianna.

Celine held a finger to her lips, and mented, "This paper. It's addressed to *me.*" She walked a full circuit of the room, searching for any sign or clue, but found nothing that spoke of danger. "How is this possible? Who even knows we're here?" she thought to Fianna.

"Perhaps West got word to one of her friends. I don't smell or sense any danger," replied Fianna. She, too, scanned the room, nostrils flaring.

"Neither do I," responded Celine. She sat in one of the simple chairs and unfolded the single sheet on the table before her, treating it as if it might suddenly explode. She gasped again; "It's in Pleiadean!"

"Please read it to me," said Fianna.

Celine nodded and began to read aloud:

> My Dear Princess Celine,
>
> We are honored that you and your dragon friend have come to assist us and our planet.
>
> Please make yourself at home here in this safe place. Eat, drink and take rest. You have had a long and dangerous journey, and another lies ahead.
>
> We are relying upon you to save us all, and beg to be allowed to help in any way we can. Please accept our deepest thanks for your coming.
>
> > May God bless you,
> > Your humble servant,
> > Father Thaddeus Greer XXIV

"Oh! You must be right — West must have gotten word to him," said Celine, smiling. She looked again at the food and clothing that had been laid out for them, then back at the paper in her hand. "Fianna, I'd say things are looking a bit better!"

The two ate a hearty meal, cleaned themselves up, and bedded down for the night; they were soon sleeping soundly. Hours later, they awoke to a very faint, low-pitched growling sound. "What was that?" asked Celine, instantly alert.

"It sounded like a dragon," replied Fianna, excited. "It came from far away; probably much deeper down the tunnels. There! I heard it again. It is most definitely a dragon — a dragon in pain! We must go to help."

"Wait. It could be a trap," insisted Celine. "We'd better go prepared." She hastily gathered their things, along with some of the food Father Greer had left them. "Okay, I'm ready. Let's go check it out."

Several tunnels led off from the chamber, in different directions. They made their way farther down the one they'd followed to reach the chamber. After just a few yards, Celine could sense that the hex that protected the chamber had relaxed to permit their exit. It closed again after they'd taken a few more steps.

As they made their way through miles of tunnel, they heard, every so often, faint, moaning growls. The sounds grew gradually louder, the farther they travelled. They seemed more like sounds of pain than of menace.

Finally, rounding a bend in the tunnel, they stopped short, staring. There, a few dozen yards ahead, were two adult dragons. They were chained to heavy metallic rings, set in the native rock of the tunnel wall. A pair of Repts was beating the larger of the two with heavy clubs.

"My parents!" roared Fianna to Celine, mentally — careful not to attract the Repts' attention by speaking aloud. "They are alive! How *ever* did they come to be *here?*"

"Just a moment," Celine cautioned. She crept along the tunnel wall to within ten yards of the oblivious Repts, quietly spoke an incantation, then stabbed her incant-baton toward them. A blue-white flash flew from the end of the baton, and the creatures instantly dropped to the cavern floor, unconscious.

"Quickly, Fianna!" said Celine — aloud, but voice tightly controlled. "We've got to free them and get out of here. Quietly, though; there may be more guards around."

Running to her chained parents, the white dragon called out, "Father! Mother! I am here — Fianna!" There was no response; the elder dragons just regarded her vacantly, dazed.

Celine shouted a word of power and struck at their shackles with her incant-baton; the bonds flew apart in a cloud of exploding dust. The dragons were free. Yet they just turned slowly and sat against the wall, giving no sign of recognition.

"They've been beaten almost senseless," said Celine. "Maybe I can help them." She pulled out her small grimoire, flipped a few pages, found what she was looking for and began a fervent chant. Fianna's parents stiffened slightly, their eyes closed, and each gave a low moan. Seconds later, they sat bolt upright. Their eyes opened, then widened in sudden recognition.

"Fianna?!" exclaimed her mother, Dini. "Fianna! It is you! It *is* you, precious daughter!" The three dragons fell together in a tearful family embrace. Even Celine was teary-eyed with joy and relief.

"Mother! Father! I am so very happy to find you! But how did you come to be here?" asked Fianna. "You have been gone for so very long; I almost cannot believe you still live." The family embraced again.

Before Fianna's parents could respond, Celine interrupted: "You both look like you're badly in need of some food and water. Your wounds should be tended, too. Let us take you to the cavern where we've been staying — I can help you there, I'm sure. But let's get away from here, fast! Before more Repts come!"

"Mother, Father, this is Celine," said Fianna. "As I am certain you have sensed, she is my Companion. She is also strong in the ways of magic. She has released you, but are you able to walk?"

"Let us see," answered her father, and he took several tentative steps. "I seem to be all right, though slow." Addressing his mate, he said, "And you, my dear?" Dini stumbled at her first attempted step, but caught herself, then managed several more, her certainty and grace increasing with each one. "It appears I am still mobile," she smiled. "But, Fianna! This is incredible. How did you *find* us?"

"Come, I will explain when we have reached a safer place," the younger dragon replied.

Celine led the party up the tunnel and back toward the cavern they'd come from, with Fianna bringing up the rear, watching and listening for any hint of pursuit. The tunnel sloped upward, and their progress was slower than Celine liked. The injured dragons needed frequent rest breaks, compounding the girl's concern. It was more than two hours before they reached the cavern.

As soon as they arrived, Fianna's parents hobbled as quickly as they could to the fountain, where both drank deeply. When their thirst was satisfied, they settled to the ground, exhausted and plagued by a myriad of pains.

"We don't have much to offer, but you should eat," said Celine, bringing out the fish remaining from Fianna's meal of the night before, and what would have been her breakfast. Then she went to the fire pit beside the ventilation shaft, lit a small fire under the hanging cauldron, and prepared an herbal salve to treat the elder dragons' many wounds.

When the mixture had been applied, she cast a healing spell. The dragons, relieved and grateful, settled down to rest. Celine made no objection — but she had a terrible sense that their time was desperately short; they must move on, and soon.

While they were eating, and submitting to Celine's ministrations, Fianna talked with her parents. "Father, Mother, please tell me what happened. How did you come to Earth?"

"Well, as you will remember," answered her father, "we had travelled to the far hemisphere to gather herbs. One morning, after our morning meal, your mother had settled in a grassy spot to preen, when a dragon — a huge, *red* dragon, with *two* necks and heads —sprang from a copse of trees, grasped her tail and began dragging her away. We both fought as best we could, but the two-head was at least twice my size and power, and a fire-breather. As we struggled, the mouth of a vortex appeared — as if from nowhere — and moved steadily toward us.

"We stopped struggling against the red one and attempted to flee, but in seconds the vortex mouth was upon us. All three of us were drawn into it. Your mother and I have long experience with tube-chute travel, so we managed to keep oriented and alive, but we had no idea where we were being taken. The red dragon appeared to be faring well, too. It was clear he was no stranger to vortex travel, and he seemed not at all surprised that this one had so suddenly appeared.

"After many hours, the tube-chute deposited us in a strange place — first me, and then your mother and the red dragon. We were so weak and weary from the passage that we just lay where we had landed, catching our breath and trying to get oriented. Then we suddenly realized where we were. The smell of the air, the color of the sky, and the deep vibrations of the planet itself made it plain that we were somewhere on Earth, our favorite vacation place. Clearly, though, this was no vacation.

"Within minutes of our arrival, up strode a Rept, or rather, a Rept-human hybrid. He was incredibly excited to see us — even more so when he discovered we were mates. Later on, your mother and I pieced together what we could recall of his maniacal jabberings and concluded that he was obsessed with having his own dragon eggs.

"Back to our arrival, though. With the strange red dragon's help, the Rept shackled us, led us to what looked like the base of a cliff, perhaps a mile from our arrival spot. There he chained us to a sheer rock wall. We eventually realized that the "cliff" was but one wall of an enormous underground cavern.

The Rept-hybrid — whose name is Soader — kept us captive

there for all the years since. He treated us well enough. I suppose he knew that there would be no eggs if he harmed us or neglected our health. But we were prisoners nonetheless. In all our time there, we could never discover a way to escape."

"That is horrible. Unspeakably *horrible!*" cried Fianna. "But, I am confused. There is no such cavern here. How did you come to *this* place?"

"Just this morning — at least, it seems to have been this morning — Soader and the red dragon came to us. Soader announced that the red one would be taking us to another place, and threatened that if we did not cooperate, we would pay dearly, with something more precious than our own lives. We suspected what he might mean, and agreed to do his bidding."

Both Fianna and Celine wondered what the venerable dragon might mean by "something more precious than our own lives," but they kept silent and let the elder dragon continue.

"Soader went on for a while, sliding into bizarre, incomprehensible ravings. We caught only bits of it — blatherings about tunnels and hostages, and bargaining chips, books, and revenge. At last he calmed, and ceased his ranting. He said something to the strange dragon; we couldn't hear what. The red brute nodded, and stepped closer to us.

"The red one struck an odd pose, then stared off into space, as if taken by a trance. His body hunched over like some sort of hulking, primordial beast, and both heads began an eerie, moaning chant. We could do nothing but watch and wonder.

"Suddenly, the mouth of a vortex appeared — very like the one that had transported us to the cavern, so many, many years before. It moved toward us; Soader stepped well away from its path, and laughed his brutish laugh.

"The vortex approached and engulfed us; your mother and me, and the red dragon too. After a relatively short passage, we found ourselves in this place. There were several Repts waiting for us. Before we could resist or escape, they seized us and chained us to the wall where you found us. Most of them departed, but for two who remained behind to guard us.

"Then, for no reason we could discern, the two began beating us mercilessly. The red dragon looked on, both faces smiling. After a little while, I heard him say something about 'return to the master.' Then he fell back into his weird, moaning trance; the vortex appeared again, swallowed him up, and vanished.

"We were left to the wicked Repts and their clubs. As our injuries became more and more painful, we began to protest, moaning and crying out. The Repts seemed delighted at this. They beat us all the harder, shouting, 'Go ahead, sure, sure! Moan an' cry! Screech an' groan! No one can hear you. Not here! No one gonna know 'bout yer poor, poor pains an' sufferin's! Not now — ha! But the boss says the white bitch and her girlie-girl friend gonna find out. Oh, yes — they finds out when the time be juuuust right! An' pay a pretty price to save yer sorry carcasses, too!" The dragon mimicked the churlish guards' speech almost perfectly.

"We had no idea what they were talking about, but in our agony, we were beyond caring.

"Then, suddenly, there was a brilliant flash, the beatings ceased and the Repts were gone. And there you were in their place, thank all the Gods!"

Just as Neal finished his account, a sound like a dragon's scream of rage welled up from deep, deep in the tunnels they had just left. Celine shot Fianna a sharp look of alarm; the white dragon mirrored it, and turned to her parents.

"Father, Mother, are you able to fly?" she asked.

"Yes, I believe we can," answered Neal. He watched with concern, though, as Dini opened and flapped her wings, too stiffly for his liking.

"I am in fine shape, when all things are considered," the matronly dragon asserted with a smile. "Celine's salve and magic have done their work admirably."

"This is good," said Fianna. "Now you must fly to a place of greater safety; you cannot remain here. Please follow us."

"But, our eggs! We cannot leave our eggs!" cried Dini.

"Your eggs? You have *eggs?*" gasped her daughter, incredulous.

"Yes, child. We have six precious eggs. Each was taken from us after it was laid, but later Rept guards began bringing them back to us several times a year, demanding that we bring them to hatching. We tried, of course, as one always must, but without success.

"When Soader threatened 'something more precious than our lives' today, we were certain he meant the eggs. We would have agreed to any demand.

"As the Repts you stunned were beating us, one of them told us that the eggs had been brought here, too. He did not say when or how, but that they were safe, and close by. He threatened that if we did not behave, there was no telling what might happen to them."

Another shriek reverberated up from the tunnels below. It was still far off, but seemed to have moved closer. "Now! Hurry! You *must* go!" cried Celine. "Fianna and I will go back for the eggs, once you're safely away!" The two led the parents toward the tunnel to the mountain's entrance.

"Follow us! Stay close!" Fianna insisted. "They cannot follow us in this tunnel — it is protected — but they may know another way out. You must get out and away as fast as you can."

Up the tunnel they all rushed, Celine leading the way. After a frenzied dash, the entry chamber and doors were finally in view ahead of them.

Suddenly, Celine had a terrible realization; Fianna caught

her Companion's thought the instant it was formed: *They had no idea how to open the doors!*

As if with a single voice, the dragon and the girl cried out, "NO!" in an agony of despair.

Then their cry was cut short as quickly as it had begun. The doors were sliding open before them!

They had no idea how this could be, but they had no time to waste in wondering. They rushed through the opening and out onto the ledge at the tunnel's mouth, the elder dragons only paces behind. Celine and Fianna anxiously scanned the skies above, the surrounding mountainsides, and the Vogelsberg Valley below. They saw no sign of danger. Yet.

"Do you know the way to Loch Ness?" Fianna asked her parents.

"Yes, from our vacations on this world. But, what of our eggs?" queried Neal. "And will you not fly with us?"

"No, we cannot. Not now," replied Fianna. "There is much that we must do before we can rejoin you, but I promise upon my life that we shall recover the eggs and bring them to you safely. Go. Find Nessie. She will keep you safe. If we do not arrive in two days' time, you must travel to Nibiru without us. We will follow as soon as we can, bearing the eggs."

"No, Fianna! No!" gasped her mother. "We must all..." but her entreaty was interrupted by a furious roar; it seemed to come from far below them and to their left. The dragon pursuing them had found another way out of the labyrinth of tunnels.

"Mother! Father! Now! You *must!*" cried Fianna.

"The eggs! Please, please, save the eggs!" Dini implored them, one last time. Then she and her husband leapt outward and snapped their great wings wide.

Another roar pierced the air, though the raging dragon still had not come into view. The two elder dragons, wings pumping furiously, disappeared into the gray cloud cover above.

Celine knelt, bowed her head and cast a spell of protection around the fleeing pair — the most powerful spell she knew.

Once the spell was cast, the companions rushed through the portal and into the entryway. Just as inexplicably as they had opened, the doors slid shut and sealed. At the same moment, a hard-flying dragon charged into the sky above, from around the mountainside. Ready to destroy what it was sure would be easy prey, it was baffled to find nothing but a barren, windswept slope.

"They'll make it, Fianna. Don't worry," said Celine.

"I know. I know they will," replied the white dragon.

CHAPTER 24

Turkey

When Celine and Fianna reached the priest's cavern, there was an old man sitting quietly at the table. A sturdy, enclosed crate rested on the floor beside him.

"I am Father Greer," he announced. "It was I who opened the portal for you just now, and sealed it behind you when you had achieved your worthy purpose. I sensed your urgent need, and spoke the words of opening and of closing when the times were ripe.

"The dragon eggs you seek are within this crate. I shall care for them until you return."

Fianna and Celine stood silent, astonished. "Th-thank you, Father," said Celine, "but, what...how...?"

The priest was not listening, though. He was hurrying around the cavern, from tunnel opening to tunnel opening, stopping at each and listening intently before dashing on to the next. Finally, he turned to the pair and announced, "You must go at once to Turkey. Follow this tunnel. It is safe, for the moment. It will take you to the far side of the mountain. From there you will begin your flight to the land of the Turks."

Fianna and Celine nodded agreement, but they were still somewhat dazed at the sudden turn of events. Agitated, the old priest urged them: "Hurry. You must hurry. There is no time to be lost. The red dragon will come again."

Celine felt there must be some sort of formal reply she should make, but all she could do was to bow and say, "Thank you for your kindness and generous help. We'll be back for the eggs as soon as we can. Can you tell us where to go when we reach Turkey?"

"You must go to the Third Portal, in the southeastern quarter of the city of Derinkuyu. On the quarter's main avenue, you will find an elderly beggar woman, sitting outside a yellow shopfront. She will give you further instructions for finding the Portal. Now go. You must leave at once!"

They thanked the priest and rushed down the tunnel he had indicated. It was hard going; rocks and debris slowed their progress, as did occasional potholes in the tunnel floor. It was particularly difficult for Fianna, who sometimes had to crawl to fit beneath a low stretch of ceiling. Eventually, they could see the faint glimmer of sky at the tunnel's end. When they had almost reached it, Celine stopped short, raising a hand for Fianna to do the same. "Wait!" she cautioned. "Before we go out there, we've got to make sure there's no one waiting for us." They stood — Celine with her knife and incant-baton in hand — and listened fiercely into the night. When both were satisfied it was safe, they stepped up to the opening.

"I do hope that my parents are all right," gloomed Fianna.

"I'm sure they are," replied Celine, "but when we're in the air, I'll call Jager and West. I'll get them to send someone to make sure they arrive safely."

"I thank you, my Companion."

"You are surely welcome, dear one. Now, we'll have to leave

right away if we're to arrive in Turkey before daylight. Are you able to continue?"

"Of course. Climb aboard," answered Fianna. Soon the two were high above the fleecy cloud deck, Celine hunkered down in the saddle and Fianna flying her hardest.

"West! Jager! Please help!" mented Celine. "Please hurry!"

"Celine! What's happening? Are you hurt?" asked a worried Jager.

"I am here, Celine," replied West. "How can we help?"

"No, we're not hurt, but we found Fianna's parents," replied Celine. "Soader has been holding them captive for years, under Dulce. Today he had them brought to the Vogelsberg tunnels, apparently to use them as hostages — bargaining chips. We discovered them and set them free, though. So much for his great plan. They're in poor condition, but able to fly. They are on their way to Scotland right now — to Nessie. I cast a spell to help them, but it may not last the night. West, can you help keep them safe?"

"Yes. We shall shield and safeguard them," replied the Mentor. "Are you travelling to Turkey?"

"Yes," answered Celine. "Soader has a dragon-locator device, and knew we were in Germany. I'm sure he'll guess that we're heading to the Turkish tunnels, to look for the treasure and the books.

"I suspect he'll leave us alone for the moment, but once we have the books, we'll be in serious danger. My guess is that he will let us do all the hard work, then hit us when we've found what he's after."

"You are very likely correct. We shall help as much as we can," replied West. "We're overwatching you now, but can only shield you while you're in the air. Once you're inside the tunnels, we will no longer be able to protect you. You will be on your own."

"Thank you, West," replied Celine. The two flew onward silently, each caught up in her own troubling thoughts. They talked with Jager and West a few times as they flew; otherwise they were silent. After many hours, they drew near to Derinkuyu at last.

"I'm afraid," said Celine. "I'm really afraid. I don't know if we can do this."

"Little One, I am fearful as well. That is to be expected—but there are many kind and powerful beings helping us. Do not forget that."

"You're right," replied Celine. I was happy to hear West say your parents are safe with Nessie. It must have been terribly hard to send them away, when you'd just found them after so many years."

"Indeed, very hard it was — but I know we are doing what will be best for all. We are following the legends, so I am certain that I shall see them again.

"We are very near to Derinkuyu now. Please be watchful for Soader and that red savage. I believe you were right in your guess that he will not strike until we have the grimoires, but we must still be cautious."

"That's the truth; I'm watching!" replied Celine. "Oh! There are the town's lights; and over there is the southeastern quarter. The beggar women should be waiting for us."

They landed among some trees on a small hill outside the town, near several tourist signs pointing out entrances to the ancient underground city.

"It's going to be difficult finding the Third Portal; there are so many!" said Celine. "I'll go look for the beggar. Wait here." After exploring a few streets, Celine found the one she guessed was the area's main thoroughfare, tiny though it was. Sure enough, within a hundred yards, there was a weathered yellow storefront. An old woman was seated before it, on a small

wooden bench. Celine approached.

"A friend from Germany sends his greetings," she said to the beggar, who appeared to be sleeping. She was not. She lifted her head, and held out a gnarled hand. Celine took out a gold coin the priest had given her, and placed it in the outstretched palm. The woman accepted the gift. Then, without a word, she gestured for Celine to go behind a tall wall to her right.

Celine mented Fianna, who was patiently waiting at the spot where they'd landed. The dragon stole through the streets following Celine's telepathic guidance, finally stepping out from the shadows to stand beside her Companion. The beggar did not flinch as dragon and girl walked past her and ducked behind the wall she'd indicated.

Down the pair went, descending a stone stairway into the dank tunnels below. "So that was the Third Portal," thought Celine; "not very impressive, for something so important." She pulled out her light-orb to help find their way; few lights shone in this part of the underground city. Soon there was no light at all, other than hers, and the only sound was their own footsteps. They agreed to mental communication only, until they were safely out of the tunnels again.

"Where should we look?" mented Fianna. "It is difficult to guess where the treasure could be, if no one has been able to find it for centuries. Father Greer's only advice was to look where we think we should not. Confusing."

"Confusing, yes. But I think he also gave us a hint," said Celine. "He mentioned more than once that we must take time for a drink from the special waters of Derinkuyu. I'm guessing he was alluding to the treasure's hiding place. In or near some water. I know he had to speak in riddles, in case someone overheard, but I think he meant to give us a clue."

"Once again, I believe you are correct. I have a fine nose for finding water, so let us put it to work," replied Fianna.

Several hours passed as the two investigated every room and passage they came to, every well and watering hole, and anyplace water was or might be stored. When they reached the city's lowest level, far beneath the surface, they sat down to rest.

Once they had settled, Celine became aware of a nearly imperceptible flow of moist air, wafting from the seemingly solid rock wall beside her. She got up and held her light-orb for a closer look; she peered up and down the wall's surface, from floor to ceiling and back again. She was surprised to find that a large section of the "wall" wasn't a wall at all. It was a masterfully fitted door, obscured by layers of dust. The door was locked, not with a physical mechanism but with a spell. She pulled out her grimoire and flipped through it by the light of her orb. Fianna looked on, intently.

Finding the spell she sought, Celine stood tall, placed the spread fingers of her left hand lightly on the door's cool, dusty surface, and recited a seven-line incantation. There came a faint creaking, and the door moved just enough on its fine, inset hinges to become easily visible. She gripped its edge, opened it wide, and with no hesitation, crossed its threshold. The dragon followed close behind.

Just inside the door was a landing of about a dozen feet, leading to the head of a gently sloping stairway; down they went, brushing aside ancient cobwebs, Celine's light-orb held before her. The stairway descended for dozens of steps, then ended in a large room that resembled a church refectory. A long table ran parallel to one wall, benches on either side. It was set with dishes, all covered in layers upon layers of dust. There was an air shaft near the entrance, so the air was breathable, if not very fresh. Judging from the dust, the place hadn't been disturbed in centuries.

Along the far wall, they saw an opening in the rock. Chest

high, a couple of inches in diameter, and modestly adorned with a ring of small, yellow tiles. A feeble trickle of water dribbled from the orifice and fell into a stone basin, several feet in diameter and resting on the floor. Its interior was glazed in the same yellow color as the ring of tiles above. Clear, cool water filled the basin nearly to the brim. Celine admired it briefly, then continued her tour of the chamber.

An old, old oil lantern sat on the table. There was no fuel for it, but Celine dusted it off, placed her light-orb inside and picked it up. "Nice!" she thought. "Probably historical, too."

Suddenly, a new thought struck her. She carried her improvised lamp back to the water basin and examined it more closely. The flow of water into the vessel was continuous, but slow. Yet the water level remained constant. Evaporation here certainly wouldn't be fast enough to maintain that kind of equilibrium, so why was there no overflow?

Kneeling beside the basin, Celine ran her hands over its smooth outer surfaces. They were dry, and she found no evidence of any outlet for the water within.

Fianna sat quietly, observing her friend's explorations. What had her so interested in the basin?

Suddenly, a wondering smile lit Celine's face. "Could it be?" she thought. She stood, and to Fianna's surprise, stepped gingerly over the lip and into the basin. She stood at its center for a moment, looped her lantern's lanyard around her neck, then sat straight down in the chilly water. Now she reached out her hands to either side, placed them against the smooth inner surface of the basin, and pushed.

Nothing happened.

She pushed again, harder this time.

Fianna gasped in horror. With a *whooosssh*, her Companion had vanished!

"Celine!" cried the dragon, rushing toward the basin. She

had nearly reached it when there came a loud splash. Peering over the basin's edge, she saw that its bottom had disappeared, revealing a smooth chute that angled sharply downward. At the bottom of the chute stood Celine, dripping wet and standing in a puddle, smiling like a lunatic.

"WE FOUND IT!" she cried, dancing a crazy little dance of joy. She held up her lantern so the dragon could see her. "I'm in a big chamber, and the treasure is here! It's beautiful — and there's so *much* of it. Gold and jewels, statues and carvings — it's amazing. And, oh! There's a chest that must contain the books!"

"Oh, Celine! You are brilliant!" exclaimed Fianna, craning her neck to get a better view.

"I'll get the books and bring them up," said Celine. "We've got to hurry. I have a bad feeling, as though something awful's about to happen. Watch out!"

The girl made her way through the heaps of treasure to the chest she guessed must contain the precious books. Reaching it, she dropped to one knee, said a brief prayer, and lifted the heavy lid. At first, her heart sank. The chest was filled with more jewels, and precious metals — coins and small, stamped bars. Where were the books?! Then she realized that the lid seemed heavier than it should be. She lifted it higher and looked up inside. There, strapped to its inner surface with jewel-studded leather bands, were two books.

She tipped the lid back as far as it would go, carefully unbuckled the straps, and brought out the books they had held.

Here they were. In her own hands. The Book of Mu, and the Book of Atlantis. She could scarcely believe it. There was no time to lose, though. She would have to examine them later.

Removing her bodypack, she took out a large piece of soft cloth she'd been carrying for this very purpose, and carefully wrapped the books. She slid the precious package into the pack and strapped it back on.

"I have them," she mented, as she made her way back to the spot where the chute had deposited her. "I don't see a ladder or stairs, so I'm not sure how to get out. Could you lower your tail so I can grab it, then pull me up?"

Fianna laughed. "I doubt any dragon has ever been asked for such a favor — much less a member of the Nibiru royal house!" she teased, but lowered her tail as she spoke.

It was too short. "I can't reach it," said Celine. "Give me a moment to figure this out." She found a stool in a corner of the chamber, positioned it under the dangling tail-tip and stepped up. She could just manage to get a firm grip. "All right — I have it! Pull me up, please!"

Fianna hoisted her Companion out of the lower chamber and deposited the girl by her side.

"Thank you, thank you!" smiled Celine. "Let's get out of here now — West said she and the Mentors can't protect us until we're up on the surface again." The pair clambered up the staircase toward the secret door that concealed it.

When they had passed through the hidden door, they shut it behind them; then Celine cast both an invisibility hex and a barrier spell, to further secure it. Now they had to make it back to the surface — fast.

They began the treacherous trek up the network of tunnels and stairways, moving as quickly but cautiously as they could. Finding the treasure had been the easy task. They feared that getting their precious burden out of these tunnels and back across a whole continent to Scotland would prove much more difficult.

"We're almost back to the surface," said Celine. "As soon as we're above ground, I'll call West to shield us. Are you ready to fly, once we're outside?" Fianna nodded. "Good."

In less than a minute, they had reached the portal to the

outside world. "All right, here we are," said Celine. She clambered into the saddle at once. "As soon as we've pushed the barrier open and passed through, let's go straight up. Ready? Push!"

CHAPTER 25

Invader Spell

Fianna shoved at the large door; it burst open and she raced through, Celine hunched down low and clinging tightly. Even before her tail-tip had cleared the barrier, the dragon snapped open her wings, pushed off with her massive hind legs and heaved downward in a mighty wing-stroke. They were airborne at once, arrowing straight up and away from the sleepy Turkish town.

Suddenly, winged disaster struck. The huge red dragon, both mouths gaping in a terrible double roar, dove at them from above and behind. "Fianna!" screamed Celine. The white dragon instantly dodged to the right and downward — just in time to avoid a full-on collision that would surely have been fatal. As it was, the red dragon's glancing blow spun Fianna out of control, stunned.

By pure instinct and muscle memory she pulled out of the spin. Her head cleared, and she frantically scanned the sky all around her for a glimpse of their deadly foe. Celine spotted the red fiend first, and mented her perception directly to Fianna.

It was above and to their left, heading into a tight turn to begin a fresh attack. Both Fianna and Celine realized that what happened next would be the true test of their hundreds of hours of training and practice.

The red dragon dove again, and again Fianna dodged — but the red anticipated her move and struck even harder than before. This time Fianna was not able to right herself before smashing into a hillside. Dragon and Companion tumbled over the grass and brush, narrowly missing a jagged outcrop that would surely have mangled them. They came to a stop, dazed but not badly injured. There was a tear in one of Fianna's wings, and Celine had collected some painful bruises.

"Are you injured?" gasped Fianna.

"Not...badly," grunted Celine, holding her abdomen. "Just... had the...wind...knocked out of...me. Few bumps...scrapes. You?"

"One of my wings is damaged, but that is all. Back into the saddle — quickly!" she urged. "Hang on. He returns!"

The red was diving on them once again. It would have driven them into the hillside, but Fianna managed to leap out of the way just in time; it struck the grassy surface and skidded to a stop less than fifty yards away. Soader, perched in a black saddle on the red's broad back, laughed maniacally through it all.

"West! West! Please! We need shielding!" called Celine. Before the Mentor could respond, the red beast leapt toward them, covering the distance in two bounds. Fianna, no match for the terrible creature in direct combat, feinted to her left, then jumped sharply to the right. The red's intended strike missed, but one of its heads swung round in time to sink its teeth into Fianna's right shoulder. It lifted the white dragon from the ground and tossed her as if she were a limp fish. She and her Companion would have been dashed into a rocky ridge, but West enwrapped them in her shielding just yards above the surface. The pair were spared the full impact, but still tumbled violently across the hillside and came up hard against a stout oak, dazed.

The red dragon had taken flight and now circled above. It sensed the Mentor's shielding — a new factor to consider. Spiraling upward, it weighed its options — all the while ignoring Soader's curses and screams of protest.

Soader was horrified that the blood-maddened beast might kill the girl — who he *must* capture alive — and the priceless white dragon, too. Worse still, the creature's fire-breath might destroy the irreplaceable grimoires!

Sprawled on the rocky mountainside, it was several moments before either Fianna or Celine moved or spoke.

"Thank the Gods for West's shielding!" Celine finally groaned, carefully assessing her body for serious injuries. "Now we *have* to get out of here. Can you still fly us back to Germany?"

"Yes, I believe so," replied Fianna. She got painfully to her feet, then shook herself tentatively, taking careful stock of her condition. There seemed to be no major trouble, so she leapt up into the air to test her airworthiness. "The shielding is helping to support me," she reported. "I can fly, but not as fast as I normally could — my wing and shoulder are weakened. If they hit us like that again, I fear it might finish me. I am not concerned about the dragon's fire-breath — Soader will not permit it, for fear of damaging the books. But we are still perilously vulnerable."

"You're right, but I have a plan. I learned a spell from Schimpel's grimoire that might be exactly what we need." Turning aside in concentration, she began reciting the chant for the Invader Spell, struggling to keep her voice even and her intention sharply focused on their foe.

Meanwhile, high above, the red dragon had decided that, shielding or no shielding, he could batter the white bitch and her pitiful Companion to death by hammering at them again and again. He cared nothing for Soader's foolish insistence that they be kept alive. He spiraled upward, reaching for enough altitude to achieve a devastating dive speed.

Celine was now nearing the end of the third repetition of her incantation, as Schimpel's instructions had specified. As she reached the final phrases, she raised her incant-baton and aimed it at the red dragon, high, high above. She completed the chant. If she had done her work well, the power of the spell was now poised for release at her final command.

Menting to West, she asked the Mentor to drop the shielding when she gave the signal, then restore it after a pause of five seconds. West agreed. All was in readiness. Celine strained to see the red dragon, thousands of feet above.

There he was — turning to the left in a wide arc, wings pumping mightily. It was hard to tell from this distance, but he appeared to be climbing.

Abruptly, the great dragon seemed to halt in mid-air. It became a mere dot — a tiny, ruddy dot, barely visible against the bright, blue sky.

Now the dot began to grow. Almost imperceptibly at first, but more and more rapidly with each passing second. The dragon was diving on them, at a terrible speed. Using skillful flicks of its wingtips and tail, the dragon had achieved a power-dive — descent at a greater velocity than even the most streamlined free-falling object could attain.

Celine suppressed the frantic impulse to call out to West, to release her protective shielding. Not yet! She steeled herself to grim patience, all her attention fixed on the red menace flashing down at her.

Mere seconds passed, but to Celine they seemed to crawl.

She was experiencing the slowed perception of time's passage in a crucial situation, a phenomenon familiar to consummate athletes and warriors.

Suddenly, she knew the moment had arrived. "NOW!" she flashed her thought to the Mentor. She sensed the shielding field vanish. Stabbing her incant-baton skyward, directly at the plummeting, double-headed demon, she shouted the word that would unleash the spell.

One instant, the dragon and his half-Rept rider were hurtling earthward at terrifying speed, the monstrous red beast bent on dealing their targets a fatal blow. The next, they were frozen, utterly motionless, in mid-air.

There was no shock, no jolt, as if the immutable laws of physics had been suspended. Their motion simply ceased.

They hung there for perhaps five seconds. Then, just as suddenly as they had halted, they began to fall. Neither dragon nor rider could move a muscle. Their hearts functioned, they continued to breathe, but they were otherwise utterly paralyzed — and utterly terrified to find themselves plummeting straight for the hard, hard ground below. There was nothing whatever they could do about it. Not even scream.

It took a moment for Fianna to register what was happening. When she did, she needed no urging. She launched herself skyward, nearly dislodging Celine from the saddle with the force of her leap. West's shielding had enveloped them again, but it did not interfere with her flight. If anything, it seemed to help, slightly reducing the air's resistance to their progress.

She flew as fast as her wounded body could manage, straight for Germany and the safety of Vogelsberg. The pair flew for hours, Celine helping Fianna as best she could with spells and charms. The Mentors' shielding helped buoy the dragon and kept them safe. At last they spotted Vogelsberg's familiar, conical mass rising to greet them.

Jager had been in near-constant contact with Celine throughout the flight, and was almost as exhausted as she by the time dragon and Companion neared the safety of the tunnels. "When we land, we're going to rest," Celine told him. "We'll be inside the shielded tunnels, so I won't be able to contact you. I'll come out and call you and West as soon as we're ready to head on to Scotland."

"That's good. *Queen Asherah* will arrive at Earth soon; we should be able to give you cover during the last leg of your flight."

"Okay, but...," answered Celine, "...but, my dad — how are you going to convince *him* to help? Doesn't he think he's coming to pick me up and take me home? What's going to happen when he sees Fianna? Unless we figure out how to convince him she's okay, he's not going to let me fly with her to Scotland, or Nibiru, or anywhere else. She's a *dragon!* He won't want me anywhere *near* her! What can we do?"

"Hold on, hold on — don't worry, sweet one. I'm sorry, but I forgot to mention that Major Hadgkiss and I have everything under control with your dad. Don't trouble yourself about him — or anything. It'll be all right. You just make sure you and Fianna get lots of rest and heal as well as you possibly can. And stay safe until we arrive! Okay?"

Celine sighed, "Oh, Jager, thank you! What a relief. Thoughts of Dad have been eating away at me for days, and I still don't know how to deal with him. I don't know how you and Major Hadgkiss managed it, but I trust you. Thanks again. Thanks a million."

"You're welcome, dear — that's what boyfriends are for. But hey, I just had a great idea! Maybe we could transbeam you and Fianna up to *Asherah*, and then back down — directly to Loch Ness. Or maybe even beam you straight from Germany to Scotland."

"Oh, that's a fabulous idea!" replied Celine. "Do you really think it's possible?"

"I'm not sure if *Asherah* can beam Fianna aboard," said Jager, "but I'll check into it. It would be great if we could. I'm partial to beaming you aboard first, and then back down. That way we could meet up at last! Even if it were only for a minute...well, think of it! I really don't know what's possible though, and we also have to go with whatever will be best for your mission. Even if your dad doesn't know exactly what the mission is!"

"Yes, do find out," she said, giving it her best businesslike tone. "If we could go directly to Scotland, it would be ideal. We must get back to Nibiru as quickly as we can, and travelling the tube-chute vortex is exhausting and dangerous. So any time and energy we can save is priceless. I'm not looking forward to dealing with Dad, though. The truth of it is, I really don't know how. If being face to face with him can be postponed until all this is over, that would be so much better."

"I agree. I'll go see Major Hadgkiss right now, and we'll work out the best way to go."

"Great — and thank you! At least some things are looking better and better," replied Celine. She sensed Fianna struggling, and went on, "I need to help Fianna now. We're almost to our landing spot, and as soon we're down I've got to tend her injuries."

"Okay. I'll arrange the transbeaming, if it's possible. In any case, I'm going to be in the landing party. I want to personally be sure Doc Deggers has given you two the thumbs-up before you risk that trip to Nibiru."

"Landing party? Doc Deggers?" asked Celine. "I don't think that will be necessary. I can get us in fine shape with healing spells. He doesn't have to go to all that trouble."

"There'll be no arguing, young lady," said Jager. "I insist, and that's that. You're both going to be checked out by the ol' Doc.

Period. Hells, maybe I can come with you to Nibiru to help. But whatever transpires, we'll be there in about six hours, so call me as soon as you step outside. Do you have a timepiece, so we can synchronize?"

"No, but that's a good idea," answered Celine. "I'm sure Father Greer will have something to keep time. If he doesn't, I'll count the minutes myself. I'm very precise, you know."

"I don't doubt it, girl. Look, I'll arrange it so *Asherah* jump-shifts precisely at 07:05, Erra baseline time. That's six hours and fifteen minutes from now — about 03:00, your time. I hope that will give you enough time to rest up. It will still be dark there, so you'll have better cover if Soader shows up."

"That's perfect, Jager. Or as close to perfect as we're likely to get. I'll make sure we're ready."

"Good. I'm going to get some rest too, as soon as we've worked out the transbeam plan. I've been up most of the past two days. If I sleep through my alarm so I'm still snoozing when you call, just call again, but shout!"

"That I will." She wanted to say more; after all, they were about to meet for the first time! She was just too exhausted, though, and her thoughts too easily fell into jumbled confusion. She settled for "Thanks again, Jager. For everything. I'll see you soon. I'm so glad you're here to help us."

"Always," he replied. "Now, go rest."

"Okay! Bye," she said, and swung her full attention to the dragon. "You're doing *so* well, Fianna. We're almost there."

Making her final approach to the mountain ledge, Fianna tried to angle in gently. But in her pain and exhaustion, she came in too steeply and fell, more than landed, hard on her side.

Celine tumbled out of the saddle and rolled to a stop against the mountain wall. She was desperately tired too, but had only minor injuries. For a moment, the two lay where they'd come to rest, breathing heavily. There was no time to waste, though. Soader could show up at any moment.

The bone-weary travellers hauled themselves to their feet and dragged their way to the spot where the tunnel entrance should appear. It opened when they were just a few feet away; once again, Father Greer had sensed their presence and need, and commanded the portal to admit them.

They staggered through the entryway and on down the tunnel toward the old priest's cavern. For the hundredth time, Celine checked the saddlebag. The Atlantis spell book and Book of Mu were still there, safe and secure.

"We've got to rest, Fianna, and I have to heal our wounds," said Celine. "If *Asherah* can't transbeam us, we're going to have to be ready to fly on to Scotland. The way we are right now, there's no way we could do that, let alone make the trip through the vortex. But listen to me — lecturing you on the obvious! I'm sorry."

"There is no need for apology, my Companion," Fianna replied. "I understand completely."

The two sat down to lean against the tunnel wall, for a few minutes' rest before making the final push to the caverns.

Suddenly, a voice came out of the shadows ahead. "You need not worry, my friends. I have gifts of healing that will mend your weariness and wounds in good time. Come now with me. You have nearly reached my refuge."

Celine turned to see Father Greer standing calmly in the tunnel before them. She did not have the energy to stand and bow properly, but dipped her head in thanks and respect.

"Thank you, Father," she whispered. "Do you have a timepiece?"

"Yes, and I shall inform you when the time draws near to 07:05, in the reckoning used upon Erra," he replied, smiling as the girl's eyes grew wide in amazement.

"How...?" she began; but the priest had already turned his attention to Fianna.

"And do not trouble yourself about the great ship's ability to transport you. I shall mend your hurts, and you shall be well refreshed for your flight, if fly you must."

"I thank you, good friend. I fear I am in worse condition than I thought," said the dragon. She turned from the priest to address Celine. "I am sorry, dear Companion, but in our pausing here, I have seen that I shall need at least two days' repose, and powerful healing help as well, before my wing and shoulder will be able to bear the strain of the flight and vortex passage. It was only by the virtue of your help, and West's, that I was able to come this far."

Celine nodded her understanding, then reached up to give Fianna a gentle hug.

Father Greer addressed them again. "There is no need to travel farther just now. We can continue to my caverns soon enough. For the moment, be at peace."

They watched as the old priest approached, stopped directly before them, closed his eyes and raised his slender, gnarled hands. After a few moments' silence, he began to chant in a language they didn't recognize, his breath faintly visible in the chill, moist air.

Within seconds, both travelers felt the warming, soothing effects of the man's magic, spreading from one cell to the next, pervading their entire bodies.

At first, Father Greer gave most attention to the worst of Fianna's injuries, then broadened his focus to their general weariness, and the depleting effects of their recent ordeals. Soon both were lying still, nearly dozing, on the cold tunnel floor — as comfortable as if it had been a deep feather cushion.

Celine was amazed at the power of the priest's magic. She knew it would have taken her an hour or more to effect the healing he had rendered in mere minutes.

His chant completed, Father Greer lowered his hands and opened his eyes. He smiled as Celine stood and bowed gratefully; Fianna followed suit.

"I don't know how to thank you for your kindness and help," said Celine. "I hope that our presence here hasn't put you in danger — and that you'll be safe when we have gone."

"You needn't be concerned for us here — we are safe enough. And your efforts and those of your friend here are more than thanks enough for me and for my brethren," he replied. "If you succeed in your quest, you will have done much to stay the tragic downward spiral of morals and ethics on this planet. It will be I who must thank *you*." He smiled again, and bowed deeply to the weary pair. "Come now. I'll prepare you a warm meal before you bed down."

Celine and Fianna bowed once again as he turned to lead them on down the tunnel to his home.

CHAPTER 26

Feelings

Back in Father Greer's cave, the old priest went about preparing food while Celine removed Fianna's saddlebags and saddle. As the dragon carefully stretched and ruffled, delighted to be free of the burden, Celine retrieved a long, stout stick from the priest's woodpile and began scratching the dragon's back and flank, taking great care to avoid bruises and wounds. She knew just the right places, and the perfect pace and pressure; Fianna was soon purring like an immense, white kitten (never mind the wings, fangs and talons). The two were quiet in their thoughts as they indulged in the little end-of-the-day ritual they'd come to love.

A while later, the humans' dinner prepared, Father Greer called Celine to the table, then opened a large barrel of fish that sat close by. The humans sat and ate in silence, while the great dragon dined as daintily as she could manage, hungry as she was. Their meal over, Celine and Fianna headed to their beds, hoping that when they awoke and made their way outside, Jager would relay the news that he could transbeam them to

Scotland — or at least up to *Queen Asherah*. Neither liked the thought of a long flight to Loch Ness, and hoped it wouldn't be necessary.

Fianna curled up on a deep pile of sweet, fresh straw, while Celine crawled into the comfy bed she'd enjoyed on their earlier visit. Both were asleep before they could even thank their host and say good night.

A few hours later, something woke Celine. Unsure of what had roused her, she raised up on one elbow and reached out with her senses. She could only hear an occasional soft sound from Father Greer, tending a pot at the fireplace. There was also the slow, steady rhythm of Fianna's breathing, but nothing more. There were no out-of-place smells or other signs of danger, so she relaxed.

Father Greer, hearing her stir, turned and smiled.

She felt safe, for now. Sinking back into the comfort of her bed, she turned to her thoughts. She wanted to concentrate on important issues, like how she would learn the spell that would lift the hex on the dragons' eggs — but thoughts of Jager kept getting in the way.

Her feelings surprised her. Just thinking about Jager warmed her cheeks...and more. She used to be embarrassed at such sensations, but over the past few days, her attitudes seemed to be changing. She wasn't sure what was happening, and trying to examine the situation from different angles didn't help a bit. She felt maybe it all had to do with past-life experiences and relationships with Jager, but couldn't pin down any details.

Somehow, she felt more...complete. Yes. That was the word for it. Complete, yet it was also as though she were becoming more than just a single person. The concept was tenuous; she knew she couldn't have explained it to anyone else, not even Fianna. And the closer the time came to meet Jager, the more intense the feelings became.

She'd first noticed the changes a few days before, when she and Fianna arrived on Earth. Contacting Jager for the first time in more than a year, she was delighted, of course — but there was also a completely new physical sensation. New to this lifetime, at least. As the days passed, the sensations had intensified, affecting her only physically at first, then, by degrees, mentally and spiritually as well. Now, as she lay snug under the warm furs and savored these new feelings, something sudden and unfamiliar occurred. It was as if a switch had flipped on, and an unfamiliar new energy had begun to flow; alive, pulsing through her nerves, complementing and reinforcing her thought waves ten-fold.

This energy resonated at a wavelength she suddenly recognized: the wavelength of aesthetics. She felt compelled to experience the energy completely; to dissect it; to understand its every nuance. Fascinated by how this exhilarating energy was affecting her, she pulled the furs completely over her head and lay in the warm darkness, trying to see if she could control the sensation — amplify it, diminish it, alter its character.

To her surprise and delight, she found she could. She began to play with it, using it to mock up images and objects in the crisp air above her. Her head fully covered, she would create an image outside her blankets — then yank the furs aside to find the precise image she'd pictured only in her mind now clearly perceptible to her normal vision, floating a short distance above. She practiced this new skill — or was it just a sort of trick? — for quite some time, until she heard Fianna begin to stir.

"How are you feeling, Fianna?"

"As a dragon should!" her friend laughed; Celine joined right in. "I would certainly love more rest, though. Much more. And more of Father Greer's wonderful healing magic as well. I suspect he put something in our food, too!" she smiled, winking at the priest who'd been watching them as he puttered about. "I am sorry, Celine — I do not mean to belittle your fine healing skills."

"Oh, don't worry!" laughed the girl. "I'm just a dilettante, compared to Father Greer. I could use a few more hours of rest, too. I felt like I hadn't slept in a week, and I don't think I've really caught up quite yet. I'm afraid we'll have to wait, though. At least until we're back on Nibiru."

"I feel the same, my Companion. Have no worries, though. I shall be all right," replied Fianna. "I believe I will be ready to fly in another day, or perhaps two, with more of Father Greer's help. I would need that time in any case; in my present condition, I could not travel the vortex, whether we were transbeamed to Scotland or not."

"Please don't worry, Fianna. It's okay. I'm sure we can stay here as long as we need," said Celine. She looked to Father Greer, who nodded agreement.

Then he announced, "It is nearly time for the great ship to arrive."

"Thank you, Father," said Celine. She turned to Fianna; "I'll head up the tunnel to see if *Asherah* is here. If she is, I'll transbeam aboard to talk with my father and Jager. You stay here and rest. Okay?"

"No, I will not," insisted Fianna, struggling to rise. "I will not allow you to go outside without me. There may be dangers there."

Fianna became more agitated as she spoke, and continued her attempts to stand. It was no use, though — her forelegs folded under her, and she groaned and winced at the persistent pains in her shoulder. Still she managed to scold Celine; "You could be trapped out there. And Soader and his red beast could be waiting for you as we speak."

"Please pardon my interruption," said the priest, "but I do not sense the Rept-hybrid or his poor, misshapen dragon. I believe that for the moment it is safe for Celine to step outside the tunnels' protective shielding. I can control the entrance from the inside, and will wait with her until she is transported to the great ship. Then I will wait one hour for her return. Does this plan meet with your approval?"

"Yes! Oh, thank you, Father Greer," said Celine. Fianna shrugged in reluctant agreement, wincing again at the stab of pain even that simple movement evoked.

Celine hugged her friend warmly. "I love you, Fianna, and I thank you for caring so. I'll be back. Please don't worry. Rest! We need you well and strong."

Celine followed Father Greer up the tunnel, struggling to ignore the mental waves of Fianna's distress. Celine's own injuries nagged at her as she walked steadily upward, but far less than she'd expected they would. Fianna must have been right — there *was* something in that food! Curious, she rolled up a sleeve to examine what had been a large, ugly bruise only hours before. Now there was just a tinge of yellow, and even that seemed to fade before her eyes.

Soon the girl and priest stood at the hidden entrance. What seemed an ordinary tunnel wall of stone suddenly transformed into a pair of doors, which slid silently open to reveal a moonlit mountainside panorama. The two stepped cautiously out onto the broad ledge before the entrance. "It is safe, my child," reassured the priest. "We are the only creatures present. I shall wait with you until *Asherah's* arrival."

"Thank you, Father. I'd like that," replied the girl. She started to say more, but stopped short when the huge, shimmering bulk of the ship appeared high in the sky above them, reflected moonlight glinting from its side. "It's the *Queen*," gasped Celine, jumping like a child. "Jager! Are you there?"

"Yep — here at last!"

"Oh. Oh! This really *is* happening," she said, half to herself.

"Yes, my dear, it is!" With an effort to be businesslike, Jager continued; "Now, how would you like to go about dealing with your father?"

"I've been thinking about that a lot, I can assure you! Fianna won't be able to fly for another day or two, so here's what I think might work. First, can you tell me if Dad is aware of our menting ability, and that we've been in touch?"

"No, he doesn't know. I've kept it secret from everyone but Major Hadgkiss."

"Oh, good. That's a relief. I was worried he might know. It's okay that Major Hadgkiss does, though — that will help with what I think we should do. I only have part of a plan, though, so I need your help."

"Okay, shoot."

"I don't think Dad should know about Fianna yet. No matter what we might say, I think he would try to keep me away from her — and I can't imagine he would allow me to go back with her to Nibiru. But we *have* to go."

"I've been thinking the same thing," replied Jager. "Your father believes you've been helping 'a friend' find her brother, so maybe we could say you haven't found him yet. How does that sound?"

"Yes. I was thinking along those lines, too. But I probably shouldn't talk to him directly. I just don't think it would be smart. I'm aching to see him, and you, too — but that doesn't seem like a good idea now either."

"Ohhh! I'm hurt, Celine!" said Jager, playfully.

Knowing he was only teasing, she continued; "I'm so sorry, but I don't want to beam aboard right now. It's just that I know my dad. No matter what, he would try to keep me on the ship, and he'd forbid my leaving to help Fianna. He'd put me in the brig if he had to. I don't want him to beam down here, either. Do you have any suggestions?"

"Hmm. You've brought up some good points. That's smart. How about this: I'll talk with Major Hadgkiss; I'm sure that between us, we can come up with a good reason to keep you and your dad apart. For now, anyway. Maybe we'll convince him to let Major Hadgkiss lead a landing party to see you, instead of himself. I'll let the major deal with that."

"Okay, that sounds fine."

"But why don't you want me to transbeam down, Celine?"

"I...I...I do, Jager," she stuttered. "I just don't know if we should be together in the same place right now, without West present. You know — because of the ancient stuff and all. It would be like putting the password for a top-secret account on full display, so to speak."

"Ohhh, okay. That makes sense," laughed Jager. "I thought maybe you were just playing hard-to-get or something, sweet cheeks. Or that maybe you had another boyfriend on the side."

Celine blushed, realizing Father Greer was probably hearing everything. She decided to use the man's presence to change the subject. "Jager, I want you to meet Father Greer, one of West's friends. He's been helping me and Fianna."

"It's a pleasure to make your acquaintance, Father Greer," said Jager. "Thank you for helping our little universe traveler."

"You are most welcome, my son," said the priest. "I am sorry if I seem rude, but I must agree with Celine. The two of you should not be together in the same location. Not yet. When West and her sisters have returned, it should be safe. Until then, I believe that your plan to have Major Hadgkiss beam down with a small landing party to 'find Celine' is a wise one.

"The major could remind Celine's father that as *Queen Asherah's* commanding officer, joining such a landing party would violate Lesser Repts and Humanoids Policy. To be specific, L.R.H. Policy 425.236, paragraph two, which states: 'During times of war, no vessel's commanding officer may set foot upon the surface of any primitive planet until an advance landing party has performed a thorough site inspection and verified that the immediate area is safe.' The major should say all this in the presence of the bridge crew, so that the commander will have no choice but to comply."

"Wow! You're so full of surprises, Father!" laughed Celine. "That's a perfect solution."

"I agree. What a great idea," said Jager. "I'll go talk to the major right now. He and the party should be there soon, so don't go anywhere, sweet cheeks."

Celine blushed, knowing the priest was receiving everything she and Jager said. "I wish I could come along with them," added Jager.

Major Hadgkiss had been waiting quietly while Jager contacted Celine. The moment Jager called on his private comm link, Dino stood and walked off the bridge, into the map room. Less than a minute later he emerged, and requested permission to enter the commander's ready room.

"Enter," said Zulak, without looking up from his console. The major entered, and the door slid closed behind him.

"Hello, sir," said Major Hadgkiss, "I'm here to..." but the rest of his words were drowned by the commander's shouts.

"It's here! Right here! Celine's locater chip! She's here!" yelled Rafael, pointing excitedly at his screen. "You're in command, Dino. I'm transbeaming down to get her. Now!"

"Raff, wait — I don't think you should," said Dino, softly but firmly, grasping his commander's shoulder in friendly restraint.

"What the blazes are you talking about?!" barked Zulak. "Are you crazy?"

"Raff," replied Dino, "I don't have to tell you it's totally against regulations for a CO to go planet-side before the area has been deemed safe. I know we've skirted that rule before, but this time I don't think it's wise at all. The risk is far, far too high. Besides, don't you think there's a better way for the two of you to meet, after all that's happened these past eighteen months?"

"What I think is that you've lost your precious little mind, Dino," growled Rafael. "I'm going down there. She's still a child! *My* child! *Your* goddaughter, for the Gods' sakes!"

"I understand, Raff. But step back and take a cold look at this. Soader was involved in her disappearance, and there's every chance he's involved with whatever's going on here, too. We don't know that that's a legitimate signal. We don't know it isn't all a trap. You've got to admit it's exactly the sort of thing Soader would pull. I can see *you* coming up with such a trick in similar circumstances — and chances are good that you'd pull it off, too.

"Let me lead a party down there to find out what's *really* going on," Hadgkiss continued, "and we'll go from there. That's per regulations, and under the circumstances I happen to think the regulations make damn good sense. It's bad enough that Celine's been missing. I'm not going to risk losing *you* now, too. And just imagine what the admiral would do to both of us if we went off book and fell for such a stinking obvious ploy."

Zulak stood silent over his console for a while, staring at the screen. Then he slowly lifted his head to look at his loyal friend. "All right, Dino. You're right. We'll go with the book this time. But when I get my hands on that girl, I'm not letting go until she's home and safe. And look, if she's there — and I damn well hope she is — give her this comm stone."

"Aye, commander. I think your plan should be most effective," replied the major, with a smile and a wink. He pocketed the stone, saluted his friend and strode from the ready room, calling for his regular landing party to meet him at once in Transbeam Station 3.

The group assembled, orders were given, coordinates were set, and they were ready to go. Just before they were beamed down, though, Major Hadgkiss very quietly gave his team an unusual final order: "Switch off your comm pickups. I'll explain later."

As Celine and Father Greer sat watching the setting moon, five white-uniformed figures materialized on the ledge, to their right. Celine jumped up and rushed to her godfather, both crying tears of love and joy as they embraced. Doc Deggers, Madda, Sreach and Jessup stood silently by, watching and grinning. Each gave Celine a hug in turn. She introduced the team to Father Greer, who opened the tunnel and led them inside, Celine walking arm-in-arm with her godfather.

Safely inside with the entrance sealed, Dino called for attention. Speaking first to his team, he said, "Thanks for switching off your comm pickups. I know that's unusual, but this is no usual situation. That will soon become clearer." The major looked from one crewmember to the next; he could see they were all with him, even if they didn't yet have a complete grasp of what was going on. He'd earned their trust in their years of close and often hazardous work together.

"If you'll excuse me for a moment, I need to speak with Celine in private. Stay at the ready, though; we'll return to the ship shortly." The team nodded, and Dino and his goddaughter stepped aside to a small alcove.

"Jager says you're not hurt. Is that correct?" asked Dino.

"That's right. I'm fine — but my friend was hurt badly and needs time to heal before we continue our quest," the girl replied.

"All right. And it's okay — I know Fianna is a dragon. I know a great deal of what's going on; Jager filled me in. Including the fact that you need more time before you head home."

"Oh! What a relief! I imagined you knew, but I had to be sure."

"I'm so proud of you, Celine," he said, gripping her shoulders. "But we've got to deal with your father delicately, as I'm sure you're aware." Celine nodded, and the major continued. "In a minute, I'm going to beam back up and tell your father we've found you. I'll explain your situation in a way he should understand. He won't like it, but I think he'll agree. I'll explain that you and Fianna are sworn 'blood sisters,' bound in a solemn ceremony and pledged to mutual assistance. Despite his fatherly misgivings, he'll understand and respect the honorable aspects."

"Whoa, that's perfect. Better than I could have come up with," said Celine. "I suspect you might just have done this sort of thing before," she added, with a conspiratorial smile. "Best of all, it's essentially true," she laughed. "If it weren't, it wouldn't work! Dad's too smart, even if he can be awfully silly sometimes." The major returned her grin. "Thank you so much, Dino. What a relief. Dad's still going to be mad and give me hell, but I know he'll see sense, and agree."

"He'll give you hell, all right. But yes, I'm sure he'll also agree and send you on your way. Probably on the condition that you be quick about it."

The pair rejoined the waiting landing party. "Okay, here's what we're going to do," began the major. "I'm going to leave you all here with Celine and beam back aboard. I'll have a talk with the CO — I expect it will take less than an hour. Then the two of us will return."

Major Hadgkiss and Celine followed Father Greer back out onto the ledge; the rest of the landing party remained inside. Dino smiled at his goddaughter as he disappeared in a transbeam swirl.

The girl and old priest sat in the shadows, waiting for the major and her father to arrive. Father Greer sensed Celine's anxiety and kept quiet, ready to respond if she spoke, but content to remain just a comforting presence as they waited.

CHAPTER 27

Honor

O nce back aboard, the major rushed to meet the command-er in his ready room. "What the hells, Dino?" barked Zulak. "Why didn't you respond to my calls?"

"Sorry, Raff. The whole area is shielded. No normal trans-missions get in or out. Fortunately, the system is so ancient it doesn't interfere with transbeaming."

"Well, it must not block locator chips either — lucky for you, I could see you were all still there and alive, or I'd have vapor-ized the place. But to hells with all that. Why isn't Celine with you? And where's the rest of your party?"

"Celine is safe. She's still down there, with the landing par-ty. Raff, she's fine — she's all right. She's just not ready to go home yet."

"What in all the Gods-damned hells are you talking about, major??" howled Rafael, pounding a fist on his desk. "What do you *mean*, 'she's not ready to come home?' You are to trans-beam directly to the surface and return with her. At once!"

"Respectfully, sir," Dino replied, "not until you've heard me out. You know I understand how important this is to you, and you know I would not act in any way that might endanger the girl. So please listen to what I have to say. Sir."

Rafael regained a bit of his composure. He knew Dino was right. "Out with it, then. This had better be good."

"Celine is not ready to go home, because she hasn't finished what she pledged she would do. She is honoring a solemn commitment."

"Are you *serious?*" the commander yelled back. "*What* Gods-damned commitment? That's my *daughter*, and she's in *danger*. Don't you *care?*"

"Of course I care, Raff. Don't be absurd. But take a step back and look at this. You should understand it better than anyone. You raised the girl. You taught her her values. You made it clear those values were sacred, and set a fine example of how to live them. You can't argue that now, and you can't violate it. You should be *proud* of what she's doing. And at her young age! She's honoring a pledge. A pledge to someone who saved her *life*. Interfere with that and you'll make nothing of everything you've taught her — and she'd be justified if she never forgave you for it. That girl was missing for *months*, Rafael. She's only asking for a few more days. That's not going to mean the end of the bloody universe."

"Okay, okay. I get it. You're right. But you're not the one who'll have to deal with Remi. I can just hear her. Believe me, you won't want to be within a light-year when she gets going."

"You're absolutely right. And that's precisely why she will never know a thing about it. Why should she? She's not here. She's not monitoring you. You're not under orders to report to her with every detail of every decision you make or action you take. The *objective* is to get Celine back. And you will. *How* you do it is *your* business. And think about this: If you over-ride Celine's decision and force her to come with you, you'll be making a colossal mess, as we agreed just a minute ago. How do you think Remi will respond to that? I'll tell you how: you'll be in deeper trouble with her — *and* your daughters — than ever."

Zulak sighed. "Right. Right again, damn it. But if anything happens...if Remi finds out I had the chance to bring that girl home and didn't take it..."

"IF that happens, I'll tell Remi that it was *my* decision," said Dino. "And that will be the truth. I'll handle her. Remi isn't already mad at me, and she'll listen. She'll scream her head off and probably bust up some furniture, but she'll listen, and she'll see sense — just like you're seeing it right now. Okay?"

Zulak sat, slumped and silent, for nearly a minute. Then he wearily raised his head and gave his loyal friend a long look. "All right. You're right about everything. As usual. Thank you. But look — the ship can't stay here while she takes care of this commitment of hers. We'll have to come back for her. So, if I let Celine do this, you've got to assign someone to monitor her. I know that's against regs, but I don't give a damn."

"No, that's a fine idea, Raff — regulations or no regulations."

"All right, then," replied Zulak. "But even though I'm saying that, I want you to know I'm not happy about any of this. I'm only agreeing because I think your judgement under these circumstances is probably better than mine. Listen, though: if I find out Celine's in any danger, we're coming straight back and extracting her, commitments be damned."

"Aye, sir," agreed the major. "So, let's beam down there so you can at least see her for a bit before we leave."

The two made their way to the Transbeam Station, and soon stood on the ledge before the tunnel doorway. There was Celine, a blanket thrown over her shoulders and clasped at the neck as a cloak, to hide the sorry condition of her uniform.

Father and daughter rushed together and held each other

close, tears of relief and happiness flowing freely. Finally, Rafael pulled reluctantly back and looked his little girl over. "You're thin," he observed, gruffly.

"Yeah, my friend isn't as good a cook as Mom. And I've been exercising lots."

"Hmph. Look, are you really okay?"

"Yes, thanks. My friend took a nasty fall and hurt herself, but she should be okay soon. And as soon as she is, and we've found her brother, I'll be ready to come home."

"So I hear," he replied.

"We heard a rumor that Fianna's brother was seen near here last week, so I have a feeling we'll find him within a few days."

"Good."

"Yes — it's great. His family misses him so badly. Thanks for understanding, and letting me stay to finish what I promised."

"You're welcome, Precious. But look — this is between you and me. Please don't tell your mother about it. Okay?"

"Of course, Daddy. We'd never hear the end of it!" laughed Celine.

"No, we wouldn't," he smiled. "Do you need anything? Anything at all?"

"Not really, but thank you. I'll be home in a matter of days, so I can wait," she said, smiling back at her father. "When I do get home, I can't imagine anything I'd like better than one of Mom's suppers — with the family all together."

"Okay. You keep safe. We won't be able to check on you daily, so I'm trusting you to take care of yourself. In exactly three days' time, we'll be back here to collect you. Mark this moment exactly."

Father Greer heard the commander's order, and assured the man that he would set his timepiece accordingly.

"I understand, and I'll take care, Dad. Thanks again for letting me do this. I love you!" They embraced briefly before the commander backed away, spoke into his comm pickup and vanished as quickly as he had arrived. Celine looked wistfully at the spot where her father had just stood, then rejoined the major and priest.

"How did you convince him?" she asked Dino.

He smiled and winked; "You're not the only one who knows how to charm your father." They both had a good laugh, as they followed Father Greer through the entrance. Rejoining the landing party, they all trooped down the tunnel to the priest's home.

Celine had mented Fianna to let her know they were on their way, and not to be startled at all the company that was about to appear. When the group reached the warm, fire-lit room, Fianna was standing ready — though a bit unsteadily — to greet their guests. Dino had briefed the party on what to expect, so they weren't shocked to be welcomed by a dragon.

Fianna bowed to them graciously, and Celine made introductions all around. The formalities completed, Fianna apologized, and asked if they would excuse her to lie down again, explaining that she was still not completely herself.

Letting Fianna get her rest, the group gathered quietly around the fire pit, relaxing on the curious collection of furniture Father Greer had assembled for them: a couple of old, over-stuffed chairs, and some sturdy benches. The priest offered each a mug of hot tea, which they gratefully accepted. After a few minutes' relaxation and reflection, the major brought their attention back to business.

"Celine, when do you and Fianna plan to return to Nibiru?"

"That depends on how quickly Fianna can heal and rest up," she replied. "Father Greer has been helping her with some healing magic, and that's going very well. My guess is that she'll be ready within a couple of days." Celine paused, a distant look coming over her face as the dragon spoke to her mentally. A moment later, the girl smiled and addressed the major again. "Fianna says she will be ready for the flight in two days — possibly a bit less. She's still concerned about the vortex, though, so she'll need all the help Father Greer and I can give her."

"All right; that's good. Father Greer, are you willing to take care of these two until they are ready to make the trip — even if it takes a bit longer than they expect?"

"Of course, my son. We are delighted to have them as our guests, and they are welcome for as long as may be needed."

"Thank you. You are most gracious," replied the major. "Celine, stay here for as long as it takes to be certain you're both ready. I'll figure out some way to keep your father from interfering with your plans."

"Okay — if you really think you can!" replied the girl. "You know how incredibly stubborn he can be."

"Ohhhh, yes. I surely do. But I've been with him long enough to know how to make him see sense. Even when sense is the furthest thing from his mind.

"I have to tell you, though," Dino continued, "he made me promise a few things before he would allow you to stay here at all. One was that one of our crew would have to be with you until we return."

Celine looked puzzled. "But you're the only ones here — and aren't you all essential personnel on the *Queen*? How could one of you stay?"

"Not a problem. Not a problem at all," said Hadgkiss. "I'd like you to meet Spacer First Class Chip O'Disk." He pointed to a small cylinder of shiny black plastic that Madda had just placed on the bench beside her. "'He' is a monitor-recorder. He reports directly to me, continuously, and he'll be staying with you while we're away." Everyone had a good laugh — Celine included.

"So, we'll jump back to Erra now. We'll be back here in three days, just as the commander ordered. If the engineers can do it safely with the ship's equipment, we'll transbeam the two of you to Scotland — to the spot where you can access the tube-chute. If there's no way to beam you, we'll at least cover you through your whole flight, and right up until you've entered the vortex.

"Oh — one last thing. Your father wanted you to have this." He reached into a pocket and pulled out the comm stone. "He knows it's of no use between here and Erra, but at least when we're in orbit or on-planet, he can reach you."

Celine smiled and took the warm purple stone from her godfather. "Thanks, Dino," she said, giving him another hug. "Tell him how much I appreciate it. But Dino, I feel like I'm deceiving my parents and being a terrible daughter."

"Shhh. None of that! You're doing what needs to be done. I've known you all your life, Celine, and I have no doubts about your judgement. Neither should you. Sometimes doing the right thing means someone gets hurt, and some things get busted or bent. Judging from what I know about what's going on, and all that's at stake here, I back you with no reservations. I'm certain your father would, too, if he didn't have such an emotional involvement. Same for your mother. They're amazingly good and strong people — but I think you know that."

Celine nodded. "I understand. And you're right."

"You're just as amazing as they are, you know. I can hardly believe all you've done so far. I couldn't be prouder to call you my goddaughter. So, look: I know it can be hard, but stay positive. Be kind to yourself. Trust yourself. Do what you know is right. Make the best choices you can, and learn from the results, good or bad.

"But enough of that. You get it. Do what has to be done, Celine. I'll do my best to see your parents don't worry. Well, not too much, anyway." They both laughed. "Seriously, though:

are we agreed?"

"Yes. We are. Many thanks, Dino."

"One more thing, before I forget," said the major. "I know Jager cares deeply for you. Very deeply. I'll make sure he's safe." The major smiled again, and winked.

"Th...thanks," she said, thinking his comment strange, but brushing it off for the moment. She had too many other things to think about right now.

"It's time for us to get back to the ship," said the major. "Father, would you be so kind as to let us out?"

"Of course, of course," said the priest. The team gathered their gear and headed for the entrance, Father Greer and Celine leading the way.

Once outside, the whole group exchanged hugs and good-byes. "We'll be back in three days," said the major. "We'll wait in orbit until we hear from you. Until then, stay strong, stay safe." He spoke briefly into his comm pickup, and moments later the landing party was gone.

Staring at the empty space where they'd all just stood, Celine couldn't fight back her tears. She gave up and let them run freely, wishing that just for a little while she could be just a kid again, back on Erra, doing kid things.

Father Greer's gentle words brought her back to the present. "We should get back inside, child. The sun is rising."

"Okay. But please, just another minute. I want to say good-bye to Jager." The priest smiled and nodded. Celine called to Jager, who responded instantly.

"Hiya, sweet thing. Did you miss me?"

Hearing her once and future lover, Celine's melancholy evaporated. "Yes, I did. And you know it!" She hesitated, then spoke again, blushing. "Jager, of *course* I've missed you. For months! I might not sound or act that way, but that's just because of everything else that's happening. I've missed you terribly."

"I know, Celine. I think you can tell I've missed you just as badly. But I also think you're doing something fabulous, and I'm way beyond proud of you. Everyone is. Well, that's not true — almost no one knows what you're doing, and how outrageously important it is. But they all *would* be proud, if they knew. And they will be, when this is over. Oh...except probably Mia."

The two had a good laugh; Mia would always be Mia, and that was something they could admire about her. She was more consistent than anyone they knew.

Jager continued, "I'm here for you always, Celine, don't forget that. I'm sorry our meeting has to be postponed, but maybe the wait will make it even better."

Celine smiled, "You might be right! I've got to go now, though. Thanks again, for everything. I'll talk to you soon."

"Okay. Be safe."

Celine, silent and deep in thought, followed Father Greer back into the mountain and down the tunnel to where the dragon slept. The girl knew she had to clear her head, and figured following her friend's example was the best way to go about it. She climbed into bed, curled up under the warm furs, and fell quickly asleep. Her dreams were full of the better days she hoped would come.

The pair slept half the day, not even stirring when Father Greer worked his healing spells over them, every hour.

CHAPTER 28

Meeting

Celine woke to the smell of cooking. She was famished. She sat up, stretched, and was surprised at how great she felt. Her injuries were just memories, and her energy seemed fully restored. She dearly hoped Fianna felt the same. Turning toward the dragon's bed, she caught a glimpse of something out of the corner of her eye, spun round to face it, and froze.

"Good morning, Celine," said Father Greer, as though everything were perfectly normal. "How are you feeling today?"

"Fine..." she muttered, completely on automatic. Her attention was riveted on something utterly unexpected: an enormous, jet-black dragon, standing in the center of the cavern, regarding her with great, glittering eyes. The immediate shock passed, and she snatched up the incant-baton and knife from where she'd laid them, just beside the bed. Even as her hands made the move, though, she knew there was no need — the dragon intended no harm. If anything, it radiated a friendly interest. Father Greer seemed totally indifferent to its presence, too. But, what the hells...!

"Greetings, Companion Celine," said the creature, in a deep, resonant voice, clearly male. Its accent seemed to echo Fianna's.

"I am truly honored to make your acquaintance." He bowed, the end of his handsomely-formed snout nearly touching the smooth stone floor. Rising again, the dragon explained, "I am Ahimoth, elder brother to Nibiru's White Princess, Fianna."

"Hello, good dragon; the honor is mine," managed the still-incredulous Celine, sneaking a quick glance to Father Greer for reassurance. The priest smiled and nodded.

"Father Greer has related at least some of what you and my sister have been through. I pledge you my every assistance in your quest, and in defeating the abomination, Soader."

Celine bowed again; "I thank you for your kind and generous pledge." She turned briefly toward Fianna; the white dragon still slept peacefully. Her whiteness now seemed even more dazzling, in contrast with her brother's satiny black. "Fianna has spoken of you a number of times," she said, turning once again to Ahimoth.

"I can only hope that what she said wasn't entirely unfavorable. I am afraid I have given her just cause to think ill of me."

Celine hesitated only slightly before responding, "Not at all, though she's mentioned some of the difficult times you shared, long passed."

The two were momentarily startled at a particularly loud snore from Fianna; they both swung their heads round to look at her, then back at each other. The ice was broken — they smiled widely and shared a hearty laugh, the great creature's deep tones reverberating through the cavern.

"Well! Hearing that my little sister has had at least something favorable to say raises hopes that she may forgive me. I was not a good brother; I have considerable amends to make, for grave transgressions against her."

"I understand," said Celine, "but the Fianna I know does love you, despite anything you may have done. I'm sure the two of you can work it all out. My guess is that she will consider that helping us right now would go a long way toward making things right between you."

Ahimoth bowed, saying, "I understand why you have been chosen as the Companion; you are wise beyond your years."

Celine was confused at this, but had no time to consider it further — Fianna had awakened.

"Ahimoth? Ahimoth!" she cried. "I heard your voice, and thought it was but part of a dream. Yet here you are! I can scarcely believe it!"

"Yes, little sister, it is I," replied Ahimoth, "your Brother of Death — and I must tell you what I have discovered about the name I once despised so."

"Oh! Yes, yes — please tell me."

"As you know, my name means 'brother of death' in the language of the ancient Hebrew people, of this very planet. I had always thought it an evil name. A curse. Yet I could not complain or object, since its use is a long tradition among our people. I have learned that I was wrong about its meaning. Or, rather, that my understanding was woefully incomplete. I now know the name's full meaning; its complete significance, the responsibilities it places upon me, and how it defines my life."

Fianna listened, fascinated.

"My name does not mean that I am fated to be bringer of wanton, random death and disaster," Ahimoth continued. "No, it describes my role and my calling: to deal out death — literal or figurative — unto any who would harm those whom I most love in all the worlds: my family. It is a name of noble aspiration, worthy of pride — not a curse or deserving of shame."

"Oh, Ahimoth! I am so happy! This explains so very much!" cried the white dragon, stretching up nearly to the cavern's roof, with an exuberant ruffle. A tear of joy ran down her cheek.

Ahimoth beamed with pride and shared joy. Then, abruptly, his smile shifted to a look of wide-eyed amazement. "Your leg!" he shouted, "Your *leg!* It is *whole!*"

Fianna couldn't help laughing at her brother's expression. "Yes! It is perfect, and better than perfect. My dear Celine has healed it for me!"

Ahimoth stared at the limb in silent awe — and now a tear made its way down his own cheek. Turning to Celine, he bowed as deeply as he could manage, and remained so for a full minute.

Celine's face warmed in a mix of pride, and embarrassment at all the attention.

"I can never thank you enough, nor repay you for what you have done, Companion of my precious sister," the black dragon rumbled. "You have undone the most horrible act of my reckless young life — an unspeakable thing that has scarred my soul ever since, and for which I could never begin to forgive myself." He remained in his deep bow, silent, for another full minute.

Finally, rising, he smiled a humble smile at Celine, and turned once again to his sister. "I have news of our parents. When Father Greer told me that they were alive, and awaiting you at Loch Ness, I went outside and called to them. They are safe, and as well as can be expected. They are anticipating our arrival, so that we may all return home as a family reunited."

"Oh, thank you, Brother! That is wonderful news. I have worried about them so," said Fianna.

"When I first called to them, they thought someone must be playing a cruel trick," laughed Ahimoth. "They would not believe it was I. I managed to convince them, though, reminding of them of family details no one else could know. When they finally accepted it, they were so excited that they could hardly think clearly! I learned that Nessie has been caring for them, and that they should very soon be ready to travel the vortex back to our home."

"Thank you for this good news, Brother" said Fianna. The pleasantries, news and revelations over, the room's four occupants now stood in uncomfortable silence. The air was heavy with the one matter that remained unresolved.

Ahimoth recognized it was up to him to speak next. "Fianna, I was overwhelmed when I learned that you and our parents were alive, and that there might be some chance of our becoming a proper family again." He fell silent for a few moments, and then continued, "I was a terrible brother to you. Truly terrible. I cannot excuse it. I cannot even fully understand it, though learning the truth of my name has helped. I can only apologize, and hope that I may somehow make right a small part of the harms I caused. I am truly, truly sorry. I was confused, and I was shamefully jealous of you, for no sane or sensible reason. The thing I regret most is hurting you so terribly." He lowered his head in anguished shame.

Fianna stood for a long moment, gazing in silent reflection at her brother's bowed head. At last, she responded. "I *do* forgive you, my brother Ahimoth. I understand, and I forgive you." The black dragon raised his head and returned his sister's gaze. The air seemed suddenly fresher, the firelight brighter. Ahimoth was about to respond, but he paused, sensing Fianna had more to say.

"I was immature — vain and silly. I flaunted myself, thinking I was oh, so special: the White Princess of Nibiru, fine and wonderful simply because I existed. How foolish. 'Fine' and 'wonderful' come only from what you *do* in the world and how you affect others, not from the happenstances of your birth," said Fianna. "So, if you felt resentment or jealousy, you cannot be faulted entirely. I deserved your hostilities. I should have sought to understand them — to discover how *I* might have inspired them — so that I might then mend my own ways, and thereby make your life a happier one, and our family whole and harmonious.

"Let me say, then, that I too am sorry. I do love you, and want nothing more than to see you proud and happy. And I want you to come home with us, so we can be a family once more."

Ahimoth crossed the cavern and embraced his sister. The two stood together in silence for a happy while, as Celine looked on in wonder. Now it was the young girl's turn to shed a joyful tear; a double stream of them, in fact — one down each cheek.

The dragons finally stood apart, and Fianna addressed her Companion. "Dearest Celine, I would like you to meet my cherished brother, Ahimoth." Though the two had already met, Fianna felt the need to observe the proper formalities, gracing the relationship between her brother and her Companion with the sanctity of dragon tradition.

"It is a great pleasure to meet you, noble Ahimoth," said Celine, with a broad smile and gracious bow.

"The pleasure is mine, Companion Celine," he replied, returning her bow. The three laughed, in spite of themselves.

Ahimoth turned again to Fianna. "Father Greer was kind enough to tell me about some of your recent adventures. I must say, I am so proud of you, sister. You are a true warrior of Nibiru. As are you, Celine!" He bowed to his sister and her Companion.

"I'm jealous of all the fun you have been having," he laughed. "It is still hard to believe that you are here — *and* that Mother and Father are alive. Until a few days ago, I believed them to have passed on, and that you were a prisoner. Now here I find you, not only free, but with as fine a Companion as a dragon could desire." Celine smiled at the siblings, sharing their happiness. At the same time, she felt wistful. If only she and Mia could have shared such a bond...

Fianna and Ahimoth laughed and continued recounting the highlights of their years and years apart. They had a great visit, scarcely slowing down as they enjoyed the meal Father Greer had prepared. Their tales weren't all happy; Fianna was deeply saddened to hear of Ahimoth's decades of suffering as Soader's prisoner.

Celine sat quietly as the dragons talked, fascinated at everything she heard. Now and then she jumped in to offer a comment, or to gently steer the conversation toward happier subjects, when things became too solemn or serious.

Enjoyable though the chat was, the threat of Soader and the red dragon lurked always at the back of their minds. At last they acknowledged this fact, and agreed it was time to get down to the serious business before them. They began working out the details of their return to Nibiru, and how they would deal with the inevitable confrontation.

After an hour of intense discussion, they had a plan. Ahimoth stood and summarized their decisions. "Very well, then. It is settled. I shall fly ahead to Loch Ness, to be with our parents and to keep them safe until you arrive. I shall also ensure Nessie has everything in readiness to open the vortex for us. You will travel to Loch Ness — either on the wing, or using the spaceship's transbeam device — as soon as Fianna has recovered fully. You will carry with you the precious cache of eggs, and the ancient books."

When it was time for Ahimoth to leave, the siblings could scarcely bear to part. They ended up in another hour's conversation, their bond growing even deeper. Finally, they realized that Ahimoth must go, and that Fianna should return to her all-important rest and recovery.

The goodbyes were difficult, but they were overjoyed at their reunion, and grateful to have healed old wounds. Before Ahimoth could leave, though, Fianna announced one final stipulation — one last task her brother must pledge to complete, as amends for his misdeeds of old.

"Anything. Anything at all," he promised, suddenly solemn and repentant.

"Very well," his sister intoned, now stern and imperious. "You must pledge that throughout the winter that follows our return to our homeworld, you will allow no snow to accumulate before the entrance to my cave." Struggling mightily to keep a straight face, she continued, "Further, you must vow to keep my fish basket continuously stocked with fine, fresh fish. Finally, you must clean my cave each week, and keep my bedding ever fresh."

Ahimoth nodded his agreement, taking every word of Fianna's pronouncement seriously. "Of course. Of course, my sister," he promised. Finally, he looked up, only to see Fianna straining to suppress laughter. Puzzled at first, it suddenly dawned on him that she was teasing. The dragons burst into gales of laughter, and Celine and Father Greer laughed right along with them.

"I was only partially joking, I hope you realize," said Fianna, when she had finally caught her breath. "I really *would* love it if you would do those things, at least for a while."

"Well, my wicked little sister, I was not joking in the least when I agreed to do them, and do them I shall. I solemnly pledge it, before these witnesses!" All four collapsed into a fresh round of laughter.

At last it truly was time for Ahimoth to go. Long past time, in fact. The black dragon, the priest and Celine headed up the tunnel for the mountain portal, and Fianna settled down in her straw bed for another solid round of sleep.

Once they emerged from the tunnel, Celine held out the comm stone to Ahimoth. "Here, please take this," she said. "Once you reach Loch Ness, you and your parents must go back to Nibiru at once. You mustn't wait until Fianna and I are ready. Please go quickly now, and take this comm stone back with you to Nibiru."

"No, Celine," answered Ahimoth, briskly. "I shall not leave this world without the White Princess."

"It'll be okay, Ahimoth, I promise you," replied Celine. "I have very powerful friends who will protect us. Please, don't fight with me on this."

Ahimoth, conflicted, stamped his feet and huffed, smoke jets bursting from his flaring nostrils. Eventually he calmed enough to speak. "No. No. I am sorry. I do not doubt you, but I will not leave Fianna here. I shall convince my parents to travel the vortex without us, and to take your stone along with them. It will not be easy, but I know I can convince them to do this, with the assurance that I will follow immediately, escorting you and my sister."

"All right, Ahimoth," replied Celine, still reluctant. "If that is what you feel you must do, I won't argue further. When you give the comm stone to your parents, please tell them that it contains a holding spell, to help keep the eggs back on Nibiru alive. It's important the eggs be protected with the spell until I arrive with the ancient books. I don't have time to explain, but please believe me.

"Also, tell your parents that it's safer for their crate of eggs to travel through the vortex with Fianna and me; that's why we haven't sent them with you. While Fianna is recovering here, I'll start learning the hex-reversing spell from the ancient grimoires. That way I'll be able to cast the spell as soon as we arrive back on Nibiru. It'll be best if I cast the spell with all the eggs together — the ones now on Nibiru, and those we'll be bringing from Earth."

Ahimoth agreed, and slipped the comm stone into a small pouch inside his cheek. Bowing deeply, he thanked Celine for taking care of his sister and especially for repairing her crippled leg. Celine's response surprised the big dragon: she walked directly up to him, wrapped her arms around his right foreleg and hugged it long and hard. That wasn't the end of it, though. Next, she asked him to lower his head. Puzzled, he complied — and she planted a big kiss right on the top of his handsome black snout.

Ahimoth was speechless, opening and closing his mouth over and over, without a sound. Eventually he managed to say, "Companion of my dear sister, I pledge to guard and protect you with my life — *always.*"

Then, with no wait for a reply, he leapt into the early evening sky. With just two powerful pumps of his wings, he vanished into the clouds.

Celine quickly called to Jager, who was delighted to hear from her. He hadn't heard from West, but told the girl not to worry; he knew the Mentors were just busy with a matter of great importance, and that they'd soon return. After a few minutes' chat, they said their goodbyes, and Celine and Father Greer returned to the cavern.

Fianna greeted them from her bed of straw. "Ahimoth will be safe, yes?" she asked.

"Yes, Fianna," said Father Greer. "He is strong and wise, and knows well how to take care of himself. Just to help out, though, I placed a shielding all around him. No one will be able to detect him as he travels to Scotland — not even with a dragon-locator device. You may both be wondering why I did not shield you in the same way, for your journey to Turkey. I would have been happy to do so, but I am only able to shield a dragon I can see directly. I was not able to accompany you to the tunnel's mouth when you left here, and so could not cast the spell."

"I thank you for protecting my brother," said Fianna. "I completely understand why you did not shield us. Thank you for explaining. These are good things to know. And, of course, it was through no fault of yours that I sustained these hurts!"

Now the dragon gave a cavernous yawn. "I am sorry, Celine; I must take more rest. I never realized just how much sleep we dragons need, when we are healing! I am certain that the process is very nearly complete, though. I hope so; I am anxious to be on our way. We have important work to do — and I fear we may soon exhaust Father Greer's good humor, and his stores of food, drink and fresh straw as well!"

"No need to be sorry, Fianna," replied Celine. "I understand — and it gives me more time for deciphering the spell books. Maybe Father Greer could even help me." She smiled at the priest, who was nodding agreement. Fianna curled her long tail forward and around her forelegs, then rested her snout across it and fell almost instantly asleep. Soon her resonant snore was the only sound in the cavern, but for the fire's faint cracklings.

Celine went to the niche where the saddle and saddlebags had been stowed, carefully brought out the precious books and carried them to the table. Father Greer had cleared a space; the two settled in, side by side, with the books open before them, and went to work.

CHAPTER 29

Re-United

To reach Father Greer's cavern the day before, Ahimoth had flown almost non-stop from the American Southwest. He had been exhausted, but managed to hide his weariness from Fianna and Celine. After leaving the girl and priest on the mountain ledge, he'd flown up into the clouds, out of view, then circled back. Before emerging from the clouds, he peeked earthward to make sure they had gone back inside. Satisfied they wouldn't see him, he flew downward again, skirting the mountainside until he came to an abandoned castle he'd spotted the day before. He landed, anxious to bed down for some badly-needed rest. First, he called to his parents to say that he would join them the next evening.

The old castle was little more than a ruin, with huge gaps in its roof and walls. It was out of sight of human settlements, though, and sound enough to protect him from the weather while he slept. A few small animals scurried frantically away at the sight of him, but they needn't have feared. The dragon had fed well as Father Greer's guest, so his appetite was quiet for the moment. He found a good spot to rest, curled his shining black bulk into a comfortable and compact arrangement, and was soon fast asleep.

He woke to the sound of falling rain. The frigid downpour was interrupted now and then by flurries of hard-driven snow. Scattered patches of slush had formed about the chamber. He certainly hadn't missed weather like this during the years of his captivity!

Despite the cold and wet, he felt refreshed and revitalized; sleep had worked its ancient magic. He uncurled and then stretched mightily, suppressing the urge to let out a good, roaring yawn, too.

He scanned what he could see of the skies through the gaps in the roof and walls, searching for any sign of an enemy. "Not much chance of seeing anything in this weather," he thought, "but that means not much chance of *being* seen, too."

Satisfied it was safe to go, he made his way outside and leapt into the chill, damp air. Straight up he flew, into the dense, gray overcast, then burst through to be greeted by a glorious cloudscape, lit dramatically by the rising sun. He made a banking turn in the direction of Loch Ness and set a strong, steady rhythm of wingbeats that would carry him there as quickly and efficiently as possible. Though glad to be on his way, he was also troubled by the feeling that unseen eyes were watching him. He kept his senses sharp, and constantly scanned all around, above and below, for any sign of danger.

A stronger flyer than Fianna, and bearing no burden, the black dragon made the trip to Scotland in just under half the time it had taken his sister and her Companion to cover the same distance. He located the loch and began spiraling downward to land, calling to his parents as he descended. Though still high in the sky, his keen eyes picked out the glint of his father's golden scales on the lakeshore far below. Just to one side, his mother's rainbow hues sparkled, too.

At the sight of them, he broke from his conservative spiral and plunged straight downward, pulling up and landing with a skid on the sand beside them. The three rushed together and embraced in a tearful reunion, purring and cooing, wings and necks stroking and caressing. Nessie watched from a few meters out in the waters of the loch. She glowed at the heart-warming sight — as did the many other water dragons who'd gathered close to shore. News traveled fast among the deep lake's dragon people.

When in Germany, Ahimoth hadn't told Celine that his parents weren't yet strong enough to travel the tube-chute. Nor had he mentioned that he could send the comm stone through to Orgon on its own, even without a courier. He thought to keep things simple, and avoid unnecessary discussion or arguments. For the same reasons, he hadn't told her of the powerful premonition that had convinced him he must return immediately to Germany, once he'd seen his parents and delivered the comm stone.

Begging his parents' pardon while he tended to a pressing task, Ahimoth asked Nessie if she would open the tube-chute vortex so that he could send something important through to Orgon the Wise. Nessie agreed, and soon she and the rest of the water dragons were assembled, ready to perform the incantation that would open the portal, as soon as the moon had reached the proper point in the sky.

With the arrangements made, Ahimoth returned his attention to his parents. "Fianna is doing well," he explained. "It is surprising to behold her. She has grown so, since we were last together, both in size and in wisdom. The most wonderful thing, though, is that she has forgiven me for being such an awful brother and mistreating her so very badly when we were young."

Neal beamed at the news, and Dini gave her son a warm hug. Neal said, "Son, we are both deeply grateful for the blessing of our reunion, and look forward to Fianna's arrival. We have missed you both so much."

The happy conversation continued as the moon crept up the sky toward its peak for the evening. The elder dragons were more joyful and at peace than they could remember, though they wished Fianna had been able to make the journey from Germany with her brother. Ahimoth assured them their daughter was safe with Father Greer, and that she'd be here in just a matter of days — as soon as she had fully recovered.

"Fianna and Celine have your eggs. They are all alive and safe," he continued. "We decided that it would be best for Fianna to bring them here, and to travel the vortex with them, rather than for me to carry them in my clumsy claws." The older dragons laughed, agreeing that the eggs were probably safer in Fianna's care.

Taking the comm stone from the pouch in his cheek, Ahimoth showed it to his parents. "This is a special stone, given me by Celine, to be sent on to Orgon. It is for this small thing that Nessie and her water dragons are preparing to open the vortex. Celine placed a spell upon the stone; when it reaches Orgon, it will speak, explaining how the last eggs on Nibiru may be kept alive until Celine can travel there to break the hex entirely.

"Orgon is to place the stone with the eggs in their cache; there it will chant a spell of protection and healing over them. It will continue its chanting until Celine and Fianna arrive. Even now, Celine is working hard to decipher and practice the Books' spells for ending the hex, and rekindling our precious eggs — and our race."

Dini and Neal nodded their understanding, solemn approval and wonder at the news.

The reunion continued until the moon was high in the sky. At the proper moment, Nessie gave the water dragons the signal to begin their chant. Ahimoth and his parents watched and listened intently as the ritual progressed. Finally, the swirling, glittering mouth of the vortex appeared, and Nessie nodded to Ahimoth — all was in readiness.

The black dragon advanced to the opening and cast in the comm stone. For a moment, the swirling intensified; then, just as suddenly as it had appeared, the opening vanished with a sharp crack, like a miniature thunderclap.

Ahimoth thanked Nessie and her companions warmly, then returned to his parents for a few more minutes of conversation.

"The time has come for me to return to Fianna. Wait for us here, rest and heal. In a few days' time, we will return with Companion Celine and the eggs, ready to travel homeward. Do you feel you will be well enough to make the journey?"

"Yes, we should be ready quite soon," replied King Neal. "Hurry back as soon as you may. And thank you, my son."

"For what, Father?"

"For protecting and caring for Fianna," he said, to Ahimoth's surprise. "I am so pleased and proud to see you assuming your role as a true Prince of Nibiru, and as my son. One day you shall make a fine king. But go now. Fly safe, fly strong. We love you."

Ahimoth was moved to silence. He simply nodded his understanding and thanks, embraced his parents once more, spread his black wings wide, and leapt toward the silver-white disk of the moon. He prayed that they would be safely back together soon, and that nothing would disrupt the fairy tale his life seemed to have become.

Driven by his dire and insistent premonition, Ahimoth turned his full attention to the flight. Back to the sister who needed him. Back to the enemy who no doubt awaited: Soader, whose death he so deeply wished to hasten.

SAFE FOR THE MOMENT IN the depths of Mount Vogelsberg, Celine was plagued by worries and premonitions of her own. The most troubling was the persistent dread that Soader and his terrible red dragon were waiting for her to emerge from the tunnels again. "Nonsense," she told herself. "I stopped them cold in Turkey, and no one has seen or sensed any sign of them since. Not me, not Fianna, not Father Greer, not even Jager or the Mentors."

As she lay curled in her blankets, she relived the battle in Turkey, and her surprising success at wielding the Invader Spell. Her thoughts wandered here and there, until they settled — and stuck — on Jager. Her cheeks and body warmed at the thought of him. Warmed beyond comfort. She hopped from the bed to find something to do. Anything.

Celine's cheeks would have warmed even more, had she known how apprehensive Jager was at the prospect of meeting *her*. His self-assurance — which seemed unwavering to any casual observer — was actually wavering like a willow in a windstorm. And the closer it came to time for *Asherah*'s jump-shift back to Earth, the worse his jitters grew, and the harder they became to hide. Dino wasn't fooled in the least. He knew his "nephew" too well. He had been teasing the young man mercilessly all day, whenever no one was around to hear.

They had just finished working with several of the crew, finalizing preparations for the trip, and were on their way to the ship's training facilities for a workout. "What the hells, Jager," teased Dino, "did you get your *hair* cut this afternoon? You did! I wouldn't have thought it was possible to cut hair any shorter than yours already was! And just why did you feel you needed a haircut? Trying to impress someone, perchance?" He laughed as Jager took a swing at him. They chased around and over the gym equipment, jumping, dodging, wrestling and sparring, then breaking apart to chase some more.

"Okay, okay," laughed Dino, when Jager finally had him pinned. "You win! You win! I promise to keep your secret safe. I swear I will NOT inform the commander that my 'nephew' has the incurable hots for his youngest daughter."

Jager tightened his hold on the older man, but Dino just laughed all the harder. His bionics trashed any possibility of a fair fight, though he hadn't really brought them to bear up to this point. Now he broke Jager's hold with just a shrug, and stood up.

"Ohhh, and was that a new uniform I saw you with, too? You might want to be a little more discrete, lover boy. The commander's likely to notice your efforts to look like an image-clip star. He's got that sixth sense fathers have, when it comes to their precious daughters. Maybe you should keep out of sight until Celine is aboard, and he's had his chance to talk with her."

Jager smiled ruefully — then sprang at Dino in a fresh attempt to pin him to the deck.

Celine was the subject of similar teasing from Fianna. When the dragon had quietly awakened that morning, she'd inadvertently overheard Celine's thoughts of Jager. When the two rose from their beds, Fianna couldn't resist teasing her Companion — and the good-natured pokes continued right through breakfast.

Father Greer quickly caught on, and was thoroughly amused at the by-play. They all had a good laugh over it, glad for the break from the growing tension over what the next few days might fling their way.

The day passed, with Fianna getting the last of the rest she would need, and Celine poring over the grimoires, struggling to unlock their secrets. Though the work was exhausting, it was an exhilarating challenge at the same time — and Celine was thankful for the engaging distraction from the looming events she preferred not to confront.

It was fortunate she had dug into the books at the first opportunity. She'd quickly discovered that there would be a lot more work involved than she had imagined.

Her task was composed of several steps. First, she had to locate the spell she needed from among the hundreds detailed within the Book of Atlantis. The book listed each spell's distinctive name, followed by a summary description, then the spell itself. Since the names and descriptions were all deliberately vague and trickily worded, just locating the correct spell was a daunting task all by itself.

Once she had the proper spell in hand, the real work began. The text of each Atlantean spell was presented as a series of numbers and symbols. Each number-symbol combination corresponded to a specific riddle or puzzle catalogued within the Book of Mu. To decipher an Atlantean spell, one had to take its first number-symbol, locate the corresponding puzzle or riddle in the Book of Mu, and solve that puzzle or riddle. The solution would be a word or phrase. When this process had been worked through for all the number-symbol combinations given in the Atlantean book, the resulting list of words and phrases, in sequence, combined to form the precise wording of the spell in question. The system — designed to help safeguard the ancient knowledge — was brilliant. Brilliant, confusing, and a lot of hard work to solve.

CHAPTER 30

Departure

The allotted days passed. With Father Greer's patient help and wise insights, Celine had made excellent headway on deciphering the spell that would free the dragon eggs from their hex. Just as important, the girl had gained sufficient insight of her own to be able to continue and complete the task without further help. The job would not be a quick one, but it could be done.

Thanks once again to Father Greer, Fianna had almost entirely recovered. She was at least fit and fresh enough to make the flight to Scotland, and travel from there to Nibiru through the tube-chute vortex.

Now it was just two hours before *Queen Asherah* was to reappear above Earth — and for the dragon and her Companion to leave the priest's generous care, in the safety of the mountain tunnels.

As Celine finished padding and strapping the crate of dragon eggs to Fianna's saddlebags, her thoughts turned to her father. She hoped it would be possible for the ship to beam them directly to Loch Ness. If not, she would have to go aboard. That would mean dealing with Rafael directly.

Whether she had to go aboard or not, how could she possibly convince him not to interfere with what she knew she must do? For all the thought she'd given the problem, she still had no plan. She knew how passionate and forceful Rafael could be, when he'd decided how something should or shouldn't be — especially where his family was concerned. Yet she could not let anything or anyone, not even her father, stop her.

Suddenly, she felt a rush of relief. She had a plan. One she hoped would cover any eventuality. When the ship arrived, she would call to Jager at once, and ask whether they could transbeam her and Fianna directly to Scotland. If so, she would tell him that Father Greer bore a message for her father, and ask that Jager either transbeam it aboard, or come retrieve it himself.

If the ship could not transbeam them directly — if it would be necessary to beam them aboard and then back down to Loch Ness — she would refuse to be transbeamed at all. There was too much risk that her father would try to hold her aboard the *Queen*. Instead, she and Fianna would leave at once and make the journey to Scotland on the wing. But she would still insist that Jager retrieve her recorded message and relay it to her father.

She gave the saddle, saddlebags and crate one final check, then took off her bodypack and opened its topmost compartment. In a moment, she'd found the recorder button; she sat down against the cavern wall and began recording, composing her message as she went along.

As concisely but completely as she could, she explained to Rafael what she was doing, and why. She apologized for keeping all this hidden from him, and for leaving without confronting him directly.

She explained her fear that in his kind concerns for her welfare, he might try to prevent her from doing what honor demanded. She was a grown person now, and — just as he had taught her — she must maintain her integrity above all else.

She must be her own advisor, keep her own counsel, select her own decisions, and never compromise with what she knew was right.

She hoped he could understand this, accept it, and possibly even forgive her. If he refused to agree, she would respect his choice — but she would carry through on her *own* choice, regardless.

If he thought he could transbeam her aboard against her will, he needn't bother trying. She would already have surrounded herself and Fianna with a spell that would block the transbeam.

If he attempted to intercept them at Loch Ness and prevent them from entering the vortex, he would have four angry dragons to contend with, one of them a mature fire-breather. Not to mention Nessie and her legion of water dragons.

No, the future of an entire noble race was at stake. She had pledged her help, and she would not be stopped.

And if he so much as *attempted* to interfere, she would never forgive him. Never. No matter how righteous and noble he might believe his own motives to be.

She concluded her recording with a heartfelt plea for his understanding and respect, signing off with, "I love you, Father. Always."

Locking the button so its contents couldn't be accidentally erased, she slipped it carefully into a pocket. Next, she explained her plan to Fianna in every detail. The dragon nodded her understanding and agreement.

Celine's new plan relieved one whole source of stress she hadn't even considered: now it was certain that she would not have to meet Jager face to face — not just yet. Not in the middle of everything else!

THE TIME HAD COME. Father Greer, Celine and Fianna made their way up the tunnels to the mountainside portal, but left the entrance closed. They would not open it until the exact time agreed upon for *Asherah's* return.

Waiting for the appointed moment, Celine reflected on all that had happened in the past week.

Against all odds, they had found the Atlanteans' ancient treasure, and recovered the priceless Books.

Ahimoth had been reunited and reconciled with his sister.

The dragons' parents, long thought to be lost forever, had been found alive, and were now about to return to their homeworld.

Celine, Fianna and Ahimoth would return with them, bearing the precious cargo of living dragon eggs.

They would also carry the spell that would finally lift the vicious hex, laid down long ago upon all the eggs of Nibiru, dooming the planet's entire dragon race to oblivion.

She had also been reunited with her dear stepfather, after nearly two harrowing years.

Finally, she had found the strength, courage and wisdom to do what she knew to be right, no matter what anyone else might think or say, and no matter the consequences.

She was confident she could overcome her father's almost certain disapproval, once she'd fulfilled her pledge to herself and to the dragons. He would finally see the sense and honor in her decisions, forgive her, and perhaps even be proud of the daughter he'd so faithfully raised.

Father Greer's fine old timepiece chimed softly. The moment had arrived. Celine and Fianna stood at the spot where the entrance would appear and glanced at each other, full of nervous anticipation — and a healthy dose of fear.

Celine turned to the priest and nodded. He opened the portal, and a brisk gust of evening air greeted them.

All three stepped through the doorway and out onto the ledge. Moments later, *Queen Asherah*'s sleek, shining under-hull appeared, high in the sky, directly above them.

"Jager are you there?" called Celine.

"Yes, Celine — we're here," her young soulmate replied.

"Good. Good. Now, please tell me: will *Asherah* be able to transbeam Fianna and me directly to Scotland?"

"I'm sorry, but no — we will have to beam you aboard first, then beam you back down to Loch Ness."

"All right. I was afraid that might be the case. Please listen carefully. I apologize for what I must do now. I..."

"What?? What do you mean, 'apologize'?!" shouted Jager.

"There's no time. Listen to me! Father Greer has something you must come get. You must give it to my father. Please, please do this for me. I *must* go now. I'll see you soon. I love you, Jager."

With that, she shut her mind against further contact and rushed to Father Greer, hugging the priest so hard it nearly cracked his poor old bones. Pushing the recorder button into his hand, she explained: "Jager will come for this. It's for my father. Thank you again — for everything."

She ran to Fianna, leapt to the saddle and hunkered down tight, ready for the jolt when the dragon took flight.

Then, just as Fianna crouched to make her skyward leap, both dragon and Companion glimpsed a flashing blur of wicked scarlet above them, and felt, more than heard, a screaming *whoosh* of rushing wings.